THE SEEKERS OF GENESIS

EMPYREAL ROOTS

THE SEEKERS OF GENESIS

EMPYREAL ROOTS

C. J. WALTERS

The Seekers of Genesis: Empyreal Roots

Available in these formats:
978-1-7364832-0-6 (Paperback)
978-1-7364832-1-3 (eBook)
Library of Congress Control Number: 2021902721

Editing: Writer Therapy
Cover Design: Casey Gerber Creative
Publishing Services: Dragon Tales Press, LLC

www.dragontalespress.com

For Joey, who made me believe in the existence of magic long before the world could convince me otherwise.

TABLE OF CONTENTS

Decisions, Decisions

A soft gust of wind brushes my bare arms, sending icy shivers through my body. Goose bumps rise on my skin, even though our sun, Zon, shines down warmly. But the balmy breeze isn't what chilled me.

Tonight marks the beginning of the end.

The unwelcome thought descends upon me like a dark omen. It's happened before, these flashes of clairvoyance, especially just before life-changing moments. And my Path Ceremony certainly constitutes one of those.

I rub my hands back and forth across my forearms—dissipating the raised bumps—before grasping the waist-high granite wall on the roof of our home, Spektrolith. Ignoring the foreboding in my heart, I focus on the Hyggelig Mountains in the distance. Their shimmering sapphire peaks are an ideal audience, allowing me to practice my Path Ceremony lines in private.

"I should have known this is where you would be, brother. Off in fairyland, reveling in your great purpose."

So much for being alone. My twin, Dameaon, has joined me, casually reclining against the west tower's wall. Dressed in black cargo pants, a V-neck T-shirt, and scuffed leather combat boots, he's a dark blemish on the roof's golden granite surface. His uneven, choppy hair—as dark as the shadowy depths of the Abyssal Sea—falls over his forehead and into his eyes, making it impossible to read his mood. Not that it matters; he's always full of hostility and wrath. Especially around me.

"Did you need something?" I ask, keeping my tone light.

"No," he says. "The house is too noisy to think."

"Everyone's getting ready for tonight."

"Yep. All for the big day."

His tone is flat, so I can't tell if he's serious. "Well, it is a big day for us."

He hoists himself up onto the roof's wall, balancing on the five-inch granite ledge. His serpentine movements are akin to the oily ankerias that dwell in the Shadow Grove, slinking down from vine-covered branches to terrorize those brave enough to enter the forest's domain. "Yeah, sure. A big day for you. For Mom and Dad. And maybe even the powers that be. But me, I don't care."

"How can you say that? You get to choose your Path tonight and become a Seeker. That's one step away from being an official member of your Class."

His mouth twists into a smirk. "I turn sixteen and I'm magically supposed to know what I want to do for the next hundred years. I don't even know what I want to do tomorrow."

I clench my jaw. "One hundred years is insignificant when you're immortal. And we're fortunate to have a choice. Not everyone is so lucky."

"Oh yeah, I'm so lucky."

I sigh. "I think—"

My twin hops off the wall and takes a step toward me. "You don't think, and that's your problem. You accept things the way they are, and don't question how they should be. I want to be free to do what I want, when I want. To live day-to-day, making it up as I go along."

"You're so focused on what you want, you've forgotten it's our duty to contribute to the universe in some way," I say. "I'm glad you're choosing the Path of a Soldier. It suits you . . . and your flippancy."

He crosses his arms. "Being a Soldier is just as important as being a Guide."

"Being a Guide requires discipline and sacrifice. Being a Soldier requires nothing more than muscles and the ability to swing a sword."

"I'll make sure to tell Dad how you feel about his Chosen Path."

I shake my head. "Father is an exception, which is why he was the best Soldier ever. And why he's our governor now."

"He's governor because Mom throws the best parties in Belkin."

"Whatever, Dameaon. I don't have time to argue about frivolous nonsense. Leave, so I can be alone."

"You don't own the roof. Go to your room if you want to be alone."

"I was here first," I say. "And you said it yourself. The house is noisy, and I need to practice. I actually care about the Path Ceremony, so you go."

My twin moves closer, his face inches from mine. His hair falls into his unnaturally lit amber eyes, but it does little to shield me from their intensity, even more pronounced with his anger. We glower at each other, and I steel my spine, determined not to be the first to look away. Eventually, he breaks eye contact and heads toward the stairs to the house.

I smile; it is a small victory, but a victory nonetheless.

Dameaon's voice echoes back to the roof. "Be careful, brother. Being a Guide takes compassion and an open mind, neither of which you have. I predict you'll botch your Guidance duty and end up in Rehuido, shamed and lonely."

His admonition causes the air to stall in my lungs. I place my palms against the railing to support my shaking legs. He's just trying to rattle me—I know that—but my trepidation has returned, beating wildly inside my chest.

A chilly breeze induces another spell of goose bumps. Zon is already half set behind the mountains, and our three moons, Meta, Hermes, and Yars, are just beginning to shine in the dimming violet sky—evidence that there isn't much time before the Ceremony.

I steady my legs and head toward the stairs.

Cheerful lyrics from my favorite musical, *Beacon of the North*, play from the Axaftin Orb on my desk. I tap my fingers against the desk's obsidian top, drumming along to the sanguine rhythm. Normally, this soundtrack cheers me up, but not now—not when conversations echo up from the foyer below as telltale signs of the gathered crowd.

I swipe my hand from left to right over the top of the Axaftin Orb, and the volume increases, dulling the voices to faint murmurs.

That's better; now I can think.

I navigate across my plush navy carpet to my king-size mattress and flop down. My ceiling is a painted mural of our galaxy's stars and moons as a reminder that Glanchings are responsible for harmony across the universe. With my Path Ceremony minutes away, that responsibility feels more like a burden, invisibly bearing down on my chest, making breathing virtually impossible.

It's not the way I wanted—or expected—to feel this evening. Not when I've been preparing to be a Guide since I was eight. All of my schooling and additional reading focused on the knowledge Guides need to be successful. While my peers were having fun, I was volunteering as an assistant for the Guide department at Moudrost, my school, completing menial tasks for the Gurus in return for their mentorship.

And it's not just me. My parents have supported my Path since day one, and Moudrost's professors agree I will excel in this Class. It's a good decision—perfect, really—and everything was going according to plan, until Dameaon's threatening words tore into my self-esteem.

I rub my fingers against the back of my neck and then crack my knuckles. Letting him jar my confidence is laughable. While I excel at everything, he blunders through life with barely acceptable behavior. Chances are, if anyone ends up shamed and lonely, it will be him.

But . . . what if he's right? What if being a Guide is a big mistake? Sure, any Seeker—regardless of Class—who fails training is banished for eternity to the district of Rehuido to mine Magical Ore at Buhler's Crest. But Guides have additional stakes the other Classes don't. If they fail, the Oldungur Council obliterates the Seeker's planet. Knowing an Original Species will live or die because of me is suddenly overwhelming.

There are other Paths I would enjoy. Easier ones. I'd be a good Mage, learning how to summon Reos's Elements to protect our planet, or I could create magical potions as an Alchemist. And it isn't too late; the rest of the Oldungur Council is here tonight. I could ask for a meeting with the head of another Class . . .

A sharp knock at my door interrupts me. I prop up on my elbows as my father, Lord Drasko, strides in.

His forehead is furrowed, and his mouth is drawn in a tight line. But it's not surprising. By his own admission, he's all business, all the time. It's brought him success in every aspect of his life during his five hundred years on Reos. He outflanked the other Glanchings in his unit during his tenure as a Soldier, he was relentless in his pursuit of my mother to win her heart and hand in marriage, and he demonstrated his strong conviction and beliefs to become governor of Belkin. Anything he has came from hard work and commitment. He's the paragon of an upstanding Glanching and everything I aspire to be.

He stops when he sees me. "Villow, what are you doing in bed? Your Path Ceremony starts in five minutes."

I roll to the side of the mattress, swinging my legs over the edge. "I know."

"Are you all right?" he asks, charging into my walk-in closet.

"I think so," I say, loud enough for him to hear me through the walls.

He returns with my Path Ceremony robes. "You think so? This isn't the time for uncertainty."

I place my arms through the robe's silk sleeves and tug it onto my angular shoulders. "I guess I'm just a little nervous."

"No reason to be nervous. You're a Verchant. You will achieve greatness."

"But . . . what if I'm not meant to be a Guide? What if I'm meant to fulfill my purpose another way? There are easier Classes—"

"Easier?" he says, scrunching his squinty caramel eyes. "Since when do you do what's easy? We've been planning for you to be a Guide since you were ten."

I walk over to my full-length mirror in the right corner of my room, fastening the robe's clasp near my neck. "I was eight, actually. But Dameaon said—"

"Dameaon. Of course. Your brother revels in flustering you. You know that. The only time a Glanching fails is when he chooses the wrong Path. Do you honestly believe you're not meant to be a Guide?"

"No. I know I'm meant to re-create an Original Species."

He takes the red-gold braided belt off my bed and stands behind me. In the mirror's surface, my father's reflection towers over mine; at a little over six feet tall, he's got at least five inches on me, and his shoulders are much broader. His black suit is in stark contrast to my robe, but his tie is a perfectly matched scarlet, in honor of the Ceremony.

"Then it's settled. A Guide you shall be." He ties the belt around my waist and steps back. "Look at you. So grown up. I couldn't be prouder, son."

His kind words are a sponge, sucking up the anxiety and doubt inside of me. I hug him. "Thank you, Father."

He returns my embrace and then straightens the robe's hood, laying it flat against my shoulders. "Oh, I almost forgot. There's been a small change of plans. Master Oldungur Cassandre is leading your Ceremony tonight."

I still; that news is far from a "small change of plans." Three days ago, Oldungur Mekhi, the Guide Class representative, traveled from Kapitala to Belkin, our district, to confirm I was a suitable Guide Seeker. Once he approved my Class choice, we practiced my Ceremony, and I was comfortable with him.

"W-W-Wait, what? I thought Oldungur Mekhi was leading my portion of the Ceremony."

"He was. But when the rest of the Oldungur Council arrived a few minutes ago and Cassandre suggested leading both Ceremonies, I gladly accepted. This is quite the honor for our family."

The clock strikes eight, and my stomach churns. I need time to process this—to prepare—but I don't have it. Frantic, I search for something to give me strength to leave my room.

My eyes lock on my desk. I open the bottom drawer and pull out a navy velvet pouch, loosening the strings and turning it over. My lucky friendship bracelet drops onto the desk. I slip it on my wrist and pull the robe's sleeve over it.

"Ready?" my father asks, opening my bedroom door.

I breathe in deeply and take a step toward him.

This is it.

I'm ready for this.

I have to be.

THE FOYER LIGHTS ARE OFF FOR THE CEREMONY, BUT BISTER flowers are strategically placed on the floor. Their petals' golden hue offers enough illumination to safely navigate to the top of the staircase, where Dameaon and my mother are waiting.

My father clasps my twin's shoulder. "Good luck, Dameaon," he whispers and turns to my mother. "You ready, Actavia?"

She kisses my cheek, and they start down the stairs, my father on the right and my mother on the left. They rejoin on the landing, and arm in arm, their silhouettes disappear into the blackness, joining our hushed guests below.

Alone with my twin, a sense of camaraderie overcomes me, as if we're about to engage in a joint battle.

"Good luck, Dameaon," I whisper.

He stares straight ahead, either not hearing or ignoring me. Probably the latter, and I regret saying anything.

The orchestra starts playing, and the Sympohoe, our district's most prominent choir, chants, "Dunaphasorre, dunaphasorre, hernaseephonee," over and over to the beat of the music.

"So it begins," Dameaon says and starts down the left

staircase. Cursing silently, I race down the right side's first three steps to catch up. Then we descend slowly, our steps in sync, until we meet on the landing. The perimeter's square railing has bister flowers wound around it, making us visible to the crowd.

Master Oldungur Cassandre rises from the void below like an enchanting chimera. She smiles at me, and my forehead moistens with sweat. While her beauty is undeniable, so is the shroud of power surrounding her. The few times I met her before tonight—all when she was the Oldungur Mage representative and not the Master Oldungur—made me jittery and unsteady on my feet.

Cassandre's thick jet-black braid skims the ground as she steps up to the podium. She grasps the microphone and addresses the crowd in a loud, commanding voice. "Good evening, fellow Glanchings. Thank you for joining us at the Verchants' charming home for the celebration of their sons' Path Ceremonies. From the moment of creation, a Glanching's life is a gift. With our eminence, we are honored to dedicate part of our lives to helping the universe. Dameaon and Villow are eager to share how they plan on making this impact, so let us begin." She turns to face me. "I ask Villow Verchant, son of Drasko and Actavia, to join me and declare your desired Class."

Even though I knew it was coming, I shudder at my name. As the eldest, Dameaon has control over the order we declare our Paths. He opted to go second, probably speculating going first would rattle my nerves. It was a correct assumption. I'm frozen, as if I accidentally cast Ice Magic on my legs.

In the foyer's inkiness, a single golden beacon shines.

It's Katarin De Legard, my fifteen-year-old best friend, conjuring a fireball in her hands. The flame illumes her smiling face, gleaming against her unbridled emerald eyes. She manages to do what she's always done: find a way to reach me, even across the darkness.

My body unclenches. Kat's support ignites my inner courage. I can do this; I was created to do this.

Master Oldungur Cassandre gestures for me to join her with her left hand, the tips of her long red nails brandished like phoenix talons in the flowers' light.

I take a deep breath and step up to the podium.

This close, the heady scent of her jasmine perfume encases me, and my vision blurs. As if she can sense my muddledness, she places her hand on the small of my back and pushes me closer to the microphone.

The darkness below offers a weird sense of isolation and gives me courage to begin, shakily. "I, Villow Verchant, do on this day, pledge my life to the higher order of all Glanchings, to serve others and enhance the lives of those around me, to make choices for the greater good, and to renounce selfishness and personal need." I hit a stride, my voice steadying. "I vow to live according to our Rules and the Glanching Code of Conduct. On this day, I choose the Path of a Guide, to be responsible for another planet and its inhabitants. I vow to lead my Original Species with integrity and develop a society full of peace and love. If I do not live up to these vows, may the Oldungur Council bring its judgment upon me."

Cassandre lifts the hood of my robe over my head, indicating her acceptance of my Chosen Path. Then she hugs me from behind—one arm around my shoulders and the other around my waist. Her embrace shackles me, draining the air from my lungs, and I fight the urge to shake her off.

"Congratulations, Villow," she whispers. "I expect many great things from you."

She releases me and claps her hands. The crowd joins in, erupting into cheers. Out of her embrace, I'm no longer frozen, and I can breathe again.

An impish smile twitches on my lips. I did it. I'm a Guide Seeker.

As the crowd's applause diminishes, I return to my spot by Dameaon.

Master Oldungur Cassandre approaches the podium, saying, "Dameaon Verchant, son of Drasko and Actavia, please join me and declare your chosen Class."

My twin steps up to the microphone without hesitation. He becomes an outline, but his booming voice resonates. "I, Dameaon Verchant, do on this day, pledge my life to the higher order of all Glanchings, to serve others and enhance the lives of those around me, to make choices for the greater good, and to renounce selfishness and personal need."

He's saying all the right words, yet his inflection makes a mockery of the Ceremony. He spits the words "personal need" like they're poison in his mouth.

He pauses, throwing a glance at me over his shoulder. "I vow to live according to our Rules and the Glanching Code of Conduct. On this day, I choose the Path of a Guide . . ."

He continues, but for me, everything stops. The blood in my veins turns into icicles, chilling every bit of me. I never realized one small word could shake me to my core.

Guide.

Dameaon just said *Guide.*

Movement brings me back to the present as Cassandre lifts my brother's hood over his head, accepting his choice. She embraces him—just as she did me—and the crowd cheers.

Releasing my twin, she speaks into the microphone. "Fellow Glanchings, may I present Dameaon and Villow Verchant, the newest members of the Guide Class."

Everyone applauds again, and the foyer lights turn on. I step forward, clutching the graphite marble railing. The crowd below is so dense that not an inch of the speckled gray marble floor is visible.

Dameaon steps up next to me, leaning against the railing. "Interesting turn of events, huh, brother?"

It takes all my strength not to walk away, but our peers are watching. Instead, I offer the crowd a small wave, doubling their applause.

"What exactly are you trying to prove?" I ask through clenched teeth.

He doesn't answer, and our father ascends to the landing, his eyes shrouded with darkness; he's not happy about Dameaon's ambush either.

My father steps up to the podium. "Members of the Oldungur Council, my fellow colleagues, and other esteemed guests, thank you for joining Lady Actavia and me to celebrate our sons' journeys to purposeful lives. If you head out to the backyard, we will continue the festivities with great food and entertainment from the Sympohoe."

He locks eyes with me and shakes his head, silently communicating that this isn't the time to talk about

Dameaon's mishap. Then he starts down the steps, joining the crowd below.

"You are in so much trouble," I whisper.

Dameaon shrugs. "We'll see."

He charges up the stairs, leaving me on the landing alone. I find Katarin in the swarm below, and she mouths, "Hurry up."

I nod, heading up the right staircase to change for the party.

I'M INSIDE MY CLOSET WHEN THE ENORMITY OF WHAT HAPpened hits me. I grab the hangers with my party attire and return to my room, perching on my bed.

Dameaon is a Guide Seeker. My selfish, undisciplined twin chose the most selfless Path possible. But why?

Perhaps it's his idea of a joke or a prank. Leave it to him to do something idiotic during our most important ritual. But his insolence only goes so far; even he wouldn't risk something so brazen.

And he must know he won't be successful. An Original Species will suffer at his hands until the Oldungur Council deems him a failure. Then he will be forced to mine Magical Ore at the southern part of Reos—forever.

Worst of all, the Verchant name—one of the most prominent in Belkin—will be tarnished. When I was nine, it happened to our family friends, the Rosemalds. Their daughter failed her third trial as an Alchemist and was sent to Buhler's Crest, but the rest of the family suffered too. Everyone avoided them, as if their child's failure were contagious. Eventually, the Rosemalds moved to another district, never to be heard from again. Now, because of Dameaon, that will probably be the Verchants' fate.

I rub my fingers against my forehead. Maybe he'll come to his senses. The Oldungur Council grants Seekers three days to request a Class reversal, just in case a Seeker has a change of heart. It doesn't happen often, but it does happen. Although it's not ideal, it could be worse. Dameaon would survive that. Our whole family would.

But it's wishful thinking; I know my twin. He's too arrogant to admit he made a mistake. That means he will be a Guide, and he will fail. I bend my head forward and close my eyes, drawing in deep breaths.

"Things didn't go well, I gather?"

I glance at the door; it's still closed, so I scan my room. Our family's pet wyvermalkin is perched on top of my bookshelf.

"Hello, Cinders. I didn't realize you were in here," I say, moving across the room to reach up and stroke his soft cheek. He shoves his petite, angular face into my fingers, demanding more affection.

"How long have you been here?" I ask.

"That's not important. What happened?"

I drop my arm to my side. "Dameaon was Dameaon. He chose to be a Guide."

He blinks his round yellow-green eyes rapidly four times. "What about you?"

"I'm officially a Guide," I say. "As planned."

"So then what are you upset about?" He licks his right paw with his pink tongue, running it against his face and the six long whiskers protruding out the side of his gray muzzle.

I return to my bed and take my shirt off the hanger. I manage to pull it on, but when I attempt to fasten the buttons, my unsteady hands don't cooperate. "Didn't you hear me? My brother is a Guide. He'll fail, and our family will be ruined."

Cinders stands. He only weighs eleven pounds, but his fluffy ash-gray fur makes his sleek body appear bigger. He extends his two wings—one attached at each of his bony shoulders—above his head, revealing their leathery gray skin. "Are you certain he'll fail?"

"Of course."

"Why?"

"Because he will."

"That's a ridiculous reason," he says, launching himself and gliding over to my lap with lithe agility. "Just focus on yourself. The rest is needless worry about things you can't control."

"It's hard to do when his decision can destroy the Verchant name," I say, lifting him off my lap and placing him on the bed. "Everything I've worked for will be for nothing. Everything my father . . ."

My father.

Of course; there's no way he's going to let my twin remain a Guide. He'll demand Dameaon change his Class, and the Glanching Code of Conduct states we must honor and respect our parents, so he'll have to comply.

"Cinders, you're a genius," I say, stroking his back several times.

"Well aware of that," he says, curling up on my navy bedspread and covering his face with his right wing. "Make sure you shut the light off when you leave."

I laugh and attempt to button my shirt again. My steady hands complete the task effortlessly now that I'm certain my brother's time as a Guide is short-lived. I put on my gray suit jacket and check my appearance in the mirror, slicking back my wavy hair—the color of coffee lightened with cream—with my fingers. Then I pause.

I've been so focused on my twin, I haven't reveled in my own success. Cassandre accepted me into the Guide Class. I will re-create an Original Species, and they will succeed because of my decisions and leadership. This time, the magnitude of that obligation falls on my shoulders, not my chest, and I'm certain I can carry it.

I won't fail; I can't fail.

The corners of my mouth turn up. My foreboding was wrong. Today isn't the beginning of the end at all; it's the start of a purposeful life.

SOMEWHERE I BELONG

My mom's party decorations have always been over the top, and tonight is no exception. But for once, I'm grateful for her frippery. The twelve-foot statues—depicting the five Classes—lining our yard's perimeter offer me a much-needed sanctuary.

My dad is furious, no doubt about it. I went against his wishes, picking the Guide Class. Which means he's going to lecture me—and I'm not in the mood. I'd skip the whole party if I could, but then my mom would complain for months, and that would infuriate my dad even more. So my goal is simple: talk to my mom so she knows I was here and sneak back upstairs before my dad sees me.

I risk peeking around the side of the silver-and-gold beveled shield I'm currently hiding behind. Directly in front of me, the Sympohoe is performing on a cyperus-tree-shaped stage. The twisted sepia branches stretch upward, as if they're trying to claw the stars out of the sky.

In the center of our lawn is a pearly canvas canopy. It's held up on each side by four slate-gray swords, each one three times my height. A few couples are already dancing underneath it, but my parents aren't among them.

Unsuccessful in the hunt for my mom, I retreat behind the safety of the statue. For the first time, I realize two crisscrossing swords are plunged through the middle of its shield. It's the Soldier Class's crest.

I chuckle to myself. The irony isn't lost on me; if I'd stuck with this Path, I wouldn't be hiding right now.

Eager to head to the roof, I slink across the thirty feet of bare lawn between the statues and duck behind the Alchemist Class's crest. This spot offers a better view of the party, but much less camouflage. The statue is primarily made up of a clear glass bottle filled with transparent orange liquid. The only solid part is the tome—inscribed with our ancient language—lying open at the bottle's base. I cower behind the book and peer over the top.

Oldungur Gregg, the Soldier Class lead, is a few feet away, talking to some of my parents' friends. I crouch even lower; he's another Glanching I want to avoid.

Continuing my search, I make my way around the yard's perimeter, pausing behind the Mage and Performer crest statues—just long enough to search for my parents. Finally, I take shelter behind the last statue. It's a lapis malaa'ig tree, with ivory feathered wings growing out of the top of the trunk.

The Guide Class's crest. My crest. For now at least.

Still unable to locate my parents but tired of hiding, I enter the banquet area. Guests are sitting at round tables with glowing centerpieces. The centerpieces' two sides are different; one is the Soldier crest and the other is the Guide crest.

I suppress a smile. My parents will have a tough time explaining the duality to their snobby friends.

"Dameaon, a word. Now," my dad says, coming up beside me.

Well, that didn't take long. "I'm a little busy, Dad."

"Now, Dameaon," he says, grabbing my wrist.

He tugs me back into the house and down the grand hallway to his study.

I hate this room. Everything about it screams banal pretentiousness. The lacquered mahogany walls have intricate murals of historic Glanching events carved into them. Except for the back one. That's a massive bookshelf filled with thousands of tomes. All of which my father proudly proclaims he has read—any chance he gets. In the far left corner, a black granite spiral staircase leads up to a second bookshelf, also full of tomes. The arches supporting the ceiling are the same mahogany wood as the walls. The only splash of color is the maroon rug in the middle of the room, but it's mostly hidden beneath plush brown leather furniture. It's all very dull, but my dad never had much of an imagination.

I pull out of his grasp. "The physical assault is unnecessary."

He closes the door and faces me, storms of wrath brewing in his eyes. "Don't be dramatic. My patience is thin. And what are you wearing on your feet? Are those your boots?"

I meet his gaze head-on. "The dress shoes pinch my toes."

He lets out a cackle. "Of course they do. How can I be surprised you picked the wrong Class when you can't even wear the right shoes?" He moves across the room to the bookshelf, adjusting the perfectly arranged tomes. "Did we or did we not decide you would be a Soldier Seeker?"

"We did."

"Yes, we did. So what were you hoping to accomplish with that brazen stunt?"

I shrug. "I changed my mind."

"You changed your mind."

"You know I just said that, right?"

He narrows his eyes. "Lose the attitude. This is serious."

I perch on the arm of a couch in the sitting area. "It always is with you."

He stalks toward me and points his finger in my face. "Dameaon, I'm warning you, you cannot be a Guide. You'll fail, and you know what happens then. You'll be sent to Buhler's Crest. Or worse. What if the Oldungur Council decides you intentionally broke your Class's Rules and finds you unworthy of existence? Do you think I want to see you annihilated?"

I offer him a lopsided grin. "You'll still have your good son."

"You're my son too. I love you," he says, tentatively touching my arm.

"Yes, but I'm not the one destined for greatness, am I?" I say, jerking my shoulder so his hand falls off me. "That honor is saved for my little brother."

"Stop comparing yourself to Villow or you will never be happy. You are meant to follow different paths. His is to be a Guide and yours isn't. Go to Cassandre, now, and tell her you made a mistake. Tell her you want to switch to the Soldier Class."

So typical, thinking he can dictate my life. "I don't want—"

"I am your father, Dameaon. You will listen to me."

"You're confusing me with my twin. He's the one who follows your every command," I say, jutting out my chin. "I won't change Classes. This is my life, and I'll live it the way I want."

My dad clenches his jaw. "You're going to be obstinate, as usual. No matter. I will have Cassandre retract her approval."

"Dad, no—"

But he's done listening to me. He charges out, slamming the door behind him.

And he says I'm dramatic.

Alone, I head over to his desk and sit in his swivel chair, spinning around a few times. A half-smoked cigar is resting in his ashtray. I pick it up and inhale sharply. It's a familiar scent—a mixture of the sweetness of cherry and the mustiness of soil. The entire room is swathed with the same aroma, albeit subtler, thanks to the thousands of cigars he's consumed in here.

There is a gentle knock at the door, and Katarin peeks in.

I place the cigar back in the ashtray. "Hey, String Bean. You lost?"

"I saw your father drag you in here," she says. "Are you okay?"

I shrug. "Why wouldn't I be?"

"I know how he can be," she says, pushing open the door and entering the room. Her long green dress's folds swish as she walks toward me.

"Well, look at you. You look nice."

She twirls a curl of long red hair around her pointer finger. "Thanks. My hair is driving me crazy, but ponytails and fancy dresses don't really mix."

"It suits you. You should wear it down more often."

"And you should wear yours back more. It's nice to see your face."

Katarin and I have flirted for years. It started when she was nine or ten and got bangs. I said I liked them in front of Villow, and it made him pout. Big mistake. Once I knew it annoyed him, I found every opportunity to compliment her when he was around. Even though the bangs have long since disappeared, the flirting has remained and is a habit at this point.

I run my fingers against my hair. It's stiff from the gel I used to style it. "Yeah, well, my mom was adamant I slicked it back or got a haircut. This was the clear choice."

"Like being a Guide was the clear choice?"

"Maybe not clear, but it was the right one."

"Why?"

I display a wide grin. "Why not? I know what's best for me."

She sits in the plush chair directly across from me. "Do you know who you sound like? Sariel."

"Your sister?"

"Yes. Sariel loves dancing, more than anything. When she turned sixteen, she wanted nothing more than to be a Performer."

I snort. "I've seen her dance. She's terrible."

Katarin laughs. "I know. She would have failed miserably. And my parents knew that too. But she's always had a skill for Magic, so they pushed her to be a Mage. And she did so well as a first-year Seeker, she's completing her second year of training at Shadowlodge, the most prestigious Mage school in Strongmist."

I tap my fingers against the mahogany surface of my dad's desk. "I'm assuming there's a point to your story?"

"My point is, my parents knew what was best for Sariel. Isn't it possible your father knows what's best for you too?"

"I won't change my decision."

"Oh, Dameaon, your pride is going to get you in trouble," Katarin says, standing. "Just promise me you won't drag Villow down with you."

I fold my arms across my chest. "What does this have to do with him?"

"Your decisions affect him. You know that. He's worked too hard to have your careless disregard for responsibility destroy this family's reputation."

I swivel the chair away from her, facing the wall. There are at least two dozen framed photos hanging on it: our family portrait from last year, a few more of my mom and dad, and the rest of Villow and his endless triumphs.

Rather than having to stare at his face, I shut my eyes. "If you're so worried about my martyr twin, maybe you should go find him and make sure he's okay."

"Dameaon, I'm not trying to fight with you. Think about what I said, okay?"

"Goodbye, Katarin."

"Ugh! You are so frustrating. Fine. Be that way."

Her dress swishes as she stalks out, leaving me to sulk.

Music and chatter echo into the study, and I glance at the door.

Thanks a lot, Katarin; she left it wide open. I'm not in the mood for any other visitors, so I shut it and collapse on one of the couches.

The leather's cool surface is refreshing—especially when the rage inside me is churning like the lava in the volcanos at Buhler's Crest. Where my dad is certain I will end up. Because failure is my only option.

Just once it would be nice if someone—anyone—had faith in my abilities. My dad is too worried about the great Verchant legacy to let me take a chance. And my mom is too wrapped up in herself to even notice me. Villow is too busy preparing for his amazing future, and Katarin is so transfixed on my twin that she's blind to everything else. In all of their senseless busyness, none of them have any time to enjoy life. It's not the way I want to live.

I only picked the Guide Class to irritate Villow, but it actually might be for the best. It's my opportunity to go to another planet. Maybe that Original Species will be more like me and I'll finally fit in. Somewhere I belong—it's a nice, but foreign, concept.

I can't let my dad take that chance away from me. I won't.

There will be time to fight with him later. First, I have to see what trouble I can stir up at my party.

AN UNWELCOME BIRTHDAY SURPRISE

EVEN THOUGH I'M CERTAIN MY FATHER WILL FIX DAMEAON'S colossal mistake, I'll feel much better once he confirms it. But our Path Ceremony celebration isn't the place to discuss it, not with other Glanchings in earshot. Besides, he's already in deep conversation with Oldungur Mekhi, no doubt about my twin.

Satisfied he's making progress toward our common goal, I join my classmates in the back of our yard.

"Okay, what was that? We weren't expecting that, right?" my friend Dexter Khan asks, shoving two cyperus-leaf-wrapped meatballs into his mouth.

"Whoa . . . don't talk with your mouth full, Chubs. It's disgusting," Colton Sturling, my least favorite classmate, taunts. "And you should probably cool it with the meatballs, or you'll end up looking like one."

Dexter's face turns red, and he glances down at the six remaining meatballs on his plate. There's a good reason Colton is my least favorite classmate; he's brazenly mean, ridiculing everyone and using their weaknesses to his advantage, guised as joking around. Unfortunately, Dexter's weakness is clear; almost all Glanchings are slender, and Dexter's plump frame is not the typical mold.

"Mind your own business, Colton," I say.

Colton's burgundy eyes turn to me. He roughly pats my back. "Sure, tough guy. Whatever you say."

I swat his hand away. "That's a cheap shot."

And it is, especially since he's six months into his two-year-long Soldier training and has more muscles in his pinkie than I do in my entire body.

Dexter runs his hand through his thinning mud-brown hair. "Can we get back to the topic at hand? Dameaon decided to be a Guide? Why?"

"What Dexter meant to say, Vil, is happy birthday, great job, and we're so proud of you," Katarin says, enunciating every word.

He shrugs. "Whatever, Katarin. You know as well as I do we're all thinking the same thing . . . even Villow. Right?"

I nod. "You're right. But I'm sure my father will fix this. There's no way he'll let Dameaon be a Guide, so let's not waste time talking about it."

Portia Sturling, Colton's younger sister, laughs, revealing the dimple on each cheek. "What's the matter, worried he'll be a better Guide than you?"

"Don't let her get to you," Colton says. "She enjoys nothing more than torturing people."

"Reminds me of someone else I know," Dexter mutters under his breath.

I'm conscious of Colton pretend-lunging at Dexter, causing him to stumble backward and drop his plate of meatballs. But I remain focused on Portia, just like I have for the better part of a year. I've memorized every detail of her face—her slightly upturned nose, high cheekbones, and plump lips. I know her mannerisms and their meanings by heart—the way she tosses her chestnut hair when she makes a point, raises her left eyebrow when she's skeptical, or throws her head back and laughs when she finds something especially humorous.

Katarin squeezes my fingers encouragingly. We've spent hours strategizing ways I can get Portia to notice me. Of course, I always recant and never act on our plans. But she did just talk to me and the band is playing a new song—a fast, upbeat tempo—providing a perfect opportunity.

"This is a great song to dance to," I say. "Portia, do you like it?"

"Not really," she replies. "I always thought it was a little, what's the word, boring."

I look down at the laces of my dress shoes; that was not the response I expected.

Katarin grabs my hand. "Well, I love it. Vil, can I have the first dance?" Without waiting for my answer, she tugs me onto the black-and-white checkered dance floor.

I lose myself in the music, enjoying the distraction from my embarrassment. At school, we take classes in a variety of subjects, including the arts, to get a glimpse of the five Paths. From dance class, I developed a little rhythm and can move reasonably well. Katarin, however, moves effortlessly. If she were beautiful, she could be a Performer, providing enjoyment and inspiration through her art. Of course, she feels the same way about Performers that I do about Soldiers and would rather "light herself on fire" than choose that Class.

The next song is "Ritzeta's Waltz," a slow dance we both know well. I bow in an exaggerated gesture and extend my right hand. Katarin giggles and reaches for it, but then she pauses, her eyes focused on something beyond my shoulder.

"Mind if I cut in, brother?"

I turn. Dameaon is directly behind me. Katarin positions her small body between us, one alabaster arm outstretched toward him and one toward me, in a preemptive measure to stop our not-yet-started fight. "Of course he doesn't mind. Plus, that means I get to dance with the best-looking guy at the party."

I clench my hands into fists; I despise how Dameaon and Katarin flirt with each other. I've confronted her on it numerous times, but she always laughs, insisting it's harmless. Even so, it's frustrating that she always seems to find some reason to compliment him.

"You heard her," Dameaon says and takes Kat in his arms.

Left without a partner, I retreat to the side of the dance floor. As much as I hate to admit it, Dameaon is a better match for Kat. He dips her gracefully, and she bends her back in a perfect arch.

From here, I see her in a different light. The ebony chandeliers strung across the canopy bring out the strawberry-blonde highlights in her curls. She's still ensnared in the awkwardness between a teenager and an adult, but she has a new elegance around her. My best friend is growing up.

"Hey there, darling," Portia says. "Having fun?"

"Yes," I say, my voice three octaves higher than normal. I try to come up with something witty, but the fact she called me *darling* makes every thought leave my brain.

She chuckles. "You're so articulate. I'm glad you're having fun, but I'm bored. And I actually like this song. Let's dance."

It's another slow song, which bodes well for me. I offer her my arm and escort her onto the dance floor. I take her left hand in my right one, hoping she doesn't notice the layer of sweat. She puts her other hand on my side, and I can barely breathe, but I manage to place my free hand above the curve of her hip. Her perfume smells fresh, clean, and airy, like the wild lupinus flowers that grow in the Summit, my favorite meadow in the Hyggelig Mountains.

I take my first step well ahead of the music, and Portia laughs, throwing her head back to display her startling white teeth. Her laughter cracks through my nervousness, and I join in. This is my chance, and I won't blow it.

Finding my rhythm, I move in time to the music. Portia keeps up with seemingly little effort. I can't help noticing how much of her olive-colored legs is visible below her strapless dress.

"You're not too bad at this," she says.

"Thanks, Portia. You're really great yourself," I reply, aware this is the first compliment she has ever given me.

"I know," she says, twirling out from me and back in.

I move to her left and place my right hand against hers, and we move in clockwise circles. Then we switch to our left hands and move counterclockwise.

"So how is your training going?" I ask.

"It's great. I'm already five months in. Look," she says, pushing her shoulder-blade-length hair away from the left side of her neck, revealing a thumb-size turquoise water droplet below her earlobe and a vivid amber fireball a bit farther back on her nape. Some of the Seekers—particularly Mages—use enchanted paint to permanently mark their skin with important moments from their training.

"They're beautiful," I say. "I can't believe you learned the Water and Fire Elements already."

"Water is my innate Element, but I learned all the Level One Fire Spells last month. Amorose took me to Kapitala to get these tattoos in celebration."

"That was nice of her. Did they hurt?"

"Nah, that's why we went to Kapitala. Deggadas, the owner of Den of Inktiquities, is the best. Most tattoo artists are former Performers, but he's an Alchemist. He used his potion-brewing skills to revamp the application process, so you barely feel it."

She drops her hair, and we resume dancing. The song ends, and she curtsies in typical Portia fashion—poised but not overstated. I bow, and when I straighten, she wraps her arms around my neck, leaning her head on my shoulder.

"Thanks for the dance, Villow," she whispers, her lips

brushing against the skin on my neck. Without looking at me, she hurries away.

I place my fingers where her lips were and close my eyes, savoring the sensation. It's painfully clear in that moment—I am totally and completely in love with Portia Sturling.

The next song starts, and I instantly recognize it. I make my way to the stage on the right side of our yard. Sure enough, my mother is there, microphone in her hand. She's in her element, enjoying the limelight.

"Hello, fellow Glanchings," she says, moving back and forth as if she's floating, a skill she learned when she was part of the Sympohoe. "I'm sorry to interrupt the fun, but if you could give me a few moments of your time, I would be forever grateful. I've sung this song to Dameaon and Villow on each of their birthdays and on this, their sixteenth one, I would like to continue the tradition."

She tilts her head back and closes her eyes as she starts to sing:

You are my gift, precious baby,
My world in ways you'll never know.
Hand in hand, we journey always,
Forever by your side to help you grow.
I will always be there,
To lift your weary soul.
I will always hold you close,
And I will make you whole.

If you get lost while on your way,
Tired and weary from where you roam,

Just follow the sound of my voice;
I will lead you home.
I will always be there,
To lift your weary soul.
I will always hold you close,
And I will make you whole.

The crowd cheers, and she blows a few kisses before descending the stage. Dameaon steps in front of me and hugs her first. After a few seconds, she releases him and embraces me. Then she races off to hold court with her friends, who are staring at her with awe. She kisses each of their cheeks warmly and smiles with more enthusiasm than she offered us.

My brother stills beside me. "Everyone thinks she's mom of the century, but I can count the times she was there for me on one hand."

I'm surprised by his reaction; he's never mentioned his frustrations with our mother before. Although what he's saying has some truth, I don't appreciate his unkind words. "She did the best she could, Dameaon. You know that."

"Of course she did. But somehow parties and friends were always more important than us."

"You know how busy she is. You should be glad she made any time for us," I argue, barely believing it myself.

He mumbles something incoherent before walking away.

I stare at his back until he disappears into the crowd and then join Katarin and Dexter at the banquet tables. The chefs outdid themselves, using the Larder of Plenty to create fantastic courses from thin air. I start with bookie-wrapped sea scallops, enoki caps filled with bramble bread stuffing, and teriyaki isys-bird skewers. For my main course, I load my plate with mountain-crest lettuce drizzled with ginger root dressing, orange-crusted trucun loin, and roasted grain potatoes with gravy. From the sea of desserts, I choose crème brûlée with graukleberry sauce. By the time I'm done, I'm certain I gained five pounds, but it's my night, so I justify it.

After letting my food digest for a few minutes, I make the obligatory rounds to my parents' acquaintances, accepting their wishes and praise. I consult with prior Guides, asking for advice on how to be successful in my new Class. Their pointers are generic: pay attention during training; think before you act; keep the greater good in mind at all times. Oldungur Mekhi congratulates me and recommends I always do my best. Like I would do anything else? As nice as it is to be part of their inner circle, I find the lack of real insight frustrating.

As the evening draws to a close, Dameaon and I stand by the front door, thanking our guests as they leave. After an hour, Katarin joins us.

"Congratulations again, Vil. Our spot, tomorrow?" she asks, referring to our tradition to meet up at the Summit after big events.

"Of course," I say.

Dameaon rolls his eyes, reaching over and hugging my best friend. "Hey, String Bean. Make sure you save a dance for me at the next event."

She giggles and hugs him back. He makes eye contact over her shoulder. Confident this exchange is meant to make me jealous, I ignore him and focus on one of my mother's friends. When I turn back, they're both gone.

My twin doesn't return, so I'm forced to say the rest of the thank-yous for both of us. By the time the last guest leaves, I'm exhausted. Even so, I won't sleep without talking to my father. I head down the hall to the study—his favorite refuge.

I raise my hand to knock, pausing right before making contact with the door; there are muffled voices inside. Uncertain of who it is, I don't want to interrupt. I turn to leave just as the door swings open.

Master Oldungur Cassandre is in front of me. Her chocolate eyes widen with surprise, but she smiles. "Ah, Villow, the Glanching of the hour. 'Twas a big day for you. I am sure you have much to discuss with Drasko, so I will not keep you." She looks pointedly at my father, who is sitting at his desk, before departing.

"Leave us," my father says.

Dameaon appears, rising from the high-back leather chair that was concealing him from view. He roughly bumps my shoulder as he exits.

I sit in the still-warm chair he vacated, directly across from my father. He moves to the far wall, standing in front of his bookcase. From my seated perspective, he appears taller and more imposing than normal.

"Villow, your timing is perfect. I need to speak with you."

"Me too. What are we going to do about Dameaon? What was he thinking? He can't be a Guide. . . . The very thought is preposterous. This is just one more example of his constant screwups. You need to fix it. You need to."

I know he heard me, yet he says nothing. Silence isn't his typical response; he's always been a Glanching of action, willing to speak his mind.

My heart pounds, and my hands moisten with sweat. I look out the window made of one-way glass to the conservatory. It's filled with exotic floras: lupinus flowers grow in clumps around the dragon statue in the middle; lycanids rest on the granite wall surrounding the garden, their petals forming fluttering butterflies; and fluffy calamus climbs up the side of the house, its rainbow colors camouflaged in the darkness of night.

The moons are fully visible now that Zon has set completely. Meta's cobalt-and-orange swirls shine the brightest, followed by Hermes's lavender and plum, while Yars's granite light is practically imperceptible because of its peers' blazing beacons. Countless stars surround them, offering a reminder that there's a larger universe at stake.

I draw strength from that and squeak out, "Father?"

He moves back to his desk, sitting down in his chair and grabbing his half-smoked cigar from the ashtray. He takes several puffs and exhales, watching the smoke wind toward the ceiling.

"I know your brother's free spirit frustrates you, and you believe he'll be a poor Guide Seeker. I agree, and that's why Dameaon and I planned he would be a Soldier. But things did not transpire as expected." He smiles, but his eyes remain dull. "I tried to get your twin to select a different Class, but he refused. Master Oldungur Cassandre wasn't aware of our concerns when she accepted his choice in front of hundreds of our peers. She's worried about how it will reflect on her if she forces Dameaon to switch Classes, so she thinks it's best for him to remain a Guide Seeker."

I rub the back of my neck. "But, Father, he'll destroy his Original Species. He's too self-centered to teach others how to live a good life, especially since he doesn't know how to be good himself."

He slams his fist down. "I'm aware of your brother's strengths and weaknesses. You don't need to rehash them for me." Softening, he continues, "That's why Cassandre and I came up with a potential solution. But . . . it's your decision."

I tilt my head to the left. "My decision? I already chose to be a Guide."

"Yes, I know. And you will be. But we thought . . . well, you and Dameaon could be co-Guides of one Original Species."

I jump up. "Father, no! There has to be another way. He'll go out of his way to destroy our Original Species just to spite me."

"Your brother would not risk his own future to spite you. Besides, we made it very clear he needs to take this seriously."

"Dameaon hasn't taken anything seriously in his entire life."

Putting his cigar back in the ashtray, my father comes around the desk and stands directly in front of me. He touches my cheek with his fingers. "Remember your oath tonight, that you would live for the greater good. This is your first opportunity to be a true Glanching. Think about the Original Species your brother would be responsible for. And our family's reputation."

My heart pounds against my chest. Suddenly, the entire night seems foolish. The Path Ceremony, the dance with Portia, talking with Oldungur Mekhi—all seem trivial if Dameaon is my co-Guide. I have the irrational urge to run to my bedroom and bury my head under my pillow, just like I did when I was young. But I'm no longer a child, so instead I force myself to stay. "What happens if Dameaon fails? I fail too, right?"

"You'll share the same Original Species, so if they are deemed evil, yes, you both would fail," he says. "Cassandre recognizes that and promised the Oldungur Council will take it into account during your report outs. She is on your side and won't forget the sacrifice you're making. But the choice is yours. You can deny Master Oldungur Cassandre's and my request."

I stifle a cackle. My father claims I have a choice, but I don't. He's right; a Glanching's life is about doing what's best for the greater good. Without me, Dameaon will fail as a solo Guide, destroying a civilization and bringing dishonor to the Verchant name. And as much as my twin's disregard for the Glanching Code of Conduct irritates me, I don't want him to spend eternity mining in Buhler's Crest, living with the rest of the outcasts in Rehuido.

I place my hand on top of my father's, which still rests against my cheek. "Okay," I whisper.

He smiles, and this time, his eyes brighten. "I have never been prouder of you. I knew you would make the right choice. You always do."

I warm at his kind words. "Thank you, Father."

"Thank you, Villow. Now get to bed. It's been a long day for all of us."

I bid him good night and head out of the study, closing the door behind me. But I don't go to my room; the storm inside my chest won't let me rest until it's unleashed. There's only one Glanching who deserves to be on the receiving end, and I know where to find him.

Sure enough, my twin is on the roof, standing where I stood just a few hours ago, before he destroyed my future.

"I hope you're happy," I say. "You messed everything up, as always."

He smiles. "Is that any way to talk to me? Honestly, brother, you need to respect me if our partnership is ever going to work."

"Respect is earned, and you've done nothing to warrant it. I'm warning you, if you stand in the way of my success, you'll regret it. What do you have to gain from all of this?"

Dameaon thinks for a moment. "A couple things. First, I thought about what you said earlier, and you're right. If I have to decide what I want to do at sixteen, at least as a Guide I won't be stuck on Reos forever. Second, this allows me to keep an eye on you so you don't create a population of weaklings. Third, and probably most importantly, I know how much you were looking forward to getting away from me, and this threw a wrench in your perfectly laid plans." He looks at the fingernails on his left hand. "All in all, I would say this is probably the best decision I've ever made."

My anger gurgles in my stomach, slowly making its way up my throat. "What did I do to deserve such a . . . a monster for a twin?"

"Temper, temper. We're co-Guides now. You really need to control your outbursts for this partnership to work." He saunters to the stairway leading back to the house, stopping on the first step. "Oh, I almost forgot . . . Happy birthday, brother."

RULES WEREN'T MADE TO BE BROKEN

I STORM INTO MY BEDROOM AND SLAM THE DOOR BEHIND ME. My desk lamp is the only light on, which normally gives the room a cozy warmth. But right now, it's a spotlight, shining on our family portrait—the same one hanging in the study. My dad is standing behind my twin, resting his hand on his shoulder. The message is obvious—Villow is the cherished son.

The rage inside me erupts into an inferno. I charge across my aubergine carpet and pick up the picture, throwing it against the opposite wall. The glass shatters, falling down onto my carpet in small, jagged pieces.

"You realize you could have hit me," Cinders says. He's curled up on my pillow, his wings pressed against his back.

The sight of him lessens my anger, just like it always does. "I'm sorry, buddy. I didn't know you were in here, but it was still reckless."

He releases a long yawn, revealing his mouth of sharp teeth. "Speaking of reckless, a Guide, huh? You keep things interesting, don't you?"

"You know me," I say, joining him on my bed. "I hate when things are boring."

"You certainly do. So now what?"

I shrug. "Now I'm a Guide."

He crawls onto my lap, and I scratch under his chin. "Do you want to be?" he asks.

I pause. "You're the first one to ask me that. Yes, I think I do."

"Then you should be," he says, shoving his head into my hand.

I chortle. "Why can't everyone be like you?"

"If they were, I wouldn't be so exceptional."

"That's very true. Are you sleeping in here tonight?"

He stands and stretches his back legs behind him. "No. The party delayed my exploring time. I need to go make sure everything is in order."

"Stop by the kitchen," I say. "I made the chefs save some scallops for you."

Cinders bumps his head into my elbow as a thank-you and then hops onto the empty twelve-inch shelf near my headboard. He continues to jump from shelf to shelf until he's sitting on the highest one, five inches from the ceiling.

He peers down at me. "Dameaon, for what it's worth, I'm proud of you. You did what's right for you, and that takes courage. More than most Glanchings have, in my experience."

I grin from ear to ear. "Thanks, buddy."

He pushes through the small door in the wall, heading

off to collect his scallops and then cause some mischief. I take a quick shower to wash the gel out of my hair.

After the never-ending disapproval I received this evening, I was certain I wouldn't sleep. Now drowsiness besieges me, all thanks to Cinders.

He's always been my only ally inside Spektrolith's walls. But that's okay. As long as I have my little wyvermalkin, I'll be fine.

FOR THE FIRST TIME EVER, I'M THANKFUL WHEN MONVREA arrives. Things at home are normally unpleasant, but dinner last night took it to a whole new level. Villow glared at me across the table like he wished I were annihilated, and my dad acted like I didn't exist. Only my mom was oblivious to the tension, prattling on and on about the success of our party the night before. By the time it was over, I was ready to disown all of them and move to a different district forever.

So, yes, I'm glad for the start of the school week. Especially since my Guide training will begin this afternoon. Still, regular, boring classes are no reason to rush to Moudrost. I take the long way—through our backyard, to the Hyggelig Mountains, and finally past the woods just south of the school.

Because of my choice of routes, I arrive at my first class—hand-to-hand combat—twenty minutes after it started. I enter the gym, expecting Professor Demetrius to yell at me. Not only am I late, he spent the better part of the last year convincing me to be a Soldier and I can't imagine he's happy with my sudden divergence.

But I'm offered a reprieve; Demetrius is visible through the glass wall of his office, talking to two of my classmates, Dougal Brendanus and Shane Coilean. He's probably recruiting them to be Soldiers. Perhaps they'll be more cooperative than I was.

I head left to the weapons wall and grab Calveras, my sword, advancing to the combat rings to partner up before Demetrius comes back. Halfway there, I stop. The rest of my classmates are gathered in a tight circle around one of the rings instead of sparring. That's odd. Practice combat is normally relatively boring. Most times, one fighter pins the other, who, in turn, admits defeat. On the rare occasion when neither fighter concedes, it evolves into a bloody, arduous brawl, ending when one opponent can't move. This fight must be the latter to have gathered everyone's attention. Pushing between two of my classmates, I reach the edge of the ring.

I picked the wrong day to be late. Colton and my twin are in the middle of an intense fight; knowing the former's pride and the latter's stubbornness, this will not end in a concession.

Colton strikes from the left, and my twin somersaults backward, landing a few paces away. Villow aims his right palm at Colton, using Ice Magic to launch frozen spikes across the floor. Colton counters with Lightning Magic, melting the icicles and a portion of the mat. He bends over, gagging from the smell of burnt rubber.

I roll my eyes; he's not the smartest Glanching in the bunch.

My brother uses the exposure to his advantage and charges. Colton straightens right before he strikes, so he feints an attack at his chest and roundhouse kicks Colton's legs. Villow launches another ice strike—this time scoring a direct hit. He lowers his blade to Colton's neck, signifying the end of a practice fight.

My brother is an idiot; there's no way Colton is injured enough to surrender.

Sure enough, Colton swings his sword upward so fast Villow can barely avert the blow. He rolls behind my brother and kicks his back—hard—causing him to stumble forward. Then lightning electrifies Villow, and he falls on his back.

Colton presses his blade against his neck. "Do you give?"

My twin shakes his head once. Good for him—at least he's got a little dignity left.

Colton's eyes glint hungrily, and he struts around the ring's circumference, holding his sword above his head like a trophy. Most of the Glanchings look away, abashed by his flashy behavior. But not Portia; she's jumping up and down, cheering loudly. Villow averts his eyes, embarrassed. I'm embarrassed for him. This is who he has a crush on? She's so obnoxious.

After his victory lap, Colton returns to finish off my twin. Villow closes his eyes, bracing for the excruciating pain of Colton's strike to his heart.

Colton raises his sword above his head and swings down with all his strength. I lunge into the ring and outstretch Calveras, meeting his blade with the clang of metal upon metal.

My twin opens his right eye a slit. When he sees me, both his eyes fly wide open.

"You owe me one," I say.

He nods, and I turn my focus on Colton. "Why don't you ever challenge someone who is your equal?"

Colton shrugs. "Because everyone is weaker than me, Dameaon. Including you. I could knock you down in three minutes."

"Prove it," I say, raising Calveras in front of my chest.

He releases a howl of fury, crouching in a fighter's stance. Ridiculous. This is practice combat, not war.

I charge him, swinging high, then low, from the right, then the left. Colton keeps up at first, but after five minutes his arms shake from the exertion.

"I think we passed that three-minute mark," I say, swinging Calveras behind my body and then forward, putting all of my weight into it.

The impact causes him to stumble backward. He jumps back on his feet, reverting to his fighter's stance. "I was going easy on you, Dameaon. Now it's time to get serious."

I've never had patience for narcissists, and he is no exception. Tired of his foolishness, I raise my left arm above my head. Purple gas spirals down, creating a flaming orb in my palm. I launch it at Colton's chest, and it explodes into electric magenta fireworks.

Colton falls onto his hands and knees, sweat dripping from his forehead. His eyes shine with hatred as he gets to his feet—jerkily.

He makes a fist and puts it against his forehead, thumb first. "You should have minded your own business, Dameaon. I won't forget this," he says, limping away.

"What is going on in here?" Professor Demetrius calls from his office's doorway.

Someone else can answer his questions; I don't have the energy for more nonsense right now. Returning Calveras to the weapons wall, I head out the side door to the school's courtyard. I walk past the Performance wing at the north side of campus and settle against a moss-covered boulder, shutting my eyes.

"Um, Dameaon."

I don't open my eyes; I don't need to. I'd recognize my twin's whiny voice anywhere. "What?"

He sighs. "Dameaon, I don't know what to say. You didn't need to jump in like that."

"I know I didn't. But Colton is becoming arrogant. Someone had to put him in his place, and it was pretty obvious it wasn't going to be you."

"I thought you might have been standing up for me. My mistake."

"That was your second mistake. The first was thinking you could beat Colton."

"Well, thank you anyway, no matter what your reasons were. It was fun to see you take him down a peg." He pauses, then tentatively asks, "So I knew you controlled the Water Element . . . but you can summon Dark Energy too?"

There is no way I'm going to attempt to explain my control of all of Reos's Magics to my brother when I don't understand it myself. I prop up on my elbows and look at him. "I saved you today because it was advantageous to me. That doesn't mean we're best friends who share their deepest secrets. Don't get confused, brother. Things are exactly the same between us. Well, except now you owe me one. And I always collect."

His face flushes. "I should have known better. You never do anything unless it benefits you."

He twists away, storming in the direction of the gym.

Oh, darn. I upset him—not that it's hard to do.

I place my hands behind my head and savor the sun's warmth on my skin. Classes suddenly seem like a lot of effort. Too much effort, especially when the boulder I'm leaning against is surprisingly comfortable.

A nap is exactly what I need to be at my best for Guide training this afternoon.

Zon is high above me when I wake. My watch confirms it's a little past lunchtime. Perfect timing, if I do say so myself.

I jog to the west part of campus and inside the Guide Seeker building, up the flight of stairs to the second floor. Thanks to my know-it-all twin, I know first-year trainees' classrooms are located here.

Unfortunately, I'm not sure which room is ours. I peek into three before I find Villow—seated at a desk in the front row.

He looks at his watch and then me, contempt written all over his face. Yeah. Because being a few minutes late is a grievous crime.

"Welcome, Dameaon," our Guru says, balancing cross-legged on top of his desk. "In the future, please try to be on time for training. If you take a seat, we can get started."

I sit at a desk in the fifth and final row—as far away from Villow as possible—and assess our Guru.

In a word, he's a mess. His wiry, platinum hair is disheveled, as if he hasn't brushed it in days, and falls in tangled clumps around his shoulders. The white linen shirt and navy pants he's wearing are so wrinkled, he must have slept in them. There's a smudge of what looks like his leftover lunch on his cheek. Unlike most Glanchings, appearance clearly means nothing to him.

It's an unexpected, welcome surprise, and I like him already.

He smiles at me, causing his slanted ice-blue eyes to crinkle. "I know Villow very well from his volunteer hours spent here at Moudrost's Guide wing, but I'm looking forward to getting to know you too. Before you arrived, Villow filled me in on the . . . circumstances that led to you being co-Guides."

Great. Not the best first impression. "I know you're our Guru, but I don't know your name."

"Ah, yes. That would be helpful. I'm Jetta. Jetta Kuo. I've worked here at Moudrost for, oh, three hundred years or so. After I completed my Guide tenure, leading the lizardlike species Lacertas to successful re-creation—"

"In a mere forty-two years," my twin says. "The average is one hundred."

Jetta smiles. "Yes, well, I was lucky. The Lacertas were naturally predisposed to goodness. Anyway, as I was saying, after completing my Guide tenure, I signed up to be a Guru, to help Seekers during their training."

I jut out my chin. "That's great, but I like results. Have any of your Seekers been successful?"

Villow turns around and shakes his head at me, as if I'm the biggest embarrassment in his life. But Jetta smiles again. "All three successfully re-created their Original Species, yes. And while this situation is a bit . . . unorthodox, I'm certain we will find success together too." He looks straight at me. "Of course, by the end of today, if you decide this isn't the right Path, we can petition the Oldungur Council for a switch. Sound good?"

I'm sure my brother is behind his suggestion. "I won't switch Classes. I'm meant to be a Guide."

Jetta nods. "That's good to hear. I don't like to waste my time and prefer working with committed Glanchings. Now that we've gotten that out of the way, let's get started. Like all Classes, Guides have their own sets of tools and secrets. You know that Glanchings are immortal and when we get injured, we heal quickly. That is because of Reos's Magic."

He takes two glowing embers from his desk's middle drawer, giving the admiral-blue one to Villow and the amethyst one to me. I hold it in my palm, and my entire body surges with power.

"After you declared your Path, our Senior Alchemists enchanted these Crystals for you," Jetta says. "Over the next couple weeks, you'll each design a piece of jewelry, so you can wear them on your planet and have a bit of Reos with you."

He pulls a chain out from underneath his linen shirt, displaying a silver amulet of an intricately designed malaa'ig tree. Its feathered wings swathe the tangerine Crystal in the middle.

"I still wear mine, almost four hundred years after my Guide tenure," he says. "It shared experiences with me that no one else has and, in some ways, is my closest confidant."

I gaze at my own Crystal, getting lost in the swirls of violet and rose churning below the surface. It consumes me, plummeting me downward into its infinity. Unnerved, I force myself to refocus on Jetta.

He tucks his amulet under his shirt and hands us each a black pouch. "Until they are secured on your jewelry, keep them safe in these bags."

I place my Crystal inside, and a strange sense of loss engulfs me, as if it's already part of me.

Jetta places a scroll in front of each of us and then returns to his desk, perching on the edge. "Before Guides began re-creating Original Species, Master Oldungur Relken and Hinnus, the first Guide Oldungur, composed *The Ten Rules for Guidance.*"

I unroll my scroll and grimace; it's so long it covers the entire desktop. The Soldier Class basically has one simple Rule: follow your commander's orders—at all times.

"There's so many," I say.

Jetta crosses his legs at the knee, adding another crease to his already wrinkled pants. "There must be, for the sake of the universe. The War of the Fiends destroyed all the Original Species, except for Glanchings. When Master Oldungur Relken decided it was time to re-create the lost worlds, he formed the five Classes to aid in the process. A Guide's role is the most important of all, so a strong set of Rules must be enforced."

"You mean the same Relken who willed himself out

of existence a few months ago?" I mutter. "I'm not sure I trust his judgment."

He looks down at the ground. Apparently, he has the same reaction as other adults when Relken is mentioned. He's silent for a moment and finally says, "Every Class has Rules, Dameaon. You know this."

"My brother didn't decide to be a Guide until two days ago, remember?" Villow says. "I'm sure he's never even looked at our Rules before."

Jetta raises his left eyebrow. "Is this true?"

I shrug; what good would come from telling him Villow is right?

He continues, "That is . . . startling. Most Glanchings are at least familiar with all the Class Rules prior to their Path Ceremony."

He stares at me expectantly, but I don't say anything. I learned a long time ago that silence makes most Glanchings uncomfortable and they will move on, even if I haven't responded.

After a moment, he clears his throat. "This will be even more important for you, then, Dameaon. You can follow along on your scroll while I recite them aloud."

> *Number One—What Is Done Cannot Be Undone. Once a decision is made, a species is created, or an action is taken, it cannot be changed or reversed. So make wise choices, for they are permanent and have lasting, unexpected effects.*

He pauses. "This Rule is more important for the two of

you than other Guides, for what one does, the other cannot change. If you work together, you'll have an advantage. But if you don't, you'll doom yourselves."

Villow turns around and narrows his eyes at me. I offer him a brittle smile, but this isn't great news. Working together has never been our strong suit.

Jetta continues:

> *Number Two—Do Not Be Discovered for Who You Are. As a Guide, you are required to live among your Original Species as one of them. No matter what the circumstances, you cannot reveal you are a Glanching.*

"Didn't you say your Original Species were scaly lizards?" I ask. "How did you fit in with them?"

"That's not quite the way I put it, but yes, that's another benefit of your Crystals," Jetta replies. "When activated, you can change your physical appearance."

"So I'll be a shape-shifter? Like, I can transform into anything?"

"Yes," he says. "Although the expectation is you will only do so when it's necessary."

This Guide thing just got even better. Maybe our Original Species will be something completely sensational.

"When do we find out who our Original Species is?" I ask.

"Can you stop interrupting?" my twin asks.

"It's okay, Villow. Dameaon is trying to learn," Jetta says. He holds up his right hand, his flat palm parallel to the ceiling, and chants, "Omna, lodna, glash."

A swirling mass of smoke appears, forming a vapor

figure. It looks like a female Glanching, minus the ethereal beauty. "She looks . . . like us," I say, unable to keep the disappointment from my voice.

"That is true, but do not be fooled by appearances. Your Original Species are called humans. Humans are born, die, and don't have magical powers." Jetta closes his hand and reopens it, transforming the smoke into a male. "Their instinct is to dominate everything around them, including one another. How you manage your Guidance duties will be essential, as humans are easily influenced, turning to darkness with little prompting."

He drops his hand, and the smoke disappears. "But we need to focus. Back to the Rules."

> *Number Three—Protect the Secret of Magic. Magic usage would reveal your differences and put your Guidance in jeopardy. Therefore, it should not be used in front of your Original Species, and never to kill.*

"Kill?" I ask. "Why would I kill them?"

"Conflict and war seem inevitable for the humans," Jetta says. "You will no doubt be dragged into their battles. But Magic gives you a distinct advantage over the humans, and you cannot use it to harm them. Moving on."

> *Number Four—Earn Your Own Way. As a Guide, you need to learn to survive in your Original Species's world. You must earn your way and not take from others to get by.*

Number Five—The Greater Good Is Most Important. During your trials, you will become attached to your Original Species and develop emotional bonds. Do not let your love of one influence you to act against the needs of the greater good.

Number Six—Intimacy Is Prohibited. Do not become physically involved with your Original Species. Although you will be disguised as one of them, you are not their species, and commingling is not allowed.

I scrunch my eyebrows together. "I don't understand. Why would I ever have a physical relationship with one of these lesser beings?"

Jetta nods again. "It might seem ridiculous now, but as you get older, it will be clearer. You'll spend most of your time on your planet and become lonely. I myself fought temptation several times during my years as a Guide, and my inhabitants were lizards. And I assure you . . . humans hold their own mystery and charm. They are capable of great evil, but also great love." He clears his throat and continues.

Number Seven—Do Not Become a Prominent Ruler. It is expected that Guides interact with their Original Species to influence their lives and teach them what is right and just. It is not acceptable to become a prominent ruler, as that is the role of the Original Species you are there to cultivate.

Number Eight—Report Outs Must Follow the Allocated Schedule. Your Crystal is programmed to alert you when your trial is over and it is time to present your Original Species's progress to the Oldungur Council. If you are certain you completed your trial prior to that, return early. If not, you must promptly return to Reos when your Crystal glows.

He pauses here again. "A Guide's first trial is for one year. Depending on how the report out goes, the next trial could be shorter or longer. Which reminds me."

Jetta heads to the back of the classroom and disappears inside the door on the right-hand side. He returns with an hourglass the size of my head, held on each side by a gold dragon's claw. The pink sand inside is flowing down at a steady pace.

"This is an Hourglass of Time," he says. "Alchemists enchanted it to magically link with your planet and control the movement of time there. Right now, the flow of sand is set to maximum speed, so the planet will develop quickly. As your civilization matures, we'll adjust it to slow things down."

He places it on his desk and continues, "There are two Rules left, but they are critically important."

Number Nine—The Truth Is Required. During your report out to the Oldungur Council, you must tell the truth regarding your behavior and that of your Original Species so they can fairly assess both your goodness and your civilization's.

Number Ten—The Oldungur Council Has Final Judgment. The Oldungur Council is the supreme judge of your inhabitants and their level of goodness. During your report outs, if they determine your Original Species has no hope of salvation, they will be destroyed and you will be deemed a failure.

The Rules—especially those giving the Oldungur Council free rein over both the Original Species's and my fate—are preposterous.

"I don't understand why we need so many Rules," I say. "I'm quite capable of making my own decisions and don't need anyone second-guessing me."

Jetta presses his lips into a grimace. "I'm sorry you feel that way, Dameaon. And I promise you, you're wrong. You'll become close with the humans and that could distort your viewpoint. The Oldungur Council provides a neutral perspective, ensuring there isn't a repeat of the War of the Fiends. Whether you agree or not, you must memorize the Rules and live by them. If you don't, you'll suffer the consequences."

"Consequences?"

Villow sighs heavily. "If the Oldungur Council determines you broke the Rules, they might annihilate you."

I draw my head back quickly. "Wait, what? That's

actually true? I thought that was just something Dad told us to keep us in line."

"How could you possibly think that?" Villow asks. "Do you ever pay attention in class?"

Jetta lifts his left hand, silencing us. "Dameaon, it is the same in all the Classes. If you simply follow the Rules, there is no need to worry." He hops down from his desk. "Enough grim talk. Let's move on to the fun stuff. Follow me."

We head into the back room. It's filled with various oddities: a gray box floating freely at waist height; a cherry-wood stand engraved with the suns and moons of the universes, holding a basin of water; a chestnut table holding a book; a shower big enough to hold three Glanchings at once; and a large black cabinet with a pewter glaze.

Jetta stops in front of the grainy square box. "This Dimensional Block is one of our secrets. It's made out of Magical Ore from Buhler's Crest and is enchanted with a Forbinder Potion. We use it to see your planet while still on Reos. To activate it, move your hand like this and recite, 'Porniti, sfera magica.'" He demonstrates, waving his umber-colored hand in a counterclockwise circle in front of it and then touching the top of the block.

It glows with a solid white light, transitions to opaque, and then disappears altogether. In its place is a rotating blue sphere. "This is Earth, your blank canvas," he says. "You will be responsible for creating species to dwell there with your humans, to help cultivate a civilization of peace and goodness."

My heart pounds against my chest; it's absolutely incredible. He gives us a moment to watch it. The only imperfection is a small brown spot in the center that disappears and reappears as Earth spins around and around.

The Rules, and the consequences of breaking them, had me down, but seeing Earth renews my excitement. We get to fill an entire planet with our own creations. That is so much better than learning proper sword techniques and battle strategies as a Soldier.

"Enough chatter from me today," Jetta says, mumbling, "Opriti, sfera magica," and waving his hand in front of the Dimensional Block in a clockwise circle. It changes back to a concrete square. "Before we part, do you have any questions?"

"When will we have our first test?" Villow asks.

I scrunch my face. "Seriously? Who asks about tests?"

"Always the anxious one, Villow," Jetta replies. "Soon. But for now, I recommend you work on your combat skills. I'm confident you'll be great Guides, but battle and war tend to be inevitable with humans."

Sparring with my twin—what a perfect way to end the day.

"Jetta, do you mind if I stay for a moment?" Villow asks. "I have a few questions concerning my assistant duties now that I'm a Seeker."

"Of course," Jetta says.

I have no interest in that boring conversation. "I'm heading to the gym."

"I'll be right there," Villow says.

I head south to the Soldier wing and take Calveras off the wall, swinging it several times through the air.

While waiting for Villow to join me, I think about Jetta's lesson today. I'm disappointed there are so many

Rules, but they seem vague enough that I'll be able to do what I want and still stay out of trouble. I'm excited about my Crystal and its power, and that we get to make a planet from scratch.

But I'm most excited about the humans. Their physical similarities to us were initially disappointing, but Jetta's description of their personalities is intriguing. They certainly sound more interesting than boring, self-righteous Glanchings.

"Humans," I say, the foreign word strange on my lips. "I think I'm going to like these humans."

TIPPING THE SCALES

I GLANCE AT THE SUMMIT'S WEST PATH, BUT THERE IS STILL NO sign of Katarin. She needs to get here; being alone with my thoughts has become detrimental to my psyche.

But how could it not be? My life was meticulously planned out to an infallible agenda. After successfully completing my Guidance duty, I would spend a century or two as a Guru in Qaflana, the Guide district. Then, when Oldungur Mekhi retired, the Council would appoint me as his replacement, making me the youngest representative ever. Portia and I would have an ardent courtship that led to marriage, becoming a power couple just like my parents.

Yes, they were big dreams, but they were achievable—until my screwup of a twin derailed everything.

A bumbler biene flies past my face, pulling me from my thoughts. It heads west, enticed by the lupinus flowers' fragrant pollen, buzzing from blossom to blossom.

Behind it, the path remains empty.

Come on, Kat, where are you?

As a diversion, I head to the east side of the Summit and dip my fingers into the stream. They glide through the cool water, making small ripples on the surface. The ripples only last for an instant before being swept away by the current, disappearing as if they never existed at all. How easily the stronger force overtakes them, smothers them, destroys them. And then they're gone—just gone.

My hand trembles, and I pull it back, wiping my palm against my jeans. Being co-Guides with my twin has not been good for my mindset.

To calm my restlessness, I move to the middle of the clearing and settle under a forty-foot cyperus tree. Its clusters of six-pointed magenta leaves block out Zon's rays. Hearing a branch snap, I turn.

Two bare feet attached to knobby-kneed legs confirm it's my best friend. She's dressed in her normal attire—a pair of baggy khaki shorts that end right above her knees and a tank top. Her flaming red hair is up in a high ponytail with one unruly piece falling across her forehead.

I sit up, relieved she's arrived. "It's about time you got here."

"You know I'm always late, Vil," she says, plopping down next to me. "What's going on?"

"Oh, nothing. Just lived through another afternoon of torture, training with Dameaon."

She tilts her head. "Torture? That isn't a bit of an exaggeration, is it?"

"No. Dameaon doesn't know anything about being a Guide, so he asks a million questions and Jetta mistakes his ignorance for interest. He's constantly praising him for his enthusiasm."

"I'm sure Jetta is just trying to encourage him."

I rub the back of my neck. "Maybe, but it's still agonizing."

"I bet," she says. "I don't understand what Dameaon is trying to prove. He should have been a Soldier."

"I don't understand anything he does," I say, offering her a small smile. "But enough about me. What's new with you?"

Her eyes sparkle. "I get to see Sariel tomorrow."

"That's right. How long has it been since you've seen her?"

"Three whole months. We talk at least once a week on our Transmission Stones, but it's not the same as living together. I can't wait to hug her."

I put my arm around her and pull her against my side. "I bet. Give her a hug from me too."

"I will," she says. Then Kat pushes away from me and scrunches her eyebrows together. "I'm gone tomorrow through Monvrea. Promise me you'll survive until I get back?"

"I think I can make it five days without you."

She grins. "Okay, but I expect Dameaon to be uninjured upon my return."

I tighten my lips and look away. It was a joke—obviously—but it hit a nerve.

"Vil?" she asks. "You okay?"

"Sorry. If I'm being honest, I guess I'm a bit jealous," I say. "Sariel and you are so close, and Dameaon and I are, well . . . not."

She puts her hand on my thigh. "I know. It's not fair."

I place my hand on top of hers. "At least I have you."

"And you always will. Tell you what, I'll take my Transmission Stone, just in case you want to talk."

"I'm not that needy, am I?"

"Do you really want me to answer that?"

There's a glimmer of mischief in her eyes and a smirk on her lips.

I grab her waist and carry her over to the thirty-foot water hole in the northeast corner, tossing her in. Seconds later, she emerges, thoroughly soaked and laughing. I jump in next to her, and we splash each other playfully. We're too old for this, but it's exactly what I need after the last couple days. Eventually, we retreat to the northern crags' granite ledges, resting in the sun's rays.

Hours later, Zon starts its daily descent. I lean my cheek against Katarin's head, savoring the warmth of her sun-soaked hair.

"We better get home for dinner," I say.

She gets to her feet, stretching her long, spindly arms upward and letting out a small squeak. Then she moves through the wildflowers toward her home, spinning back to blow me a kiss. "Don't let your brother get you down. The world is yours for the taking. You just have to be brave enough to seize it."

"Thanks, Kat. Safe travels," I say, navigating south through the jinger trees masking the trail to my home.

As I head down the trail, I think about what Katarin said. She's right; I'm allowing Dameaon to overshadow me in training with all his ridiculous questions. I need to be more assertive, to remind Jella I'm the one who has been preparing for this my whole life—the one who is destined to be a Guide.

THE NEXT SCHOOL DAY STARTS WITH SPARRING PRACTICE. I enter Moudrost and join Dexter in the gym locker room. He's sorting his potion kit in preparation for his Alchemist lesson that afternoon.

He holds up a bottle filled with purplish-blue liquid, so thick it looks like jelly. "What do you think this does?" he asks, squinting his beady, closely spaced gray eyes.

I grab the bottle, trying to determine its weight. "Hmm. Is it a Camouflage Potion to blend into the background?"

"No, those are green," he says, putting it back in the potion kit and returning it to his locker. "I was making an Illumination Elixir and I swear I followed the directions, but it's supposed to be white and fluorescent. Do you think it matters?"

I laugh. "Dexter, you're one of my best friends, so do me a favor. Don't drink that."

"I was thinking the same thing. I just wish I knew what I did wrong."

"Me too," Dameaon says, opening the locker next to mine. "We don't need haphazard potions made by mediocre Alchemists. Are you sure you picked the right Path?"

I glare at my twin. "You of all people cannot question someone's Path choice."

"So touchy, brother. Jetta thinks I picked the right Path. What was the word he used to describe me? Oh yes, a natural."

I clench my hands into fists, wanting to punch him in

the face. Instead, I slam my locker and grab my quarterstaff. Dexter does the same, following me into the gym.

"What was that about?" Dexter asks.

"Nothing," I say. "He's just being Dameaon. Look, as your friend, here's my advice. You need to relax, and making potions will come naturally."

"It's just so hard. I really wasn't expecting it to be this difficult."

I'm a bit surprised to hear him say that. As far as Classes go, Alchemy is considered one of the hardest. Alchemists craft potions that make life easier and ordinary objects magical. Some work closely with Soldiers, enchanting armor and weapons, while others draft blueprints for technological advancements like bridges, buildings, and transportation methods. They're the embodiment of Magic and science working hand in hand, which requires an analytical mind—making it perfect for Dexter.

"You're being too hard on yourself," I say, touching his shoulder gently. "It'll come to you. I promise."

The right corner of his mouth turns up slightly. "Thanks."

"Anytime. You ready to practice?"

He nods, and we hop up on the balance beam, swinging our wooden sticks at each other. Surprisingly, Dexter stays erect, matching my swings blow for blow.

After twenty minutes of sparring, we take a break. I lean against the wall, while Dexter simpers beside me.

"Okay, I give. Why are you looking at me like that?"

His grin widens. "It's better if I show you. Come on."

He leads me back into the locker room, opening his locker.

"Do you know what this does?" he asks, handing me a lime-green potion.

Small yellow curlicues swirl throughout the liquid. I recall my Introduction to Alchemy class last year, but come up blank. "I don't recognize it."

"That's because it's new. I invented it, all by myself," he says. "I'm terrible at following potion recipes, but I'm a wiz at making my own."

I collapse on the bench behind me. There are three tiers of Alchemists—Apprentice, Junior, and Senior. Only the most talented potion-makers achieve Senior Alchemist status, where it's permitted to invent new potions. Since Dexter is still a Seeker and not even an Apprentice, he's definitely out of bounds.

"What are you thinking?" I ask. "If anyone finds out, you'll be in a lot of trouble."

He hangs his head. "I know, Villow, but I don't see why. I have so many ideas and a natural talent for concocting. It seems silly to make the same old potions over and over. Other less creative Alchemists can do that."

I admire his ingenuity and the fact he found some much-needed confidence, but I can't encourage this. "I understand how you feel. But something could go really wrong. What does it do, anyway?"

"You know how I kept up with you while we were sparring?" I nod, and he continues, "I didn't become athletic overnight. But with my Rivelazione Potion—yes, I named it—I don't need to be. I poured a little bit on my quarterstaff, and now it detects my opponent's attacks and parries automatically. It doesn't guarantee I'll win, but it gives me a fighting chance. Pretty incredible, right?"

Jetta's warnings about following the Rules echo in my mind. "It's impressive, Dexter. But you're breaking the Rules. It's a dangerous road, and if you're not careful, you won't be able to find your way back. And it's not just banishment. You know what happens to Glanchings who purposely break the Rules . . . I can't even think about it."

"You're right," he agrees. "I won't do it again. But . . . this one is already made, so . . . think about the possibilities. I could put a drop on your sword, and then you could rechallenge Colton. Even if you don't win, a draw would still embarrass him."

I play his scenario out; each time I block Colton's blade, he would get more and more flustered. It would make him careless—sloppy even. I can almost smell the sourness of his sweat, pouring off his furrowed brow, as his face turns red and his desperation increases.

And Dexter is right—even if I don't win, our peers would be impressed. Especially Portia. She's seemed uninterested in me since I lost the fight with her brother, but this would change things. She would see me as strong, as her equal. It could be the catalyst to starting our relationship.

But as enjoyable as the fantasy is, it doesn't matter; using this potion is wrong, especially to deceive someone. Even if that someone is Colton.

"I can't, Dexter. Everyone would wonder how I suddenly became as skilled as Colton. And if the gossip reached our Gurus and they started questioning things, they might figure it out. We would both be in big trouble. Especially you." I give the potion back. "Get rid of the evidence and stick to your lessons. You'll get your chance to be creative eventually."

"You're right, Villow, as always," he says, placing the potion and his enchanted quarterstaff in his locker. "I'll dispose of them after school. But just once, I would like someone to put Colton in his place. I can't believe I had a crush on him when he first moved here."

I laugh. "Agreed. Now come on. Let's get back before we're missed."

We return to the gym and spar again. I knock Dexter and his non-enchanted quarterstaff off the beam seven times before class ends. Each fall, his eyes darken a little more.

"This was a lot more fun with my other staff," he admits after the final knockdown.

I offer him my hand, pulling him up. "Dexter—"

"I know, I know, you don't need to say it. I was just stating facts. I'm done. Promise."

We return to the locker room. As I shower, I contemplate telling his Guru about his misstep. But if I did, he would be in a lot of trouble. Perhaps even annihilated. I couldn't handle being responsible for the destruction of a friend. Besides, Dexter promised he was done, and he's never lied to me. There's no need to report him for one mistake. No need at all.

THE TIMBRE OF GURU JETTA'S VOICE IS SOOTHING. TOO soothing.

Regardless, I know how important his lessons are, so

I sit up in my chair and guzzle my coffee, concentrating harder.

My twin stifles a yawn behind his left hand. Jetta stares at him and drops his textbook to the floor with a loud bang. Dameaon jumps in his seat, and I smile.

"I realize you might find this tedious," Jetta says, "but it's imperative to understand Earth before journeying there. Remember, knowledge is power."

"All we do is listen to lectures," my brother says. "What good is all this information if I never get to do anything with it?"

"You'll get to use it," he replies. "But these lectures, as you call them, make you a better Guide. With so much at stake, you can't go into this blind."

My twin nods reluctantly, and I take a deep, calm breath. I knew it was only a matter of time; Dameaon is damaging his relationship with Jetta all by himself.

Our Guru picks up his book and reopens it. "As I was saying, Glanchings placed zircon crystals on the Earth, which gave it the energy necessary to be a host planet. The crystals also quelled the remaining molten rock, forcing it below the surface. Then lengthy periods of precipitation formed large bodies of water, making the planet nearly ready to support human life."

He closes the book and places it on his desk. "The final step of creating a host planet is now in your hands. As you would say, Dameaon, we are finally going to *do* something. Come."

We follow him to the table in the back room. "We spent the last two weeks discussing Guide essentials and the history of humans. Now we're ready to move into the Development Phase."

Jetta grabs a periwinkle potion and heads to the shower-like machine on the left side of the room. He pours it into the top nozzle of the shower. "This is a Teleportation Machine. The Transmission Potion I just poured into it will enable us to go to Earth."

"Wait, we're going to Earth? Now?" Dameaon asks.

"Yes, it's time for your first test," Jetta says. "In a few moments, you will create a flora. Which is good timing, since you're so bored with my lectures."

"I didn't say I was bored," my twin says. "That's a bit extreme."

Jetta smiles, enjoying the repartee. I curl my lip; just like that, Dameaon's back in his good graces.

"Here, put these on," our Guru says, handing us our Crystals, now embedded in our chosen jewelry. "They were finished for you yesterday. And not a moment too soon. They are linked to the Hourglass of Time, so we can go to Earth for small periods during the Development Phase."

I examine my amulet. Reos's Elements are strategically placed around an ankh with my deep blue Crystal in the middle. It's beautifully crafted and even better than I hoped it would be.

And I hate to admit it, but my brother's ring is extraordinary; the head is an engraved gargoyle with curved wings surrounding its simian body like a halo. His amethyst Crystal is clutched in its clawed hands.

Dameaon slides his ring onto his left pointer finger,

and I place my amulet around my neck. Jetta holds up two dull gold laptops, handing one to each of us. They're sixteen inches long and only half an inch thick. "These are Creation Claviatures. Think of them as depositories, holding the necessary components you will combine together to create all the species that will inhabit Earth." He gestures to the Teleportation Machine. "After you."

We step inside, and Jetta pushes the circular button on the front of the shower. Droplets of the potion hit my arm's bare skin, and my vision blurs, shifting to total blackness and then surging whiteness.

When I can see again, I'm on an island of dirt, no bigger than Spektrolith. The sky above me is cyan—much bluer than Reos's lavender—and the sun is more yellow than Zon's vivid orange. A cool breeze brushes my skin, and the salt it carries stings my eyes. I take a few steps forward, to where the waves crash into the island. The turquoise water surrounding me is endless.

I'm on Earth! Earth! My planet! I reach down and clutch some of the russet soil in my hands. Smiling from ear to ear, I toss it above my head.

"Can you not act like an idiot?" my twin asks.

"Come on, Dameaon, this is our moment. We're on Earth. Our planet."

Jetta nods. "Villow is right. Take a second to enjoy this. Look around. This is your blank canvas. You have the opportunity to make it a paradise for the humans."

Dameaon tosses his hair out of his eyes. "That's my point. I want to do my job, not throw dirt around."

I clench my fists; my twin is once again wrecking what

should be a great moment. "Maybe that's because you haven't been wanting this your entire life like I have."

"Sorry I'm not boring and don't plan out every single moment of eternity like you."

"Okay, boys, that's enough," Jetta says. "Today is about getting along, not fighting. Your test is to create a tree, flower, or other type of foliage to provide oxygen. You must agree on whatever you create, and I must approve it for you to pass. But don't worry. No one has ever failed this test."

"No one has been saddled with Dameaon before either," I say.

Jetta frowns. "That was unnecessary, Villow."

"Yeah, brother, how do you know we won't fail because of you?" Dameaon says.

"No one is going to fail," Jetta says, enunciating every word. "But since you brought it up, if you do, you get two more tries before you're dismissed as Seekers. Now, Villow, if I can borrow your Creation Claviature, I'll show you how to use it. Dameaon, feel free to follow along on yours. I've linked them for now, so whatever happens on one happens on the other."

I hand Jetta my laptop, and he opens it in front of him, releasing it. It magically hovers in midair. A two-foot-wide, semitransparent, lime-green square appears on the ground next to us.

"These laptops have standard keyboards and touch screens. There are different tabs to aid in creating your species," he says, demonstrating by tapping the Category tab at the top of the screen. The words Flora, Animals, Landscapes, and Create Your Own appear. "There is also a freestyle tab, where you can use the stylus to create something from scratch, but I recommend waiting on that until you've had a few successes."

He touches Flora, and the subcategories of Trees, Shrubs, Flowers, and Other appear. Jetta selects Trees, and a brown trunk pops up on the screen. An identical three-dimensional hologram forms on the lime-green square. He touches the trunk on the screen and uses the keyboard's arrows to scroll through the options. The hologram follows along, changing with each click, until Jetta decides on a smooth bark archetype.

Small color squares are arranged in a single column on the right side of the screen. He scrolls down until he reaches the browns, selecting mahogany. Then he moves on to the leaves, deciding on a teardrop shape and hunter green for color. He glances up at the hologram and nods, as if he's satisfied.

"The outward appearance is complete, but my work is not over," he says, selecting the Traits tab. "Defining your creation's traits is critically important. I want this sapling to be similar to our cyperus trees. Its leaves will change colors in the different seasons, and in the bitter cold of some parts of Earth, it will shed them to conserve energy. The zircon crystals and water will help it grow, and when it dies, it repays them by fertilizing the soil."

He types everything he just said on the keyboard, and the list of characteristics show up on the screen. "There, that should do it, I think. Are you boys okay if I approve this? It would be a nice addition to Earth, in my opinion."

"Of course, Guru," I say.

Dameaon nods, and Jetta pushes the Execute button.

An approval screen pops up. He types in a code, and the tree's hologram turns solid.

"While we are in the Development Phase, I'll set the Hourglass to advance Earth's time quickly each evening, so your approved creations spread across the planet. In some places, my sapling will thrive and multiply; in some, it will adapt to survive; and in others, it will die. But that's all part of the process."

Jetta hands the Creation Claviature back to me. "Now it's time for your test. Use your imaginations and make something inspired, but it must meet three requirements. One, it must be able to survive on Earth; two, it can't be evil; and three, it must add value to the humans in some way. And remember . . . you're a team, so you must agree before submitting your flora for my approval."

My twin has already selected Flowers from the menu and is flipping through stems. Katarin's words echo in my brain: *The world is mine, if I'm brave enough to take it.*

"I want to create lupinus flowers, like the ones in the Summit," I say. "What do you think, Dameaon?"

"I'm not surprised," he says. "How unoriginal."

Still, he flips through the stems, stopping at a thin one that mirrors the lupinus flower's. Then he selects rounded leaves. "Like this?"

I nod, pleased he's cooperating, even if he is hogging the controls. I touch the petals and use the left arrow button to flip through the choices. My brother begins pushing the left button too, scrolling so fast the screen becomes a blur.

"Dameaon, you have to let me navigate too," I say. "We're a team."

"Your brother is right," Jetta says.

My twin scowls. "I just let him pick the stems."

"You didn't actually let me do anything, though," I say.

"Fine, baby," he says, dropping his hands to his side. "Go ahead."

I ignore his dig and get to work, choosing small florets to finalize the construction of the flowers. I change the stems and leaves to grassy green and select cerulean blue for the petals.

In the Traits tab, I add notes about how the petals grow in clumps and describe their fresh, clean smell. It evokes memories of Portia's perfume, and I can't help wondering if that was my real reason for selecting them.

"Okay, that looks right," I say. "It's ready for approval."

"Not quite," Dameaon says. "I have a few tweaks."

He selects the Freestyle tab and takes the stylus from the side of the laptop.

"What are you doing?" I ask.

He begins to draw long, thin tentacles, coming out of the petals' centers. "Protecting our flowers. If humans try to touch them, these tentacles will shoot out and strike them."

I clench my fists tightly. Just when I start to believe we could work together, he does this. "Seriously? Jetta said we couldn't create something evil. Do you want us to fail our first test?"

He stops drawing and looks at me. "These flowers aren't evil. They won't hurt the humans if they leave them alone. Jetta said it himself. Humans are destructive."

I turn to Jetta. "My brother is being unreasonable. I can't work with hi—"

"And *my* brother is being a control freak," Dameaon says.

Guru Jetta puts his pointer finger against his lips, silencing us. "Boys, stop. You must work together. And Dameaon, while I agree the flower isn't evil, I would argue it's unnecessarily dangerous. Are you certain this is what you want to create?"

My twin glares at him. "You keep saying humans are prone to selfishness and harm. I'm trying to teach them there are consequences to destroying things."

"Is that really what you're trying to do?" Jetta asks. "Think long and hard before answering."

"Yep. I'm sure," he says, but he won't meet Jetta's eyes.

"This flower is not befitting for Earth," I say.

"Fine, but I'm not making lupinus flowers," Dameaon says. "That's just unimaginative and stupid."

"No, it's smart. There's plenty of time to use the Freestyle tab once we pass our test."

He shrugs. "I'm not giving in, brother."

I cross my arms in front of my chest. "Well, I'm not either."

Jetta raises his eyebrows. "If you can't agree, I have no choice but to fail you."

"Then we fail," my twin says.

I shut my eyes. I want to pass—more than anything—but Dameaon cannot bring these flowers to life. "I can't agree to this . . . abomination."

Jetta sighs. "Then there is no reason for us to remain on Earth. Intoarcere, intoarcere."

The world blurs, and we are back in the Teleportation Machine. Jetta charges out, pacing in front of us. "That was very troubling, boys. This is the easiest test you'll have. It's meant to be simple, to ease you into the creation process."

He stills and runs his fingers through his hair. "You only have two more chances to pass, and if you don't, you'll be kicked out of Guide training and sent to Rehuido. Tomorrow, you must come to class ready to partner. Got it?"

"Got it," my brother mocks and storms out.

Jetta turns to me. "The Oldungur Council is not going to be pleased. I can buy you some time, but you must get through to Dameaon. Your success depends on it."

I grind my teeth so hard my jaw hurts. Master Oldungur Cassandre is the one who forced this partnership on me and now expects me to fix it.

"It's not fair," I say. "And Dameaon has never listened to me."

"That may be true, but you must find a way to get through to him now."

I shake my head. "Jetta, you are our Guru, and I will do anything you request. But what you're asking is impossible. Surely you can influence him easier than I can."

His face sags and his shoulders hunch forward, as if I just placed an invisible weight on them.

It doesn't inspire confidence, and a chill forms at the base of my spine. "Guru?" I whisper.

He moves to the pewter cabinet, holding his hand in front of the locked doors and whispering inaudibly. Reaching inside, he returns, cradling a small garnet sphere.

"Do you know what this is, Villow?" he asks. I shake my head, and he continues, "It's an Essence Orb. All Original Species, including Glanchings, have one. After the War of the Fiends, the Oldungur Council gathered the orbs from the destroyed planets and secured them at Kapitala. And that's when they noticed something troubling. While the Glanching Orb continued to shine brightly, the others dimmed a little more each year. But when Guides successfully re-created Original Species, their orbs returned to full luminance.

"This is the humans' Essence Orb," he says, holding it out. I cup it in both hands. "As you can see, the light is barely visible. We've tried to re-create humans time and time again, but they always turn evil and have to be destroyed. Their orb is so dim now, the Oldungur Council is certain this is their final chance. If you fail, their orb will stop glowing, and humans, as an Original Species, will be no more."

My legs tremble with the severity of my mission. "Why did you give me the humans after you knew Dameaon was my co-Guide? Surely there's another Seeker who can take on this mission. Someone who isn't saddled with my twin."

He takes the orb back. "Villow, your firm convictions and caring nature will help the humans embrace their creativity and passion. But they're also selfish and impulsive, much like your brother.

"I'm not sure why Dameaon is what he is or why he chose to be a Guide, but his nature is the very reason you were assigned the humans. The Oldungur Council and I are certain he is the key to reaching them. You need to help him grow. Your success hinges on it."

My heartbeat quickens; I always considered myself a hero-in-training, but my twin is the true bridge to reaching our Original Species? It's one too many disappointments. One too many blows to my self-esteem. One too many times my brother wins. It's all just too much.

I run from the room and down the stairs, ignoring Jetta's pleas to stop. Outside, I inhale deeply, willing myself not to cry.

An unpleasant tingling develops at the base of my neck, creeping through my body. I open my eyes and glance around Moudrost. Dameaon is across the courtyard, smirking at me—as if he knows why I'm upset.

My weak grasp on my composure crumbles, and I'm overtaken by sobs. Wanting to escape it all, I run down the trail toward home.

HALFWAY TO SPEKTROLITH, I QUELL MY TEARS ENOUGH THAT I can breathe again, bringing back my ability to think. Jetta is right; someone needs to get through to Dameaon or we will fail as Guides. But he's wrong about who can do it. My twin will never listen to me. In fact, if I try, he will be more heinous out of spite.

He does, however, listen to my father . . . every once in a while. And although he won't admit it, my twin would do anything to gain his respect. If I can persuade my father to talk to him, Dameaon may comply.

It's my best chance. Quite possibly my only one.

I pick up my pace, hoping my father is working from home today. More and more, he's taken the train to Kapitala—often three or four times a week. While it's only a two-hour ride and he's always back by dinner, this is too important to wait.

I enter the foyer and place my hand against my chest; even from here, I can hear my father's deep surly voice. I head down the hall and stop outside his closed door.

"Enough excuses," he says. "I'm ready to move forward. Now."

His tone is insistent, and he's practically shouting. Intrigued, I press my ear to the door.

"Your emotions are running high," a husky voice says. It's female but definitely not my mother's lyrical resonance. "No one is stalling. But if you do not calm down, you will ruin everything. Operations of this magnitude take time to execute correctly."

"I understand, but I am running out of patience," my father says. "This is my life, not yours. And you promised to help me."

"I am helping you," the female replies. "Just give me a little more time to do things the right way."

He sighs heavily and remains quiet for a few seconds. "Yes, of course," he says finally. "You're right. I apologize for my outburst."

I back away from the door and bow my head in shame. It's wrong to listen to his private conversation, especially when it's clearly a personal matter. I'll come back later, once his guest is gone, and—

"Villow, you're home early," Jinnet, one of our housemaids, calls from the foyer. "Are you feeling okay?"

I race down to her. "Oh, I . . . Training ended early, and I wasn't feeling well. I'm heading up to bed."

"Do you want me to bring you anything?" she asks. "Some myntu tea perhaps?"

There's a negligible click behind me, but my guilty

conscience makes it as loud as the clap when Mages summon Thunderous Tempest. I shut my eyes, beseeching it's not my father opening his door.

"Villow?" he says. "What are you doing home?"

I inhale sharply and turn. "Hello, Father. I had something I needed to discuss with you, but it sounds like you're in the middle of a meeting, so it can wait."

He narrows his eyes but says, "I have time now. Come in."

His sharp tone is less than inviting, but I follow him. He's already back at his desk, writing furiously in a book.

I scrunch my eyebrows together; there's no one else in the room, but I definitely heard another voice. His Transmission Stone is on his desk to the left of the book. Of course. He must have been on a call.

"What is so urgent you had to leave school early to speak with me?" my father asks, not glancing up from his writing.

I sit in the leather chair across from him. "I didn't leave early. Jetta dismissed us, after Dameaon made us fail our first test by creating a monstr—"

He stops writing and looks up at me. "You failed your first test?"

"Only our first attempt," I say. "We get two more tries."

He leans back in his chair. "Villow, be cautious how you communicate. For a moment, I thought you failed Guide training."

"I'm sorry, Father," I say. "We haven't failed. At least not yet. But Jetta is convinced if someone doesn't get through to Dameaon, we will. Jetta asked me to talk to him, but you know that will only make things worse. I thought . . . maybe you could remind him of the consequences of failing."

He returns to his writing. "Yes, of course. I'll talk to him after dinner. Now unless there is something else, I really must get back to work."

I still; his quick dismissal is unusual, especially with me.

I pluck a piece of lint off my jeans and toss it on the ground. "Shouldn't we take a few minutes to strategize?"

"I successfully manage the entire district of Belkin. You don't think I can control my own son?"

"I do. It's just—"

"Villow, I know you're trying to help, but this is urgent," he says, pointing to his book. "I promise I'll deal with your twin later tonight. Now go. Please."

I stand, but there's an odd fluttering in my gut. "Who were you talking to?"

"Talking to?" he says, not even looking up.

"Before you came out of your study. I heard you talking to someone."

"I haven't talked to anyone all afternoon. Besides you, that is," he says. "Perhaps you mistook my music for a conversation."

His Axaftin Orb is on his desk. It's a good excuse, but I'm positive I heard his voice. I glance at his Transmission Stone again. As discreetly as possible, I touch the surface with my left hand; it's warm, which means he used it recently.

He's lying.

But why? As far as I know, my father has never lied in his life. It's in direct violation of the Glanching Code of Conduct. His secret has to be something big to warrant it. It shakes me—to my very core—and I don't want to be here anymore.

"T-T-That must be it," I say. "I'll let you work now."

"And I'll let you know how it goes with your brother," he says.

I head up to my bedroom, my arms hanging at my sides.

This day was an absolute disaster. Dameaon caused us to fail our test, and then Jetta shared that my twin is critical to our Guidance success. I asked my father for help, so I don't get banished, and he barely seemed concerned. And then he lied to me.

I take my Transmission Stone off my desk and settle on my bed. Katarin can help me figure it out. I touch the screen but pause before saying her name. I shouldn't bother her, not while she's visiting Sariel.

Besides, my father is the most upstanding Glanching I know. And experience has taught me that things are often different from how they appear. For all I know, my father's planning a surprise for our family, and he lied so he didn't ruin it.

Satisfied there must be a logical explanation, I place my Transmission Stone on my nightstand and sit at my desk to study.

THE NEXT BIG HERO

I CONJURE A SMALL ORB OF WATER IN MY CUPPED HAND AND offer it to Kitsune. He dips his pointed snout against my palm and drinks greedily, swishing all four of his fluffy white tails back and forth.

Kitsune and I have been friends for a long time. Three years ago, I started eating my lunch alone in a field north of the Performer wing. One day, an alabaster lis—no bigger than my boot—joined me. I gave him a bit of cheese, and he came back the next day and introduced himself. Within no time, Kitsune and I became almost daily lunch buddies.

"Thanks, Dameaon," he says, rubbing his velvety fur against my cheek. "Same time tomorrow?"

"Sounds good," I say.

He dashes across the field, a stark white streak against the lush green meadow. The tips of his enormously large ears poke through the tall grass as he nears the forest's edge. Idly, I wonder what he'll do for lunch when I leave for my trial.

If I leave.

As far as I can tell, I stand a better chance of ending up in Rehuido than on Earth. And it's all my brother's fault. My petty, cannot-fight-his-own-battles brother. He ratted me out to our dad instead of trying to talk to me himself. And dear old dad couldn't miss the opportunity to lecture me about the greater good and the impact my actions have on the Verchant name.

I finally agreed to compromise, as long as Villow would do the same. It was worth it to shut him up.

But yesterday, my twin re-created his lupinus flowers—without consulting me—making it clear he wasn't open to a give-and-take. So in return, I added pungent poison that caused the humans to lose their eyesight if they plucked the flowers. He threw a fit, and we reached another stalemate.

This afternoon, we have our third and final attempt at our flora test. I don't want to fail, but I won't create flowers with no protection. Not when Jetta has preached over and over how selfish humans are. Even if it means banishment.

The sound of laughter echoes behind me; someone is coming, and I'm in no mood for conversation. I scoot behind a boulder, attempting to hide.

Portia, Colton, and Nemesis Coollidge enter the east side of the field, the latter two with their swords. Fantastic. The Sturling siblings. It couldn't get any worse.

"All right, Nemesis, you ready to take another beating?" Colton asks.

Nemesis shakes his head. "I thought you were going to help me with my technique?"

Oh, Nemesis. He is a fool, like most of my classmates—but a kind fool—and Colton takes full advantage of it. Nemesis is nimble on his feet, making him a perfect candidate to be a dancer in the Performer Class. But instead, Colton bullied him into becoming a Soldier Seeker, no doubt to make himself look better in comparison. And even though Nemesis is only a month younger than Colton, they're years apart in fighting skill.

"I am," Colton says. "Watch me whup you. It'll teach you how to be a master fighter."

Nemesis shifts uncomfortably. "I really don't learn much when I'm fighting you. I'm more focused on defending my—"

Portia thrusts her hip into Nemesis, causing him to stumble to the right. "Stop being a baby and show us what you got."

Even if I didn't know Portia and Colton were siblings, I could guess it; they're the two biggest bullies I know. And poor Nemesis is too nice to say anything.

Lucky for him, I've never been accused of being too nice.

I hop to my feet and into the field. "Nemesis, if you need help with your fighting technique, ask someone else—someone who isn't such a jerk. And Portia, can you stop talking? Your voice is so whiny. It's giving me a migraine."

Colton gets so close, our noses are practically touching. "Watch it, friend. That's my sister you're talking to."

I shove his shoulder. "First of all, we are not friends. Second, find a mint. Your breath is disgusting."

He unsheathes his sword. "You have a smart mouth, Dameaon. I'm going to teach you a lesson."

Nemesis grabs Colton's shoulder. "Colton, come on. He's not worth it."

He shakes his hand off. "Stay out of this."

Portia shoves herself between us. "No, Nemesis is right. Dameaon is definitely not worth it. You're already in trouble with your Guru because of your temper. If he finds out you're picking fights, he'll kick you out of training."

Colton lowers his sword. "Okay, okay. Besides, there's no glory in beating up a Guide Seeker. They're all a bunch of losers."

I toss my hair out of my eyes. "That's funny. I seem to remember this loser destroying you last time we fought."

He lunges for me, but I'm prepared and somersault to the left. I hop up, raising my hand to the sky to conjure Dark Magic.

Portia grabs his arm, tugging desperately. "Walk away, Colton. Please. For me. I can't lose you."

He looks at her and softens. Then he turns toward me and spits on the ground.

"You're not worth it. You're not worth anything. You're always playing the hero, fighting everyone else's battles. Mark my words. One day you'll pay for it," he says, stalking off toward Moudrost.

I catch Nemesis's eyes. "You seriously need to reevaluate who you consider a friend."

He offers me a half smile but follows Colton.

Portia doesn't leave so quickly. She glares at me with

fire in her eyes. "Why do you always have to be such a downer?"

I jut out my chin. "Why do you always have to be so mean?"

She makes a fist with her left hand and places it against her forehead, thumb first, and then charges back to Moudrost.

"Yeah, well, franzleduk to you too," I shout after her.

I shut my eyes; this was not what I needed. Not right before my impending failure as a Guide.

With no time left before training, I head back to the courtyard. Colton and Nemesis are sparring, with Portia cheering on the sidelines. And my brother is there too, staring at Portia with a dopey look on his face.

I have no clue what he sees in her. She goes against everything he stands for. She's unkind, bossy, and superficial. While he's annoying and pretentious, he's also complex and honorable.

Honorable. Of course. My brother lives for the Glanching Code of Conduct. I can use that against him.

I stand at the entrance of the Guide wing, waiting for him to finish his awkward attempt at flirting. Eventually, he stops embarrassing himself and heads my way.

He shakes his head when he sees me. "What do you want, Dameaon?"

"Oh, nothing much. Just thought I would share my genius plan to save us both from banishment."

He crosses his arms. "You have a genius plan?"

"Yep. I'm calling in my favor."

"Your favor?"

"Remember when you decided to fight Colton last week and I had to intervene?" I say. "You agreed you owed me one, and I'm collecting today. I'm going to create whatever I want, and you're going to let me."

"You're insane. There is no way I'm doing that. Those two favors are not even close to being comparable."

I examine the fingernails on my left hand. "Your word is a promise that cannot be broken."

"What?" he asks, scrunching his nose.

"It's from the Glanching Code of Conduct. I know it by heart, since you're always quoting it to me. This is your chance to prove you actually follow your precious code."

He looks at the ground. "This isn't fair."

"Fair. Is that your favorite word? Life isn't fair, brother, and it's time you learned that. Decide what's more important to you: letting me make one little creature out of hundreds or your promise."

I don't wait for his answer; I don't have to. I know my righteous twin. He won't go against his word.

I'll make what I want today, no questions asked.

The Hits Keep on Coming

How did I let this happen? I'm one false move away from failing as a Guide, and Dameaon just took away all hope of his concession.

I would give anything to reverse time and refuse my twin's help during my fight with Colton. So what if I looked pathetic in front of Portia? It's nothing compared to what I'm facing now.

But Dameaon is right; I agreed to owe him a favor if he helped me. And the Glanching Code of Conduct is clear about keeping promises. Besides, even if I refused his request, there's still no guarantee we could create something we agree on. Knowing Dameaon, he would refuse to cooperate out of spite.

That means my only chance of passing the flora test lies in my unpredictable twin's hands.

The thought makes my legs quiver, but I take a deep breath and enter the Guide classroom. Jetta and Dameaon are standing by the front windows, speaking in hushed whispers.

"Ah, Villow," Jetta says, offering a weak smile. "Right on time. Now that you're both here, let's begin your test. I really hope you took my words to heart and partner to make a flora."

Dameaon snickers. "I have a good feeling. Today will be a cinch."

"I certainly hope so. You both have such promise," our Guru says, running his fingers through his hair. "I would hate to see you waste your talent mining Magical Ore for eternity. Do whatever it takes to pass. Please, for me."

"Hear that, brother? Whatever it takes," Dameaon says.

I avert my gaze. Jetta's pleas are a dose of reality. He's right; I have to do whatever it takes to pass, and that means letting Dameaon create whatever he wants. If not, we will be banished. And as frustrating as my twin is sometimes, he can't want that.

Unless . . . What if that's been his plan all along? Perhaps he'd sacrifice himself, just to destroy me. He's so fickle, nothing would surprise me. If so, there's a very good chance this is my last day as a Seeker.

This can't be how it ends.

If we fail, I'll beg for Master Oldungur Cassandre's mercy. Maybe she can convince the Council I deserve another chance, this time as a solo Guide. After all, it's her fault I'm in this situation in the first place. If she hadn't requested I be co-Guides with Dameaon, I would have passed my test the first time. It's unfair we are being held to the same Rules as single Guides.

That's it.

The Rules can't be broken, but maybe they can be reinterpreted. "Guru, why have there never been co-Guides before?"

"Well . . . your circumstances," he says, nodding slightly at Dameaon, "were unique."

"I understand. But this can't be the only time co-Guides would have been advantageous."

"I'm sure you're right," Jetta says. "But Master Oldungur Relken was very strict. He never would have allowed it," Jetta says. "Cassandre is a bit more . . . unconventional."

I nod. "Based on that, don't you think it would make sense to look at the Development Phase a bit differently?"

Jetta lifts his right eyebrow. "Villow, if there's a point, I wish you would get to it."

Dameaon snorts. "He's just stalling."

I ignore him. "I know the Rules say the test is to create one flora. But they were written for a sole Guide Seeker. Since there's two of us, doesn't it make sense that we each make our own creation and pass or fail based on its merits?"

"Two creations?" Jetta says, tilting his head. "Why, it's never been done before."

I push back my shoulders, standing my ground. "Because there's never been co-Guides before."

Jetta brushes his fingers against his amulet's chain. "There is merit in what you're saying, but—"

"Merit?" my twin says, stomping his foot. "My brother is always preaching about following the Rules, but now he wants to change them because it suits him."

I shoot him a murderous look. "Quiet, Dameaon. This benefits both of us. We would have an actual chance to pass our test and remain Seekers."

"Boys, please. Stop. I need to think for a minute," Jetta says, closing his eyes and rubbing his forehead. "The flora test has always been one creation, but Villow is right. The Development Phase Rules were written for one Guide. It's reasonable to assume two Seekers should get two creations. Very reasonable indeed."

He opens his eyes and claps his hands once. "Okay. It's decided. Each of you will create a flora. If you pass, I'll need to get Oldungur Mekhi's approval for dual creations on future tests, but I'm certain he'll see the logic. Now that we've settled that, let's not waste any more time. To Earth," he says, heading to the back room.

Alone in the classroom, Dameaon elbows my side. "You think you're so clever, don't you?"

"No, I think I just saved us both from banishment," I say, walking toward the back room. "By the way, consider your favor collected."

"Wrong," he says, but I don't argue. There's nothing he can say that will make a difference now that Jetta has agreed.

We collect our Creation Claviatures and teleport to Earth. The once-bare island is an attestation of our failure. Jetta's tree—the only creation in sight—has multiplied and covered the circumference, blocking out the salty breeze. Hopefully, my flora will soon populate the island as well.

I get to work immediately, re-creating the lupinus flowers without Dameaon's input. Feeling confident after my victory, I risk adding white centers to the cerulean petals and rename them bluebonnets.

Satisfied, I push the Execute button.

Jetta takes my laptop and reviews the tabs. He types in a code, and my hologram shifts from semitransparent to solid.

"Congratulations, Villow," he says, slapping my back. "You passed."

The tension from days of worry melts away, and I feel ten pounds lighter. I did it! I passed my first test. I'm still a Seeker and didn't tarnish my family's name.

With my own safety secured, I check on Dameaon. He's still working at his laptop, but his hologram looks promising. It's a delicate flower with velvety bloodred petals and a teak-brown stem. The latter has small points on it.

"Dameaon, what are those pointy things?" I ask.

He continues working, not even glancing my way. "Thorns."

I sigh. "For what purpose?"

"If humans touch the thorns, their poison will kill them."

There is no way Jetta will approve his flower, not with the poison. Part of me wants to say nothing and let him fail. I already passed, so there's a good chance the Oldungur Council would let me be a Guide by myself. That's all I ever wanted, and suddenly, it's a real possibility.

But as much as Dameaon infuriates me, I couldn't live with myself if I didn't try to get through to him.

"Jetta said we couldn't create something evil," I say. "You're not going to pass."

"Here we go again. My roses aren't evil, brother. The thorns won't hurt the humans if they don't touch them."

"But if the humans *do* touch them, they're dead. Seems pretty evil to me." I turn to Jetta. "My brother isn't thinking this through."

My twin frowns. "I thought we agreed to make our own flora. Mind your own business."

Jetta shakes his head. "Dameaon, while you could argue your rose isn't evil, I would suggest it's unnecessarily deadly. Are you certain that's what you want to submit for my approval?"

My twin glares at him, but Jetta returns an equally fierce look. Dameaon breaks eye contact. "Fine, I'll get rid of the poison, but the thorns stay."

He hands his Creation Claviature to Jetta. Our Guru completes his review and approves his flora.

I press my hand to my stomach and let out a slight moan. Dameaon passed. I'm relieved—for his sake and our family's.

"Nice job," I say.

Jetta releases a boisterous, booming laugh. "Nice job indeed. I won't lie. You had me worried. But you both passed, in large part because of Villow's suggestion. I cannot express how proud I am. Of both of you. You now have free rein to make flora for the rest of the Development Phase. The only time I will intervene is if a creation is truly disastrous."

"Oh joy. More opportunities for my brother to dissect everything I do," Dameaon mutters.

"Don't do anything stupid and I won't have to criticize you," I say.

Jetta scrunches his forehead. "Boys, stop the bickering. Our work on Earth is done for now."

We teleport back to Reos. I say goodbye to Jetta and head to the east part of campus. Portia expressed interest in my test, and I want to share the good news with her. Unfortunately, I don't see her anywhere. Based on the time of day, she could still be in Mage training, so I decide to hang out for a few minutes.

Glancing around to entertain myself, I notice Dexter—sitting alone at a picnic bench in the Alchemist wing.

Perfect. I've been meaning to talk to him privately.

He offers a small wave as I approach. "Hey, Villow. I'm assuming from your smile it's good news?"

"I figured out a way to pass our first test, so things are looking up," I say, sitting down across from him. "At least for now. How's training going for you?"

He frowns, gesturing to the potion kit on the table. "No matter how hard I try, it's still so difficult."

"Just keep with it. You don't have your first test for another month, right?"

"Yes, thankfully, Alchemy Seekers don't have their first test until month five. If it was as soon as yours, I would be in Rehuido right now."

"I'm sure you're exaggerating," I say, shifting on the bench. "Look, I've been meaning to ask you something. It's a bit awkward . . . but I feel like I need to."

He scrunches his eyebrows together. "We've been friends forever. You can ask me anything."

"I just . . . want to make sure you stopped creating your own potions."

"I told you I would."

"I know, but I just need to hear you say it one more time. You did, right?"

He opens the lid to his potion kit and pulls out an opaque tan potion. "See this? It's a Hibernation Elixir. And this," he says, taking out a solid lilac one, "is a Quell Ailment. Both training-level potions. Both mixed by me. Happy?"

I lick my lips. "You didn't actually answer my question."

"Yes, Villow," he says, his voice just above a whisper. "I've stopped creating my own potions."

He's disappointed in me—as am I.

I drop my chin so low it's touching my chest. "I'm sorry, Dexter. It was unfair to ask you again. You're a good friend and deserve better."

"Forget it," he says, putting his potions back in the kit and standing. "I'll see you tomorrow, okay?"

"Dexter . . ." I say, but he slinks away, not looking back.

A sour taste fills my mouth, and I squeeze my eyes shut. What is wrong with me? I just accused one of my best friends of lying, with absolutely no proof. Working with Dameaon must be affecting me more than I realized. Not every Glanching is conniving like him. I'll apologize to Dexter again tomorrow and explain my behavior. He'll understand—he has to.

I take three deep breaths and start home. Just as I enter the woods, Portia's distinctive laugh reverberates through the branches. After my disastrous talk with Dexter, I could use a win, so I head back toward Moudrost.

Portia is standing next to the Mage Seeker building. I

start toward her but pause when I realize she's clutching the arm of a shadowed figure near the building.

It must be Colton.

I shuffle my feet, unsure if I have the strength left to deal with him.

But then the shadowed figure places his hand on the small of her back and leans into the light.

I fall to my knees.

It's *Dameaon.*

Portia kisses his cheek, and I resist the urge to vomit. Instead, I force myself up, dashing down the path.

Tears flow down my cheeks as I wander aimlessly through the woods. Until now, I didn't know I could mourn the loss of something I never had. But then, I've spent endless hours daydreaming about my relationship with Portia. Once I got the nerve to ask her out, we would go on a few awkward dates. Over time, we would realize how much we have in common and commit to each other, staying faithful even while I was on Earth. Then we would get married, and the Oldungur Council would grant us a son. It would be an epic love story—envied by our peers.

But my selfish, worthless twin has taken that from me. Out of all the horrible things he's done, this is the worst. He knows how I feel about Portia and he claims to despise her—and yet, he's letting her kiss him. No wonder she's been avoiding me. She's moved on . . . to Dameaon.

No more. For too long, I've let my brother ruin my life. It's time to take back control.

Digging my fingernails into my palms, I plot my revenge. I'll steal everything from him, starting with his

Guidance duty. Every time he makes a mistake, I'll point it out to Jetta, and eventually, he'll *have* to agree my brother is a failure. Meanwhile, I'll become the best Guide ever and Portia will come running, begging to be with me.

The tides are going to shift, but this time, in my favor.

DUN-DUN-DUN-DUN-DUN.

My Transmission Stone's ringing pulls me away from studying for my history test. I glance at the surface and do a double take.

It's Katarin.

I didn't think she would call from Strongmist, but she's probably checking in on me. I press my fingertips against the Stone's glossy surface, and her face pops up on the screen.

"Hey, Kat. I didn't think you'd have time to . . ." I stop; her cheeks are splotched with red patches, and her eyes are puffy. "Kat, are you okay?"

"Sariel is missing," she says, bursting into tears.

"Missing? What do you mean, missing?"

"She's gone, Vil. We planned on meeting at her apartment, but she wasn't here." Kat wipes the bottom of her nose with her sleeve. "I waited an hour and then I checked with Shadowlodge. They said she hasn't been to class in five days."

I glance down, uncertain of what to say. Sariel used to skip classes at Moudrost frequently, so her news isn't too surprising.

"I know what you're thinking, Vil, but she's changed.

She loves school and would never miss one class, let alone five days. Not unless something bad happened."

I still have my doubts, but there's no reason to share them with my best friend.

"I'm sorry, Kat," I say. "What can I do to help?"

"My parents already took the train to Strongmist and are here with me. We've checked with Shadowlodge, but no one knows anything, and they're not taking this seriously. They said students disappear sometimes, but they always come back. But Sariel would never do that. Especially not with me coming. I know it's a lot to ask, but could you see if your father can find out anything—you know, with his government connections?"

"Yes, of course," I say. "I believe he's home now. I'll call you back shortly."

"Thanks, Vil. I'll be waiting," she says, hanging up the call.

I press my lips together. I made it sound easy, but I've been avoiding my father for two days. I still haven't figured out how to confront him on his lie—or if I even want to. But now I need to talk to him, for Kat's sake.

I find him inside his study, sitting on his couch.

"Father?" I say from the doorway. "Do you have a minute?"

He looks up. "Villow, of course. Come in. I feel like I haven't seen you in days."

"I'll get straight to the point," I say, sitting down on the other end of the couch. "I need your help."

He shuts his book and places it on the ottoman. "This sounds serious."

"It is. Katarin just called. She went to visit Sariel in Strongmist a couple days ago. But she's missing. Kat's really wor—"

"Sariel. That's her older sister, right?" I nod, and he continues, "Wasn't she a bit . . . wild?"

I had a similar thought, but it won't do any good to share that with him. "Yes, but apparently all that changed when she became a Mage Seeker. She got into Shadowlodge, so that says something about her dedication."

"I'm glad she is taking her training seriously. I'm hoping being a Guide will do the same for your brother."

I bite the sides of my cheeks; if he saw Dameaon's behavior today, he wouldn't be so hopeful. "Only time will tell. But if we could get back to Sariel . . . Kat was hoping you could ask Strongmist's governor to investigate?"

He shakes his head. "What could a government official do? The De Legards should be working with the school to locate her."

"Katarin said Shadowlodge isn't doing anything."

"Probably because there's nothing to be done."

"Kat doesn't think that's the case, Father, and she is gen—"

"Even so, it's best not to get involved with things that don't concern you, Villow. It's how you stay out of trouble." He picks up his book and returns to reading.

His brush-off is the final crack in the dam holding in my frustrations. Every decision I make is for the good of our family. Now, when I ask him for a favor, he dismisses me, just like I've seen him dismiss Dameaon hundreds of times.

My anger bursts out in the form of an accusation. "So I

guess it's not my concern that you lied to me about talking to someone two days ago."

He snorts. "We already discussed this. You heard my music."

"Your Transmission Stone was still warm. I felt it," I say, hanging my head. "We've never lied to each other before. Please don't lie to me now."

My father breathes in deeply. "Sometimes I forget how much you've grown up. All right. I will tell you, but only if you promise to keep it secret . . . for now."

I slide forward to the edge of the cushion. "I promise."

He places his thumb and pointer finger over his closed eyes, rubbing them roughly. When he opens them, they're clouded with sadness. "I'm not certain how to tell you this. I didn't want you to find out this way. The truth is, I want a divorce."

In the hundreds of scenarios I played out, this never entered my mind. "A divorce? That's . . . that's insane."

"It's not insane. Your mother and I have been growing apart for quite some time."

"Growing apart," I mutter.

I heard what he said, but it makes no sense. My parents have been acting exactly the same way they've always acted. At least once a day, they get into some silly fight, but they make up almost instantly. On rare occasions, they get into heated arguments that last for days, but then my father grovels and buys her a ridiculously expensive gift. And I can't even remember the last time that happened. What has changed that he is suddenly unhappy in their marriage?

"Villow? Talk to me."

I lock eyes with him. "Who were you talking to on your Transmission Stone?"

He winces, but he answers, "Master Oldungur Cassandre."

I fall off the edge of the cushion and jump to my feet. "Why would she care about your marriage?"

"You know how much Glanchings disapprove of divorce. Cassandre is helping me manage the situation so I don't lose my position as governor. She's very supportive of my career and the good work I do for Belkin."

A hard lump forms in my stomach, as if he punched me hard. In a way, he did.

"This is unbelievable," I say. "Cassandre forced me to be co-Guides with Dameaon, and now she's helping you get a divorce. She's poison to our family."

My father's mouth falls open. "That's blasphemy. She is the Master Oldungur and deserves your respect. And don't rewrite history. You agreed to be Dameaon's partner." He places his hand on my arm. "Look, I know it doesn't feel like it now, but this means good things for you and your brother. Once I'm divorced, I'll spend more time at Kapitala, making connections that will help you get anything you want."

I pull away from him. He doesn't know me at all if he thinks that entices me. "Anything I want? I want my parents to stay together. I want you not to break my mother's heart. I want Dameaon to act like a normal Glanching. I want to be a Guide Seeker without him bringing me down. Everything I want is impossible, so don't make empty promises."

I almost make it to the door before he speaks. "You

don't have to support this, but you cannot tell anyone, especially your mother. There's a greater good you need to think of. Promise me you'll keep my secret, even if you don't agree."

I turn, but I can't look him in the eye. "I won't tell Mother, but I demand something in return. You will help find Sariel. It's the least you can do."

"Fine," he says. "We're agreed."

"One more thing. You need to think about what this will do to Mother. You're her whole world, and she loves you, even if she doesn't act like it sometimes. This is not okay, and you know it. If it was, it wouldn't be a big secret."

With my point made, I run to my room and launch myself onto my bed. I lie in silence, focusing on my rapid breathing and attempting to return it to a natural pace.

This is inconceivable. How can he want a divorce? He preaches about the Glanching Code of Conduct all the time, and it clearly states once you choose your partner, you commit to them for eternity. And I know my father; he takes his vows very seriously. At least, I thought I did. Perhaps I don't know him at all.

On top of that, learning that Master Oldungur Cassandre, our supposed moral compass, is helping him, is beyond disappointing.

A cold tremor arises from deep within me, and I begin to shake. Even when I crawl under three layers of blankets, it doesn't stop. It's as if something inside me has frozen solid from my disillusionment. What if I never find a way to feel normal again? That thought makes me tremble even more.

I close my eyes and roll onto my side, trying to block everything out. A faint hum fills my ears—so faint I wonder if it's my imagination. But then velvety fur strokes my cheek and a warm body curls up against my chest.

Cinders.

I stroke his small body, grateful for his company. His purring vibrations have a magic of their own; they soothe me, warming my chilled insides, until the smallest glimmer of hope emerges.

My father wants to keep the divorce a secret. He claims it's to protect his reputation, but perhaps some small part of him isn't sure it's what he really wants. He's having a moment of weakness, but in the end, he always does the right thing.

When I've lost my way, he's always steered me down the correct path. Now it's my turn to do the same for him. I'll talk to him tomorrow, the first chance I get, and help him remember who he truly is.

He'll change his mind. He has to.

With my hope in my parents' marriage somewhat renewed, I'm able to function again.

I kiss Cinders's forehead and slip out of bed. My mouth is dry, so I head to the bathroom for a drink. Even after consuming a full glass of water, I'm still parched and slightly dizzy, but it doesn't matter. I owe Kat a phone call. I return to my room and dial her on my Transmission Stone.

She picks up after one ring, as if she was waiting by it—which she probably was. I promise her that my father is looking into her sister's disappearance and I will be in touch as soon as possible. When we hang up, I take a deep breath.

"I'm sure that was difficult, but you did good," Cinder says. "Especially considering the circumstances."

"What circumstances?"

He stares at me with unblinking eyes. "I know everything that goes on in this house."

"So you know my father . . ." I can't even say it.

"Wants a divorce, yes. I've known for a while."

I cross my arms. "You've known and didn't tell me?"

He stands and arches his back. "Why would I tell you?"

"So I could do something about it."

"There's nothing you can do. Your dad needs to do what makes him happy."

"No, he needs to do what's best for the greater good. That's staying married."

Cinders stretches his wings toward the ceiling. "Thinking like that is exactly why I'm glad to be a wyvermalkin."

"Glanchings are considered the highest moral compasses in the universe," I say. "We must be doing something right."

"I suppose. But I spend every day doing what makes me happy. Which would you prefer?"

"Why can't I have both?"

He cocks his head. "I suppose you can, but to be blunt, you don't seem very happy."

I press my fingers against the base of my neck. "I'm happy."

"If you say so. I'm going to explore now," he says, heading through the small hole in the bottom of my door cut just for him.

I stare at the wall, pondering what he just said. How can Cinders think I'm unhappy? Sure, Dameaon is the worst brother ever, Portia completely betrayed me, and my father's recent admission was a real blow, but I have my work, my friends, and I'm a Glanching.

Maybe I'm depressed right now, but anyone would be after the day I had. How could they *not* be? I crawl back under the covers, pushing away the lingering doubts that occupy the shadowy depths of my mind.

MIRRORED IMAGES

A long time ago, I learned the only Glanching I could rely on is me. But there's too much at stake right now to not ask for help.

I clear my throat.

Jetta looks up from the Hourglass of Time. "Oh, Dameaon, I didn't realize you were here. Give me a second. I'm trying to adjust the sand's flow for your test today."

I leave the doorway and join him by the back table. "That's why I'm a little early. I'm worried about—"

"Yes, yes," he says, "No need to worry. Just remember my lessons and you'll do fine."

"I'm not worried about the test, Jetta. It's my brother."

"Oh? Is he sick? I certainly hope not. I would hate to postpone things."

"No, it's not that. He's been . . . weird. Moody. Short-tempered. Cynical. It's starting to affect our training. He's overly critical of everything I make."

Jetta fiddles with the bottom of the Hourglass and places it back on the table. "There, that should do it." He looks at me, his left eyebrow raised. "Don't you think some of your creations the last couple weeks could be the reason for his moodiness?"

I shake my head. "I've dealt with my brother my whole life, so I know how judgmental and condescending he can be. But this goes way beyond that." I move over to the Dimensional Block—currently in globe form. There are yellow and brown blotches intermixed with the blue water. "Look how much land there is on Earth now, thanks to my volcanos. But did my brother support them? Nope. They were too dangerous, what with the eruptions and lava."

Jetta scratches his jaw. "In fairness, Villow's islands accomplished the same thing without the adverse by-products."

I toss the hair out of my eyes. "Okay. Not the best example, but I have more. What about my poison ivy? He said the oozing sores were unnecessarily cruel. My cacti's spikes were barbaric, and my sharks' razor teeth were deadly weapons. And my black mambas' poison w—"

"Your point has been made, Dameaon," Jetta interrupts. "But let me offer a dissenting opinion. The criticism has been mutual. I seem to recall you saying his sycamore trees were dull and unimaginative."

I grin. "Come on, they're just jinger trees with a different name. At least half his creations were stolen from Reos."

"What about his giraffe? You said its neck was much too long to be practical."

"It's an accident waiting to happen, Jetta."

He clasps my shoulder. "The point is, you've both been critical of each other. You came to me, so let me offer you some advice. Tone down the hostility, and Villow will follow suit. You can be a great team, if you find a way to get along."

I jut out my chin. "He's too pompous to change. We'll never get along."

Jetta pauses for a moment and then pulls his necklace out from under his linen shirt. "Dameaon, do you know why I chose the malaa'ig tree for my amulet?"

"You really like trees?"

He laughs but instantly becomes serious. "While that's true, it's not the reason. Eons ago, Glanchings didn't even know Magic existed. During his time at university, Relken Harding developed a radical theory for his thesis project. He argued that when Glanchings used their minds, they only used half their natural abilities. For a Glanching to transcend to his true potential, he also had to master the power of the heart.

"His classmates, Hinnus Nebule and Magica Leaching, believed in his vision. Together, they learned to meditate and link their hearts to Reos's Elements, in an attempt to control them. Since the casting process was unpredictable, they would travel to the Shadow Grove to conduct their experiments in private.

"During one of those experiments, Magica attempted to merge her heart with the Lightning Element but was overcome by her fear and pain. Hinnus and Relken tried to awaken her, but she was in too deep of a trance. They watched helplessly as she exploded into light molecules that struck a nearby cyperus tree, charring it to bits."

"Wait, I thought Glanchings were immortal."

"We're immortal, not invincible. Why do you think Mage training is so structured? Summoning any Element that isn't your innate one is dangerous and must be taught by a Guru inherent in that specific Magic," he says. "Anyway, the tragic loss of Magica affected Relken deeply, and he abandoned his thesis project for six months. He spent most of his time wandering in the Shadow Grove, searching for answers to quell his guilt.

"During one of those walks, he came across the charred cyperus tree. But something magical had happened. The tree had found new life and, this time, grew more beautiful, with feathered wings sprouting from its trunk. Its resilience, even in the face of total destruction, awakened something in Relken. He realized no matter how bleak things can seem, hope is not lost if there is still life left inside you.

"Relken and Hinnus restarted their experiments and were successful in mastering their innate Elements. They named the power of the heart Magic, after Magica, who gave her life for its discovery. When Relken became the Master Oldungur, he assigned Hinnus as the first Guide Oldungur. Hinnus chose the malaa'ig tree for the Guide Class's crest, as a reminder there was still hope for the Original Species so long as their Essence Orbs burned."

I glance down, focusing on a small scuff on my boot. "I imagine there's a lesson I'm supposed to take from your story?"

Jetta nods. "Hope is not lost for you and Villow. You are both still here. If you want a better relationship, take the first step."

"I don't care about having a good relationship with him. I'm here because it's affecting our training."

His lips turn up into a slight grin. "My mistake. It's okay to want things to be different with . . . Well, hello, Villow."

For a second, I worry my twin overheard us. But then he glances at the clock on the wall and scowls. "Am I late?"

"No, no, you're right on time," Jetta says.

Villow presses his lips into a thin line. "What were you two talking about?"

"Nothing important," Jetta says, covering for me.

My chest swells with gratitude; over the course of our training, Jetta has proven candid but trustworthy. It's made being a Guide Seeker much easier, and I'm thankful he's our Guru.

My brother narrows his eyes suspiciously—he's many things, but stupid isn't one of them.

I need to make something up, or he will harp on this for days. "Jetta was just telling me how much better of a Guide I am than you."

He crosses his arms and frowns. Apparently, he's not in the mood for sarcasm.

I sigh. "If you must know, I was getting final tips from Jetta for our Original Species test today."

Villow looks at our Guru, and he nods. "Dameaon wants to make sure he creates the perfect Founder."

My brother's arms fall to his side, and the tension

wanes from his face. "It's about time he was serious about something."

I turn to Jetta and raise my eyebrows in an I-told-you-so gesture.

Our Guru bites his lip to suppress his smile. "Now that you're both here, let's complete the necessary prep work so we can head to Earth. I already set the Hourglass to mirror Reos's time while we're there. As soon as we return, I will adjust it so Earth ages five years overnight. You will pass or fail your test based on your Founders' goodness tomorrow.

"Before we head out, you need to decide where your Founders are going to live." He carries the Dimensional Block to the middle of the room and chants, "Acopera acest spatiu." It transforms into a flat four-foot map.

"In this format, the Dimensional Block is interactive. Touch any part of it and you can see a close-up." He demonstrates by placing his fingers against a yellow patch. A small semitransparent square appears perpendicularly above the map, filled with golden sand, cacti, small lizards, and tumbleweeds. A number—08478—is at the top of the square. He lifts his fingers, and it disappears. "Take your time and explore. When you've decided on a suitable location together, place your hand on the map, and say, 'Anseo.'"

Villow paws at the map, touching spot after spot. I take a moment to think about our lessons; the ideal location needs to be on land, have food and water nearby, mild temperatures, and some sort of shelter.

I touch a wooded peninsula on the upper left, and the map zooms in. Sure enough, it meets every criteria.

"Anseo," I say, pressing my hand against the map. My location expands, taking up the entire space.

Villow throws his hands in the air. "Really, Dameaon? You didn't even let me see the area before you picked it. Jetta, do something."

"'Jetta, do something,'" I mimic. "Fight your own battle. For once."

"You're right," he says, lifting his chin and shoving me—hard.

I stumble backward two steps before regaining my footing. I lunge forward, but Jetta steps between us.

"Settle down, boys," he says. "Dameaon, you should have consulted Villow. You know this. Thankfully, your location appears to be a good one. It has a cave for shelter, nearby fruit trees, and a river with fresh water."

I push my shoulders back and offer Villow a cunning grin. "I know."

My twin cracks his knuckles, probably wishing he could hit me.

Jetta checks the number on the map and types it into the keypad on the front of the Teleportation Machine. "There. Now we will teleport right to the Founders' soon-to-be home."

He hands us our Creation Claviatures and picks up a container of mudlike mixture off the back table. "This is Creazione Sludge, found in the wettest part of the Shadow Grove. Its Magic allows us to re-create Original Species. Once I approve your Founders, we will use it to bring them to life." He glances around, as if he's looking for something. "I believe that's it. Let's go."

We teleport to Earth, appearing in the small clearing.

The dense forest surrounding us fills the air with the invigorating sweet scent of pine. The river isn't visible, but I can hear its babbling to my left. The cave is even bigger than it appeared and will offer ample protection for the humans.

Jetta nods with approval. "Yes, yes, this will be a wonderful home. A few reminders before you begin. Founders are the predecessors for all other humans, so it's imperative they have positive attributes and high morals. For the Original Species test, you must only select components from the Founders tab, and the Freestyle tab is off-limits. Once you're done, I still have to approve your creations. Villow, why don't you make the female, and Dameaon, you take the male? Remember my training and do your best."

I open my laptop and get to work, starting with his face. After scrolling through every option, I select an angular style with a prominent nose and sunken cheekbones. For his eyes, I choose a straight, oval shape and almond brown for the hue. I keep his hair short—with a bit more length at the front—and color it jet black. I select a solid but lean build and deeply tanned skin that will protect him from the sun's strong rays.

Happy with his appearance, I move on to the Traits tab. I think about the skills I value and give them to him—a strong determination, to succeed even in tough circumstances; a sense of adventure, to discover more about the world around him; and a love of animals, so he will live in harmony with the creatures of Earth. Finally, I give him self-confidence, so he will stand up for his convictions.

Satisfied, I hit the Execute button and gesture for Jetta to join me. He reviews my Founder on my Creation Claviature and moves to my hologram. He places a mound of Creazione Sludge at the base and then enters his approval on my laptop.

Jetta puts his arm around my shoulder. "Your Founder is exceptional, Dameaon. I'm so proud of you."

Villow glances over, scowling. "He created a human version of himself."

Now that he mentions it, my human really does look a lot like me. Not that I'll admit it. "You're insane. His eyes are a completely different color."

"And you're ridiculous," he says, returning to his laptop.

A deer wanders into the southern part of the meadow, munching on the dandelions in the grass. It lifts its head and spots us, slinking back between the trees.

"Jetta, I'm going to explore while he finishes," I say, heading toward the woods.

"Don't go too far," he calls behind me.

Once I'm inside the thicket, I stop and listen for clues as to which way the deer went. An abrasive scratching reverberates in the red cedar tree above me. I glance up and grin from ear to ear.

In homage to Cinders, I created numerous species of wyvermalkins, minus the wings. One such variant is right above my head, sharpening its claws against the tree's trunk. It looks down, revealing its spectacular eyes; the outside rims are amber, surrounding olive irises with black pupils in the center.

"You're a strange fellow," the tiger purrs, and I identify him as a male. "What might you be?"

I laugh and hold my hand up, stroking his cheek. "Yes, I suppose I *am* strange to you. I'm Dameaon, the one who created you."

He stares at me—unblinking and unimpressed. I stifle a smile; apparently, he's also inherited Cinders's personality.

"How do you like living here, tiger?" I ask.

"My name is Jasper," he says. "And it's quite nice. There are lots of fruits and berries to eat. And a nearby river to swim in and drink from. I'm sure you'll like it just fine."

"Thanks. I'm only here for a quick visit, but there will be two creatures, called humans, who look a lot like me in that clearing," I say, pointing north. "Perhaps you could give them some pointers?"

Jasper rests his chin on his front paw, extending his razor claws. "I suppose. If it doesn't interfere with my nap time."

"Dameaon?" Jetta yells. "Where did you wander off to?"

"Coming," I holler.

Jetta's lectures about humans echo through my mind. I look up at the tiger, who still has his claws out. "It was very nice to meet you, Jasper. Promise me, if the humans ever try to hurt you, you'll defend yourself?"

He lashes his long orange-and-black striped tail behind him. "Hurt me? Look at me. Who would ever hurt me?"

I shake my head. "They won't, but just promise me."

"Whatever you say," he says, licking his left paw and rubbing it over his ear.

I bid him farewell and rejoin Jetta and Villow. My brother is smirking; his Founder must have been approved too.

I glance at her. "Wait. You made fun of my Founder, but you've made a Portia replica."

He snorts. "You would see Portia, wouldn't you?"

I scrunch my eyebrows. "What's that supposed to mean?"

"You know exactly what it means."

"Boys, please," Jetta says. "Let's focus on what's important. You created Founders who have a real chance of creating a strong lineage."

He pulls the Essence Orb out of his sleeve, and I absently wonder if it's been up there this whole time. "To ensure the humans are re-created as an Original Species, we use their Essence Orb to form the Founders' hearts." He holds it above his head and chants, "Straluceste puternic in puterea ta."

It floats in the air, vibrating with a gentle hum. A soft ruby light encases our Founders' chests. The hair on my arms stands straight up. This is it—the exact moment of humans' re-creation. It fills me with a sense of purpose for the first time in my life.

"Can I stay here tonight?" I ask.

Jetta shakes his head. "I appreciate your enthusiasm, Dameaon, but there needs to be separation between you and the humans from the very beginning. It helps you stay neutral and make better decisions as a Guide."

The thought of leaving makes my rib cage tighten so much I can barely breathe. "I can stay here and still remain neutral."

He tilts his head, softening his expression. "I know you think that, but you must trust the process."

"Fine," I mutter, looking at the ground. "Let's go, then."

"Dameaon, it really is for the best," he says. "Besides, I promise, if you pass your test, which certainly looks promising, you'll get to interact with them tomorrow afternoon."

"What?" I ask. "Tomorrow?"

Villow shakes his head in disgust. "Passing the Original Species test marks the completion of the Development Phase."

Jetta smiles. "Villow is right. If you pass, you move into the Influencing Phase, the final chapter of preparation before your first trial. Your first test in this phase is to interact with your Founders, encouraging them to follow a path of kindness."

I widen my eyes. "And then what? We have our first trial?"

"No, the Influencing Phase normally lasts three to five months," Jetta says. "We will age Earth and travel here many times, for many tests. Each one has a specific goal, and you will pass or fail, based on meeting them. We will continue that way until the Oldungur Council and I agree you are ready to be on your own, or you fail three times and get banished. But first, you have to pass the Original Species test. So let's head back to Reos and regroup tomorrow."

I nod. I've waited this long for somewhere to belong; I can wait one more day.

"AND YOU KNOW I ADORE LEELA AND HAROLD, BUT TANGERINE place mats with blush plates? It's so gauche."

I roll my eyes; we're already on our second course, and my mom hasn't stopped talking for an instant. Family dinners are the worst; my mom gossips about all her so-called friends, my dad says as little as possible, and my twin gloats about everything. I much prefer the nights when my parents are busy and I can eat in my room.

My mom finally pauses for a breath, and my father interjects, "How's Guide training going?"

He didn't address the question to either of us, but, of course, his gaze went right to Villow.

"Best day so far," my twin says. "We re-created our Original Species. I made a really strong Founder. Jetta said so."

He won't get all the glory. Not this time. "I created the male human and mirrored him after myself. Jetta said he was—what was the word he used, brother? Oh yes—exceptional."

Villow scowls. "Well, I drew inspiration from those I value most, not just myself."

I finger my roll, considering tossing it at his head. "Apparently, the only Glanching you value is Portia."

My dad raises his eyebrows, and Villow's face reddens. I stifle a laugh; for once, I'm not the one being questioned.

"She does bear a physical resemblance to Portia," Villow says. "However, she possesses a curiosity and enthusiasm for life that was motivated elsewhere. As I said, I drew inspiration from many sources."

My dad stabs his shecker filet, and blood squirts onto his plate. "Listen to your brother, Dameaon. He thought about his human from all perspectives, not only the physical. You can learn a lot from him."

"And using Portia for inspiration isn't a bad thing," my mom adds. "She's quite a beauty. I'm sure she's just lovely." She glances at me. "I'm sure yours is nice as well, Dameaon. Now, where was I? Oh yes . . . so Harold, of course, was mortified that . . ."

I still; my mom's feeble compliment came out more like a criticism. Villow draws his brows together, compassion in his eyes. Uninterested in his sympathy, I snarl my lip, and he looks away.

The rest of dinner drags on, revolving around the typical topics—my parents' busy schedules, gossip, and strategies for my father's political gain. I don't say another word and sulk up to the roof as soon as dessert is done.

In the nighttime sky, the Hyggelig Mountains have turned into unfamiliar, abstract mounds, making me feel even more lost. My throat thickens with unshed tears. I swallow a couple times, attempting to return it to normal.

Normal. Not that normal is good. Normal for me means loneliness. Emptiness. Criticism. Especially in this house. I'm doing just as well as Villow in Seeker training, but my dad doesn't see it. No matter what I do, I'll never measure up to my twin.

But I have the Founders now. And soon, there will be

lots more humans. My parents won't matter so much, not when I have them. Earth holds the promise of what I've always wanted—an undefined future, full of adventure and excitement. That's what I need to focus on.

Eager for tomorrow to come, I head down to bed. Within minutes, there's a soft purring in my left ear. Cinders has decided to share my pillow. He reminds me of the tiger and his fierce beauty.

I stroke his back a few times and whisper, "I love you, buddy."

A hissing wheeze implies he's already asleep. I shut my eyes, matching my breathing to his.

My little wyvermalkin is always good company. The best kind, really.

JETTA IS PERCHED ON HIS DESK, CROSS-LEGGED, FACING THE doorway. When he sees me, he grins. A good sign. I smile back as Villow pushes past me into the classroom.

"Did we pass?" he asks.

Jetta's smile reaches from ear to ear. "Why don't you go see for yourselves?"

I head to the back room, but Villow gets there first, hogging the Dimensional Block's map. I shove into his shoulder, pushing him over so we can both see.

Not that it matters. The humans aren't in sight. Subtle modifications show they've been busy; there's a vegetable garden cultivated from forest seeds, two loosely woven wooden baskets brimming with fruit on the right side of the cave's entrance, and ten halved gourds full of water on the left side.

"They seem like they're adapting well," Villow says.

"They are," Jetta says. "They've used the natural resources to make their lives easier. Dameaon, your location was a wise choice."

I toss the hair out of my eyes. "Obviously. I told you, I know what I'm doing."

"You still should have consulted me," my twin says. "And I would argue it was luck, not your . . ."

His attention shifts to the map. Our Founders emerge from the cave, squinting in the sudden brightness. The female releases my Founder's hand and takes off running. She makes an about-face around a tree and then charges forward. The male rushes after her, grabbing her waist just before she reaches the cave. They fall to the ground in a mess of tangled limbs, kissing warmly.

"Their progress is encouraging. It's evident they have a great love for each other," Jetta says. "I spoke to Oldungur Mekhi this morning, and he is extremely pleased. We agree that you passed. This is really great work, boys."

Excitement courses through me; we get to go to Earth now. "Grab the Transmission Potion, Jetta. I'm ready to do some serious influencing."

Jetta slumps his shoulders. "Unfortunately, that will have to wait until tomorrow. The Oldungur Council requested my presence at Kapitala at once, and I need to leave in a few minutes."

"Can we just go introduce ourselves?" I ask.

"It's a good thought, Dameaon," Jetta says, "but it's a waste of a Transmission Potion."

Villow rubs his neck. "Can we at least watch from here?"

Jetta nods. "Of course. You can stay as long as you want. I know this is disappointing, but I promise, tomorrow will come quickly. Enjoy your time with them, boys. Please close the door when you leave."

He heads out, and my stomach churns from disappointment. But Villow looks worse than me; his face is ashen, and his eyes are glazed over.

"Brother, are you okay?"

He licks his lips. "I can't believe . . . He promised . . . No one ever lives up to their word."

I shrug. "It's not like Jetta had a choice. You know if the Oldungur Coun—"

"I'm so sick of it," he interrupts.

"Sick of what?" I ask, but he's not listening.

He heads to the table and adjusts the Hourglass of Time. Then he moves to the locked pewter cabinet, holding his hand in front of it. "Deschide usa magica, deschisa," he says.

"What are you doing?"

He heads to the Teleportation Machine, pouring his just-procured potion in the top. Then he enters a code in its keypad. "What's it look like I'm doing? Going to Earth."

"Without Jetta?"

He steps inside the shower. "He promised we could go if we passed. And we passed. Are you coming?"

A deep laugh escapes my throat. My twin—who never does anything without an exhausting amount of preparation—is being spontaneous. This is a Villow I can get behind.

"I'm in," I say, stepping inside.

He narrows his eyes. "Technically, there are no Rules

around observing the humans without Jetta . . . so as long as we stay out of sight, we should be fine."

And there he is. The Rule-following downer returns—much too quickly for my taste.

"Let's go," I say.

"Not until you promise. No interacting, just observing."

I offer him my sweetest smile. "Whatever you say, brother."

He nods and pushes the button, sending us to our Founders' camp.

A SNAKE IN THE GRASS

I PRESS MY PALM AGAINST THE BRIDGE OF MY NOSE, TRYING TO quell the sudden throbbing behind my eyes. What was I thinking? Jetta is going to be furious when he finds out we came to Earth without him. And how could he not be? The Rules are clear; Seekers do not interact with their Original Species without their Gurus until their Guidance trial. We have to go—

A smack on the side of my head pulls me from my thoughts. A crimson apple is on the ground near my sneakers, and Dameaon is a few feet away, leaning against a tree.

I reach down and pick it up. "Did you just throw this at me?"

He plucks another apple off a branch above his head. "You looked like you were having a meltdown."

"I am. I-I made a huge mistake. We . . . we have to go back. This is . . . I mean . . . Jetta is going to be so mad."

"Uh-huh," he says, biting into his apple and crunching loudly.

I rub the back of my neck. "This is serious. Do you know how much trouble we're in?"

"You're forgetting something important."

"What?"

"We're only in trouble if we get caught."

"Um, are you forgetting about the Tome of Commemoration? It transcribes everything we do as Seekers."

He takes another bite, swallowing before he answers. "The Tomes are more for our sake than Jetta's. Besides, as far as he's concerned, we're on Reos right now, behaving like good little Glanchings. There's no reason for him to look at it."

I hate to admit it, but Dameaon is right; while our Tome is useful to Jetta when the Trial Phase starts, right now its primary purpose is for us to review and learn from. The chances Jetta will look at today's notes are slim. "Good point. We can go back right now and just forget this ever hap—"

"Are you insane?" he asks, tossing the half-eaten apple over his shoulder. "There is no way I'm going back. We just got here."

I grab my ankh amulet. "We're going back, Dameaon. Intoar—"

"Stop!" he says, tugging his gargoyle ring off and throwing it into the nearby bushes, disappearing into the woods before I can react. Without his Crystal, I can't summon him back to Reos.

"Dameaon, get back here!" I say.

His voice echoes through the trees, "I'll meet you back here in an hour. Keep my ring safe until then."

"Dameaon!" I scream, but there's no answer.

This isn't good. I should go back to Reos right now, but leaving my twin here unsupervised is a bad idea. He could get us in a lot of trouble. Especially since he just ran off without his ring. What happens if an animal finds it? Or one of the Founders? I do a thorough search through the thick foliage, but it's nowhere to be found.

The babble of water to my left gives me an idea; based on the location code I used, the Founders' camp should be just north of here. Dameaon said he wouldn't be back for an hour, which is more than enough time to observe the humans. Besides, there's a good chance that's where he is headed.

Using the river's gurgling as a compass, I reach its banks in no time. I follow it north, arriving at the Founders' clearing moments later. I stay hidden in the woods, protected by their leafy camouflage.

My twin's Founder is working in the garden, whistling as he uses the gourds to water the plants. When all the containers are empty, he brings them to the river. This close, his similarities to Dameaon are eerie, although his brown eyes have an innocence my brother's never had.

The faint melody of laughter echoes through the trees to my right.

Perhaps it's my Founder.

I creep through the woods, dodging branches and thicket, emerging into an orchard. Sure enough, my Founder is standing underneath an apple tree at the far end. I slink from tree to tree, getting as close as I can without being seen. When I'm fifty feet away, I risk peeking around my current hiding spot's gnarled trunk.

I inhale sharply, overwhelmed by her beauty. Dameaon

was right; she does look exactly like Portia. My heart aches all over again, reliving the incident of catching my twin and her together. But after watching for a moment, I'm able to uncouple her from Portia. My Founder's mannerisms are different; they're more animated—overly enthusiastic even. She giggles and twirls in a circle, peering up into the apple tree's foliage.

Intrigued, I risk creeping behind a closer tree. A violet snake is coiled around a low branch above my Founder, its head inches from her face. They're too far away for me to hear the conversation, but the snake's body vibrates, and I'm pretty sure it's laughing. She caresses its head, and in return, it picks an apple for her with its fangs. I'm aware she takes it, but my eyes remain focused on the snake. Its serpentine movements are familiar, as are its glowing amber eyes.

Dameaon.

I bare my teeth, rage brewing inside of me. My twin looks over her shoulder and smiles, which is incredibly disturbing in his current form. I want to rip his wormy body off the branch and stomp all over it, but I can't. Not with my Founder here. To prevent myself from charging forward, I clutch the tree's trunk so tightly that pieces of bark flake off in my hands.

They talk for another minute, and then she heads west, probably back to the clearing.

I wait until she's out of earshot and then charge toward Dameaon. "Are you out of your mind? You promised you would only observe."

My brother—the viper—slithers up the tree, the black triangles on his back moving from side to side. "I *was* observing, brother. I was minding my own business, when she said hello to me. It would've been rude to ignore her."

"Don't be coy, Dameaon. What did you say to her? And what's with the snake form?"

"Another person would have been much more alarming to her than a snake. You should have altered your appearance too."

It's a cutting gibe; while he's excelling at our Metamorphosis lessons, I'm struggling. "I didn't need to transform because I'm smart enough to stay hidden. What did you say to her, Dameaon?"

"Nothing of importance. I just asked how she likes living on Earth. She said that she enjoys it very much. And she's very curious. Very curious indeed . . ."

"You broke the Rules. Jetta is going to discipline us for this."

He snickers. "Ohh, I'm trembling in my skin. Besides, he won't find out. Unless you tell him."

"This isn't something I can keep hidden."

"Don't be such a goody-goody. Nothing I did changes anything—"

"It changes *everything*! Who knows what damage you did? Jetta might be able to fix it."

He slithers down to a branch level with my face, narrowing his eyes. "Because my influence couldn't possibly do something good, right?"

I shake my head. "There's a reason we don't get to interact with our Founders alone. We're not ready yet."

He flicks his tail from side to side, creating an obnoxiously loud rattle. "I'm more than ready. Wait and see."

A flash of amethyst blurs on the tip of his tail. Of course. In order to transform, he needs to have his Crystal.

"Intoarcere, intoarcere," I say, and the air thickens, blurring my vision.

We reappear on Reos, Dameaon still in snake form. He mutters, "Emorta, umuday," and a soft white light surrounds him, shifting him back into his Glanching form.

He throws his hands up. "You had no right to do that!"

"I had every right. You broke your promise by talking to my Founder."

My twin scowls and heads toward the door. "Franzle-duk to you, brother."

"Wait. Where are you going?"

He shrugs. "Anywhere but here."

All the blood drains from my face. "We can't leave. We need to monitor our Founders and make sure they're not acting differently."

"Observing is not my style. Seems like a good job for you, brother," he says, leaving.

I sigh heavily. He is the worst. First, he breaks his promise not to interact. Then he leaves me to clean up the mess.

I head over to the Dimensional Block and zoom into the Founders' clearing. Both humans are working in the garden, tilling their plants. After an hour, a tiger emerges from the southern woods. The Founders stop working and greet it warmly, stroking its chin and back. All three of them head to the river, swimming and splashing in the water. Eventually, the tiger heads back into the woods, and the Founders disappear into the cave.

I only observe them for a couple hours, but Dameaon

is right; his influence doesn't seem to have changed anything. Bowing my head, I sag against the wall. If we're lucky, the only record of our unapproved excursion will be in the Tome of Commemoration.

The Tome.

Of course. Maybe it can offer some clarification of what Dameaon said. I take the mulberry-covered book off the back table and flip it open to the last entry.

> *3:18 p.m., Frusrea, 16th of Osteren, Year of 10,064M*
>
> *Villow and Dameaon Verchant teleported to Earth at location 98443. Dameaon removed his Crystal. At location 98733, Villow observed the male Founder. At location 98324, Dameaon transformed into a snake and interacted with the female Founder, telling her humans are the heirs apparent of Earth while Villow observed. Villow and Dameaon teleported back to Reos.*

I place the book back on the table. The good news is it doesn't say anything that makes me panic; the bad news is, if Jetta does read it, we'll be in so much trouble.

But there's no reason for him to check the Tome, and the Founders don't seem any different. Perhaps Dameaon is right about not telling our Guru. I don't like lying, but the truth will create a lot of drama over nothing.

We have a good chance of getting away with this. And if we do, I'll never do anything so foolish again.

The next afternoon, Dameaon is waiting outside the entrance to our Seeker building. He grabs my arm and tugs me around the corner.

"What is your problem?" I snap.

"Possibly nothing," he says, releasing my arm. "I'm making sure you're not going to do something stupid."

I look down at the grass, remaining silent.

"You're going to tell him, aren't you?" my twin asks.

I nod. "I have to."

"Why?"

It's a fair question—one that I spent most of the night debating. Ultimately, I knew I couldn't keep this secret and remain true to who I am. Regardless of the consequences, Jetta must know.

I make eye contact with him. "The Glanching Code of Conduct is clear. Do not lie or keep secrets, as it weakens fortitude."

Dameaon shakes his head. "You're an idiot."

"Perhaps, but that doesn't mean I'm wrong," I say, shoving past him and into the building.

Jetta is leaning against the wall by the classroom's front windows, staring out into the courtyard. My twin comes up behind me and grabs my arm, trying to drag me into the hall before I can speak.

"Jetta, I have something I need to tell you."

He turns and faces me. His eyebrows are scrunched together so tightly they look like one long caterpillar. "In the name of all that is good on Reos, what were you thinking going to Earth without me?"

"H-H-How did you find out?"

His nostrils flare. "It wasn't difficult. I got back from Kapitala last night and came to see how your Founders were doing. That's when I saw the Hourglass was set to Reos's time."

I grimace; I can't believe I made such a rookie mistake. But then again, I'm no expert on sneaking around.

Jetta gestures for us to follow him into the back room. "I fixed the Hourglass to mature the Founders five years overnight. When I arrived this morning . . . well, see for yourselves."

The map—still zoomed into the Founders' clearing—illustrates a very different tale than yesterday. The humans have traded in their braided-leaf clothing for fur garments. The extremely pregnant female stretches a deer skin across a string near the cave entrance. Next to her, a baby rests in a hollowed-out log transformed into a makeshift cradle. The male stands in the river, inspecting a semicircle of closely placed branches stuck in the bed's mud. He grabs a fish trapped between the sticks and stabs it with a sharp piece of bone.

"Why are they dressed like that? And why did he just kill that fish?" I ask.

Jetta frowns. "Dameaon awakened the female's ego, and she, in turn, did the same for her partner. The belief that they are superior to the creatures around them enabled them to kill."

His revelation rattles me to the core. My animals are defenseless, while most of my twin's are equipped with some type of weapon; it's as if he knew this would happen—or made it happen.

"What exactly did you say to her?" I ask Dameaon.

"His exact words aren't important," Jetta says. "It's the result that matters."

I turn to Jetta. "Let me go back to Earth. I can fix this. I know—"

He holds up his hand. "The damage is done, Villow. The Founders' innocence is gone and cannot be reclaimed. They lost their ability to communicate with animals. And it's not the only consequence. The Oldungur Council and I discussed the situation at length this morning. As punishment for your blatant disobedience, your Metamorphosis options have been restricted. You can only transform into humans now. In addition, Dameaon's interaction counts as your first failed attempt in the Influencing Phase. That only gives you two more tries."

I place my hand against my forehead; this is unbelievable. Dameaon's careless actions cost me so much already. Now, his reckless attitude is going to make me fail Guidance training.

"This is all his fault," I say, glaring at my twin. "It's not fair."

He shrugs. "You're the one who said we should go."

"You're both to blame," Jetta says. "And I wouldn't complain. Your punishment could be much worse. You went to Earth without your Guru's permission. But the Oldungur Council knows this is the humans' last chance at re-creation, and Cassandre implored the Council to show you leniency."

Dameaon's laugh has a sharp edge to it. "I'll make sure to thank Cassandre next time I see her."

Jetta shakes his head. "Your sarcasm is not appreciated,

Dameaon. I hope this is a lesson to you both. You must take the Rules more seriously, if you want to be successful.

"I will age Earth one thousand years overnight, and we will attempt your Influencing test again tomorrow. Together, with a real civilization. For now, leave me so I can calm down."

"Whatever you say, Guru," my twin mutters, storming out.

Jetta lowers his head, closing his eyes. He looks defeated—broken even.

Tremors surge through my body; my actions caused his pain. I need to find a way to explain how this happened. I owe him that. "J-J-Jetta? I know you want me to go, but . . . I need to apologize. I mishandled the situation yesterday, but Dameaon made things so much—"

"Villow, stop," Jetta says. "Do not blame your brother for this. If you don't take responsibility, you will make the same mistakes again. You went to Earth without me."

"I know, but he made it so much worse."

"Your brother is impulsive. Reckless even. You know this. Normally, you are the voice of reason. But lately, you've made rash decisions too." He touches my shoulder. "Something is going on with you, Villow. You know you can talk to me about anything, any time."

Part of me wants to tell him everything—that my family is falling apart, that I've lost all faith in my father, that Dameaon stole the Glanching I love—but I can't unload on Jetta, not after disappointing him.

"It's Guide training. It's harder than I thought, especially because of my twin."

He presses his lips into a thin line. "Are you sure that's all?"

I can feel the tears forming in my eyes, but I don't deserve his compassion. I nod and make up an excuse about needing to leave, rushing out of the room. On the way home, I recite a silent mantra—I do not break the Rules—over and over, until I'm certain I will never make this mistake again.

SINCE MY FATHER'S DIVORCE REVELATION, OUR RELATIONSHIP has shifted from warm admiration to coldly civil. Thankfully, my parents had a gala this evening, so I was able to eat in my room and avoid the whole uncomfortable mess.

Lying stretched out on my mattress, I count the stars on my ceiling. I'm up to 104 when there's a sharp knock at my door. The clock on my nightstand confirms it's a little before midnight; this can't be good.

Before I say anything, my father charges in.

"Father, what's wrong?"

He sits on the edge of my mattress and places his head in his hands.

This definitely isn't good. "Did . . . Did you tell Mother?" I ask.

"What?"

"You know . . . about the . . . divorce?"

"Oh, no, Villow. It's much worse than that." His heavy tone causes my heart to pound in my chest. "Strongmist's governor, Dresla, called me this evening. She finally received news on Sariel. Oldungur Hana checked the Estatua Building in Kapitala." My father looks at me with dark eyes. "Her Olemasolu Statue is gone, Villow. You know what that means."

Glanchings' Olemasolu Statues are created when they are, and hold their very life essence. So if Sariel's Statue is gone, she is too.

I prop up on my elbows. "What? That makes no sense. Katarin said she was happy and doing well in training."

My father shakes his head. "The Level Two Elemental spells were difficult for her, and Sariel was afraid of failing her next trial. Oldungur Hana surmises she couldn't handle the shame that would bring to her family, so she willed herself out of existence."

Hearing my father say it makes it real. Sariel is gone. Bright, lively, free-willed Sariel. She was a blinding force, full of energy and life.

Katarin is going to be devastated—her whole family will be.

"Do the De Legards know?" I ask.

"They were notified this evening." He squeezes my foot underneath the covers. "I know you're dealing with your own family matters, but Katarin is going to need you—now more than ever. You must be strong for her."

"Of course," I say, my voice cracking. "I won't let her down."

He stands. "When things like this happen, they remind you what's important."

I raise my eyebrows. "Does that mean you're reconsidering divorcing Mother?"

He shifts uncomfortably on his feet. "No, it means I love you and hope things can get back to normal between us."

I think about what he's saying. What if I lost him, like Kat lost Sariel? Would I really want our last conversation to be strained? Of course not, but I just can't let his selfishness go.

"I love you too," I manage to offer. "But right now, I can't stand the sight of you."

My father offers me a brittle smile. "I understand. Good night, Villow," he says, shutting the door behind him.

I spend the next hour trying to come up with the best words to comfort Katarin, but everything sounds hollow and flat. I attempt to relate to what she's going through; if I lost Dameaon, how would I feel? Even with our strained relationship, I suppose I would miss him—or, at the very least, miss having a sibling. There would be something hollow about knowing I was suddenly an only child.

But Katarin's situation is different. She loves—correction—loved Sariel. What can I say that will help her? That won't feel disingenuous? Nothing will be good enough, not when her big sister is gone forever.

In the end, I determine the best thing to do is just be there for her and listen.

Katarin isn't in class the next morning, and I try calling her during lunch, but there is no answer. I leave a message to meet me at the Summit after school, but her lack of response fills me with trepidation.

What if she's gone, like Sariel?

It's a silly thought, of course. She'll be at the Summit. She has to be.

I block it out and enter the Guide Seeker building; today is too important to be distracted. If Jetta found a suitable opportunity, we'll have our second Influencing

Phase test. He's standing in front of the map when I arrive. Dameaon is to his left, dressed in all black and looking especially devious. Not a good omen.

"Hello, Villow," Jetta says. "Join us. Please. I've put yesterday's unpleasantness behind me, and we are going to start again. Fresh."

I press my hand to my stomach. "You mean, you're going to let our gaffes go? Just like that?"

He smiles warmly. "If you carry the burdens of the past around, you won't get far in the present."

I let out a huge breath; knowing Jetta forgives me lifts my spirits immensely, returning my confidence.

"I've chosen the spot for your next Influencing Phase test," he says, pointing at the map. It's zoomed into a small village surrounded by a crudely constructed rock wall.

"This is Adevarul, a small civilization of three hundred humans," Jetta says. "It's primitive, compared to Reos, but quite advanced by Earth's standards. The square wall surrounding their village keeps them safe. When the river floods after heavy storms, it protects them from the rising water, and it keeps their hostile neighbors from invading. It also makes it the perfect location for our test. It isolates them . . . just in case things don't go well."

I wince. Jetta said he let go of our mistakes, yet he's still preparing for the worst. Obviously, he hasn't let our missteps go—not like he claimed.

"Your goal is simple today," he says. "The teenagers in Adevarul are becoming restless with the confining walls of their civilization. You need to find a way to encourage their current lifestyle. Our backstory should help you with this. From time to time, the Adevarulians give shelter to citizens fleeing Agopo, a hostile civilization to the north. We will be three such defectors. Follow my lead and don't worry. If you get off course, I will redirect you. This should be an easy win."

He takes the Transmission Potion off the table and pours it into the Teleportation Machine. "A few more things. While their language is the same as ours, they've added their own . . . spin to it. Try to adapt. And review how they're dressed before we leave. Use your Crystals to transform your appearance to match theirs."

Dameaon peers down at the map, scrunching his face like he ate a brambleberry. "Their fashion sense leaves a lot to be desired."

He's right; the men and women are dressed alike, in shapeless white wool garments that fall to their knees and simple leather sandals.

I transform my clothes into an oversized T-shirt and sandals, and lengthen my hair so it falls down to my shoulders. Dameaon and Jetta complete their own alterations, although my twin doesn't change his hairstyle.

When we arrive on Earth, the sudden change in temperature hits me hard; the sultry air creates an invisible hand, choking the breath from my throat. Even the sun appears hazy from the humidity. I'm thankful for my sandals; the ground must be blistering. It's clear why the Adevarulians built so close to the river; they must consume a lot of water.

Jetta smiles at us. "Remember, follow my lead and you'll be fine."

We make our way south, reaching the village's walls in a few minutes. A brute of a man—as wide as he is tall—stands in front of a lopsided wooden gate at the northwest side of Adevarul. The planks of the gate are crudely laid against one another with large gaps between them.

"Salutari'," Jetta calls to him. "We're hopin' fer a bit o' food before continuin' on to Kunnoka."

Dameaon titters—no doubt from Jetta's modified dialect—and I elbow his side.

The gatekeeper looks us up and down. "Where ya be from?"

"Agopo," Jetta says. "We were fleein' from der hostil lifestyle. Would ya let us rest fer a minute or two?"

The brute nods, accepting the explanation, and I realize how prepared Jetta is. I push back my shoulders; with his help, there's no chance of failure.

"Comin' in," the man yells, and the wooden gate moves from right to left, creating a small opening. He leads us inside the walls.

The village is even less impressive in person. It's no bigger than Moudrost's campus, and the floor is dirt with sprigs of dead grass. There are small makeshift stone huts scattered about, each the size of our Guide classroom. I hate to say it, but I can see why the teenagers are antsy.

The gatekeeper talks in hushed whispers to a teenage girl, while the other Adevarulians near the entrance stare at us with mild interest. Then the brute heads back outside. Three teenage boys move the gate into the opening, pushing a large boulder against the back to secure it.

The teen girl approaches us, smiling to reveal crooked teeth. "Salutari', trav-lers, I'm Mercia, daughter ta Adevarul's chief. Welcome ta our humble village." She turns to the three boys who just moved the rock. "Tregs, git des men some water. Harum, find dem somethin' ta eat. Frash, alert ma fadder ta our guests."

The three scurry off, and she heads over to a grouping of flat rocks surrounding what appears to be an unlit fire pit. I can't imagine it ever getting cold enough to need a blaze; every inch of me is covered with sweat.

"Rest yaselves," Mercia says, sitting down on a rock.

Dameaon sits down on her left, and Jetta sits across from him. I take the empty seat to her right. Tregs returns and hands us each a hollowed-out gourd filled with water. Harum brings us some fresh raspberries, also in gourds.

"May we join ya fer a bit?" Harum asks.

"Certainly," Jetta says, and the boys sit down.

Mercia cocks her head to the side, gazing at my twin. "Ya hair is so diff-rent. So pointy."

"What can I say, I'm-ma trendsetter," Dameaon says.

"Trend . . . setter?" Tregs asks. "What's dat?"

Jetta narrows his eyes. "Dameaon's always bene a bit . . . adven-trous. In life and in style."

Mercia leans forward. "Adven-trous. Tell us. Wha's it like, out der?"

"I have me own opinions," Jetta says, "but I assume ya would rather hear from da young ones."

That's his signal; this is the start of our test.

"It's very big," I say. "You're . . . I mean, ya very lucky ta have such a nice village to be part of."

"It's also very exciting," Dameaon says, flashing a smile at Mercia. She blushes. "Me brother has never been one fer risk-taking."

"It's dang-rous," Harum says. "Dat's why we stay 'ere, behind da walls."

"Ya lucky ta be safe," I agree.

But Dameaon shrugs. "Lucky? Perhaps. But walls sound a bit like a cage ta me. And what is life without freedom?"

I shut my eyes and take a deep breath; is he trying to make us fail?

"A life o' safety is a long-lived one," Jetta says. "Ya would all be advised ta remember dat. All o' ya."

Dameaon nods slightly, understanding his message. But Mercia stares straight ahead, looking unconvinced; Jetta's words were not enough to reach her.

"Jetta is right," I say. "We've lost many friends ta the dang-ers we've seen."

"Very true indeed," Jetta says. "It's a—"

Frash clears his throat behind us, interrupting the conversation. "Da chief would like ta talk to ya, trav-lers."

Jetta stands. "Ya, o' course. And den we will need ta head out. We have a lot o' ground ta cover before dark."

Mercia stands and tugs my twin's arm, pulling him to his feet. "O' course. I'll git some supplies while ya talk to me fadder. Dameaon kin help me."

I clench my hands into fists; of course she picks my twin over me. But Jetta shakes his head. "Villow will help ya, Mercia. Dameaon, come wit me."

My fists unclench, and I offer Jetta a crisp nod. Mercia might be smitten with my brother, but it's clear who Jetta trusts more.

"As ya wish," Mercia says, disappointment dripping from her words.

Jetta offers me a knowing look before heading off with Frash, but he doesn't need to; I won't screw this up. Not after the last debacle.

Mercia leads me over to a makeshift supply closet on the west side of their village. It's a three-sided mud-brick structure with four crooked wooden shelves. She keeps stealing glances at me as she packs a small bag with berries, bread, and some sort of meat. I feel bad, taking their meager supplies when we don't have a need for them, but we must keep up the charade.

"May I ask ya somethin'?" she says.

"O' course," I say.

"We're taught we mus' stay 'ere in the village ta be safe. But ya travel. See more den jus' walls. Do ya really agree wit' dis way o' livin'?"

I know how a proper Guide would answer. I should tell her to live for the greater good of her people. That it's her only option, especially as the chief's daughter, and she must be an example for them.

But the words catch in my throat.

My entire life, my father has preached about the importance of the greater good. Yet he is divorcing my mother. Whose needs—besides his own—does that serve? And Sariel is gone now, but she was a free spirit who really experienced life—for the short time she had. Can I say the same?

I search Mercia's unsuspecting face and something inside me breaks. How can I tell her how to live when I'm not even sure I know what it means?

"I cannot answer dat. But I'll tell ya dis. Each of us must decide what's right for us. Ya have one life, and it's short. So make it count. Be happy. Because if ya don't—"

"Villow!"

I turn; Jetta is behind me, his face flushed with fury. Dameaon is smirking from ear to ear.

"J-J-Jetta. You're done already?"

Jetta clutches Mercia's shoulders. "Don't listen ta me friend. He is young and doesn't understand da true reason fer living. Ya are a leader, a future chief. Ya mus' protect da good of ya village, always. Ya can do dat by keepin' dem safe. Do ya understand, Mercia? Dis is important."

She nods but looks far from convinced.

Jetta turns to me, shaking his head in disappointment. "We mus be goin' now. Come, boys."

We fall in line behind him, heading out of Adevarul. I glance back at Mercia. Her lips are pursed, as if she's deep in thought. We exit the village and travel south against the wall.

Dameaon shoves my shoulder from behind. "Great job, brother. Really. Quite the showing."

"Shut up," I say.

Jetta turns around. "Quiet, both of you. We will discuss this on Reos."

Once we've passed the southwest corner of Adevarul's wall, Jetta chants, "Intoarcere, intoarcere," and we teleport home.

Dameaon steps out of the Teleportation Machine. "I'm going to head out—"

"You're staying," Jetta says. "You and Villow are a team."

My brother rocks on his feet, as if he's contemplating making a run for it. I can't blame him. Jetta is furious, and it's all my fault.

I bow my head. "I'm sorry, Guru."

He flares his nostrils. "I thought your brother was the wild card. That I could leave you alone with a human and it would be fine. And I made this test easy. All you had to do was encourage her lifestyle. But instead, you added to her doubts."

"So does that mean . . . we failed?"

Jetta throws his hands up. "Yes, Villow. If it wasn't clear, you failed."

"I'm sorry. I just have—"

"I don't want to hear your excuses," Jetta says. "You're dismissed."

"I'm sorry," I say again, bursting out of the classroom and racing toward the Summit.

A QUICK GLANCE AROUND THE SUMMIT CONFIRMS KATARIN isn't here yet. I sit down next to the stream and dip my legs into the cool water. Wiping the sweat off my brow, I remind myself there could be plenty of reasons she didn't show; maybe she's too sad to get out of bed or her parents need her. Perhaps she didn't check her messages. There's no reason to worry, not until I know more.

After a few more minutes—that feel like hours—I'm so anxious I can barely breathe. I need to know Kat is okay—even if I only see her for a moment. I stand to head down the trail to her home just as she emerges into the Summit.

Unshed tears well up in my eyes. I stumble back a step before running to embrace her.

"You got my message," I whisper into her hair.

"I got your message," she says, giggling.

I release her. She's . . . smiling? I prepared for almost every scenario, but happy Katarin wasn't one of them. "A-Are you okay?"

"I'm great," she says. "Now tell me about your day. How was Guide training? Are you getting alo—"

I grab her arm. "Kat, stop."

She looks up, blinking rapidly. "What?"

"Don't you want . . . to talk about your sister? My father told me about her Olemasolu Statue."

She shakes her head. "There's nothing to talk about. Sariel is fine, Vil."

I tilt my head to the side. "Um, she's not fine."

"Sariel and I are connected," she says. "I can still feel her. She's alive."

She must be in denial. I need to find a way to get through to her. "Kat, I know this is hard, but her Ole—"

"She. Is. Fine." Her eyes widen—so much so, she appears a bit crazed.

Kat needs her false hope, at least for now. I won't take it away from her. Not yet. "Okay, if you say Sariel is fine, she's fine."

She offers me a lopsided grin that increases her unhinged appearance.

"Fill me in on what's happening," she says, tugging me over to the stream.

Settling on the bank with our legs in the water, I tell her about my recent snafu.

"It's so unlike you," she says. "What do you think caused it?"

Kat's been back from Strongmist for weeks, but I haven't told her about my father's divorce, hoping he'll change his mind. We have, however, spoken at length about Dameaon and Portia.

I sigh. "You know what my problem is."

She pulls her legs out of the stream and turns to me. "Vil, don't you think it's time you confront Dameaon? I really don't think he's with Portia. He doesn't even like her."

Hearing her name out loud makes my heart ache like it was stabbed. "He doesn't have to like her. He'd do anything to hurt me. And if I confront him, he'll just find a way to make me feel worse."

"How are you so sure?"

I shrug. "History has proven it time and time again. Look . . . I appreciate you listening, but I really think we have more important things to discuss. Are you sure you don't want to talk about . . . you know, Sariel?"

"There's nothing to talk about. She'll show up any day now, laughing about how worried we were over nothing."

"Kat—"

She hops to her feet. "I'm fine, Vil. Everything's fine. I'll see you tomorrow, okay?"

"If you say so," I agree, standing and heading toward the trail to Spektrolith.

"Vil?" she calls from across the Summit. I turn back, and she continues, "Promise me you'll think about what I said. Talk to Dameaon. You never know until you try."

I nod and start down the trail.

You never know until you try.

That might be true most of the time, but I've learned that when it comes to my twin, the less I try, the better.

THE LAST CHANCE TO GET IT RIGHT

Water is my innate Element—or at least the first one I could conjure. Maybe that's why I have such an affinity toward it in any capacity. I've spent the last thirty minutes in the hottest shower stream possible, filling the room with steam. It drums against my scalp, warming my core and turning my skin bright red.

A furry gray paw sneaks around the shower curtain, batting at my toes.

I suppress my laugh and pull back the curtain quickly. "Boo!"

Cinders's eyes grow as large as Meta, and he puffs his tail, racing out of the bathroom. I chuckle; he's fully grown but still loves to get into mischief. I suspect that will never change.

Stepping out of my shower, I dry off with my thick amethyst towel. Cinders returns, winding between my legs. I bend down and stroke his head a couple times.

Then I brush my teeth while he sits on the counter, batting the dental floss.

"Cinders, you need to let me get ready," I say. "I'm already late."

He flicks his silver-tipped tail back and forth—in and out of the sink. "I'm helping."

I scratch behind his ears. "If this is your helping, I would hate to see your hindrance."

"They look surprisingly similar," he says, following me into my closet while I get dressed.

"Shocking," I say, pulling on a black T-shirt and cargo pants. "What are you up to today?"

"I'm going to visit my clowder, followed by a long nap."

I pull on a pair of socks and head into my room. "Want me to open the window?"

He stretches his wings above his head, flapping them several times. "Sure. I plan on napping here this afternoon."

I push up on the window, opening it enough so he can get in and out easily. "There ya go, buddy. Tell your family I said hi."

He hops up on the sill, turning to face me. "You're my family too, Dameaon. Do whatever's necessary to pass your test today. I would miss you if you didn't come home."

He leaps out the window, soaring up into the violet sky. My vision blurs from the tears in my eyes.

Even though Cinders lives with us, he visits his wyvermalkin clowder in the Hyggelig Mountains a couple times a week. The first few times, I worried he wouldn't come back—but now I know he always will. I'm his chosen family, and he is mine. I can't get banished and leave him. I'll do everything I can to pass our test today—even if it means babysitting Villow.

Leaving the window open for him, I head to Moudrost. After an excruciatingly boring morning of classes, it's finally time for Guide training.

Jetta and Villow are in heated conversation by the Teleportation Machine. I remain in the doorway, hoping to avoid getting dragged into their argument.

"You already said you were sorry, Villow, but you must do better," Jetta says. "You have two failures. If you don't pass every remaining test, you will be banished. I honestly cannot believe we're in this situation. What is going on with you?"

It's a fair question. Besides his odd behavior, my brother looks terrible; he has dark circles under his eyes, and his hair is greasy, like he hasn't washed it in days.

Villow takes a deep breath. "There's something I haven't told any—"

He locks eyes with me, stopping midsentence. He points to the door, and Jetta turns.

"Dameaon, there you are. Join us," Jetta says. I move into the room, and he continues, "After your influence, things went very badly for Adevarul."

I clench my jaw. "After *my* influence? Pretty sure this was all my brother's fault."

Jetta shakes his head. "This is not the time to place blame, Dameaon. You are a team."

Cinder's fluffy face flashes before me. I need to pass—for him. "Sorry. I'm listening."

Villow draws his head back quickly. "Since when do you apologize?"

I jut out my chin. "Since your shoddy performance put me one move away from banishment."

"Boys, stay focused," Jetta says. "You're both making mistakes. A lot of them. And the humans are the ones paying. This time, it was the Adevarulians. Villow, after you influenced Mercia, she snuck out of her village to see the world. Unfortunately, she went to the war-loving village of Agopo. When Agopo's chief realized she was the Adevarul chief's daughter, they kidnapped her and demanded ransom in food."

"I-I never meant for that to happen," Villow says.

Jetta nods. "I know you didn't, Villow, but unfortunately, it did. The Adevarul chief refused their ransom request, putting the needs of his people before his daughter's. The Agopos tortured Mercia and then killed her, sending her heart to Adevarul. The grief was too much for her father. He led his men north and invaded Agopo. The Agopos were stronger and killed the Adevarulian men. Then they marched to Adevarul, burned down its gate, and took over their village."

I think about Mercia; all she wanted was an adventurous life. She shouldn't have died for that. "Good work, brother. You single-handedly destroyed an entire village."

"You're . . . right. It's all my fault," he says with a deadpan tone. "I killed them all."

"I appreciate you owning your actions, Villow, but don't blame yourself for everything," Jetta says. "Mercia was selfish and would have been a weak leader. In addition, the Agopos food sources were running out, and they were becoming desperate. It's very possible Adevarul would have met the same end, regardless of your actions. What's most important is you learn from this. Your words, no matter how trivial they may seem, can create a tidal wave of change."

"What's left of Adevarul now?" I ask.

Jetta lets out a long, low sigh. "While the majority of the humans are Agopos, there are some remaining Adevarulians, and the two civilizations are coexisting. After Oldungur Mekhi and I deliberated, he convinced the Council there is still hope for their future and to spare the village.

"What's imperative now is you focus on your influencing today and leave whatever personal problems you have on Reos. You must pass the test today, boys."

I glance at Villow. He looks limp, like he'll fall over at any moment. Not exactly the embodiment of confidence we need. "Brother?"

He stares straight ahead, like he didn't hear me. I wave my hand in front of his face. "Hello?" He shakes his head and looks at me—with terrified eyes. "We can do this," I tell him. "We just have to follow Jetta's instructions."

Our Guru offers me a small smile. "Dameaon is right. If you follow my lead, you should pass this test no problem." He leads us to the Dimensional Block—still in map form. "Almost five thousand years have passed since Adevarul. Civilizations have grown, prospered, and died."

He zooms in to a small island. At the southern tip, there are at least a hundred humans dressed in brown robes. Some are fishing, some are hunting wild pigs, and some are gathering firewood, but all of them are working.

"These humans are nomads who have no place to call home. They wander across the island, following the migrating animal herds. Their only purpose is to survive. Your goal is simple: help them believe in something . . . more."

"More than what?" Villow asks.

"More than the belief that survival is the only point to life," Jetta says. "It's no way to live."

My stomach tightens into a knot. Jetta is right; it's no way to live. I should know—it's what I've done for sixteen years. Survive, and hope against all odds something more will come along.

"Nightfall arrives soon on this part of Earth," Jetta says. "The nomads will make camp, providing a good opportunity to influence them. Members of their group come and go all the time, making our infiltration easy. You know the drill. Change your appearance to fit in, and we'll head out."

I clutch my Crystal and mutter, "Emorta, umuday," changing my T-shirt and cargo pants into a brown robe. After Mercia's focus on my hair, I lengthen mine to shoulder length, matching most of theirs.

My brother has also transformed, but he looks far from ready. His eyes are glassy, and his chin is trembling, like he's ready to burst into tears. Not the game face I was hoping for, especially when my future depends on his success. Passing this test is up to me.

Prep completed, we teleport to Earth, arriving on a grassy knoll. The air is chilly, and I'm grateful we're dressed in long robes. Jetta leads us north, saying we will run right into the nomad's temporary camp.

"Why don't we gather some firewood and bring it with us?" I ask. "You know, make it seem like we belong."

Jetta nods. "A very good idea. Let's get some timber."

We each gather an armful of small branches and make our way to the nomads' camp. A few of them glance at us, but no one says anything. We add our wood to their pile, and Jetta leads us to the food line. One of the nomads hands me a wooden bowl filled with wild pig meat, mushrooms, and blackberries.

Jetta gestures to three teenage boys sitting in a semicircle. "They look like a good possibility for influence."

I glance at my twin; he's staring at the ground in a daze. No help there.

I take the lead, heading toward the teens. "Can we join you?"

The closest one—a handsome, dark-haired boy—nods. "Gyse. Habben't seen ye before."

Oh goody. Another group of humans who butchered our language. "We're recent additions to ye camp," I say, sitting down.

I make small talk while Villow sits, doing nothing. The humans are no older than me, but all three have life partners, and the blond one—who is named William—has two kids. I can't imagine being saddled with a family already, but humans don't live forever, so I suppose they have to grow up faster than we do.

When the dark-haired one—who I now know as James—admits the endless travel wears on his female partner, I decide it's a good opportunity for influence.

I glance at Jetta, raising my eyebrows. He nods slightly, giving me the okay.

"I must biddan," I say, attempting to mirror their dialect. "Don't ye want to stay put for a while?"

"Stay put?" William asks.

"Not travel. How offen do ye live in one place?"

Lincoln, the short, sunken-faced one, shrugs. "We don't keep track o' time. How would we?"

I scratch my jaw. The nomads have no concept of time. I try to imagine a life without days, weeks, or months. It's impossible to comprehend. No wonder they wander aimlessly.

"Understanding where ye are in the scheme of time is a valuable thing, I assure ye," I say. "Maybe ye could move less."

"How?" William asks.

I point to the sky. "Use the tools ye have. The sun rises and falls each day. At night, the moon and stars appear. Ye can use dat somehow."

James looks up, studying the stars. "The sky. Gyse."

Lincoln shrugs. "I don't understand what it will do for us. We live, we work, we die. Dat's it."

Villow shakes his head. "Dameaon is right. It matters. It will give ye a sense of purpose. And who's to say dis is it?"

I offer him a small smile; it's good he's finally joining in.

"What else could dere be?" James says. "We live, and den we're gone."

Villow shrugs. "Perhaps. Or perhaps dere is something more. Some greater purpose to ye lives. Ye are so busy chasing food, ye can't even think." He holds up one of his berries. "Find berry bushes and uproot dem. Make a garden in fertile soil, where ye can tend to dem. They will grow food for ye. And the wild pigs ye hunt? If ye can corral dem, ye can keep dem. They will mate and produce more pigs. With more food, ye can stay in one place longer."

Lincoln tilts his head to the side, pondering Villow's advice. He's the only one with brains.

"He's right, Lincoln," I say. "We've seen civilizations like this. Their lives are easier. And look," I say, pointing to a mound of boulders and rubble. "Ye even have rocks nearby to build structures to live in."

Jetta stands. "Lots of good conversation, boys, but we need to be up with the sun. I believe we should retire for the evening."

"Gyse," James says. "Thanks for the company."

We say our goodbyes and retire to the ground, pretending to sleep. After ten minutes, Jetta taps my shoulder and points to the woods to the west. We slink between the trees, and he transports us back to Reos.

His massive grin is a good sign. "See what happens when you work together? I couldn't be prouder of either of you. You backed up each other's ideas, and the nomads listened."

My brother raises his eyebrows. "So does this mean we passed?"

Jetta laughs—a full, deep howl. "Yes, my boy, you passed. Not only that, you couldn't have done better. Everything you said was perfect. Oldungur Mekhi is going to be so pleased. I can't wait to see what happens with the nomads. I'll age them ten years tonight, and we will check on them again tomorrow. For now, class is dismissed. Take tonight off. You earned it."

I say farewell and head out, eager to share the news with Cinders. At least for today, I'm staying in Belkin.

Outside Moudrost, Katarin's red ponytail blows in the breeze. I can't believe she's here, after finding out about Sariel's death yesterday. They were so close; I expected she would take weeks off—not a day. I jog over to the Mage wing, interrupting her conversation with Sophie Cantata.

"Hey, String Bean."

"Hi, Dameaon," Katarin says. "How's it going?"

Sophie looks down at her sneakers. "I-I gotta go, Katarin. Talk to you later." She turns, practically running away.

I tilt my head. "Another one of my adoring fans, I see. What did I ever do to her?"

Katarin scrunches her nose. "You can't be that clueless."

"Try me."

"Sophie has a crush on you."

I snort. "She doesn't even talk to me."

"Because she's too nervous around you. Why don't you ask her out?"

It's an interesting question. Sophie is a year younger than me and seems sweet, but reserved. As far as I can tell, she spends all her time practicing the piano and violin, vigorously pursuing becoming a Performer Seeker. Not exactly a good match for me.

"No thanks."

"Why not?"

"She's not my type."

She puts her hands on her hips. "You mean, like Portia?"

I scrunch my eyebrows together; Katarin knows Portia drives me insane. "If I had to choose any of my classmates to go on a date with, I'd pick the feisty redhead."

She giggles, and I'm glad she hasn't lost her sense of humor.

"Look, all joking aside, I wanted to check in," I say. "How are you doing?"

She shrugs. "I'm fine. Class is going well, and I only have two months left before I have to choose my—"

"You can't be fine, Katarin," I interrupt. "You and Sariel were close. I'm sure losing her is hard."

"I didn't lose her, Dameaon. Training just got too tough, so she had to take a break. But she'll come home soon. Any day now."

"Who told you that?"

She touches her chest. "My heart."

I press my fingers against the bridge of my nose and shut my eyes. Katarin is in denial. Not that I blame her—losing someone you love must be the worst pain in the universe—but avoiding reality is not a good idea. In my experience, it only makes things worse.

I touch her cheek with my fingertips. "Katarin, Sariel willed herself out of existence."

She shoves my hand away. "No she didn't."

"Then where is her Olemasolu Statue?"

"In the Estatua Building. Oldungur Hana is lying. It's still in Kapitala."

I shake my head slowly. "I love a good conspiracy as

much as the next Glanching, but you've got to face the truth. Your sister is gone, and she's never coming back."

Her eyes blaze with a fiery rage. "Villow is right. You are vile."

"If getting you to accept the truth makes me vile, so be it."

She launches herself at me, beating her small fists against my chest.

"Hit me as long as you want," I say. "It doesn't change the fact your sister is gone."

Katarin punches my chest for a few more minutes, until fatigue takes over. Then she looks up, searching my face for hope. Whatever she sees in my expression makes her emerald eyes gloss over with unshed tears.

"She's gone," she whispers.

I wrap my arms around her, and she releases her tears, sobbing against my chest. I stroke her back, whispering, "It's okay," over and over.

Finally, she pulls away, looking at my chest instead of making eye contact. "I'm sorry I cried on you. Your shirt is soaked."

"It's just a shirt, Katarin."

She wipes her cheeks with her palms. "I must look like a mess."

"I've seen worse," I say with a small smile. "But seriously, you okay? We could go somewhere if you want—"

"No, I'm okay," she says. "Well, maybe not okay, but at least I'm facing the truth now. My sister. I'm never going to see her again, am I?"

I squeeze her arm. "No. But Sariel always had a reason for what she did, even if it only made sense to her. Find peace in that."

"She was an enigma, wasn't she?" she says, tears welling up in her eyes again. "I'm going to head home now, to have another good cry in the privacy of my bedroom."

"I'll walk with you. You shouldn't be by yourself right now."

She shakes her head. "I want to be alone. Besides, Villow wouldn't like it."

I still. "This isn't about him. Worry about yourself for once."

She drops her chin to her chest. "He tried to get me to see the truth yesterday, but I wasn't ready. It would hurt him, knowing you were the one who got through to me."

I run my fingers through my hair; I can't believe Katarin is worried about Villow's feelings. But she doesn't need an argument. Not right now. "I'm not going to tell him, Katarin. It's never been my style."

"I know. I appreciate it," she says, squeezing my hand. "And thanks."

"For what?"

"For making me face the truth."

I smile. "The truth's all we have."

She nods and leaves me, heading home. I replay my words: *the truth's all we have.*

I've been avoiding Villow for far too long. His mopey attitude is affecting our Guide training and almost got us banished. It's time I forced him to be honest—even if he doesn't want to be.

My twin's clumpy steps echo down the hall, announcing his arrival. I prop up on my elbows.

He enters his bedroom and clenches his jaw. "What are you doing here?"

Apparently, he's not happy to see me. I smile. "I live here, remember?"

He tosses his shoulder bag onto his desk. "You always have to be sarcastic. I'll clarify. What are you doing in my room?"

"Are you blind? I'm hanging out with Cinders," I say, pointing to the gray fluff-ball curled up between my legs.

"I can see that," he replies, pressing his lips together. "I didn't realize our wyvermalkin was a traitor."

Cinders lifts his head and blinks several times. Then he jumps down and saunters out, refusing to look at my brother.

"Okay, what is your problem?" I ask. "You've been moodier than normal and now you're being mean to Cinders."

"You're my problem, Dameaon."

"*I'm* your problem? I'm the reason we passed our test today."

"It's not about that," he says, sitting in his desk chair. "I know you don't like me, but I didn't think you would stoop so low as to steal my girlfriend."

I choke back my laughter. "Since when do you have a girlfriend?"

"I did . . . well, almost did. Until you stole her from me."

"Who exactly did I take from you?"

He crosses his arms. "Portia . . . Who else? You knew I liked her and you went after her anyway."

I stand. "Once again, you have no idea what you're

talking about. Get your facts straight before accusing me of nonsense."

I move to the door, but he grabs my shoulder, spinning me around to face him.

"You don't want to fight me, brother," I warn, flaring my nostrils.

"That's exactly what I want," he says, shoving my shoulders.

My welled-up frustration surges to the surface, and I push him—hard. He stumbles backward but steadies himself and charges at me.

I sidestep and pin his arms behind him. He struggles, but it's useless; I've always been stronger.

"Have you gone insane?" I ask.

"If I did, it's your fault."

I release his arms and shove him forward. "Stop blaming me for everything that goes wrong in your life."

Villow covers his face with his hands. "You don't get it." He drops his arms to his side and looks at me with wet, dull eyes. "Why did you go after Portia? Do you really hate me that much?"

I throw my hands in the air. "I already told you, I have no idea what you're talking about. Why do you think I'm with Portia?"

"I saw her kiss you at Moudrost a few weeks ago. In the courtyard."

I rack my brain for a reasonable explanation but come up empty. "I would never let Portia kiss me."

"I saw you, brother. She kissed your cheek."

"You've been a complete jerk for weeks because Portia

kissed my *cheek*? Grow up, brother. And I promise you, she's so not my type."

"Portia is everyone's type. She's perfect."

"Sure, if you think superficial, self-centered snobs are perfect. I prefer Glanchings with a little more depth."

He collapses in his desk chair. "B-But . . . this makes no sense. If she isn't dating you, why isn't she with me? She's barely talked to me since the Path Ceremony."

"Maybe she doesn't like you. Or maybe because you're dull. Or a killjoy. The reasons are endless. But she's not with me, so you'll need to ask her. Just prepare your fragile ego for the answer. And stop being so self-absorbed or we'll fail our Guide training," I say, brushing against his shoulder as I leave.

JETTA IS GRINNING WHEN WE ARRIVE TO CLASS THE NEXT DAY. The Dimensional Block is still zoomed in to the grassy knoll. The nomads moved the giant rocks into a circular position, stacking some of them on top of each other.

"Your advice made quite the difference," Jetta says. "The nomads planted crops and domesticated pigs, just like you told them to. Dameaon, your explanation of time's value inspired them. Just look. They created rock formations to track the hours of the day. And that's not all. Villow, you made them question if there was something beyond Earth. They discovered faith, believing in a better place after death. The rock formations also serve as graves, used to celebrate the dead's passing. This truly is a turning point for humankind."

Villow nods. "You did good, Dameaon."

Perhaps it's his way of apologizing for last night. "Not so bad yourself, brother."

Jetta slaps both our backs. "I have exciting news for you. Oldungur Mekhi and I talked this morning. We both believe you are ready to be on your own, my boys."

My twin's eyes widen. "You mean . . . we're ready for the Trial Phase? That's a little soon, isn't it?"

Jetta nods. "It is. But the Oldungur Council has concerns about the humans' Essence Orb. It dims a little more every day."

Goose bumps spread across my neck. I can't believe it. I'm going to Earth—without Jetta.

"I'm sorry," Villow says, "but it feels like the Oldungur Council is setting us up for failure. I mean, the Rules clearly dictate we should spend months in the Influencing Phase."

"The Rules say you pass the Influencing Phase when I believe you're ready," Jetta says. "Do you honestly think I would let you go if I thought you wouldn't succeed? Have some faith in me, Villow. And yourself. The leadership you both showed with the nomads was so impressive, I know you'll be fine."

"We got this, brother," I say, offering him a smile.

He returns it, and my heart warms.

"As soon as I find a suitable civilization, you'll head to Earth for a year," Jetta says. "There's nothing left for you to do here, boys. Go enjoy your last couple days on Reos with your loved ones. I will let you know when I've found your civilization."

I head home and share the news with Cinders. He insists he'll be fine while I'm gone and makes me promise

I'll come back. As soon as our mom finds out about our pending departure, she launches into party-planning mode. Our entire dinner is a discussion surrounding decorations and guest lists.

Later that evening, I head up to the roof and sit on the granite ledge. Under the light of the three moons, I think about my life.

Two months ago, my brother criticized me in this very spot, claiming I was destined to be a Soldier while he would be a Guide. That criticism made me change my Class, and in turn, my life.

Being a Guide Seeker has brought me more excitement and happiness than anything else ever did. The humans fill me with a sense of belonging I've never felt with the Glanchings. For the first time, I believe in destiny. This is what I was meant to do, and Villow helped me get here. As much as he infuriates me, I won't forget it.

Not that I'll ever tell him that.

SOME GOODBYES ARE HARDER THAN OTHERS

THE LAST TWO DAYS HAVE BEEN A BLUR. BETWEEN HELPING MY mother plan our going-away party and extra lessons with Guru Jetta, I haven't had a moment of free time. But I promised Kat a private goodbye. So, even though I have a hundred things to do, here I am, waiting for her on the Summit's northern rock crags.

Zon's rays reflect off Katarin's flaming hair, alerting me to her arrival. I start my descent, dropping the last several feet to the soft grass as she emerges from the mountain path.

"I was beginning to think you forgot about me," I say.

Her face pinches. "It's not funny, Vil."

"Sorry, Kat. Is everything okay? I'm sure you're still upset about Sariel."

She tightens her ponytail, high on the back of her head. "It's still really hard. My parents cry all the time, and there's nothing I can do to make them happy. And it's not just that. It's . . . well, you're kind of my best friend, and I like having you around. When I didn't know exactly when you were leaving, it was easy to avoid reality, but now it's hitting me hard."

"Cheer up. I'm still here for another day," I say, grabbing her waist and lifting her off the ground. I spin her so fast that her legs fly out behind her, and she laughs—loudly.

When I put her down, she keeps her thin arms clasped tightly around my neck.

"I'm going to miss you," she whispers into my chest.

"I'll miss you too. Come on." I lead her over to a cyperus tree close to the stream. We retire under its branches, lying on our stomachs, arms bent at the elbows.

"You know, a year isn't that long," I say. "And you'll start Mage training soon. You'll be so busy you won't even have time to miss me. It's a blessing I'm leaving so I can preserve my fragile self-esteem."

"This isn't the time to joke," she says. "I'm trying to tell you something, and it's hard enough without your teasing."

I sit up, crossing my legs beneath me. "Sorry. I'm listening. I swear."

"Okay . . . let me try to explain. Do you see those rocks?" She points at two flinty heads in the stream. "As the water flows over them, they change . . . gradually. So slowly, you don't notice it from day to day. But if you didn't see them for a long time, the change would be obvious.

"You and I . . . we're like those rocks. We see each other almost every day. But . . . now you're leaving for a year. What if we don't recognize each other when you get back?"

"It's one year, not one hundred. We won't change that much."

She sighs. "This isn't coming out right. Let me try again. I've been meaning to talk to you since you danced with Portia at your Path Ceremony. I didn't know how to bring it up. Honestly, I still don't. But losing Sariel taught me that we need to say things, while we still can."

The mention of Portia provides the clarity I need. Katarin hasn't been impressed by her behavior lately. "Kat, it's okay. I know where you're going with this. And I think we're on the same page."

She springs to her knees, grasping my hands in hers. "Oh, Vil, you don't know how happy that makes me! I was certain you wouldn't feel the same way."

I laugh at her exuberance. "Honestly, things have been different since the gym incident with Colton. I saw a side of her I'm not sure I like. And we haven't really talked in weeks, so—"

She scrunches her nose. "Her?"

"Portia. Who else?"

She drops her shoulders. "Of course you think this is about Portia. Sometimes I wish you weren't so clueless."

"Okay, enough of the vagueness," I say, throwing my hands up. "What's this about?"

"Are you this naive? Haven't you noticed things have been different between us? That we haven't been spending time together like we used to?"

"What do you expect? I've been busy lately. Plus, I've had a lot going on with my family. You don't even know all of it."

"Not everything is about you and your precious

problems." Kat pauses, taking a deep breath. "Sorry . . . I know you've been busy . . . but that's not it.

"Listen, and please don't interrupt. I've been trying to talk to you since the Path Ceremony. When I saw you dancing with Portia, I was happy for you. But I was also jealous. Which is silly, because you're my best friend. And that's when I realized I didn't want you to be with her . . . because . . . you should be with me . . ."

I jump up, striding a few paces away from her. If she continues, it will change everything between us, and I don't want that; our relationship is the most positive constant in my life. And I'm mad at Portia, but that doesn't mean I've ruled out a future with her forever.

"S-S-Say something, please," she says.

"What do you want me to say? You know I care about you, but as a friend."

She touches my shoulder from behind. "Well, I love you, Vil. I've probably loved you for longer than I even realize. And I think you love me too, but you're just too scared to admit it. Look at me. Really look, and you'll feel what I feel."

I turn and start at her bare feet, moving my gaze up her body: knobby knees, khaki shorts, a jade tank top, slim neck, and five freckles across her cheeks and nose. Begrudgingly, I peer into her emerald eyes—windows to her pain. There's no spark, no attraction. Without a doubt, the only love I have for her is as a best friend.

"Kat, I don't want to hurt you, so please don't make me say it."

A tear runs down her left cheek. "Okay. I guess that's what I needed to hear," she says, brushing it away. "I believe in us, Villow. You don't see it yet, but you will."

I snort. Another Glanching who thinks they know more about me than I do. "Trust me, I'm not going to change my mind. You're like my little sister."

She balls her fists. "Like your little sister? Like your little sister!? You're not that much older than me, and a lot less mature. You've been spending too much time with Dameaon. Here I am, bearing my heart to you, and all you can do is be cruel."

"And you have never been less of a good friend. It's unfair to spring this on me right now," I say. "I thought saying goodbye to you would be the hardest part of leaving. Now, I'm certain it will be the easiest."

She steps back, as if my words pushed her. "I hope being away teaches you some humility. See you in a year . . . that is . . . if you stop being such a jerk." She races down the mountain trail, her balled fists swinging at her sides.

"Don't count on it," I scream after her, storming out of the Summit.

Katarin just gave me another reason to be glad I'm heading for Earth tomorrow; hopefully, the time apart will bring her to her senses.

I STARE ABSENTLY AT MY BEDROOM WALL, TRACING THE INdentations on my ankh amulet: the top of the loop has a sideways Z for Lightning; the right curve has a four-leaved plant sprouting from a triangle, denoting Earth; the left curve has two parallel lines with spiraling right ends for Wind; a plump raindrop on the transverse bar's left side represents Water; the right traverse bar's three rippling heads symbolize Fire; and a jagged blade signifying Ice resides at the bottom of the cross.

There's a knock at the door, and Jinnet peeks in. "Sorry to interrupt, Villow, but your mother wants you downstairs, now."

"Tell her I'll be right there," I say, placing the amulet over my head. My admiral-blue Crystal in the center warms my chest.

Jinnet nods and closes my door, presumably returning to the party. Even though I said I was coming, I don't follow her. Her intrusion jogged a memory of my tenth birthday, and I let the scene replay in my mind.

I was in this exact spot, anxious and trying to summon the energy to head to my party.

Jinnet—who was our housemaid even then—already came to retrieve me once, so when there was another knock at my door, I expected it was her. Instead, it was Katarin.

Her ear-to-ear smile disappeared when she saw me. "Uh-oh. Are you okay?"

"No, I'm not okay," I said. "This party is all for appearances. Like I want to spend my birthday with a bunch of my parents' friends. And Dameaon's been so mean all day."

"Oh, Vil, I'm sorry."

"I should be used to it by now, but I guess I'm still hoping for something to change. Did my mother send you up here?"

"Huh? No. I have your birthday present. Close your

eyes," she said, grabbing my hand and placing something in it. "Okay, you can look."

In my palm was a kumihimo band, braided with dano worm thread, dyed four shades of blue—iris, cornflower, cyan, and azure.

"It's a friendship bracelet," she said. "It's a reminder I'm here for you. Always."

I put it on and held out my arm. The bracelet dangled several inches below my wrist. "It's great, Kat. But it's a little big."

She laughed, but only for a moment. "I know, I know. I made it big enough to fit when you're an adult. This whole best friend thing is forever, ya know?"

"Promise?" I asked.

"Of course. You're stuck with me."

In response, I tackled her with a giant hug. Even after I opened my endless gifts, the friendship bracelet was still my favorite. It symbolized Katarin's affection for me, and that was a big deal. A really big deal. It changed everything. I had her, and that was enough. Enough to make me stop caring that so much of what my family did was for show. Enough to make me stronger. Enough to make me believe in myself. I was certain nothing would ever get in the way of our friendship.

Now, with one conversation, we're on the precipice of losing each other forever. Even though Katarin exasperated me, I could have been more understanding. I need to fix things with her. Tonight.

I check my reflection in the mirror, smoothing out the wrinkles in my graphite linen pants.

"How long are you going to admire yourself?" Cinders asks from the top of my bookshelf.

I adjust the collar of my sky-blue button-down shirt. "I'm so glad you woke up to share your opinion, but I wasn't admiring myself. It's important I look nice tonight. I am the guest of honor after all."

He stretches his wings and glides down to the floor, rubbing against my legs. "There are more important things than looking nice."

I stroke his velvety head. "Like what? Petting you?"

"Among other things."

I laugh. "I'll miss you, Cinders, but something tells me you'll be fine without me."

He wraps his tail around my ankles. "Of course I'll be fine. A bit of advice: learn to love yourself. If you do, you'll never be lonely."

"I do love myself."

"If you say so. I'm going to get some food at 'your' party. See you downstairs," he says, sauntering out.

"I do love myself," I call weakly, but his words remain with me.

If I really do love myself, why am I still up in my room? That's not the behavior of a Glanching with high self-esteem.

It's this fight with Katarin. My nerves are getting the best of me because things aren't right between us. I'll feel better once we make up. But the only way to do that is to go downstairs and find her.

I take my friendship bracelet out of my bottom desk drawer and slip it on my wrist, adjusting the cuff of my shirt to hide it. Then I take a deep breath and head down to the party.

It's already in full swing, packed with Glanchings celebrating our send-off. To my left, guests are sitting in sand-colored chairs embellished with pearls, placed around seashell-shaped tables. Ahead of me, the Sympohoe is performing on a wooden-plank ship hull with square cotton sails as a backdrop. Center stage, the lead singer, Laulja, croons into the helm's hidden microphone.

I wander over to the dance floor. A few couples are already on the sapphire marble floor speckled with frothy white paint to emulate ocean foam. That includes Portia, who is clutching Nemesis warmly. That's unexpected; maybe he's the reason she's not interested in me.

Blocking them out, I resume my search for Katarin. Dameaon and my father are to my right. My twin raises his drink in the air, and I smile weakly; like it or not, I'm stuck with him. My mother joins their conversation, and my father takes her hand. She beams up at him, kissing his cheek.

Hope renews inside me. Maybe he decided not to divorce her after all. It certainly looks promising. I take a step toward them, but someone grabs my arm.

"Hey there, darling," Portia drawls beside me.

Her off-the-shoulder dress is adorned with aquamarine and teal sequins that glisten like fish scales. Its short hem, paired with her high heels, makes her toned legs appear even longer.

"Portia," I say. "You're like the sea come to life."

"That's exactly what I was going for. Don't you know that's the theme your mother chose for your party?"

"Yes, but I'm surprised you do."

She squeezes my arm. "I'm just full of surprises."

"I'm sure you are. It's part of your charm. It makes my last night on Reos even better."

She laughs, displaying her dimples. "You are so dramatic. It's not your last night. You'll be back in a year."

"Of course," I say. It's exactly what I told Katarin hours before.

Katarin.

I glance around, but her vivid red hair is nowhere to be found.

"I came over here looking for a dance partner, but if you're too distracted, I'll find someone else," Portia says.

"You want to dance with me?"

"Duh. I just said that."

I abandon my search and offer her my arm. "Sorry. I'd love to."

We get to the dance floor as the band begins "Ritzeta's Waltz." I place my hands on her waist. She leans her head on my shoulder, and we move in unison across the floor. Holding her in my arms is mesmerizing, and I don't speak, afraid it will ruin the moment.

When the song is over, I catch a glimpse of Colton over her head. He's glaring at us with more hatred than I've ever seen.

I freeze; my sudden standstill alerts Portia that something is wrong.

She turns around. "Franzleduk. My brother told me to stay away from you."

"What? Why?"

She tugs me off the dance floor and toward the woods

to our left. "He's still mad about Dameaon interrupting your fight."

I scrunch my face. "Like that's my fault?"

She grins. "In case you haven't noticed, Colton isn't exactly reasonable."

We enter the woods and wander down the mountain trail. In the silence of the boscage, it hits me; it's not my fault she's been avoiding me—it's Colton's. Which means she might actually like me after all.

The muscle near my left eye starts twitching. If Portia likes me, I have a reason to be nervous again. I rack my brain for something clever to talk about.

"So . . . how's Mage training going?" I ask lamely.

She giggles. "It's good. I learned how to cast Ice Blast yesterday."

As proof, she rubs her hands together and pushes them forward, like she's shoving an invisible object. A frosty blast shoots from her palms into a nearby tree, and the frozen leaves clack against each other.

"See. Now I'm like you," she coos, pursing her frosted pink lips.

I absently wonder if they taste like cake. "You're like no one else I know."

She smiles at the compliment but says nothing else, and the conversation ends. After my last pitiful choice of subjects, I don't try to engage her again.

We arrive at the Summit, and Portia wanders around, taking everything in. "So this is the famous Summit. Not too bad, I suppose. Of course, Katarin built it up so much, it's a little disappointing."

I bite my bottom lip and grimace. Bringing her here is a violation of my friendship with Katarin, especially when we're fighting. I point back at the trail. "We should probably return to the—"

"So are you excited about tomorrow?" she interrupts.

"Yes . . . I've been waiting for this as long as I can remember. It's my chance to do something good. Something substantial. I'm sure you feel the same way about being a Mage."

Portia waves her hand dismissively. "Yeah, sure. What secrets has that old coot Jetta taught you?"

I recoil; she knows better than to ask about my Class's secrets. And it's rude to call Jetta an old coot.

She must sense my tension because she grabs my arm again. "Hey. I was only teasing. You're so sensitive."

And now she's insulting me. There are so many things I should say: that asking me to share Guide secrets is not appropriate; that she's being disrespectful; that I'm no longer in love with her—in fact, I'm not even sure I like her; and more than anything, I need to find my best friend and apologize.

"I think we should go—" I start but never finish the sentence; Portia's lips smother my words.

My initial thought is she does, in fact, taste like cake. Then, realizing I'm standing like a statue, I close my eyes and press my lips against hers. The scent of her perfume mixes with the nearby lupinus flowers, and I'm certain I'll never smell them again without returning to this moment.

My first kiss.

I lean in, and her arms tighten around my neck. Our noses bump awkwardly, so I tilt my face slightly to the right and she opens her mouth, entangling her tongue with mine. Every sensation is intensified, and I'm more aware of my own heartbeat than ever before; it's beating fast and hard against my chest.

Eventually, she pulls away. "We should get back before anyone realizes we're gone."

I nod, and we walk back in silence, Portia's hand resting in the crook of my arm. Even when we rejoin our friends, Portia doesn't release me.

Our classmates' reactions are mixed. Amorose Hart, her best friend, smiles broadly; Nemesis grimaces as if he's in pain; Sophie giggles behind her hand; and Dexter stares blatantly, his mouth agape. Only my twin remains practically unchanged, scrunching his eyebrows so slightly I may have imagined it.

"Uh, Villow, c-could I get a minute with you? In private?" Dexter asks.

"That's a good idea," Portia replies, finally letting go of my arm. "I need to talk to my brother anyway."

Colton is on the other side of the yard, glaring at us, his eyes ablaze with fury.

"Sure," I say. "Dexter, why don't we go up to my room?" We head upstairs, and I gesture at the bed. "I'm sorry we didn't get more time together the last couple days. Things have been crazed."

"I don't care about that. What's going on with you and Portia?" he says, leaning against my mattress.

I smirk. "I'm not sure myself. But I can tell you one thing . . . she's an amazing kisser."

His eyes widen. "You kissed her?"

"Well . . . technically, she kissed me."

He whistles—one long note. "Wow. I didn't see that coming."

"Me neither. I don't think I'll ever be able to predict what she'll do next. But that's part of her charm. Speaking of Portia, I don't want to be gone too long, so what did you want to talk about?"

He pulls a wrapped gift from his messenger bag and places it on the bed. "I have something for you."

I unwrap the navy paper to reveal a hinged walnut box. Inside are six unlabeled potions.

I cover my mouth with my hands. My insides are suddenly frozen. "I'm assuming these are your own creations?" I ask. He nods, and I slam the lid shut. "Dexter, we talked about this. You promised to stop."

He touches the top of the box. "I lied. Look, I know you have Rules you need to follow. But I'm asking you, as your friend, to take these to Earth with you."

"I'm not supposed to use Magic on Earth. Besides, they aren't labeled. How would I know when to use them if I don't know what they do?"

"Listen to your heart. Mine told me to make these for you, so I did." He stands, walking backward to the door. "I'm sure you'll do great as a Guide, Villow. You're good at everything you set your mind to. I-I'll miss you and s-see you when you get back."

Dexter leaves, and I stare at the errant box. I need to get rid of it, but disposing of potions—particularly those whose contents are a mystery—is no easy feat; it's not like I can pour them down the sink. Right now, I just need to hide them. I place the box under a pile of T-shirts in my closet and head downstairs, rejoining the party.

The rest of the night flies by uneventfully, concluding with Dameaon and me bidding farewell to our guests. On her way out, Portia whispers, "A year isn't that long, darling. We'll pick up where we left off when you get back," making me warm from my head to the tips of my toes.

After the last guest leaves, I start up the foyer stairs, but Dameaon calls after me. "It begins tomorrow."

"What does?"

"Our real lives."

I step down, rejoining him. "I suppose that's true. It's a little sooner than I'd like, but what choice do we have? Are you ready?"

"I'm always ready, brother. It's you I'm worried about. Get it together before we leave," he says and heads out the front door.

I hunch my shoulders. Every time things start getting better between us, he has to act like that. He's probably still punishing me for my accusations surrounding Portia. Still, his harshness drains what little energy I had left.

But it doesn't matter how tired I am. I need to know if my father is reconciling with my mother before I leave. Begrudgingly, I head to his study. He's at his desk, smoking a cigar.

"Father?"

He looks up. "Villow. What a nice surprise. It was a wonderful party. A perfect farewell."

"Mother always plans perfect parties. Speaking of, I saw you with her tonight. You looked so happy. Did you decide to do the right thing and stay with her?"

He puts down his cigar. "Things have not changed,

Villow. I told you, I have to keep up the appearance of a good husband. For the sake of my job."

"What about Mother's sake? You're playing the role of the doting husband too well. She won't see this coming. It's not fair."

"You're too young to understand. Life isn't always fair, and eternity is a long time. Too long to be unhappy."

I have the sudden urge to hit him. Instead, I give him my coldest stare. "Life is fair, if you play by the Rules. I thought Dameaon was the biggest disappointment in the Verchant family. Turns out it's you."

Completely forlorn, I charge out of his study and crawl into bed without changing my clothes. The emotional toll of the day hits me hard, and my eyelids are too heavy to keep open.

Sometime later, I jolt as if I'm falling.

The positions of Meta, Hermes, and Yars indicate it's the middle of the night, but I'm suddenly wide awake. My heartbeat stops, and I curl up into a ball under my covers.

Katarin didn't show up to my party.

Her behavior is something I would expect from my twin—or, if I'm being honest, Portia—but not my best friend. Even if I were furious with her, I would never let Kat leave for another planet without saying goodbye. But that's exactly what she did.

It's not important—it was still the best night ever. Katarin and I are growing up. Moving on.

I yank the friendship bracelet off my wrist and throw it across the room.

Determined to sleep, I close my eyes again, mentally

chanting, "It's not important," until I convince myself it's true.

KATARIN DIDN'T SHOW UP TO MY PARTY. IT'S MY FIRST THOUGHT upon waking—the same one that kept me up half the night. I roll out of bed and shuffle to the shower. The deluge of hot water relaxes my muscles and revitalizes my skin but does nothing for my weary mind.

I shamble down the foyer's left staircase, driven by the delicious aromas drifting out of the dining room. My parents are already there, eating breakfast.

"Good morning, Villow. I hope you slept well," my mother says. She looks vibrant in her loose canary-yellow dress.

"Yes. The party wore me out," I lie, scooping a variety of foods onto my plate from the buffet.

"It was quite the party, wasn't it?" she says. "And you were completely charming last night. All my friends were so impressed at how much you've grown up."

"They must not have been looking at the same Glanching as me," Dameaon says as he enters. He's still in his pajamas and his hair is unkempt, but he appears well rested.

"And of course, they said the same thing about you, dear," my mother says. "It was exceedingly important for your father and me."

I sit down, my cheeks flushing with frustration; once again, she made a momentous event in my life about her. Then I remember her world is about to explode and soften.

Dameaon flops onto the chair across from me, setting his overflowing plate down on the table. He picks up his erdberry pancake with his fingers and chomps it like a savage.

"You know you have silverware, right?" I ask.

In response, he opens his mouth, displaying his half-chewed food.

"Villow, Dameaon, I'm sure you're nervous about today, but don't argue," my mother says. "You're lucky you get to share your Guidance experience." She takes a sip of her tea. "Drasko, perhaps you have some advice for your sons?"

"If the boys don't know what to do at this point, nothing I say will make a difference," he replies, not glancing up from the paper.

"Nothing you say matters anyway," I mutter, rubbing the back of my neck.

He scowls. "All right, you want some advice? If you make decisions for the greater good, you'll succeed."

Blissfully unaware of our father's plans for divorce, Dameaon continues shoveling food into his mouth. But I know too much to let it go. "That's good advice. Do *you* follow it?"

He slams his paper against the table with a loud smack. "Yes, Villow, I do," he says, his volume rising with each word. "You will not question me in my own house."

My mother nervously tugs her garnet ring over her knuckle and back into place. "Honestly, Villow, what is wrong with you? Your father exemplifies living that way."

I bite the side of my cheek to prevent myself from screaming at her. How can she defend him when he doesn't care about her at all? When he's planning on divorcing her? When he's the biggest hypocrite I know? But screaming will only hurt her, and I can't bring myself to tell her the Glanching she loves is a fraud.

"Forgive me, Mother. The stress of today is getting to me," I reply, standing. "I'm meeting Katarin at the Summit before school, so I better get going."

Another lie, but I can't be in the same room as my father a moment longer.

"Oh, good," my mother says. "I noticed she wasn't at the party."

"Yes, she had a bad headache last night, but I'm sure she'll be better today," I fib. My third lie of the day, and I've been awake less than an hour.

"You better hurry," my father says, returning to his paper.

"Don't worry, I'm leaving, and you won't see me again for a year. I'm sure that will help ease your conscience."

I march to the foyer with my mother trailing behind me. "I don't know what's gotten into you today. I'm sure you're nervous, but that doesn't mean you can disrespect your father. You go back and apologize right now. You don't—"

"I'm sorry, but I can't," I say. "Besides, I have to go."

"Goodness. I don't like your attitude. Don't lose track of what's important now that you're a Guide. Family is still the most important thing." I shrug, and she opens our front door. "I'll tell Drasko you said goodbye and that you're sorry. I wouldn't want him to think I raised a wretch for a son. Ta-ta, dear."

And there it is—the world's worst goodbye.

With nothing left to say, I head out.

While my mother's send-off was as shallow as I expected, I had imagined the heartfelt moment between my father and me endless times. He would offer me sage advice and tell me how proud he was. But that was before I discovered his secret. It makes me long for my best friend even more. I hurry my pace, hoping she really is waiting at the Summit.

As I pass through the jinger trees, rustling ahead makes my heart pound.

"Kat, I knew you'd be here," I cry out, rushing into the clearing.

Two nibblers—the cause of the noise—stop grazing and stand on their hind legs. They playfully dive into the lupinus flowers, their fuchsia noses and long ears poking out between the petals.

My exuberance drains, and I fall to my knees next to the stream. I can't believe she isn't here. I press my hands to my temples, trying to dispel the forming headache.

The rippling water summons her analogy about how we would change. She's right; I don't know what's going to happen on Earth, but I will come back different.

One thing is certain—if I don't make up with her today, she'll stay mad for a year. That anger could turn to hate, and that's the last thing I want.

Plunging my hand into the water, I pull out a smooth oval stone—a memento to take to Earth—and place it in my shoulder bag before heading to Moudrost.

In the courtyard, Dameaon is talking to Portia and Colton. Portia smiles and waves, but her brother practically drags her to the gym.

I join my twin. "What was that about?"

He leans against a twisted cyperus tree. "It wasn't about you."

"That's not what I asked."

"Yes, you did. Maybe not directly, but it's what you meant."

Rather than wasting my time arguing with him, I start toward the general studies building. Dameaon steps in front of me. "She's not here."

"Who?" I ask, idly thumbing the friendship bracelet on my wrist that I retrieved from my bedroom floor this morning. He shrugs, but I know he's talking about Kat.

"Let's go, brother," he says softly. "It's time to meet Jetta."

Dameaon heads to the Guide Seeker building. A lump forms in my throat; I'm not going to get a chance to apologize before leaving. I walk a few paces behind my twin, trying to stop my tears. By the time we reach the classroom, I've regained my composure enough to plaster a wooden smile on my face.

Jetta is leaning against his desk, tapping his foot impatiently. Yet he beams when he sees us. "Good morning, my boys. Today's the day. Your day. We have a few things to discuss before you depart. Come. Please."

We follow him to the back room where he points at the Hourglass of Time. "I've adjusted it so Earth and Reos's times mirror each other, as will be the case for your first three trials, until you graduate from Seekers to full-fledged Guides.

"The reason is twofold. First, your teenage years are formative, so it allows you to age at the same rate as your peers on Reos." He moves over to the cherrywood stand in the right corner. The water in the basin is magically linked to our Crystals, so it currently shows the three of us in the back room. "Second, it allows me to use the Viewing Sphere to check your progress daily. If matters go too off course, I'll call you back early. But this is all about you surviving alone as Guides, so I'll only do so if things go very, very wrong. Otherwise, your Crystals will alert you when your year is up. You have them, correct?"

As confirmation, I pull my amulet out from under my T-shirt. Dameaon holds up his left hand, displaying the white-gold ring on his pointer finger.

"Good," Jetta replies. "Remember, every time you alter your appearance or heal yourself, it drains some of your Crystals' energy. Away from Reos, they won't recharge, so if you use their energy up, you won't be able to utilize their abilities until you come home to recharge them. Now, let's review Troy quickly."

He leads us to the Dimensional Block, zoomed in to a walled city next to a large body of water. Jetta chose patriarchal Troy for our trial for a couple reasons. First, most of its nine thousand citizens are working class, while a small percentage belong to the noble class. They are predominantly good humans, doing their best to contribute to their society and live simple lifestyles. This makes it a relatively easy population to influence.

Second, they're a civilization with a real need for Seekers. Their barren soil makes them dependent on trade with nearby cities for a majority of their food. The trade deals rely heavily on King Priam's relationship with the other cities' kings. His only son is weak and may not be able to keep the deals in place upon Priam's death, leaving the citizens of Troy to starve. It's the perfect opportunity for us to change their fate.

"Remember to spend your first couple days gaining more insight into your professions." He zooms the map in to four structures on a hillside north of the city but still safe inside the walls. "Villow, visit the temples and learn more about oracles. The Trojans' belief in the immortals will provide a good opportunity to influence them."

He glides his fingers over the map, moving to a small bar at the southern end of the city. "Dameaon, to help you as an orator, spend time at the local bar, Sailing After Dark, listening to the patrons' stories. They base a lot of their lives around their history and fables."

"The bar? Tough work," my twin says.

"I figured you would be disappointed," Jetta says with a grin.

He moves the map to the center of Troy, where there is a large crowd of Trojans, moving from store to store in the market. It's set up in four quadrants with intersecting roads dividing them. The upper left quadrant sells food and wine, the upper right sells red clay pottery, the lower right sells armaments and bronze armor, and the final one sells cloth—mostly white wool with a few colorful silk pieces—along with a couple other miscellaneous shops.

A raging pyre burns in the center of the market. The Eternal Flame, as it's called, is important to the Trojans' survival. They don't have a power source, so the humans light their torches in the Eternal Flame, bringing its fire inside their homes for light and to cook.

"The shop is a good place to visit to gather information

about what's important to the Trojans," Jetta says. "Once you earn some drachmas, visit and purchase your own items. Finally, don't forget to follow the Rules for Guidance."

He looks pointedly at Dameaon, and I know his warning is meant for him.

Sheepishly, I adjust the messenger bag on my shoulder where I hid Dexter's potion box. For the hundredth time, I remind myself bringing them doesn't break the Rules, only using them does—and I have no intention of doing that. Just knowing I have them provides me a sense of much-needed security.

"Oh, there's something else," Jetta says, handing us each a fluorescent cherry-red potion. "Interestingly, as the humans spread out, their languages evolved. Now there are numerous dialects across the globe. But have no fear, these Speech Potions will instill their tongue in your mind. As fair warning, they are bitter, so I recommend drinking them quickly."

I take his advice and swallow mine in two gulps, my face puckering. He's right; it tastes like unripened brambleberries.

He leads us over to the Teleportation Machine and gestures for us to get inside. "Oldungur Mekhi had his operatives place a Teleportation Machine on the peaks of Mount Ida. It's in a location that is much too cold for the humans and has a high density of zircon crystals, so your teleportation should be smooth. When you arrive, head west until you reach the coast. Follow it north, and you'll run right into Troy."

Jetta pours the Transmission Potion into the top.

"While you're on Earth, promise me you'll stay together. You're stronger united than apart. Be safe and be the Guides I know you can be. See you in a year, boys."

I smile weakly. His parting words exhibit more concern for us than both of our parents combined. It's not fair—for either of us. "I promise, Jetta."

Jetta pushes the button, and the showerhead emits droplets that sizzle warmly against my skin.

"Don't screw this up, brother," Dameaon says.

I glance over, but he's nothing but a shadow as my vision blurs. "It's not me I'm worried about."

He scoffs in response, but it doesn't matter—in fact, nothing does. Because in that moment, everything becomes dark.

My vision returns, blurry and unfocused. Blinking several times, I can still only see six inches around me, as if the air is full of static. I hold out my hand, and tiny floating particles land on it, melting from my palm's warmth. Although I've never seen it before, I know exactly what it is—snow.

I bend down, tossing handfuls of fluffy powder above my head and watching it drop in clumps to the ground. Falling backward, I swoosh my arms and legs, creating an imprint in the milky blanket.

"If you're done acting like an idiot, could we get moving?" Dameaon says.

At the sound of his voice, I sit up. His amber eyes penetrate the swirling snow, reminiscent of the monsters in my childhood fairy tales—only this time, my brother is the villain and I'm the prey. That thought chills me more than the frigid temperatures, which is silly. Just because the blizzard conceals everything but his glowing eyes doesn't mean he's a monster.

To prove it, I jump to my feet. "Come on, Dameaon, celebrate with me. We're on Earth! Not just for a test with Jetta but for real this time."

"That doesn't mean we should act like children."

I refuse to let his aloofness ruin this moment. Using his eyes as an anchor, I crouch and roundhouse kick where I estimate he's standing. Sure enough, there's a loud thud as he hits the ground. I whoop loudly, and he crashes into me, knocking me onto my back.

"Do you admit defeat, brother?" he asks, hurling wet precipitation in my face.

"Never," I shout, throwing him off. I pound handfuls of snow into a ball, tossing it in the direction I launched him.

His cursing confirms it made contact, and a retaliation snowball hits me in the temple. I fall backward, but I am on my feet quickly, packed snow in hand.

I spin in circles, but he's disappeared. Suddenly, I'm hyperaware of everything around me. Each falling snowflake seems like it's trying to smother me. The chilled air seeps inside me, making me numb. What's worse, there are zero background noises—no chirping, hissing, buzzing, gurgling, or whooshing. I never experienced complete silence before, and it's eerie.

I clench my jaw. "Okay, Dameaon, you were right . . . We need to get moving. I call a truce."

He doesn't respond, and my pulse races. "Come on, Dameaon, this isn't funny. Let's go."

Suddenly, I'm attacked from the left and on the ground again.

My twin is holding down my shoulders. "No truce, brother. Do you give up?" he asks, chuckling.

His laughter—so infrequent—is contagious. "All right, I give. You win."

He stands.

"Let's get moving," he says, offering his hand to help me up.

Kat was right about confronting Dameaon about Portia. Things are different between us. Better. More brotherly. My best friend is always right—except about us as a couple, that is. Remembering our fight makes my eyes well up, so I block it out and focus on Earth.

We start down the mountain, going west like Jetta suggested. I try to keep up with Dameaon, but as my adrenaline subsides, the frigid temperature takes its toll.

"Wait up," I holler when he pulls far ahead.

He stops, crossing his arms impatiently. "Is there any particular reason why you're so slow?"

I shiver. "I can barely feel my legs. Aren't you freezing?"

"No, that's what this is for," he says, holding up his left hand to display his glowing Crystal.

"We're supposed to use our Crystals sparingly. Being cold doesn't constitute using them."

"Sure it does. But if you don't want to comply, I'm not waiting for you," he says and begins descending even faster.

It takes all my strength not to toss another snowball at his head. But that would be far from productive, so instead I grasp my amulet and mouth, "Nihmiurgma."

Warmth flows through my entire body, and I'm able to keep up.

We make good time, traveling two miles down the snowy peak in thirty minutes. Here, it's much warmer, so I touch my Crystal to turn it off. Unfortunately, there's no sign of Troy or the coast—just rolling hills, speckles of trees, and mounds of boulders.

"Now what?" I ask.

"Shh," my brother says, moving around a jagged edge of rock.

On the other side, ten goats—six adults and four kids—are munching on grass. A tiny black one headbutts an adult, who reciprocates with a stern look. The kid searches for a new target, lowering its head and charging at my twin. Dameaon kneels, and it leaps onto his lap.

"I guess you made a new friend," I muster, unable to keep the jealousy from my tone.

My brother smiles from ear to ear and scratches the white tuft of hair on its forehead. "I will admit, it has a certain *spunk* I can relate to."

The young goat hops to the ground, darting ahead and back to us.

"I think it wants us to follow it," my twin says, taking a few steps.

Sure enough, it sprints forward, turning only once to make sure we're coming. Our inability to speak with it is frustrating, but the goat still finds its own way to deliver its message. It charges around another large rock, bleating with pleasure. Following it around the boulder, I immediately retreat, pulling Dameaon with me. I hold my finger up to my lips, warning him to be quiet.

The goat brought us to a clearing with at least fifty sheep. More importantly, it led us straight to a human. I peek over the top of the boulder as the goat bounds up to him.

He drops his wooden staff and squats. "Αντιμετωπίζετε και πάλι προβλήματα, δεν είστε εσείς, Aegidius?" he asks, stroking the goat's chin. *You're causing trouble again, aren't you, Aegidius?* His odd dialect is understandable, thanks to the Speech Potion.

I point up the mountain to regroup, but Dameaon is staring at his Crystal and chanting silently. A glowing light surrounds him, and his linen shirt and pants morph into a white chiton. His gaze rakes my body, indicating I should follow his lead.

I sigh, annoyed he's making decisions without my input. But what choice do I have? I can't argue with a human nearby. Acquiescing, I grasp my amulet in my right hand and mouth, "Emorta, umuday."

As my Crystal's power encircles me, I alter my jeans and T-shirt, transforming them to mirror the shepherd's loose white wool chiton—comparable to a one-shoulder dress—falling to my knees and cinched by a brown leather belt. My sneakers change into leather sandals, and as a final touch, I transform my canvas shoulder bag into a leather one. Its thin strap rests on my left shoulder and crosses my chest, securing the bag on the right side of my waist. Pleased with my transformation, I turn back to my twin, but he's already in the clearing.

The human stands when he sees him.

"Χαιρετίσματα," Dameaon says. "How are you, friend?"

"Friend? Do I know you?" he asks, cradling Aegidius protectively in his arms.

I curse silently and join them. "Sorry to startle you. We don't mean you any harm. We're just a little lost and hope you can direct us to Troy."

"It is a two-day journey that way," he says, pointing northwest.

"Thanks," I say, starting in that direction.

"Halt!" he cries. "Please . . . halt. I offer you a fair deal. I will provide detailed directions in return for you camping with me tonight. It is a bit lonely on this mountain."

"I'm sorry, we—"

"Of course," my twin interrupts. "We'd be happy to."

"—need to get to Troy," I finish. "We've already lost several days and shouldn't waste any more time."

"Nonsense. We can spare one night," Dameaon says.

"It is settled," the human says. "Shall we set up camp?"

I sigh, knowing I've lost. "Fine. One night. But then we really must get to Troy. I'm Villow, and this is Dameaon."

He waves his hand dismissively. "We can exchange names when the work is complete. The sun is almost gone, and the fire must burn by then."

"Why?" my twin asks.

He squints his chocolate-colored eyes. "You have been lost on Mount Ida for days, no? Surely you have encountered wolves at night. Without a fire, we are at risk, especially my flock."

"Luckily, we lit a fire each night to stay warm," I reply, raising my eyebrows cautiously at my twin.

"For certain, luck is not the reason. The gods must favor you. We must get to work. Villow, can you collect enough firewood to last the night, while Dameaon and I catch our dinner?"

I nod and venture into the nearby woods. I busy myself collecting fallen branches, attempting to silence the echo of Jetta's voice: *Spend your first couple days observing, so you can create a good backstory to fit in.*

We've only been on Earth for a few hours, and we've already gone against his advice. When he finds out, he'll be so disappointed—maybe even angry. At both of us. Even though it was Dameaon's idea, I could have opposed it more. But spending time alone with the shepherd was too great of an opportunity to pass up, and I have to believe Jetta will understand that.

My arms full of thin, dry timber, I head back. In camp, the human places half the sticks in a pile and lights them with flint and steel. Then he cooks the freshly caught fish, browning both sides.

"Have you ever been to Troy?" I ask when we sit on fallen logs to eat.

He nods. "I lived there my whole life. Until becoming a shepherd."

I sit up; our luck couldn't be better. "What's it like?"

He takes a gulp of goat's milk from his cup and passes it to Dameaon. "It is typical of a city."

"Could you give us a little more information?" I ask. "We're pretty excited to learn about Troy."

He crosses his arms. "It is not a subject I enjoy talking about."

Although I'm intrigued, I don't push it. "We all have things we would rather not talk about. Besides, it seems like you found your place."

He surveys his flock gathered around the fire. "Yes. The immortals blessed me with finding my purpose. I turned sixteen a few months ago and needed to choose my profession. Since I am fond of animals, being a shepherd was a wise choice, but I miss home more than I thought I would. Maybe in time I will find my way back." He clears his throat and continues, "But tell me. Your speech is less formal than I am used to. What brings you to Troy?"

Since it was my twin's idea to spend the evening with him, I tilt my head at him in a go-ahead gesture.

"You're correct. We're from a city far from here," he says. "Our mother, who raised us by herself, recently passed away. Our entire lives, she told us our father died before we were born.

"On her deathbed, she admitted he was actually a Trojan vagabond. Their romance was short-lived, and he left before she knew she was pregnant. With her last breath, she begged us to go to Troy and find him. So that's why we're here."

Leave it to Dameaon to concoct an elaborate story rather than something simple, like we're traveling the world. I jump in. "Which is why we were so lucky to run into you. With your directions, we'll reach Troy in no time."

"The blessings of the gods brought us together," the shepherd agrees. He stifles a yawn. "It is later than I realized. Let us retire. And think, soon, if the gods allow, you will meet your father. I pray he is everything you want him to be."

I think about Lord Drasko and what a disappointment

he is. "Yes, it would be wonderful to have an honorable father."

Dameaon gives me a puzzled look but doesn't say anything, and we retire to the ground. It's hard, but it's one of many sacrifices required to be a Guide.

I glance up at the night sky. The single moon of Earth shines down on me. My throat thickens with emotion. I never appreciated how much I loved Reos's three moons until this moment. Or my soft bed with warm covers. I shift, trying to get comfortable without a blanket or pillow.

The nearby sheep bleat softly, and I glance at the shepherd.

I've been so focused on my personal life that I've forgotten being a Guide is my true life's purpose. The shepherd is my purpose. I have the opportunity to save humankind. That's so much bigger than all the drama waiting back on Reos.

The distant howls of wolves make me grateful for the brightly burning fire. I focus on the dancing flames rather than my racing thoughts, and soon my heavy eyelids drop into total darkness.

An Unexpected Opportunity

I LEAN OVER VILLOW, MY FACE INCHES FROM HIS. HOW HE CAN sleep so soundly on the ground is beyond me. Growing impatient, I shake his shoulders roughly and he jolts awake.

"Nice of you to finally wake up, brother. Are you going to sleep the whole day, or can we head for Troy?"

He opens his mouth to reply but changes his mind, standing and stretching instead.

I gesture to the human on the nearby hill. "He woke up at dawn with his flock. And I've been up talking to him. I'm taking this Guide thing a lot more seriously than you."

"Enough, Dameaon. Just because I slept later doesn't mean I'm not taking this seriously. What did you talk . . ." he says, trailing off. His eyes focus on something beyond my shoulder. "Who are they?"

"Who are who?" I say, turning. In the distance, five men on horseback are galloping toward us.

"Let's ask the shepherd."

I nod, and we race up the hill.

"My friends, I know you are eager to get to Troy, but surely there is no need to rush," he calls.

I point to the horsemen. "Are you sure about that?"

He glances in the direction I indicated and scowls. "We need to run. Now!" he screams, clambering toward a grove of trees.

I pause uncertainly. My twin is also frozen, and for a moment, we stare at each other. Then I start after him with Villow close behind. He's the only human we know, and that counts for something.

"Who are they?" I ask when we're close enough for him to hear me.

"Soldiers," he yells. "We cannot let them catch us."

I jump over a small stream, landing on its muddy bank.

"Why? What did you do to make soldiers chase you?" Villow asks.

He ignores him, skillfully darting between the trees. My brother and I mimic him, dodging fallen branches and logs. Although we're barely winded, the shepherd's breathing is heavy, and his pace is slowing. Still, he pushes onward, and we finally reach our destination—a cave.

He pushes the large rock away from its entrance and gestures at the dark hole. Villow shrugs and dives inside. I follow him, and we pull the rock back into place, plunging ourselves into total darkness.

"Hold on," the human says. "I left flint, steel, and a torch in the back, just in case."

I'm not in the mood to wait. I place my hand against the side of the cave, using it to safely navigate to the back.

I reach into the darkness and find the large piece of wood leaning against the wall. With no clue how to light flint and steel, I summon a fireball in my hand, holding it to the end of the torch. It ignites, illuminating the darkness.

My twin is a few feet away, glaring at me. Oh, darn; he's upset I used Magic.

I turn to the human. "You have some explaining to do."

"I suppose I owe you the truth, since you did not abandon me," he says, his voice raw with emotion. "I was not lying when I told you I needed more time to figure out my life. But my father, who does not care about anyone's opinion but his own, had plans for me. That meant I could stay in Troy and do what he wanted, or run away. So I bought some sheep and goats and escaped to the mountains. My father must have figured it out and sent his troops after me."

"Those men looked pretty serious," my twin says. "Is your father a man of influence?"

"You could say that. I know you barely know me, but will you help me escape? I cannot be trapped in a meaningless existence forever."

I soften; I'm an expert on feeling like life is meaningless.

"I'm sorry," Villow says. "We need to find our father, and this isn't our fight."

The shepherd closes his eyes. "Of course. It was foolish to ask." He pushes the rock away from the entrance. "May the gods lead you safely to Troy."

"If we run into the soldiers, we won't tell them where you are," my brother promises before exiting the cave.

I think about the conversation I had with the human this morning. If I play this right, taking his place could be advantageous to me. "You know they will never stop pursuing you, right?"

He leans against the wall. "I just want to be left alone."

"If you truly want to escape, I can help you."

He tilts his head. "How?"

The Rules are clear about using Magic in front of humans, and I have no intention of getting called back to Reos. "The immortals blessed me with great powers, but you must close your eyes."

He does, and I use my Crystal to transform into his mirror image. "Okay, open them."

He takes one look at me and drops to his knees. "I have never seen such sorcery. Are you certain you are not a god?"

"No, I'm just good friends with them. And I promise, if you accept my help, I will take care of the Trojans," I say, pausing. "But I will be giving up my own freedom. As such, I have two demands. First, you must promise to never return to Troy unless I come find you. Second, Aegidius comes with me."

"You want my goat?"

"Aegidius and I bonded, and I need a friend," I say, offering him my hand. "Do we have a deal or not?"

He narrows his eyes, thinking for a moment. "You promise to take good care of the Trojans?"

"You have my word."

"All right," he says, grasping my hand. "We have a deal."

"Best of luck, shepherd," I say, pulling him to his feet.

"You too, Dameaon."

I hand him the lit torch and head out of the cave. Villow is nowhere to be found; apparently, he grew tired of waiting. Oh well—at least I'm spared from another one of his lectures.

I set out for Troy, stopping every now and then to listen for my twin. As I near our campsite, voices echo through the trees. I veer east, making a quick detour to check it out.

Sure enough, the five soldiers have taken over our camp, sitting on the logs around the now-extinguished fire. My dimwit brother is on his stomach, crawling into the clearing toward his shoulder bag. He reaches for the strap, just as one of the soldiers looks over.

"What are you doing?" he shouts gruffly, striding toward my twin.

Villow jumps to his feet, clutching the bag behind his back.

The soldier snarls, revealing crooked yellow teeth. "Have you seen a shepherd, close to your age? Do you understand me? Are you mute?"

One of the soldier's companions shoves him away from my twin. "Please ignore Dareios. He has no manners," he says, pulling off his helmet to reveal damp black curls. "We are looking for our friend and thought this might be his flock."

Villow looks at the ground. "I-I haven't seen anyone."

He is the worst liar ever; guess it's up to me to save him. I step into the clearing, twenty feet behind my twin.

"Are you sure?" the soldier asks. "I was told he was a shepherd on Mount Ida and—"

His piercing blue eyes focus on me, and he pushes past Villow.

"Paris, it's you," he says, pulling me into a giant hug.

"It's good to see you too," I reply.

"I'm sure it's a bit surprising as well," he says. "Your mother wrote about your sudden disappearance and begged me to help. So I boarded a ship and traveled from Sparta, all to bring you home."

"I'll come back readily, but we must bring my new friend along," I say, pointing at my twin.

"Didn't you have two new friends?" Villow asks.

I shake my head. "Nope, just you."

"That's not true. My brother was with me, and I won't leave him behind," he insists.

I appreciate his loyalty, but he's screwing up my plan. "Honestly, Hector, stop making up stories. You told me you were an only child," I say, giving him the name of an infamous Guide who failed in re-creating the Geitenmensen, hybrid goat-men.

He scrunches his forehead and looks at my left hand, spotting my gargoyle ring. He shakes his head, but I ignore him, turning to the handsome soldier. "If you help me find my goat, we can get going."

He laughs. "Wait . . . you want to bring a goat to the palace? Aren't you in enough trouble already?"

"The palace?" Villow asks.

I shut my eyes; I was hoping it would be a bit longer before he found out the truth.

"You didn't tell your friend who you really are? It's not polite to keep secrets, Paris. Or should I say Prince Paris," he says, turning to Villow. "As he is next in line to be king, I'm sure you understand why his parents were so upset when he ran off. But fear not. I, Achilles of Sparta, succeeded where the Trojan Guard failed. And it wasn't easy, I promise you." He turns back to me. "Who is this again?"

"This is Hector the shepherd."

The soldier looks him up and down and sneers, clearly unimpressed. "As I said, I am Achilles of Sparta. Paris and I went to military camp together when we were twelve and have been like brothers ever since."

"That's because I was the only person who could kick your butt," I joke. It's risky, since I have no idea what really happened at camp, but he laughs.

"It was one fight, and I ate bad fish the night before."

I chuckle. "Still counts. You're just mad I tarnished your perfect record."

Achilles hooks his arm around my neck, placing me in a choke hold. "Whenever you want a rematch, just let me know."

With my Glanching strength, I could easily escape. But that would be suspicious, since Achilles has at least fifty pounds on me and double the muscles. So instead, I pretend to struggle until he releases me.

Out of nowhere, Aegidius bounds into the clearing. He charges to me, not fooled by my change in appearance.

"Your goat friend, I presume?" Achilles asks. I nod, and he smacks his hands together once. "Then our party is complete, and we can head for Troy. Soldiers, ready for our departure."

His men untie the horses from nearby trees and bring them over. I walk a few paces up the hill, staring down at

Paris's flock. He will join them soon—free to live the life he wants. I'm giving him that.

In return, I get to be a prince and help the Trojans—even more than I could as an orator. It's a win-win, really.

"Paris," Achilles calls.

I glance at the flock once more and return to the camp.

Achilles hands the reins of a regal ebony stallion to me. "I brought Phlegein along, expecting we would find you. I figured you'd want to ride him home."

I hold my hand up to the horse's muzzle, letting him get used to my scent. Then I stroke his thick black mane. Cradling Aegidius in the crook of my left arm, I use my right hand to boost myself up.

Achilles frowns at Villow. "You'll have to ride with Paris, since we didn't plan for you. It will slow us down, but so be it."

"I'm not going to slow you down," he says. "Two of your soldiers have to share a horse too."

Achilles looks at me. "Are you sure we need to bring him?"

I ride over to my twin, nodding at Phlegein's back. "He's not so bad once you get to know him."

Villow clenches his fists for a moment before pulling himself up.

It's appropriate he's riding behind me. I'm excelling at being a Guide—I've got a best friend, a horse, and a goat—and so far, all he's done is make an enemy out of Achilles.

WE RIDE MOST OF THE DAY, REACHING THE BASE OF MOUNT Ida by sundown. While the other men venture out to hunt and gather firewood, Achilles and I feed Aegidius wild alfalfa. Villow is nowhere to be found, no doubt off sulking somewhere.

When the soldiers return, I chip in, stacking their recently found firewood into a small pile by the fire.

"What can I do to help?" Villow offers, appearing out of nowhere.

Everyone keeps doing what they're doing—starting a fire, skewering rabbits, or dragging logs into the clearing—and doesn't acknowledge him in any way. As we gather around the fire, Villow ends up alone on one side, peering across the flames at everyone else. As the social outcast for our entire lives, I can't help but smile; maybe now that he knows how it feels, he'll be nicer to me.

"Without Achilles's charm, we could not have found you, Paris," Dareios says. "The shepherd you bought the flock from kept his promise and acted like he never met you. But his daughter . . . well . . . one smile from Achilles, and she offered up the truth. Of course, who can resist a dimpled man in shiny armor?"

"What's the matter, Dareios? Jealous?" Achilles ribs.

"Sure," he admits. "You've got brains, brawn, and wealth. The gods blessed you, in every way. Who wouldn't be jealous?"

Achilles pushes out his chest. "I won't argue with you."

"You forgot to mention his modesty. Or lack thereof," I add, and the soldiers laugh. It's so easy, being with them; it's like I belong here.

"Sounds a lot like you, Paris," Villow says, and the conversation ends abruptly.

The Spartans exchange glances, and when we resume talking, he doesn't say another word. Once dinner is over, the soldiers pass around five bottles of wine. As the night wears on, they break into song, belting out upbeat ditties at the top of their lungs. By their seventh number, the wine slurs their speech so much I can't understand what they're saying, but it doesn't matter; all the songs are the same: a Spartan faces a terrible foe, is victorious, and spends the rest of his days as a hero.

A few songs later, I realize Villow is being excluded from the wine drinking. Part of me wants to ignore it; after all, he never included me with his friends back on Reos. But the other part of me—the side that knows what it's like to be the outsider—wins out.

When one of the bottles comes back to me, I walk over and sit next to him on the other side of the fire.

"Hey," I say, offering him the bottle.

He ignores it, crossing his arms instead. "You've really done it this time. What were you thinking, taking Paris's place?"

I take a swig from the bottle. "I was trying to help him. He didn't want to be found, and I had the ability to make that happen."

"You're pretending to be a prince," he whispers. "You know the Rules say you can't be a leader."

"Blah, blah, blah. All you ever do is criticize me. For your information, I didn't know Paris was the prince when I agreed to take his place."

"It doesn't matter. You know what the Rules say. 'Do not let your love of one influence you to act against the needs of the greater good.'"

I jut out my chin. "Love? I don't love Paris. I barely know him. I saw an opportunity and I took it."

"Well, it was the wrong move. Once they fall asleep, we need to sneak away. You can change back to your Glanching form, and we—"

I shake my head. "We don't even know what being a prince means."

"Jetta told us the king is in charge of Troy and the prince is next in line. And that King Priam will die soon."

"He said the king will die someday, not soon. I'll probably be back on—"

"What are you two whispering about?" Achilles says, towering over us.

I was so focused, I didn't realize the men stopped singing. I recover quicker than my twin and pat the log beside me. "Nothing important."

He plops down. "If you say so. Are you ready to face your father tomorrow?"

"I don't have a choice, do I?"

"No," he says. "Running away was not the wisest decision. But then, you've always made bad choices. Remember military camp? You persuaded me to sneak out in the middle of the night and go swimming. My foot was bitten by a snake, but we couldn't go to the infirmary because we broke curfew. When we finally went the next morning, you had to carry me because my leg had swelled to double the size. Thank the gods I didn't end up losing my foot."

The real Paris sounds like someone I wouldn't mind being friends with. I nod, pretending to recall it. "We've certainly had our share of adventures, haven't we?"

"We've been through a lot together," Achilles agrees. "Speaking of, would you regale us with the song you taught me that year? About Herakles?"

I pause. "That was a long time ago."

"Not that long ago. And it's your favorite song."

I look at Villow for help.

"I think Paris is too tired to sing," he says.

Achilles furrows his brow. "Since when do you let a working-class citizen speak for you? And address you so informally?"

I hold up my hand. "Hector didn't know I was a prince until today. I'm sure he'll adjust. But he's right. I am very tired, and I have a lot on my mind. Perhaps you could sing it, if you remember?"

There's a glimmer of doubt in Achilles's eyes, but he nods and stands. His golden armor gleams in the firelight as his deep voice rings out:

Along the shores of Troy, deep in the Aegean Sea,
There was a serpentlike creature called Hydra,
Who made its home near the city's quay.
Stalking ships with the speed of enhydra,
Its screams filled the air like a banshee.

Lethal venom dripped out from Hydra's forkèd-
tongue mouth,
Killing the seamen, every death gorier.
Soon fleets diminished and fear was routh.
Troy prayed to the gods for a warrior,
As hope for freedom became drouth.

The king offered great riches to the souls who
would fight,
And slaughter the monster with deadliest breath.
Heroes came and fought with all their might,
But decapitation did not cause death,
Instead two heads grew at its site.

Then mighty Herakles sailed out to grapple the
beast,
His sharp golden sword against Hydra's heads
brushed,
Causing each of its domes to increase.
Thirty mouths struck and his vessel soon gushed,
Filled with water, winning was weest.

To an island of boulders, bravest Herakles went,
Fastening large rocks to his wreckèd ship's lines.
With this tool, success he did augment,
Launching the rocks, trapped his foe in seine,
Till it commenced its last descent.

The Trojans, released from the evil monster once
feral,
Sang their praise for Herakles, the new victor,
And his valor that saved them from peril.
He received wine, wealth, and women galore,
Living the life of a hero.

"Achilles, that was quite an emotional performance," Dareios says.

"Jealousy does not become you," Achilles says. "Now, let's retire. Paris is tired, and we have a long day of riding ahead of us."

We follow his advice and get to sleep, resuming our journey after breakfast. The flat terrain provides a smoother—but duller—ride than yesterday, and the miles of brown pastures quickly become redundant.

Just when I'm certain the tedium will drive me insane, Achilles points to a gray dot on the horizon and shouts, "Troy is glad to see you, Paris."

The blob takes shape as we get closer, morphing into curved stone walls, easily five times taller than me. When we approach the gate, it lifts in front of us, as if by magic.

Entering Troy, we fall into a single line behind Achilles. Our horses' hooves clomp against the stone streets as we travel the southern route through the city. The few humans who cross our path wisely stay out of the way, bowing as we pass.

We continue until we reach another wall, and Achilles hollers, "Guards, open the gates. I have returned with your prince, as promised."

There is a faint sound of grinding metal as the door in front of us rises. Inside is a courtyard filled with trees, flowers, statues, and fountains. A gigantic gray-and-white marble building surrounds us.

We dismount, and Aegidius runs circles on the lush grass, bleating loudly. Apparently, he's happier than I am to be back on his own feet.

"Avoiding your father, Paris?" Achilles says.

I nod. The truth is, I have no clue how to find him in

this labyrinth. "I suppose I am. But maybe if you go with me, it won't be so bad."

"As you wish. I'd like to see his reaction anyway," he says, moving to the ivy-covered wooden door in the middle of the building. He's knocked backward as it springs open.

A woman rushes forward and throws her arms around my neck. "By the gods, I never thought I would see you again," she says, tears flowing down her cheeks.

"Queen Hecuba, you are making a spectacle of yourself," Achilles says playfully.

So this is my new mom. In just a few seconds, she's shown more warmth toward me than my real mom has my whole life. Her genuine embrace warms my chest, and I wrap my arms around her.

"It is not every day my only son returns," she says, pulling Achilles into our hug. "Oh, Paris, flesh of my flesh, you are home. I have you to thank, Achilles."

"It was my honor to serve you," he replies.

"Troy owes you a debt," she says, releasing us.

She looks past me, noticing my twin for the first time. "I did not realize we had company. Paris, who is this?"

Achilles puts his arm around Villow's shoulders, steering him toward us. "You haven't met Paris's new friend yet? He's a shepherd."

She narrows her eyes, deepening the wrinkles on her forehead. "Really, Paris, a shepherd has no place here." She turns to Villow. "I am sure you understand that working-class citizens are not welcome at the palace and you must be on your way."

Villow shrugs his shoulders, moving out of Achilles's embrace. "I appreciate that shepherds and princes do not mix. But I am no shepherd. I'm an oracle. I was on Mount Ida meeting with the gods when your son stumbled upon us. The gods made him identify himself and, once they knew he was Prince Paris of Troy, demanded I stay with him until he found his true purpose. They brought us together, and our journey isn't over yet, so I cannot, in good faith, leave his side."

Queen Hecuba's expression changes from contempt to disbelief. She raises her eyebrows at me. "Is this true? You met the gods?"

"I suppose," I say noncommittally.

"Then why did you tell me he was a shepherd?" Achilles asks.

Villow steps forward. "He was protecting me. I asked him to hide my identity until we were safely in Troy."

"Hector's a little paranoid," I say.

"Paranoid?" the queen asks.

"Worries a bit too much, about everything," I say. "But yes, he's an oracle."

Achilles drops onto his left knee. "By the gods, forgive me. I never would have treated you so poorly if I would have known."

The queen places her hand on Villow's shoulder. "Forgive us both, Oracle Hector. You are welcome at the palace as long as the gods require. Achilles, escort him to the guest quarters across from your room so he can get settled."

He nods, and she continues, "Come, son. Let us go

see the king. You have some explaining to do, but your debacle was not without reward. Your new friend is a gift from the gods and will surely smooth things over."

I look at my brother. He narrows his eyes and shakes his head, displeased I'm pretending to be the prince of Troy. Luckily, I don't have to answer to him.

"Coming, Mother," I say, following her into the palace.

PARTIES ARE FUN, RIGHT?

ACHILLES'S MUSCULAR LEGS CHARGE FORWARD, LEADING ME down corridor after corridor. Left, right, left, left, left, right—the palace's marble hallways are relatively indistinguishable, so I enumerate the turns, hoping it will help when I venture out alone. Eventually, we stop at a wooden door at the far end of a passageway.

He looks at his feet instead of me. "Per the queen's request, this is the best guest room. I'll leave you to get settled."

Before I can respond, he's sprinting away, probably mortified for how he treated me prior to my oracle declaration. After a stressful couple days, I'm thankful to be alone. I wipe my sweaty hands against my chiton and open the door.

Yikes . . . If this is the best guest room, I would hate to see the worst. It's not much bigger than my closet at home, and a lot less cheerful. Sparse wooden furniture, bare marble walls, and a single window—covered by dull gray shutters blocking out the midday sun—make for a rather melancholy ambience.

Disappointment saps my remaining energy, and the single bed practically summons me. I skim my fingers against the cobalt wool blanket and recoil from its scratchiness. Tossing it back, I climb between the soft cotton sheets. The goose-feather mattress is lumpy, but it's a definite improvement over the ground. Recalling where I slept the last two nights makes my cheeks burn with shame. So what if the room isn't lavish? It has the necessities, and it's a place to call my own. Besides, this isn't a vacation; it's my job.

One that I'm not doing very well. Thus far, my performance has been lacking, while Dameaon seems to be excelling. Watching his easy rapport with Achilles made my heart ache.

The pitiful truth is, I miss Katarin so much it hurts. I close my eyes and grip the friendship bracelet on my wrist, imagining what she'd say right now: *"Dameaon's fitting in because he's pretending to be someone else. Give it time . . . You'll find your own way to make connections with the humans."* Almost instantly, my heartbeat slows to a normal rate. My imaginary Kat is right—I just need to put forth a little more effort and I'll fit in.

My confidence somewhat restored, I make my way across the room to the wooden stand topped with a bowl and splash some water on my face. At room temperature, it does little to refresh me, but I head out anyway, arriving at the entrance with minimal backtracking.

"Can you open the gate?" I holler up to the nearest wall guard.

"Of course, Oracle," he says, beckoning another guard over.

Together, they crank a giant lever—reproducing the earlier grinding—and the gate's chain winds around the axle. Eager to start exploring, I duck underneath when it's halfway up.

"Just let us know when you're back, and we'll let you in," one of the guards says as the gate drops behind me.

I mumble a thank-you and then head out into the streets. Even though I rode through them less than an hour ago, we were going too fast to see anything.

This is my first chance to explore Troy, so I go slowly, taking in every detail. The capacious street outside the palace gate is wide enough to fit five side-by-side humans across it. A line of black ants parade across the cobbled road, and dewy moss permeates the cracks between the flat stones.

Directly across from the palace gate is an alluring two-story building. It's constructed with gray stones the size of my clenched fist that are held in place with hardened mud. Thriving ivy climbs the sides to its flat roof. In the verdurous lawn, a twisted-trunked olive tree's shadow has created an oasis for five huddled goats.

Another goat is curled in a nook created by two criss-crossing branches. It bleats down at me, displeased its nap was interrupted.

I laugh. "Sorry to disturb you. I'm leaving now."

It bleats again and then returns to resting. I venture onward, discovering similar structures sprinkled alongside the road. Very few Trojans pass me, and I only glimpse a few working in their yards, but they're all friendly, offering short yet polite greetings.

"I pray you to be well," a wrinkled, crooked man calls, perching on a bench outside his home. "This weather is a gift from the gods."

"It's a perfect day," I agree.

There's nearby giggling, and the old man points to the yard opposite his. "You have a couple admirers."

Sure enough, two teenage girls are peeking over a white wool sheet that is hung across a string to dry. Not wanting to encourage them, I offer the old man a quick wave and keep going, making my way north.

I come around the corner and the city's layout changes significantly. The street is half as wide, and the buildings are identical, one-story squares with only a few feet between them. The tiny dirt yards have spatterings of stubbly brown grass, and there's increased activity—with far more Trojans bustling about. This is the working-class section of Troy.

I travel down street after street—passing a myriad of small houses—until I eventually reach a crossroads. The cobbled road continues down the right fork, but the left path is made of dirt, with bountiful fields in the distance. I veer left, ambling along, enjoying the chirping birds and the cool breeze against my skin. Civilization fades behind me, and the wheat and barley stalks fill the air with a sweet aroma.

On a knoll up ahead, I find what I'm searching for: four buildings all by themselves.

The temples.

I ascend to the top. Thanks to the higher elevation, I have a clear view in every direction. The rolling hills stretch far to the north, abdicating to the city's round walls. To the west, the palace is situated behind its own wall. Beyond it, the water extends until it encounters the cloudless sky. The city is to the southeast. From here, the buildings are so small they appear to be dwellings for woodland creatures.

Eager to learn more about oracles, I turn my attention to the closest temple. It's solid marble and ginormous—rivaling Spektrolith's size. The lofty roof is held up by five pillars on each side with detailed flutes running from the bases to the top of the shafts. I stretch my arms around one, but I can barely encircle half of it. The gaps between the pillars are so wide, ten people standing shoulder to shoulder could fit—easily.

I step inside and the temperature drops at least ten degrees. It's austere, except for the twenty-foot marble statue dead center in the room. My sandals slap against the stone floor, echoing in the cavernous space as I make my way over to the statue.

It's a beautiful woman with a symmetrical face and round eyes framed by thick lashes. Unclothed, her voluptuous figure is strategically concealed by her coiffed hair and the waves she's rising out of. The plaque below her bare feet states:

Temple of Aphrodite, Daughter of Zeus and Dione
Goddess of Passion and Beauty
Protector of Lovers and Desire

Aphrodite must be one of the immortals the Trojans value most. I rush to the next temple; it's a shrine for Poseidon, god of the sea. His statue's muscular tree-trunk frame is covered by fish-scale armor, and there's a fifteen-foot, sharp-pointed trident in his left hand. After seeing Troy's docks, I'm not surprised they honor the god who is the protector of sailors and aquatic adventures. His menacing eyes—shrouded by his long hair and equally lengthy beard—make my arm hair stand straight up. I know he's not real, but I still hurry on to the next building, eager to escape his piercing gaze.

The third temple is for the goddess Artemis, protector of animals and the hunt. Dressed in a full suit of armor, her statue depicts a cunning warrior, ready to take on any foe. The only indications of her femininity are the ponytail fanning out the back of her helmet and her shapely legs beneath her pleated skirt. The loaded bow in her right hand is pointed directly at me, the arrow pulled back at the nock with her left hand. Her taut expression reminds me of my brother when he brandishes a particularly disgruntled scowl. I return her glower before leaving, irritated to be reminded of him.

The final temple is devoted to Apollo, Artemis's twin brother. Twins. I can't escape Dameaon even when I'm trying. If appearances are any indication, they're as different as the two of us; while her eyes were narrowed in concentration, his are soulful. And where her jawline was strong, his is delicate—fitting for the god of light and healing. Instead of a weapon, he cradles a lyre in his strong arms. The marble sun behind his soft curls creates an aureole, further enhancing his angelic appearance. He's one god I wish actually existed; my guess is we would be friends.

Eager to explore more, I head out the rear of the temple. There are ten stairs—which I climb—that emerge to a thirty-foot annulus composed of small square rocks placed side by side. To the right is a sunken pit, so deep I would vanish if I jumped in. Not that I want to. There are burnt sticks and ashes lining the bottom.

In the middle of the annulus is a large table of some sort. The edges are carved with intertwined Ls and sevens. Three of its sides are solid marble, but the back was hollowed out to create two shelves, stockpiled with pottery.

I grab the top plate and place it on the counter. Its face is etched with the image of a bearded man holding a lightning bolt like a javelin. I bend down, searching through the pottery, and find a jug with the same design. I remove the stopper and sniff the opening—it's filled with pungently strong wine.

The immortals are not real, so what is all of this doing here? I search for additional clues. To my left are three more annuli—one behind each temple—but not much else. Except the man rushing up the hill, that is.

I stash the jug on the shelf and duck behind the table, hoping he didn't spot me. While I want to start my oracle duties, I haven't spent enough time observing to do so comfortably.

If I'm lucky, his destination is one of the temples and I can sneak down the back side of the hill. But then he starts talking—too close to be inside—and that hope dies.

"Apollo, merciful among all gods, please hear my plea. Isidora is still ill. The doctor has tried all his remedies but offers no answers. Please, Apollo, heal her ailment. I cannot live without her."

I peek over the table. A middle-aged man is standing right in front of me, his flat palms pressed together near his chest.

I duck back behind the table, bumping it in the process. The plate, positioned precariously on the edge, topples to the floor with a loud clang.

"Oh, by the gods. I didn't realize someone else was here."

I glance up; he's staring right at me.

"I-I-I'm so sorry. I didn't mean to eavesdrop, but you didn't see me . . . and then . . ." I say, standing. "I-I promise I didn't hear anything. I'll just head out . . ."

He scrunches his forehead. "It's not polite to listen to other people's prayers."

"I apologize," I say. "I just arrived, you see, and I wanted to see the temples. I'm an oracle and—"

His eyes widen. "You're an oracle?"

As soon as the words escaped my lips, I wanted to pull them back in. But the damage is already done.

"Yes," I manage to squeak out.

He smiles broadly and comes around the table, taking my hand. "Apollo himself must have sent you. There is not an oracle to be found in all of Troy, and now here you are. I need your help, Oracle. My wife is ill, and the doctor cannot help. It is up to the gods now. Please help me beg for Apollo's mercy."

I'm at a loss. I know he wants me to talk to the gods, but I have no idea what that looks like. Still, doing *something* is better than nothing. Positioning myself in front of the table, I close my eyes and hold my arms up in a V shape. I vibrate my entire body for ten seconds before collapsing to the floor. I wait a moment and then rise to my feet.

The man stares at me, his mouth agape. "What was that?"

I rub the back of my neck. "I . . . channeled Apollo."

"I've never seen an oracle do that," he says. "At least, not a real oracle. I have heard about fakes, wandering between cities and stealing from hardworking people." He begins to back away. "I-I need to be going now."

"No, wait. Please," I call, but he's already racing down the hill.

I start pursuing him but realize that will only make things worse. Shaken, I fall to my knees; I just made a big mistake.

What if this man tells the other Trojans what I did? It will hurt my credibility. I might not be able to be an oracle, as planned and approved by Jetta, and I'll have no clue how to get my Guidance duty back on track. That means I'll have to return to Reos and consult Jetta on other occupations. It's embarrassing beyond belief that I screwed up so soon. There has to be another way . . .

Magic.

It's the simplest answer, really. Even if I don't behave

like a normal oracle, all it would take is one Ice Spell and everyone would be convinced I speak to the gods.

Except, using Magic in front of the humans would break a Guide Rule set by the Oldungur Council—a Rule that, quite frankly, makes no sense right now. One little spell would get me into the Trojans' good graces faster, saving me months and months of work.

The Council clearly doesn't understand how hard it is to be a Guide. Even Oldungur Mekhi must have forgotten, since his Guidance duty occurred so long ago. That must be it. Otherwise, they wouldn't keep a Rule that makes being a Seeker unnecessarily difficult.

But Guidance duty isn't supposed to be easy; that's why only the strongest Glanchings are successful. And I chose to be a Guide, in part, because of that.

And while the Magic Rule seems absurd, the Oldungur Council is made up of the wisest Glanchings on Reos. There are reasons for it—reasons I can't see.

Besides, I'm probably being a bit negative; while messing up with one Trojan is unfortunate, it's not the end of the world. If I learn more about oracles—quickly—I can still turn this around. Still, the last thing I need is someone else showing up and looking for help. I race back to the palace, hoping to find answers safe inside its walls.

While I was out, someone opened the shutters in my room, revealing the expansive harbor outside the city's walls. Beyond the docks, the water glows crimson, suffused by the setting sun.

The red hue transforms the room's drabness to unexpected coziness, restoring my languor. This time, I surrender, sinking into the mattress and pulling the sheets up to my chin.

As I'm fading into slumber, a loud knock jolts me awake. The door flings open, and a stranger enters. When he sees me, he drops everything in his arms.

"Oh, f-f-forgive me, Oracle. I didn't realize you had already retired," he says, bending down to retrieve the items from the floor. "I have your chiton for this evening."

"This evening?" I ask, sitting up.

"Yes. All the nobles are coming to celebrate the prince's return. And it's a great opportunity for everyone to meet you. We haven't had an oracle for months, not since Phokas died, and many Trojans need the immortals' help." He lays the articles at the bottom of the bed. "Can I help you get dressed?"

I pull the covers over my bare chest. "No, I can do it."

"Okay, I'll be back shortly to escort you to the party," he says and leaves.

I stay in bed, rubbing my drowsy eyes and digesting the news. Dameaon must have convinced King Priam he's the real Paris, or there wouldn't be a party tonight. But how hard could it have been? It's not like he was expecting an imposter—who looks exactly like his son—to show up.

Attending a party for my twin is the last thing I want to do, but I force myself up and examine the items at the end of my bed—a square of navy silk, fasteners, a leather belt, and sandals. I have no clue how to make a functional chiton out of them, but I do the best I can, wrapping the fabric around myself and securing it with the fasteners and belt.

There's a quick knock, and the stranger reenters. His eyes widen. "Oh . . . Can I help you finalize your chiton, Oracle?"

I inspect my work; my chiton is loose around the armpits and drags behind me on the floor. "It's been a while since I've dealt with such fine silk. I guess I'm a little out of practice. And please call me Hector."

Even though he's two heads shorter than me, he easily adjusts the fasteners at my shoulders with his gnarled, wrinkled hands. "Forgive me for not introducing myself earlier. I'm Natham, your assigned chamber gentleman. I'm here to help with anything you need while at the palace."

He pulls the excess material above my belt so it blouses slightly, transforming my mess into a stylish ankle-length chiton. "That should finalize things," he says, placing the sandals on the floor. "Are you ready?"

"Yes, let's go," I say, sliding my feet into the soft leather and following him into the hall. His stocky legs plow forward—surprisingly quick for his compact size—and I practically have to jog to keep up. Eventually, we stop in front of a large archway.

"Enjoy yourself, Oracle," he says and throws open the door.

"Hector," I correct, but he's already gone. Uncertain what to expect, I take a deep breath and step inside.

The room is grander than I expected—almost as large as my backyard—and it's filled with hundreds of Trojans. Thankfully, the raised entrance overlooks the sunken room, allowing me to get my bearings before plunging into the party.

Guests are gathered in small groups, chatting and imbibing wine. Dressed in vibrant silk chitons, they light the hall in an exuberant rainbow. Paintings and tapestries bedeck the perimeter, and there's a banquet table situated between two open doors on the back wall. On the left wall is a dais topped with three golden chairs.

A wave of nostalgia washes over me; the similarities to a Reos celebration are uncanny. Of course, there's a huge difference between here and home—my friends. I've never been at a party where I didn't know anyone.

What I wouldn't give for Dexter's frank observations. Or Katarin's bright smile. Or Portia's sarcastic wit. Still, I'm not completely alone. I do have my twin.

I bite my bottom lip and desperately search for Dameaon. He isn't here yet, and not a single person is alone. Except me.

Suddenly, I don't know what to do with my hands, dangling like limp tentacles at my side. I hold them in front of me, focusing on the thin veins in my wrists; they're fragile, like my confidence.

Realizing how ridiculous I must look, I drop my arms back to my side and descend the six steps into the room. To blend in, I pretend to be captivated by a nearby tapestry. The hundreds of colored threads interlace to depict a young man groveling in front of a statue of a woman. Although most of the statue is gray, her face is ivory with rosy cheeks. In the clouds overhead, Aphrodite—or at least it looks like her—sprinkles glitter down onto both of them.

"Quite a tapestry," Achilles says, coming up beside me. He's still in his armor—minus the helmet—and I'm beginning to think it's the only clothing he owns.

"That's Aphrodite, right?" I ask.

"Yes. The artist's depiction of Pygmalion and Galatea's epic romance is splendid, don't you think?" he says. I shrug noncommittally, and he continues, "Pygmalion, the sculptor . . . who fell in love with his own creation, Galatea? And Aphrodite, in her mercy, took pity on him and brought Galatea to life?"

"Oh yes, of course. It's a wonderful portrayal. I must be more tired than I realize."

He scrunches his eyebrows. "Are you sure you're an oracle?"

The blood drains from my face. "Um, I . . ."

He laughs and grasps my shoulder. "I'm teasing you. You need to lighten up. Come, join me in a glass of wine."

I clutch my forearms. "Thanks for the offer, but I'm going to pass."

Wine is the last thing I need right now; I've seen my mother imbibe too much and lose her wits, and I'm barely surviving as it is.

"Your loss. The king and queen spared no expense. No one will be your comrade if you're dull . . . even if you are an oracle," he calls over his shoulder.

"Thank you. I think," I holler after him.

Alone, I'm clumsily aware of my hands again. To keep them busy, I head to the banquet table. Just as I grab a plate, the room plunges into silence, and the guests swarm the entrance.

Queen Hecuba and a stately man with a crown—no

doubt King Priam—stand on the small platform. Plate still in hand, I move to the back of the crowd.

"I pray you to be well, guests," the king says, his voice booming to every corner of the great room. "For many years, I have appealed to the gods to help my son discover who he truly is. And after spending the last several months on Mount Ida, he has come back changed. So, while he was missed, the time away was good for him. Good for us. He returns a little wiser and much more equipped to be your prince. Join me now in thanking the gods for their blessings and in welcoming him home."

My brother enters behind them, and the crowd erupts into cheers. Once their applause dies down, all three descend into the room. The guests part to either side, making space as the royals move to the dais and stand in front of their respective thrones.

Dameaon's transformation is profound. While he looked like Paris before, his proud posture mirrors the king and queen's exactly, and his scarlet velvet robe and the gold crown in his champagne hair seem like they are part of him rather than accessories. But my twin has always thought he was superior to everyone else, so playing royalty shouldn't be too difficult.

Once the royals sit, the twenty-piece band begins playing an upbeat song. Just like that, the room springs back to life. Some of the Trojans pair off, executing overdramatic dance steps, brimming with twirls and spins.

Since I don't know their dances—or have a partner—I return to the buffet, filling my plate with barley bread, goat cheese, and grapes before heading to the far-right corner. I nibble at my food, trying not to look as uncomfortable as I feel.

After a moment, a chisel-faced teenage boy and his ashy-haired, muscular companion approach me.

"I pray you to be well," the chisel-faced one says. "I'm Oedipus, and this is Nicholas. We were told you are the new oracle. My friend could use your help."

"Where did you hear I was an oracle?" I ask.

Nicholas shrugs. "My father is one of King Priam's Elders. Is it not so?"

"No, it's true. I was surprised you knew, is all."

"News of an oracle travels quickly," Oedipus says. "As I was saying, Nicholas could use Poseidon's blessings. His family's ships return in two days' time, and they are hoping for bountiful fish."

I look over at Nicholas; he's staring out into the party as if he's bored with our conversation. "If they are Nicholas's ships, why are you the one asking?"

Nicholas meets my gaze straight on. "Immortals? The underworld? Zeus? I don't know. It all seems a bit dubious."

Oedipus narrows his brown eyes. "Nicholas, you just questioned the gods' existence in front of an oracle."

Nicholas shrugs. "I bet Hector understands. Some of what happens in our lives has to be our doing. If not, what's the point? We can't be at the mercy of the gods for everything."

I nod slightly while grinning. "Although the gods help us, everyone is responsible for their destiny. Our successes and failures are, in large part, based on our choices."

Nicholas smiles at me. "Finally. An oracle who makes sense."

Oedipus clears his throat. "Yes, well anyway, Oracle, do you think you could ask Poseidon for his blessing for Nicholas's ships?"

I nod. "I will visit his temple tomorrow and ask for his aid."

Nicholas narrows his eyes. "This is a first. Most oracles take any opportunity to show off."

"I would rather just enjoy the party," I say.

"Perhaps. Or perhaps you are the fraud Zenobios claims you are," Nicholas says. "He's our family's shopkeeper. He told me about the oracle at the temples—the one who didn't know how to channel the gods."

"I-I-I know how to channel the immortals. As I said, I want to enjoy the party." I step backward, hoping to make a quick escape out the back door.

"Kallipos," Nicholas yells, and a short, stocky teenage boy joins us. "You and Oedipus need to keep Hector here. I'm going to solve this right now."

Oedipus and Kallipos surround me, forcing my back against the wall. I could shove past them, but where would I go? Besides, I'm certain running would only make things worse.

Nicholas charges over to the royals, bowing before my brother. Dameaon steps down from the dais and joins him. My heart races so fast, and I can't breathe; this was already bad, but involving my twin can only make it worse. Dameaon glances over at me and smirks. My knees shake as Nicholas crosses the room, rejoining us.

"The courtyard. Now," he says.

His friends look eager for a fight, but I comply willingly, heading out the back door. The crisp air is a welcome change, soothing my flaming skin and allowing me to breathe again.

Kallipos squints his cornflower eyes. "What is this about?"

"You'll see," Nicholas says.

I look up at the full moon, surrounded by stars in the night's sky. This can't be the end of my Guidance duty; I won't let it be.

"We're here, Nicholas," my twin says. "Let's begin."

I turn, but he's not alone. He's brought his "parents" with him. I don't know what he's up to, but it doesn't bode well for me.

"What is this about?" I ask.

"Nicholas claims you are lying about being an oracle," Dameaon says. "As the royal family of Troy, we felt it was our duty to investigate."

King Priam crosses his arms in front of his indigo robe. "This cannot be true. No one would risk the immortals' wrath with such lies."

Nicholas bows his head. "Sadly, King Priam, it's happening in other cities. The leader of my trade caravan has seen it. Frauds claim to be oracles, stealing money from those seeking the gods' guidance."

"And what makes you believe this specific oracle is a fraud?" Priam asks.

"My shopkeeper asked for his help earlier. Hector tried to channel Apollo by vibrating his entire body. That's not right. And listen to the way he speaks. Something is off."

The king and queen look at me with skepticism in their eyes. Priam shakes his head. "Hecuba, go call the Trojan Guard. We will arrest him, until the Elders decide his punishment."

A thick layer of sweat forms on my palms. Jetta was right; I should have spent the first couple days observing. Instead, my actions have cost me, and I'm going to be labeled a fraud.

Even if I find a way to escape, being an oracle isn't an option now. The Trojans will be suspicious of anyone who shows up after word gets out about me. My only chance is to convince them I'm legit.

"No, wait!" I say, and Hecuba pauses. "I am an oracle. The gods chose me."

I glance at my twin. His smug smile makes my muscles quiver with anger. But I'm desperate—so desperate I'm willing to ask him for help. "Paris, you were with me on Mount Ida. Tell them. You know I'm an oracle."

Priam nods. "Hecuba said that you saw him talk to the gods. You are flesh of my flesh. If you say it is true, all doubt is gone."

Dameaon looks at the fingernails on his left hand. Then he extends his fingers, looking at his gargoyle ring. "I never actually saw him talk to the gods, no. But I'm sure Hector understands the *frosty* reception and would be glad to prove himself. If he demonstrates his abilities, I'm certain we will *shiver* from his power."

His word choice isn't lost on me; Dameaon wants me to cast Ice Magic.

It's really the only solution at this point, except it violates a Rule. But my twin has already used Magic, and he's still here. Besides, this conversation has made it clear how important oracles are to the Trojans. What if I never find another profession that can influence them like this one?

Jetta will forgive me for using Magic this once. He has to.

"Well?" Hecuba says, tapping her foot impatiently.

Pressured to act, I go with my instinct. I move ten feet away from the group, fully committing to the show. Raising my hands, I chant nonsense. Electricity gathers in the sky, swirling down to my palms. I bring my hands in front of me and launch my frosty orb into the fountain. The water stops, frozen solid.

Oedipus drops onto his left knee. "By the gods, I've never seen anything like that before. Forgive me."

The king places his hand on my shoulder. "Forgive all of us. The immortals must treasure you above all. We will be blessed to have you in Troy as long as you wish to stay."

Dameaon smiles at me—a knowing smile. "I knew you had it in you, Hector. Our guests will be missing us, but the king, queen, and I are pleased to know you are indeed a real oracle. Rejoin us inside, if you please."

The royals leave the courtyard, and all the uncertainty dissipates from my body. I collapse on my knees.

"Uh, Oracle?" Oedipus says. "Are you well?"

I stand on shaky legs. "That took a lot out of me, but I will be fine."

He bows his head. "I'm sorry I doubted you. If it is your will, I'll leave Troy and never return."

"As will I," Nicholas says. "Accusing you like that. We both deserve exile."

"That is not what I wish," I say. "All I ask is that you

share what you saw with your peers. Help them understand that I am a true liaison with the immortals, even if my ways are a little peculiar."

There's a moment of silence, and then Nicholas says, "We must spend more time with you. Join us tomorrow afternoon for a game of field hockey, if you can."

I shake my head. "I wish I could, but I will be too busy."

"It's a standing invitation," Nicholas says. "We meet in the north field, near the temples, almost every afternoon. Join us anytime."

"Thank you," I say.

Oedipus holds up his empty cup. "It's time for a refill. Shall we?"

They start toward the wine jugs, but I lag behind. As happy as I am they trust me now, I'm exhausted from the drama of this evening.

Oedipus turns back to me. "You aren't coming?"

"No, I—"

"You don't drink? Is that another special oracle thing?"

"No, I just need to retire. It's been a long day."

We bid farewell, and I slink back to my room. Behind my closed door, the gravity of what I've done hits me. I violated a Rule my third day on Earth. At the time, with the humans' accusing eyes on me, it seemed like my only option. Now, alone, I'm certain almost anything would have been better than using Magic.

I need to head back to Reos and speak with Jetta. He'll forgive me. I can choose a new profession and try again. But . . .

What if the Oldungur Council isn't so forgiving? What

if they find out I'm on Reos, and decide I can't come back. Worse, what if they let Dameaon stay alone? Sure, he's doing okay right now, but it's just a matter of time before he screws things up. I need to be here when that happens.

And sure, I used Magic, but I didn't hurt anyone. The Rules emphasize that above all else.

My real problem is I don't know how oracles are supposed to behave. Troy doesn't have any to learn from, but the neighboring cities must. And Nicholas owes me now.

First thing tomorrow, I'll ask him for permission to travel with his trade caravan. The other oracles can teach me how to channel the gods, and I'll come back and fulfill my role—without using Magic.

THINKING AHEAD

"ONCE AGAIN, HESIOD, YOUR VIEWPOINT IS SHORTSIGHTED AND unimaginative," I say, pacing back and forth on the stone floor. The sound of my footsteps ricochets against the walls in the vast throne room.

"I would argue it's classic and prudent," Hesiod, the lead Elder, says. "Troy has survived hundreds of years behaving this way."

"Troy has survived, not excelled," I say. "I'm talking about a new, superior reign."

King Priam shakes his head. "Hesiod is right, my son. Troy remains safe because we do not make waves. The immortals do not look well upon arrogance."

"What I'm suggesting isn't arrogance, it's shrewdness," I say. "The immortals value that. You fought against the trade expansion too, Father, but look how well that is working. The ships returned this morning, full of silks and spices like you've never seen. The entirety of our olive oil was bought or traded. Once we send our caravans to the neighboring cities, we will increase our wealth tenfold."

Elder Seleucus pounds his fist against the table. "Your trade expansions are the very reason you want Troy to build an army. We should be happy with our place in this world. The king is right. If we aren't careful, we will anger the gods. Or our neighboring cities."

I stride over to the table on the left side of the room. The king is sitting at the head, with three Elders on each side—six identical bookends, alike in agedness and appearance, except for Lycus's and Pelagios's lack of beards.

There is an empty seat directly across from Priam, but I never sit during our daily strategy meetings. Standing gives me a much-needed edge, since I'm always outnumbered in my opinions.

"Troy needs to adapt," I say. "The future is uncertain."

Elder Deiphobus shakes his head. "Paris, Troy's future will remain strong as long as Priam's descendants reign. Besides, we have the walls to keep us safe."

I grasp the back of my wooden chair. "What happens if Troy is left without a king? Walls can be breached, but an army would keep us safe."

Priam scrunches his face. "Are you planning my murder, son?"

I smile. "Of course not. But you are not immortal, as much as I wish it were so."

"And that is why I have you. You will lead once I am gone," he says, returning my smile—his genuine and full of love.

In the past six weeks, Priam and I have developed a

close relationship. He's been more of a father to me than Lord Drasko ever was.

"Ah, but I am not immortal either," I say. "Troy should not be reliant on one person to survive. Sparta understands this. Their city is surrounded by fierce enemies, but they survive because they have a strong army."

Hesiod's face turns red with anger. "We have the Trojan Guard. That's more than enough protection. I won't ask noblemen to waste their time training in an army when Troy has no enemies. Their time is better served elsewhere."

I throw my hands up. "Doing what? Drinking at the bar? Or playing field hockey? Come on, Hesiod, be honest. It's not like the nobles do anything of real importance."

Hesiod stands so quickly his chair falls behind him, hitting the stone floor with a loud bang. "The nobles do more than—"

A knock at the door interrupts him. Pavlos, my favorite member of the Trojan Guard, enters.

He bows his head. "Your pardon, King Priam. I bring urgent business for Prince Paris."

"Share your news," the king says.

Pavlos smiles at me. "The trade caravans are back, and Oracle Hector was with them. He just returned to the palace and is in his quarters."

I turn to Priam. "Are we done here?"

Hesiod shakes his head. "We still have business to discuss, my king."

"Business can wait until tomorrow," Priam says. "My son wants to see his friend. Paris, please tell him I request his guidance after dinner tonight."

"Thank you, Father," I say, racing from the room and down the corridor.

My twin is back. I can't wait to tell him everything I've accomplished in the time he was gone. I race through the palace corridors, knocking on his door and charging inside. He's in his bed—resting—even though it's mid-morning.

I crouch down next to him, his face inches from mine. "Hello, brother."

He opens his left eye a crack. "Go away. I'm sleeping," he mumbles, dropping his eyelid.

I charge across his room and open his window's shutters. "It's a beautiful day. Look at what you're missing."

"I know what I'm missing, I was just outside," he says, propping himself up on an elbow. "Paris, I'm exhausted. I don't have the energy to fight with you."

"You know we're alone, right? You can call me Dameaon. And who said we were going to fight?"

"If I call you Dameaon in private, I may slip up in public. We're going to fight because I'm still mad at you for making me use Magic to prove I was an oracle."

I scrunch my eyebrows together. "How is that my fault?"

"How is it not? All you had to do was back up my story."

"And all you had to do was be a better oracle. That's why you were in trouble in the first place." I sigh. "I came here to fill you in on all the good I've done while you were off having fun."

He throws the covers off and perches on the edge of

the mattress. "I was off learning how to be a proper oracle so you couldn't corner me into using Magic again. And I already know what you did while I was gone—some sort of screwup I need to fix. Just like always. So what is it this time?"

I drop my shoulders. It was foolish to believe he would be proud. "You always think the worst of me, don't you?"

"You screw up, Paris. It's what you do."

I jut out my chin. "I came here because I found something to help you, but forget it."

He stands and rubs his eyes. "I'm sorry. I'm tired and grumpy, but I shouldn't take it out on you. What is it?"

"Forget it," I say, heading into the hall.

I hear him stumble out behind me. "Wait up," he shouts, but I don't—not after his insults.

Still, he's following me, so why not make him remorseful for his rudeness? I charge down the corridor, out of the palace, and into an open area with small detached structures. I stop in front of the third one.

"You could have waited so I didn't have to run," he says when he finally catches up.

"The exercise was good for you," I say, inserting a key into the door's lock and pushing it open. The inside is filled with vases, jars, plates, and paintings. "Queen Hecuba redecorated the royal wing last month and stored all the old artwork here. I thought it would help you with your oracle research."

"This is perfect," he says. "It's exactly what we need to fill in the missing pieces of Trojan life. If we're lucky, there might even be some art dep—"

"This is exactly what *you* need, brother. You know . . . since you prefer research to actual living. Me? I'd rather learn through experience."

He turns to me and clears his throat. "This is a really nice gesture. I-I'm sorry I was a jerk to you."

I toss the key at him. "I'm used to it. Enjoy your art and don't forget to lock up."

"Wait," he says. "I was planning on playing field hockey this afternoon. I know you're probably too busy with prince duties, but you're welcome to join me if you'd like."

I pause; Villow has never asked me to do anything with him. Ever. Maybe it's the start of a thaw between us.

"I'll meet you in the courtyard after lunch," I say.

He shakes his head. "I plan on stopping by the temples first. Meet me at the field at the north part of Troy instead."

"Okay, brother. I'll see you there," I say and head out.

I MAKE MY WAY TO THE FRONT OF THE PALACE. AEGIDIUS IS standing in the fountain, letting the water cool his sun-soaked back. He bleats when he sees me and runs over.

"I missed you too, Butthead," I say, scratching behind his ears.

Aegidius has become my faithful companion, but I still miss Cinders every day. Truthfully, my little wyvermalkin is pretty much the only thing I miss from Reos. Earth is better than I ever thought it could be.

He hops off, joining a few other goats in the shade of a nearby olive tree. Achilles is on the left side of the grounds, shooting arrows at a straw target. Each of his launches hits directly in the middle of the target.

"Do you get tired of being good at everything?" I say, coming up beside him.

"Honestly? No," he says and laughs. "Uh-oh. What happened?"

Normally, I can hide my emotions, but Achilles is very perceptive. And we've become close in a very short time. Even so, I'm not ready to rehash my family issues, especially since Achilles isn't aware I have a brother.

"It's my father," I say, taking the bow from his hands. "He's still not convinced Troy needs an army."

He frowns. "You must find a way to persuade him, Paris."

I aim at the target and release my arrow. It sticks in the straw—a few inches above Achilles's seven perfectly shot shafts. "It's not exactly easy with six Elders fighting against me."

I hand the bow back to him, and Achilles takes aim. "You are a force, my friend. No one can beat you. Except me, that is." He releases his arrow, and it's another perfect shot. "What do you want to do this afternoon? I thought hunting might be enjoyable."

While I don't enjoy hunting, it's a source of the Trojans' food, so I do it from time to time—but only when I have to.

I shake my head. "We have other plans. How do you feel about field hockey?"

THE RECIPE FOR SUCCESS

Time flies by in the storage room, and lunchtime comes quickly. I take a step back and examine the two piles I created—one for the underworld and one for the gods and goddesses—all fragments of a story that, when decoded, will provide more knowledge about oracles.

Satisfied with my progress, I lock up and head for the temples. The cloudless sky offers no protection from the sun's strong rays. Luckily, the nearby sea generates a balmy breeze that cools the atmosphere to a bearable level.

As I travel down the road, I think about my interaction with Dameaon this morning. While I'm still mad at him for forcing me to use Magic, he seems different now. More mature. Sharing the storage room is proof of that. It seems Guidance duty is changing my twin for the better.

The temples come into view, and I realize someone is praying at Aphrodite's altar. Perfect. After my travels, I'm ready to be an oracle.

I climb the stairs, calling out as I near the top, "I pray you to be well."

The human turns; it's a young girl—no older than me—who is a bit chubby and very plain. Her chiton is made of white wool, and she has a single gold necklace around her neck. Working-class, no doubt about it.

She smiles, and it warms her entire face. "I pray you to be well. I'm looking for the new oracle."

"I'm Oracle Hector. What—"

She squeals with delight and grabs my arm. "Oracle, I heard you were back! Can you ask Aphrodite to take mercy on me? I'm in love with a man who doesn't know I exist and I need him to love me back. I'm desperate. I will give whatever Aphrodite demands in return."

"Let us go invoke her mercy," I say, gesturing for her to follow me.

She furrows her brow. "In the temple? I thought only oracles and priests were allowed inside?"

I still; I spent the last six weeks in the cities of Dardanus and Abydus with their oracles, and their citizens were allowed in the temples. The fact the Trojans don't enter theirs is ridiculous. "You're allowed, I promise. The immortals enjoy when humans visit their shrines."

She hesitates but takes one tentative step inside. When nothing happens, she dashes across the floor as if it's searing her bare feet. But she lifts the left side of her mouth, and I'm impressed by her courage.

"Before we proceed, I need to know a little more about you," I say. "It helps with my conversation with Aphrodite."

She nods. "Of course. I'm Iris, daughter of Sidirourgos,

Troy's finest blacksmith. Several months ago, my father hired an apprentice, Theos, to work for him. Since I first saw him, I knew he was the one for me. He's strong, quiet, and so handsome. But he doesn't know I'm alive. I've done everything to get his attention—worn my finest jewelry, sat in the smithy for hours—but all he cares about is learning my father's craft. My life is incomplete without him. My last hope is Aphrodite."

Ah. A love request. I saw a lot of those in Dardanus and Abydus. This will be easy.

I gesture to the goddess's statue. "If Aphrodite makes Theos fall in love with you, she will expect you to dedicate your life to him. Are you sure you're ready to do that?"

"Yes, I'm sure. I can't live without him."

"But you're so young. How can you be certain?"

"I'm not that young. I turned fifteen last month. And when you're in love, age matters little. It might be unfair to ask Aphrodite to make him love me, but I'll be the best wife ever and treat him like a king."

The intensity she conveys is authentic and makes me want to help her. "Let me see what Aphrodite has to say."

I close my eyes and bow my head. After several minutes, I blink a few times, pretending I'm coming out of a trance.

"Oracle? Did she talk to you?" she asks.

"She did, Iris. She has found you deserving, but now must ensure Theos is worthy of you. She promises to have an answer for you by tomorrow afternoon. Go home, and be good and kind. Meet me here tomorrow after lunch, and I will let you know her decision."

Iris throws her arms around me for a second and then pulls away; it's improper to hug an oracle.

"Thank you," she says. "I am certain Aphrodite will judge him well, as he is more than worthy of me. I will see you tomorrow."

She darts out of the temple, and I laugh; her enthusiasm is infectious. I hope, for her sake, Theos is interested. I'll find out soon enough, but first, I have a field hockey game to get to.

My brother is already at the field when I arrive. As is his surprise guest, Achilles. Nicholas and Oedipus leave the group to greet me as I approach.

"I pray you to be well, Hector," Nicholas says. "The prince told us you were coming. It's so good to see you."

"I'm glad I could join you," I say.

"Now that everyone is here, why don't we pick teams?" Nicholas suggests.

Oedipus points at Achilles. "I call dibs on him."

Nicholas stares at his arm muscles. "Why don't we wrestle for him?"

"Be fair, Nicholas. You're the best player," he rebuts. "It isn't reasonable you get him too."

"Boys, allow me to introduce myself. I'm Achilles. And there is no need to fight over me. Although, I don't mind if you do." He places his arms around their shoulders. "Back in Sparta, I'm famous for my field hockey skills. You know what they called my team, right?"

Oedipus shakes his head, and Nicholas shrugs.

"The winners," Achilles says, cackling loudly.

Everyone joins in with his laughter, and just like that, the bickering ceases.

"Come, we'll introduce you to the other players," Nicholas says, leading us onto the field and ticking off the fifteen other Trojans' names.

The players bow when he introduces my brother.

"There's no need for formality," Dameaon says. "I want to play a fair game, so treat me like anyone else."

They shuffle their feet uncomfortably, but they're smiling. His message is clear; although he's the prince, he's also their peer. He's won their favor. As much as I hate to admit it, I'm proud of him.

"So . . . let's get started," Nicholas says. "Oedipus, since my team has one less player than yours, why don't you take Prince Paris and I'll take Hector and Achilles?"

Oedipus stills. He made it very clear he wanted Achilles, but he can't argue without insulting the prince. After an awkward moment of silence, he nods once—curtly.

We break into our teams, and Nicholas gathers us in a tight circle to strategize. "Okay, Belen, you start off as goalie, and Kallipos and I will be the forwards. Cy, you can play striker, and Jace, you'll be the stopper. That leaves two open spots for defense. Milos, Ezio, Dion, do you mind sitting out the first half so we can give our new teammates a chance?"

That's not what I was hoping for. I spent my six weeks of travel learning how to be an oracle, but I still know very little about field hockey. "Oh, that's okay. It's been a while since I played, so I wouldn't mind watching the first half."

Achilles thrusts an L-shaped stick at me, knocking the air from my lungs. "Nice try. Hector and I are playing forwards. We want to be in the action."

"Whatever you say, Achilles," Nicholas agrees.

With no valid excuses, I take the stick and walk onto the field. Thankfully, it's a fairly simple game. Using sticks, we drive a small ball down the field toward our assigned net. Every time we successfully get the ball into our net, we score a goal, and the team with the most goals at the end of the game wins.

One thing is very clear—there are no rules on physical contact. It's only twenty minutes into the game, and I've already been elbowed in the ribs five times. Nicholas and Oedipus came to serious blows once, and Kallipos whopped his opponent's legs so fiercely with his stick he collapsed, triggering a brawl that ended with two black eyes.

But it's my twin who's taken the brunt of the blows—all from Achilles, who charges him every chance he gets. Dameaon is struggling to keep his anger in check, and when Achilles unnecessarily flattens him again, I cringe, knowing he's reached his breaking point.

My brother stands, blood flowing from his skinned knees and fury in his eyes. He rushes Achilles, knocking him on his back. Achilles attempts to push him off but fails. Dameaon punches his face again and again. The players exchange hesitant glances; Achilles needs help, but no one is brave enough to touch the prince.

Unfortunately, that leaves me. I take a deep breath and crash into my brother. Knocking him to the ground, I hold down his shoulders.

"Paris—" I whisper, but he interrupts by jabbing my nose with the heel of his hand.

Gushing blood flows down my chin, and I howl in pain. He twists his body and ends up on top, hitting me over and over.

I cover my face, hissing through my fingers. "This isn't appropriate. You need to stop." I need to find a way to get through to him, so I risk saying his real name. "Dameaon, quit punching me, unless you want everyone to realize something is off with us," I whisper.

The glassiness leaves his eyes, but he jabs my nose once more before standing. I contemplate taking out his legs in retaliation, but we have an audience—with agape mouths—so I get up instead.

My brother offers his palm to Achilles. "I took things too far, my friend. I didn't mean it."

Achilles stares at his outstretched hand like it's a dagger. "Paris, have you been possessed? It's just a game. And by the gods, I don't understand why I couldn't throw you off."

He shrugs. "Competition fuels my strength. I'm like you that way."

Achilles remains still for another moment, but then the doubt dissipates from his eyes. He grabs Dameaon's hand, pulling him into a quick hug. "All is forgiven, my friend. Let's go for a ride before dinner."

They head to their horses, and I'm left alone with the Trojans. Although my vision is still blurry from Dameaon's punches, I can see well enough to know no one is looking at me.

"I suppose I should head out as well. I need to . . . visit the temples," I offer as an excuse.

The tension drains from their shoulders; they're relieved I'm leaving. And who can blame them? All I brought with me was drama—in the shape of my twin.

"Of course. We wouldn't want to keep you," Oedipus says.

I head down the path that leads to Troy, turning back once. The players have already resumed the game without me. In the distance, Achilles and Dameaon gallop toward the woods. I start walking again—by myself.

Although my few bruises don't justify using my Crystal, they're a painful reminder of how awry things went. The fight was my brother's fault, but somehow, I'm the one left alone. So, even though Jetta wouldn't approve, I clasp my amulet and mutter, "Hura, hura, enray."

My Crystal's warmth fills me, realigning my nose and clearing my eyesight. Unfortunately, it doesn't quell the emptiness inside me. The truth is, Dameaon's time on Earth is going better than mine. He belongs here in a way I don't, regardless of how hard I try.

But being in Troy isn't about fitting in; it's about making real change. I need to focus on what's important—my Guidance duty.

The first step is finding Theos. I quicken my pace, heading toward the city.

While I have no idea where the blacksmiths work, someone in the market surely will. I make my way down the streets, turning a sharp corner to emerge into a vast open space filled with hundreds of Trojans. Most of them are dressed in wool chitons, with just a sprinkling of chromaticism mixed in.

To my left, a wide, sweating brute bangs his fist on the counter of his shop.

"This is my most premium goat cheese. Five drachmas is a steal," he screams.

A stocky man, whose head is barely visible over the worktable, snorts. "You're unreasonable. I won't give you more than two."

The brute snatches the cheese back from him. "Keep moving. I don't need your business."

"To the underworld with you," the customer says, storming off.

After that exchange, I decide to approach another vendor for help. I try to mentally picture where the weapon shops were on the Dimensional Block. If I remember correctly, they're located in the bottom left quadrant—diagonal from where I'm currently standing. I take a deep breath and dive into the commotion, dodging elbows on my way south.

Unexpected flickering orange tentacles surge above the humans' heads in front of me.

The Eternal Flame.

There's time for a brief pit stop, so I move to the edge of the raging pyre. Although it's well contained in a sunken pit, the flames still loom high above me. A boy around eight places his unlit torch in the blaze until it ignites. He skips off, holding it high above his head. In a world devoid of Magic, the Eternal Flame's brilliance feels a little bit magical.

I charge back into the crowd, reaching the weapon vendors in no time. I approach the closest human—an older man with a salt-and-pepper beard.

"May I help you?" he asks.

"I pray you to be well," I say. "Can you direct me to the smithies?"

He looks me up and down. "Might I inquire what your business is?"

I understand his concern; dressed in the silk chiton of a nobleman, there's no obvious reason for me to visit the blacksmiths. "I am Oracle Hector. The gods sent a message for a Trojan blacksmith's apprentice I must deliver at once."

He smiles. "By the gods, you're the oracle. I will take you there at once."

"No, don't leave your shop unattended. Directions will be fine."

He nods. "Okay. Take the southern route out of the market and pass three intersections. The smithies will be on your right, with swords and shields on their outside signs."

"Thank you," I say and start down the southern path.

My visits to the first two smithies—small single-room workshops—are wasted efforts. Not only does Theos not work there, they couldn't tell me where he does. I charge inside the next one, eager to find him.

It's a good size with swords and shields displayed on the wall. Unlike those in the market, their etchings are exquisite. I take the closest shield off its holder and slide the leather strap over my left arm. It's surprisingly heavy, so I clasp my wrist with my right hand to help support it. The scorpion on the forty-inch face is so realistic the tail's sharp point looks like it could sting me.

"This place is off-limits for non-blacksmiths," a teenage boy calls from the back of the smithy.

I return the shield to its holder. "My apologies. I'm looking for a blacksmith apprentice. Do you know Theos?"

"I am he," he says. "But you really can't be in here. It's dangerous."

He's Iris's love interest? Based on her description, I was expecting something . . . more. Everything about him is ordinary—average height, normal weight, unexciting face with dull brown eyes and hair. His only distinguishing characteristic is the scarlet birthmark smudged across his left cheek. But there must be something special about him for her to be so smitten.

"Ah, Theos. Would you join me for a drink at Sailing After Dark?"

He scrunches his forehead. "It's the middle of the workday."

"I appreciate your dedication, but I really must insist," I say. "I'm Oracle Hector, and the gods have asked me to deliver a message to you."

The blood drains from his face, and his cheeks turn white. "What do the immortals want?"

"Join me for a drink and I will tell you," I say.

"Yes, yes, of course," Theos says.

He locks up the smithy, and we travel down four streets to Sailing After Dark. It's midafternoon, so the bar is already crowded with noblemen, but we're able to secure a table in the left corner.

Without knowing exactly how to bring Iris up, I decide on the subtle approach, by steering the conversation toward her father.

"How is working for Sidirourgos?" I ask. "Do you enjoy being his apprentice?"

"Yes," he says puffing out his chest. "He's the best blacksmith in all of Troy, but more than that, he's a good man . . . an honest man. He took me on as his apprentice, even though I come from a family of bakers. He didn't need to do that, you know, but he saw potential in me no one else did."

"He sounds wonderful."

Theos fingers the rim of his glass. "He is."

He's nervous. But for what reason? Probably because I told him the gods sent me—and who could blame him for that?

"I'll get to the point of why I'm here," I say. "Aphrodite sent me."

His eyes widen. "A-Aphrodite?"

"Do you know why the goddess of love would want me to find you?"

He pales again. "I know why. Please tell her I'm sorry."

I rub the back of my neck. "Aphrodite is not upset with you, Theos. She only wants to help. But I must understand what is going on."

Theos chugs the rest of his wine and stares at the table. "As I already said, Sidirourgos has given me an opportunity that I never thought I'd have. And how do I repay him? I fall in love with his only daughter. I come here each night and drown my sorrows in wine, but it doesn't help. I love her all the same. She deserves a noble—someone who can buy her everything her heart desires. And that's not me."

I stifle a laugh. How are they both so clueless about the other one's affection? "You may not be rich, but your heart is rich with love. Be patient, and I'm certain things will turn in your favor. I will bring your love forward to Aphrodite, and she may help you."

Theos's smile brightens his entire face. "Thank you, Oracle."

"There is no need to thank me, Theos. Now, on to happier topics. Your work as a blacksmith is much more detailed than the wares in the market. How do you accomplish that?"

We share another glass of wine, and he explains his technique to me. By the end of our conversation, I understand what Iris sees in him; his genuineness is apparent.

They deserve a happy ending, and I'm the one who can make it happen.

The next day, I return to Aphrodite's temple to share the good news with Iris.

"I pray you to be well," a male voice calls from the front entrance.

I head outside, joining Nicholas. "I pray you to be well. Did you need counsel with the immortals?"

"No, you know how I feel about them. I was looking for you."

"For me?"

He stares at his sandals. "I owe you an apology, Hector.

The fight yesterday . . . well, it was awkward, but it wasn't your fault. You were the one who broke it up. I should have thanked you for that."

My chest swells from his apology. "Thank you, Nicholas, truly."

"It's nothing," he says. "Anyway, I was hoping you'd join us for field hockey today."

"I would like that," I say. "I'd like that very much. But I am waiting for someone. Can I come by when I'm done here?"

Nicholas nods. "See you soon."

He heads down the northern side of the hill—just as Iris races down the southern path straight toward me.

"I pray you to be well, Oracle," she calls.

"Iris, I'm so glad you made it. Please, let's go inside," I say, and we enter the temple. "I have news from Aphrodite, but she wants to be certain about your feelings for Theos. Are you sure he's who you want for the rest of your life?"

She nods. "Yes, I want him more than anything."

"All right, then." I wave my hand in front of her face. "Aphrodite enchanted your lips so that the first person you kiss will fall deeply in love with you forever. But her magic will disappear at sunset, so you must act quickly."

"I have to kiss him?" Iris says, brushing her fingertips against her lips. "And then he'll love me, just like that?"

She digests this news for a moment and then hops up and down a few times.

"Thank you, thank you, thank you!" Turning to the statue, she adds, "Aphrodite, you are blessed among the immortals. I give you my word: I'll love Theos forever."

She runs from the temple, pausing only to drop a couple drachmas in the collection plate at the entrance. I rub my hands together and release a hearty chortle. Not bad for my first success as an oracle; two people who love each other will admit it, and I earned some money.

My thoughts return to Reos, certain that Jetta will be pleased I turned my oracle duties around. I can hear his voice: *"That's the way to do it, my boy. You can succeed as a Guide and follow the Rules. Keep it up."*

My imagined Jetta is right; things are finally starting to go my way. I place the coins in my drawstring shoulder bag and head for the field to the north.

SETTING SAIL FOR NEW HORIZONS

"PRINCE PARIS, I WOULD LIKE YOU TO MEET MY SON, NESTOR," Seleucus says, holding his baby out to me. "He is blessed to have you as his future ruler."

I place my hands under Nester's armpits, holding him ten inches away from my chest. He squirms uncomfortably, not enjoying being suspended in the air.

Achilles is nearby, surrounded by the rest of the Spartan field hockey team. He laughs when he sees me. Not only do I hate when people fawn all over me, I dislike kids. Especially babies. All they do is cry and spit up.

"He's a handsome boy," I say, giving him to Seleucus and stepping back, "but if you'll excuse me, I must talk to Achilles."

Seleucus cradles his son in the crook of his arm. "Of course, Paris. Enjoy the game."

I start toward my friend, but Villow steps in front of me, blocking my path.

"Hello, brother," I say. "I trust you're ready for the game."

"How many times do I have to tell you not to call me brother?" he says through gritted teeth. "I need a word. Privately."

Based on his charming greeting, I'm in store for one of his holier-than-thou lectures. "No thanks. I'm busy."

"Now," he demands, heading over to the far end of the stadium. I trail behind him, knowing he'll badger me until I give in.

"What is it?" I ask.

"I didn't see you at the sacrificial ceremony this morning."

I snort. "That's because I wasn't there. Watching you slaughter innocent goats isn't my idea of fun."

"I don't like it either, but it's an important part of Trojan tradition," he says. "And as Troy's prince, it's your duty to attend."

"Tradition or not, you've still become a butcher. All in the name of your precious immortals. Promise me you'll stay away from Aegidius at least."

He exhales audibly. "That's not fair, and you know it. The goats' deaths are quick, and their meat is used to feed many."

"That doesn't mean I want to see it, brother," I say, backing up from him. "If you're done with your lecture, I'm going to go. You know, to do my *princely* duties."

"Don't call me, brother," he snarls behind me.

I've angered him, but it's not surprising. These days, he's always upset about something. When I get back to the stadium's field, Priam and Hecuba are perched on the dais in front of the stands. I join them, sitting on the middle throne.

Hecuba takes my right hand. “There you are. We missed you at the ceremony this morning. Where were you?”

I squeeze her hand. “Sorry, Mother, I wanted to wish the Spartan players good luck.”

“Oh, Paris, we’ve been through this,” Priam says, shaking his head. “Multiple times. You need to focus on the Trojans. You are their prince, not Sparta’s.”

“I was being a good host,” I say, knowing it’s a weak excuse.

But how do I tell him that the Spartans, especially Achilles, are easier to be around than my own people? They share my values and see life as an adventure. Spending time with the Trojans makes me edgy. They’re so . . . wooden, worried they might offend me. Truthfully, I can see why Paris ran away.

Except for his parents. I don’t understand how he left Hecuba and Priam. Besides attending the daily strategy meetings with Priam, I eat dinner with the king and queen every night. Most evenings, Hecuba and I enjoy leisurely strolls around the palace grounds, holding deep conversations that I’ve always longed for with my real mom. Paris didn’t realize what he was giving up, escaping his duty in the mountains. But I know better; I’m part of a family for the first time, and I’m not taking it for granted.

“Your father is right,” Queen Hecuba says. “You must show the Trojans you support them, Paris. You will be their king someday.”

Barring a terrible tragedy, someday will never come.

Besides crow's-feet around his eyes and a few gray hairs at his temples, Priam is still the paragon of youth. And health—except for the beginnings of a small cough this morning. He will certainly survive longer than my one year on Earth.

I smile at him. "With the gods' blessings, I won't need to be king for a long time."

"May the immortals hear your invocation, my son," Priam says. "Now, it's time for the game to start. Perhaps you could make the opening remarks?"

I adjust the gold crown on my head. "The Trojans would rather hear from you."

"You do not give yourself enough credit," he says, touching my cheek. "And for the record, there is no one *I* would rather hear from. I'll give the speech today, but I'm expecting you to start taking over."

Priam raises his palm at the captain of the Trojan Guard, alerting him it's time to begin. The captain blows into his horn, and the hundreds of fans scattered across the field file into the stands. The Spartan and Trojan teams—including Achilles and Villow—form a line across the field.

The king stands and addresses the crowd. "I pray you to be well. As king of Troy, I would first like to extend my gratitude to the Spartans for agreeing to a field hockey match before departing for home in two days' time.

"Field hockey is a demonstration of great strength and competition, and also an offering to the immortals for their entertainment. We beseech you, Poseidon, to find us deserving and, in return, deliver the Spartans home safely. I ask the team captains to embrace, in acknowledgment they will play a fair game worthy of the god of the sea."

Nicholas and Achilles hug, and the crowd cheers. My brother waves like he's some big celebrity.

What a hypocrite. He criticizes me for being the prince, but he's become famous, both from his oracle duties *and* his field hockey skills.

"Without further delay, let the game begin," Priam says, sitting.

The players move into formation and begin running up and down the field. I shift uncomfortably on my throne but do my best to look interested. Noblemen chasing a ball around a field is not my idea of a good time, and it's even duller as an observer.

When the game breaks at halftime, Sparta is ahead twelve to seven. All thanks to Achilles, who's scored ten of the Spartan goals. The Trojans huddle in a tight circle to talk strategy, their heads hung in frustration.

Another reason why I don't like field hockey; it's only a game, but nobles take it so seriously. When the second half begins, I excuse myself and join Aegidius in the grassy meadow just outside the stadium, alternating between watching the game and playfully chasing him.

Ten minutes in, Achilles manages to steal the ball from Nicholas, driving it toward the Spartan net.

"He's going to score again, Butthead," I say. "I have to admit, Achilles is a pretty remarkable athlete."

Aegidius munches on the nearby alfalfa, clearly not as impressed as I am.

As Achilles nears the net, Oedipus charges at him with the speed of a rhinoceros. The Spartan swings his stick and sends the ball flying, just as Oedipus collides with him.

The ball goes into the net, and the crowd boos, but I

secretly cheer. Achilles is going to single-handedly win the game. I turn my attention back to my little goat, but a strange calm descends over the stadium. It causes the hair on my arms and nape to lift.

Something is wrong—I can feel it. I search the field for Achilles, but he's on the ground with Oedipus crouching beside him.

Field hockey is a full-contact sport that generates some serious injuries—and even a rare death. But I never worry about Achilles. He's practically invincible. Or so I thought.

It hits me like a punch to the gut; Achilles isn't immortal like me, and he could be really hurt. Or worse . . .

I race onto the field, shoving through the players encircling him.

"Achilles, it's Paris," I say, crouching on his left side. "Are you all right?"

His eyes flutter. "I'm okay . . . but my ankle . . . hurts."

I bow my head, waves of relief surging through me. He's still conscious. And an ankle injury isn't great, but he'll survive it. The doctor joins us, kneeling on Achilles's right side.

"He says it's his ankle," I tell him.

He places his fingers against Achilles's right foot, spinning it clockwise. He grimaces, his face turning snow white. Seeing him this peaked is unbearable, so I move a few feet away, pacing back and forth while the doctor finishes his exam.

My twin breaks away from the group, joining me. "He's going to be all right, Paris."

"You don't know that," I say. "He could be really hurt. And for what? A stupid game."

"Lower your voice," he whispers. "You cannot talk like that."

"Why not? It's the truth. It's—"

"Forgive my interruption," the doctor says, standing next to my brother, "but I'm almost certain Achilles's only injury is a sprained ankle. I'm taking him to the tent to do a full exam now."

Sure enough, two men have placed Achilles on a stretcher and are carrying him south to the white tent just outside the stadium. I press my palm to my chest, letting out a huge breath.

"Thank you, doctor," I say. "I will join you."

I start forward, but Oedipus steps in my path. "Prince Paris, I didn't mean to hurt him . . . It was an accident."

I jut out my chin. "It's a bit convenient though, isn't it, injuring Sparta's best player?"

It's unkind, but I'm in no mood for kindness—not when Achilles is on a stretcher and Oedipus is still standing.

Oedipus bows his head. "It was an accident. I swear upon the immortals."

"Of course it was," Villow says, placing his arm around his shoulders. "Injuries happen. We all know that, Oedipus. The prince is just worried about Achilles, but he shouldn't take it out on you."

"I am worried about him," I say. "But you should be worried too. For both your sakes, he better be okay."

I storm off the field and into the tent. Achilles is lying flat on a cot, and the doctor is wrapping his ankle with thin strips of wool.

"I was hoping the oracle would be with you," the doctor says. "Achilles could use Asclepius's help in healing."

The last thing I need right now is to listen to my brother offer up phony prayers to a fake god. "Hector is one of the best players on the Trojan team. He's needed on the field right now."

The doctor nods, accepting that excuse. A true Trojan, he'll do anything to win the game—even if it means his patient doesn't get the immortals' help.

I move to the side of Achilles's cot, squeezing his arm.

He opens his right eye a crack. "Paris. Did we win?"

"The game's not over," I say.

"Then what are you doing here?"

"You know I don't care who wins."

He chuckles but then clutches his sides. "By the gods, my ribs hurt. Don't make me laugh again. And you should care. Troy stands a chance now that I'm out of the game."

"Maybe so, but I have no interest in watching it." I clear my throat. "You had me worried."

"You shouldn't worry. I'm invincible," he says, but shadows invade his eyes. "The doctor says I have to rest my ankle for a month or so."

"I suppose it's good you're leaving in two days then. The week-long journey home will give you a chance to heal."

"Are you sure you won't join me? Sparta is beautiful during winter."

His offer—already made a dozen times—is tempting. As much as I would enjoy seeing Sparta and spending more time with my best friend on Earth, my trial is to help Troy.

I shake my head. "I ran away from my duties once. I can't do that to my parents again."

"Who said anything about running away? Tell them you're going. Besides, forming a relationship with King Menelaus would be good for Troy. They will—" He forcibly sucks in, wincing in pain.

"You need to rest," the doctor says. "It's the best medicine for you."

"He's right, Paris," Achilles says. "Go watch the game while I sleep. You can come back and give me a play-by-play when it's over."

I plop down on the cot to his left. "I'm not going anywhere. See you when you wake up."

Achilles mumbles something about my stubborn streak but shuts his eyes and is snoring within minutes. The pain must be bad for him to succumb to sleep so quickly.

In the distance, cheers erupt from the stadium. Since most of the fans are Trojans, it means they scored.

Troy is going to win now that Sparta's best player is injured.

My brother's face hovers behind the tent's flap, beckoning me to come outside. On the cot beside me, Achilles is still sound asleep. I slip out and move far enough away we can talk without waking Achilles. The sun is already half set, cooling the air and bathing the hills in a fiery orange light.

"Who won, brother?" I ask.

He clenches his jaw. "Stop calling me that. I'm Hector, not your brother."

"Fine, *Hector*. Who won?"

"We did. The final score was sixteen to fifteen."

"Of course. Not surprising after Oedipus took out Sparta's best player."

My twin shakes his head. "You do realize you should be happy about that. You're the prince of Troy, not Sparta."

"I'm well aware of that. Contrary to your opinion, I'm not an idiot. But I don't enjoy ill-gotten victories, regardless of the winner."

"There's a reason that's set up," he says, pointing to the tent behind me. "Players get injured all the time."

"Maybe so. But from where I'm standing, Achilles is hurt, and because of that, the Trojans won. Oedipus better stay out of my way."

"I'm going to assume your threat is your leftover fear talking, because Oedipus didn't mean to hurt Achilles and you know it. But I didn't come here to fight."

"Why are you here, then?"

"The team is celebrating their win at Sailing After Dark, and it would be nice if you came."

I shake my head. "I can't leave Achilles."

"You know I don't agree with you being the prince," he whispers, "but the role has been beneficial to our trial. The Trojans value you, and it would mean a lot to them if you came. It would mean a lot to me."

I search his face for sarcasm, but he looks sincere. A warm feeling expands across my chest; Villow just admitted I add value to our Guidance duty. And on top of that, he asked me to join him at a social gathering.

"I'll see if I can stop by. But first, I need to check on Achilles," I say, heading back to the tent.

Inside, Achilles is awake with his back propped up by two pillows.

I rush to his side. "How are you feeling?"

"Better," he says, and it appears to be true; a bit of color has returned to his cheeks. "The doctor is transporting me back to the palace. While he does, go get a drink with your team."

"You overheard Hector and me?" He nods, and I continue, "The Trojans didn't win fairly. I don't want to celebrate that."

He shakes his head. "Injuries happen, Paris. You know that. Oedipus didn't mean to harm me, I'm certain."

I consider what Achilles is saying. It makes sense. And it would be good to make a showing, since it means so much to my twin.

"All right. But one drink and then back to you." I turn to the doctor. "Please have him transported to my quarters."

"Look, I appreciate the sentiment," Achilles says, "but my guest quarters are fine. Besides, where will you sleep?"

I smile. "I can use the guest room for a few nights."

"You're a good friend, Paris," he says. "Now go. Have fun."

"I'll check on you when I get back to the palace," I promise and exit.

Pavlos is outside, pacing back and forth. He stops when he sees me and bows his head. "Prince, I'm here to escort you to the palace."

Pavlos has become a trusted friend over the past three months, but he takes his job a little too seriously.

"Don't you have anything better to do than follow me around?" I ask.

"Protecting you is my duty," he says. "There is nothing more important than that."

"Fine, if you insist on following me, we have to make a brief stop before heading home."

We head to the southern part of Troy, where Sailing After Dark is located. Even from outside, I can hear rambunctious chatter and loud music. The mixture of pungent wine and sweat drifts into the street from the cracks in the wooden door.

Pavlos raises his eyebrows. "I wouldn't be doing my duty if I didn't express my concerns, Prince. This really does not seem like a good place for you. It's . . . a bit rowdy for royalty."

I laugh. "Oh, Pavlos. What are you? A year older than me? But you act like you're fifty. One glass of wine and we're out of here. Promise."

"I have no interest in drinking, but I'm coming with you."

"Suit yourself," I say, pushing open the door.

The bar is even more crowded than the cacophony implied. Every table is filled, and almost every inch of the floor is packed with men, half of them so drunk they stagger on their feet. There's a small stage straight ahead of me, where a flutist, a lyrist, and an aulete are performing. The Trojan field hockey team is gathered at a table to the right of the stage.

To my left, the Spartan players are sitting at a table,

drowning their sorrows in wine. Based on their jerky, sloppy movements, they're completely wasted. It's not surprising, since Achilles is the one who keeps them in line.

"We wez robbed," Dareios says, slurring his words. "Wherez zat Trojan who hurt Achillez?"

Drunk Spartans looking to settle the score. Fantastic. What could go wrong?

I scan the bar for Villow. He's by the communal wine bowl, talking to Nicholas. Pushing my way through the crowd, I grab my brother's arm and drag him out the side door to the street.

"While I'm glad you decided to show, I was in the middle of a conversation," he says, pulling away from my grasp.

I get straight to the point. "How long have the Spartans been here?"

He tilts his head. "The Spartans are here?"

"Yep. They're completely drunk and talking about settling the score with Oedipus. We should get the Trojan field hockey team and move their celebration to the palace before someone gets hurt."

Villow rubs the back of his neck. "Okay. Let's go gather the team."

We turn back to the door, but Pavlos is standing in front of it. "I insist you stay out here, Prince. Things inside are much too dangerous for you."

I snort. "I'm quite capable of holding my own."

"I'm sorry, my prince," Pavlos says. "But—"

"We don't have time to argue," my twin says. "Paris can stay here, and I'll get the team. I'll be back in a few minutes."

As much as I hate waiting around, he's right; it doesn't matter who gets the Trojans, as long as they leave before a fight breaks out.

I nod, and my brother heads inside. Pavlos paces anxiously, and I lean against the wall, waiting for Villow to return.

Suddenly, the band's music is replaced by shouts and thuds. I race inside before Pavlos can stop me. As I feared, the bar is in total chaos, transformed into a brawling jumble of fists and limbs.

Next to me, Pavlos unsheathes his sword. "Stay behind me, Prince Paris. I will protect you."

The last thing this situation needs is weapons.

I place my left hand on top of his, grasped firmly on the hilt. "Lower your blade. This cannot end in bloodshed."

Once he has sheathed his sword, I leap on top of the nearest table. "By the order of Prince Paris—" I scream, but no one can hear me over the racket.

Where is my twin? I scan the crowd, but he's missing. Maybe he got most of the team outside already? Then Dareios charges by me—with surprising speed for someone who was completely inebriated minutes ago.

My gaze drifts in the direction he's heading. Some of the Trojan players—including Oedipus—are on the stage, shielding the band from the fight.

Damn. I rush to the end of the table, launching myself through the air and landing as close to the stage as possible. Then I shove through the brawling mass, hoping I reach them before something bad happens.

I break through the crowd and realize a stillness has descended on the patrons near the stage. And then

I see why. My brother is kneeling on the floor, holding Dareios's head in his lap. Blood is flowing out of the Spartan's left temple.

Oedipus is standing beside them. "H-He came out of nowhere and attacked me."

The crowd is frozen, but it won't last for long. Luckily, Pavlos is as dependable as always and is right next to me. I unsheathe his sword, stepping onto the stage.

"Everyone stay where you are, by order of Prince Paris," I say, brandishing the blade. "This night has already gone too far, and I'm taking control. Now. Pavlos, the palace doctor is in my chambers, tending to Achilles. Run as fast as you can and alert him we are bringing an injured man and need his help. Immediately."

He remains still—transfixed by the pool of blood on the floor by Dareios's head.

"Pavlos!" I scream, and he tears his gaze away from the blood, looking at me. "The doctor, now. It's an order."

He unfreezes and runs out the side door. With one problem solved, I address Villow, while keeping my eyes on the crowd. "Is Dareios okay?"

"I don't know," he says. "His pulse is weak, and he's not conscious. And there's a lot of blood . . ."

The Spartans exchange angry glances; this is the second time Oedipus injured one of their own in less than twenty-four hours. I need to keep them calm, to buy myself time to figure out what to do.

"Oedipus, I am putting you under arrest by order of the prince of Troy. You are under my watch until the Elders complete an investigation into what happened here tonight."

"Paris, you can't—" Villow says.

"It is a command from your prince," I say, cutting him off. "Not another word, Oracle." Then I address the Spartans. "Justice will be served for Dareios, I promise you. But first, we need to get him to the doctor."

I take off the outside layer of my satin robe and lay it on the ground. "Spartans, help me place your comrade on this so we can carry him to the palace. The rest of you, clear out. Now. Go sleep off the drink that caused such foolishness."

The Trojans practically run for the two exits, eager to flee from this horrific scene, while the Spartans lift Dareios onto the robe. They grab edges of the fabric, carrying him toward the main entrance of the bar.

Pavlos passes them, racing toward me. "Prince . . . are you . . . all right?" he puffs. "I ran into Cadmus, and he is delivering the message to the doctor so I could come back and protect you."

"I'm fine," I say. "But I put Oedipus under arrest. Take him to the palace at once."

Villow shakes his head. "Paris, you can't—"

"It's okay, Hector," Oedipus says. "The prince is doing what he must. I'm certain the Elders will find me innocent of any crime."

Pavlos and Oedipus head out of the bar together, leaving my twin and me alone.

Villow places his palm against his forehead. "I cannot believe you did that. Dareios attacked Oedipus. He was just defending himself."

"I'm doing what it takes to keep peace with Sparta," I say. "Accidents or not, Oedipus sprained Achilles's ankle and probably killed Dareios. Sparta will demand retribution."

"What does that mean?"

"It's up to the Elders. They will decide Oedipus's fate, as they do for all criminals."

"He's not a criminal."

I shrug. "To the Spartans he is. I'm going to check on Achilles and Dareios. Why don't you go to the temple and pray to your fake gods? It's all you're good for anyway."

He scowls at me. "What are you saying?"

"Allow me to spell it out for you. If you weren't hanging out with your friends, you would have realized how drunk the Spartans were and defused the situation before someone got hurt. But you were too busy having fun. So you don't get to be sanctimonious about how I handled things. If you ask me, you're just mad I'm doing more to help the Trojans than you are."

"I've done plenty to help the Trojans."

"Not like me," I say. "Back on Reos, you're the one who excelled at everything. But not here. On Earth, I'm outshining you in every way. I have a family, real friends, and I'm making a difference. Troy has more wealth than ever because of my trade deals. That money will help them survive when Priam dies. What have you done for the Trojans, besides validate their belief in fake gods and goddesses?"

"The only reason you are doing so well is because you're pretending to be a prince," he says. "Through the Trojans' belief in the immortals, I have made them more independent. And I made a life for myself here without stealing someone else's identity. I have friends too—"

"I'm well aware of your friends. They're the reason I'm dealing with a crisis right now. I don't have any more time to waste on you, brother. I need to continue to clean up the mess you helped create."

I storm out, leaving my twin alone in the shambles of the bar.

I PACE IN THE THRONE ROOM, WAITING FOR NEWS ON DAREIOS. If he dies, the Spartans will demand justice, and I shudder to think what that will mean for Oedipus.

Hesiod enters, and I can tell by his grim face he doesn't have good news.

"Is he dead?" I ask.

Hesiod shakes his head. "Not yet, but the doctor says he won't last the night."

I collapse on my throne. "This is not good."

"Agreed. We need to get ahead of this, Prince. I will call an emergency strategy meeting right now."

"No," I say. "My father still has his cough and needs his rest. Gather the Elders and let them know we will meet at first light. I will tell the king then."

"As you wish," he says, lingering in the doorway. "One more thing. The Spartans are demanding Oedipus's life as retribution. I don't like it, but I'm not sure we have a choice. Sparta is too powerful to displease."

I rub my fingertips against each other. "Understood, Hesiod. Good night."

"Good night, Prince," he says and exits, shutting the door behind him.

I grasp the throne's arms. If Dareios really did start the fight, Oedipus is an unfortunate casualty and doesn't deserve punishment. But it won't matter; the Spartans won't care. They lost a close friend and ally and will demand a life for a life.

The Trojans have come too far to risk their safety for one person.

For the good of Troy, Oedipus must die.

"You're really feeling better?" I ask.

Achilles smiles and lifts his right foot into the air. "I'm not ready for battle, but I'll be walking in no time."

I sigh. "That means you will be leaving tomorrow, then, huh?"

"Menelaus asked me to come home to continue my service in the Spartan army. Quite frankly, I should have left months ago."

"It's just . . . I'll miss you."

He grins. "I know. Which is why you should spend the winter in Sparta."

"You never stop, do you?"

"You know me," he says, folding his hands behind his head. "I always win, by any means necessary."

A knock at my bedroom door interrupts our laughter.

Pavlos enters, looking especially serious. "Sorry for the intrusion, Paris, but the Elders must meet with you. Immediately."

Achilles scrunches his eyebrows together. "That's odd."

"Especially since we spent all morning together," I say, rising to my feet. "I'm glad you're feeling better, my friend. I'll check on you again this evening."

I head into the hallway, where Pavlos is waiting for me.

"What is this all about?" I ask.

"I'm not certain," Pavlos says, "but I heard them say something about the oracle."

Damn you, Villow. I quicken my pace and head inside the throne room. The Elders are sitting around the table, but Priam isn't here.

"Where is my father?" I ask.

"His coughing got worse, so he retired for the day," Elder Thaddaeus says. "He told us to consult you on any urgent matters."

I move over to the table and stand behind my chair. "What is so urgent it can't wait until tomorrow?"

"It's Oracle Hector," Lycus says. "He just confessed he was the one who injured Dareios and insists the death sentence is his, not Oedipus's."

Deiphobus scratches his scalp. "As you can imagine, we are uncomfortable stoning an oracle, especially when he's our only one. And we're certain the immortals won't like it."

Hesiod nods. "It puts us in a difficult position. Do we anger the Spartans or the gods? Quite frankly, I don't like our odds against either foe."

"Which is why we summoned you," Lycus says. "A compromise might be our best option. Since Hector is an oracle, we thought exile might be a more . . . suitable punishment. The immortals would not be angered, and with your friendship, Achilles might be willing to accept the terms. It leaves us without an oracle, but that can't be helped."

"Give me a moment," I say, sitting down on my throne.

My stupid, self-righteous brother's meddling just screwed everything up. Again. I should let him fall on his sword. It would teach him a lesson—a much-needed one at that.

But we're three months into our year-long trial. And even though I told him otherwise yesterday, as an oracle, he's done a lot for Troy. In the last month, he used the gods to convince farmers to grow crops outside Troy's walls, using shepherds' flocks' manure to fertilize the land. With him gone, the strides he's making would cease—or worse, backtrack. Even if he transformed and came back as a different oracle, he would need to gain the Trojans' confidence all over again. We could fail, all because he's trying to save one man.

I rejoin the Elders, standing near the table. "I remained silent until now in order to avoid influencing you, but I was at the bar that night and saw Oedipus punch Dareios. He is the one who deserves punishment."

Hesiod strokes his beard. "So Oedipus must be stoned."

I twist my gargoyle ring around my finger. "Let us learn from Hector's act of mercy and commit one of our own. Oedipus will not be killed. He will be exiled."

"Sparta will not like that," Lycus says.

"As you said, Achilles will agree because of our friendship," I say. "If exile was appropriate for an oracle, it is also appropriate for a nobleman. Give Oedipus five hundred drachmas and tell him to start over, at least three cities away."

"Prince Paris, you must reconsider," Pelagios says. "Sparta—"

"If you are so worried about Sparta, we will lie to them and say Oedipus is dead. In fact, we will lie to everyone." I place my hands on the table, leaning forward. "We must make a promise now to never share the truth with anyone outside of this room. For Troy, everyone must believe Oedipus is dead."

The Elders nod reluctantly, mumbling agreement.

"Very good. Exile Oedipus at once and let him know that if he ever returns to Troy, we will stone him upon sight," I say, starting toward the door. "Now if you'll excuse me, I have somewhere to be."

"HOW MUCH LONGER IS THIS GOING TO TAKE?" I WHISPER. "I need to check on Achilles."

"The doctor is with him," my twin says. "Besides, I only asked you to attend the gamos. Be glad you're not part of all three days of the ceremony."

I shake my head. "Three days of celebration for two teenagers losing their freedom. Seems a bit idiotic to me."

"We're celebrating two people who love one another," he says. "There is nothing idiotic about that."

"Still, I feel sorry for the groom. Promising himself to one woman in his teens? He's throwing his life away. Speaking of, there's somethi—"

"F-F-Forgive my interruption, Prince Paris, but I need Oracle Hector. The bride must talk to you at once," a teenage girl says beside us, her eyes lowered to the ground.

I smile at her. "Oh good. Hector enjoys nothing more than being needed."

He glares at me but accompanies her out of the dining hall. I head over to the wine table, wishing I would have skipped this dinner. But I promised my twin I would be here, and I need to tell him about Oedipus—before he hears it elsewhere.

I'm two glasses in before Villow reappears. Instead of returning to our table, he heads to the front of the room.

"Family . . . friends," he says, "thank you for joining us to celebrate Theos and Iris's gamos. In this vast world, it's a blessing to find someone special and a love like this is rare.

"But not so long ago, Iris and Theos were strangers. Then Sidirourgos took on a young apprentice, and their lives changed. The time Iris and Theos spent together in the smithy built a foundation of friendship that eventually blossomed into love. And today, they solidify that love and promise each other forever.

"Last evening, I had dinner with Iris and her family. As tradition dictates, during our meal, she offered up sacrifices to the goddesses. To Aphrodite, Iris gifted her girdle, asking her to keep their love strong throughout the years. She gave her favorite childhood doll to Artemis, in return for protection in future childbirth. Finally, she offered a lock of her hair to Hera, to provide many children to fill their home with laughter. A love this strong will only be strengthened with the legacy of children.

"At this time, the couple is ready to make their relationship official with their marriage procession. Iris will leave her childhood home to take residence with Theos in his house. Together, they will make it their home and build a bright future. Please join us outside now."

He nods at Iris and Theos, and they head out the front door into the street. The fifty guests follow, and I take up the rear with Pavlos. We march down the cobbled roads lit with burning torches, to ward off evil spirits.

Fortunately, Theos only lives three streets away, and we arrive quickly. Unfortunately, my brother begins talking again. "Before we allow the bride and groom to share their first night together, they wanted to share a few words in front of their family and friends. Theos, I invite you to go first."

Theos glances at his feet. "Iris . . . you're a-amazing, in so many ways, and I'm, um . . . happy to spend the rest of my life with you. I p-promise you forever."

I bite the sides of my mouth to keep from chuckling; Iris clearly isn't marrying him for his speaking skills.

"Iris, it's your turn," Villow says.

She takes Theos's hands in hers. "I remember the first time I saw you, working at the furnace in my father's forge. I watched you hammering the sword you were fashioning . . . so precisely. I was so amazed by your hands that day. Hands with the gift of artistry. Hands that work so carefully to create such beauty.

"A month later, a dove hatchling fell out of its nest in the olive tree outside the shop. I watched you approach it, slowly . . . quietly. You cradled that tiny bird in your hands so gently and placed it back in its nest. I was moved by your hands that day. Hands that take such care with everything. Hands that are so gentle, they keep even the most fragile things safe.

"A few weeks after that, we went on our first date, a picnic in the woods. Your hands shook the whole time. Nerves, I suppose. But on the way back, you summoned the courage to hold mine . . . and you didn't let go the whole way home. I fell in love with your hands that day. Hands that tremble when you're nervous, but are still brave enough to take risks. Hands you use to illustrate the kindness in your heart.

"Now, I hold your hands in mine—these amazing, loving hands—and promise you forever. I'll never stop working to make you happy and will wake up each day renewed to making all your dreams come true. You are my life, and I pledge myself to you, forever."

Theos squeezes her hands warmly. "I'm glad I went first," he says, and the guests chuckle.

Villow places his hands on top of theirs. He pauses, enjoying being the center of attention. "The favor of the immortals will lessen your burdens and ease your life together. I have no doubt it will be a beautiful journey filled with much joy. Theos, Iris, let me be the first to congratulate you on your decision to merge your lives."

Theos kisses her quickly—just once—and the guests applaud. Iris tugs him back, giving him a long, passionate kiss, and the crowd erupts with catcalls. She's my kind of girl.

Theos pulls away, bright red but smiling from ear to ear. They wave at us and then disappear through the front door.

The guests disperse, heading back to their own residences. In minutes, Villow, Pavlos, and I are the only ones remaining in the street.

I look at Pavlos. "Give us a moment."

He nods, and I join my brother by Iris and Theos's front door.

"I'm shocked you're still here," he says. "I figured you left ages ago."

I shake my head. "I needed to speak with you privately. I'm curious. Do you always have to be the martyr?"

"What do you mean?"

"Did you really think I would let you take the blame for Oedipus?"

He sighs heavily. "It isn't your decision. I'm doing this. I already gave Oedipus my word. And Nicholas."

"What does Nicholas have to do with any of this?"

"They're very close," he says. "And Nicholas is my best friend in Troy. I won't disappoint him."

"I'm sorry to tell you this, but you're going to disappoint him, brother. Oedipus was stoned this afternoon."

His eyes widen, and he covers his mouth with his palm. "No. How could you do this?"

"How could I not?" I say. "I saved you from making a huge mistake. You couldn't take the blame for him. Our Guidance trial is at stake."

"It's at stake because you're doing nothing to help me," he says. "All you do is throw parties. And use the Trojan women." I scrunch my eyebrows together, and he continues, "Oh yes, I'm aware of your use and dismissal of women for your own pleasure. Remember the Rules.

You might be living as a human, but you know what you really are."

I cross my arms. "You know better than to believe rumors. And I may be a Glanching, but right now, I'm the Prince of Troy."

"And what do you have to show for it? We're supposed to be guiding and teaching, but I can't think of a single positive thing you've done."

"Well, maybe you should look a little harder," I say. "I've done plenty. This whole oracle thing is going to your head. Don't forget who *you* are. You can't channel the gods and you aren't one yourself."

I storm away, Pavlos following at my heels.

In the heat of anger, Villow's true feelings came out. He thinks I've done nothing. Nothing! How can he be so blind? Can't he see how I've changed, how much I've accomplished?

Achilles's offer to visit Sparta has never seemed so enticing. But I need to check with my father before I can go. I race to the palace, straight to the royal suite. As always, a guard is stationed at Priam's bedroom door.

He announces me, and I enter, finding Priam in bed, even though it's only a couple hours after sunset.

"My son, what a wonderful surprise," he says. "I thought you were at a wedding."

"It's over," I reply. "Plus, I needed to speak with you on something."

"Come," he says, patting the bed beside him. "What is so urgent?"

I sit down. "Achilles has invited me to join him in

Sparta, and I would like to go. I believe it would be good for Troy to develop a relationship with their king. But I won't leave without your blessing."

He ponders for a moment. "It seems you have thought this through, and what you are saying make sense. How long would you be gone?"

"It takes a week to travel across the sea, so six weeks minimum. That would give me a month in Sparta, but it's hard to say if that would really be enough time. It could be—" Priam's coughing interrupts me. "I don't think it's wise I go, if you're still not feeling well."

"Nonsense. It is simply a little cough. A strong alliance with Sparta is favorable for Troy. And although I will miss you, I am so proud. The old Paris, the child you were before you returned from Mount Ida, would have just taken off without discussing it with me. You will be a strong king someday."

I wrap my arms around him, and he returns my embrace.

"May Poseidon keep you safe, my son," he says.

"I'll be home before you know it, Father," I say. "Now get some rest."

I stop by Hecuba's suite next, delivering the news of my departure. She sheds a few tears but wishes me luck. Finally, I alert Achilles to my change of plans and head to my own chambers to pack.

Villow is convinced he's the only one helping Troy.

Let's see how he fares when I'm across the sea.

A SURPRISING VISITOR

My entire body feels like it was burned by hot coals, thanks to the bad dreams that haunted my sleep. Every time I shut my eyes, I pictured Oedipus—lying on the ground—as stone after stone was thrown at him until his battered body surrendered to death. In my nightmares, he used his last breath to accuse me of forsaking him.

And it's true. I promised Oedipus I would save him. Instead, Dameaon made me a liar.

Even though I'm overwhelmed by sadness, I summon the little energy I have and stumble out of bed to open my shutters. The midmorning sun brightens the room, and the breeze wafts in, replacing the stale air with cool, salty freshness. I splash cold water on my face and dress in a clean chiton, readying myself for the laborious tasks before me.

My first stop is Nicholas's house, to inform him I failed in saving Oedipus before he hears it elsewhere. The news of his death will be tough on the entire field hockey team but will be especially difficult for him. Then I will head to Oedipus's parents' house. While I'm certain they have been notified of his death, they lost their oldest son last night and will need the comfort of an oracle.

I take a deep breath and head for the door, pausing to collect the piece of paper just inside my room. It reads:

> *Brother,*
>
> *Since you're convinced I'm such a failure, I decided to save you from the torture of watching me "do nothing." I set sail for Sparta this morning with Achilles and Aegidius. I don't know when I'll return, but since you're such a stellar role model, I know Troy is in capable hands. Keep up the great work, "Oracle."*
>
> *Prince Paris*

My blood runs cold. It's impossible. Dameaon couldn't have abandoned his Guidance duty. But then, this is the same Glanching who changed his Class in the middle of his Path Ceremony.

I run through the palace to the docks, hoping to stop him before it's too late.

A quick glance around confirms my fears; there are only fishing ships in the harbor, and my twin is gone. I reread the note, still clutched in my hand. *I don't know when I'll return.*

I stare out at the vast sea, willing him to magically appear. Guru Jetta's voice echoes in my mind: *"While you're on Earth, promise me you'll stay together."*

I gave Jetta my word, and now here I am—alone. He would want me to go after Dameaon—to bring him back. It makes sense, but there's risk in that too. If I go to Sparta, Troy is left Guideless.

The Aegean Sea's tumultuous waves mirror my inner turmoil. My mind races, but I'm unable to make sense of the jumbled thoughts. If only Dexter were here. His analytical reasoning could help me figure out what to do.

But maybe there's a way to channel him. I close my eyes, pretending he's beside me. His voice speaks inside my mind: *"If you stay in Troy, Dameaon will no doubt create havoc in Sparta. On the other hand, if you go to Sparta, you could lose momentum with the Trojans. That could be the difference between passing or failing your trial. And who knows if Dameaon would even come back with you? It would probably be a useless trip."*

Pretending Dexter is here, even for a moment, makes me realize how much I miss him. My eyes prickle with tears; I didn't appreciate his friendship enough—not since my Path Ceremony. I was too focused on Portia and the other drama that seemed to dominate my life.

I make a mental note to apologize and find more time for him when I'm back on Reos, before returning to my current dilemma: should I chase after my twin or not?

After what he did to Oedipus, Dameaon has proven he's capable of anything. But he's in Sparta, where nothing he does influences our trial. Whereas if I leave Troy, it could. We could fail because the Trojans were left alone.

I can't risk that. Not yet. Not when things are going so well. And distance could be a good thing—for both of us.

We can forgive and forget the harsh words we exchanged last night.

Yes, staying in Troy is the right thing, for both of us. Dameaon doesn't realize it, but he's given me a gift. I can focus on our trial and not worry about what he's doing—at least for a little while.

I crumple his note into a ball and toss it into the sea. The waves devour it hungrily, and it disappears—just like my vagabond twin.

When I get back, Natham is waiting at the palace entrance. He escorts me to the throne room, where the king and the Elders are seated around the table in the middle of a heated debate; apparently, unplanned ventures across the sea aren't princely behavior.

"This is so typical of him," Thaddaeus says. "Paris is still the same insecure, selfish child he's always been, running away from his duties."

Priam lifts his crown and runs his fingers through his hair. "That is unfair. Paris is not running away this time. He is visiting Sparta to build a strong relationship with King Menelaus. That is for the good of Troy."

"How long is his visit for?" Hesiod asks.

Priam looks up at the ceiling. "He could not say, specifically."

"Of course not," Hesiod says. "Because he is running away. Again."

"And your time on Earth is limited," Deiphobus says. "Paris should be here, learning how to be a good king."

"I understand, but I disagree," Priam says. "This will

make thi—" The king's words are overtaken by a coughing fit.

"This is exactly my point," Deiphobus says. "Listen to your cough. Put aside the love you have for your son and do what's best for Troy."

Priam sips his water. "It is a cold, Deiphobus, not a death sentence. And I always do what is best for my city. Always. An alliance with Sparta strengthens us."

Hesiod shakes his head, unconvinced, and the other Elders exchange knowing glances. He looks at me. "Perhaps Oracle Hector could share the immortals' opinion?"

I nod and shut my eyes, pretending to channel the gods. Some of the Elders' arguments were solid, but their dismissal of Priam's points was unfair. Sparta is a superpower, and Troy, while a fair city, is small. Having an ally with such wealth and a considerable army would benefit them, especially as they continue to grow their trade industry.

"The immortals side with King Priam," I say, opening my eyes. "Artemis expressed her support of a relationship with Sparta. And Poseidon has promised to grant Paris safe travels across the sea. This is a good move."

The king straightens his spine and looks directly at Hesiod. "It is settled then. Troy will not go against the immortals' wishes."

Hesiod shakes his head. "My king, you must reconsi—"

Priam slaps the arms of his chair. "You dare defy the immortals? You know how unwise that is. Troy would pay for that, much more than they could ever pay for Paris's visit to Sparta. The decision has been made, and I do not want to hear another word about it."

He stands and shuffles out the door.

Hesiod rubs his beard. "Forgive me for saying this, Oracle, but my instincts are telling me this visit will doom us all."

"The immortals are not wrong," I say. "Paris's visit will fare well for us."

He nods, but he doesn't look convinced.

"Good day to you, then," I say, eager to escape before they find new reasons to demand Paris's return. Besides, I have bad news to deliver, and I want to get it over with.

NICHOLAS ANSWERS HIS DOOR, SMILING FROM EAR TO EAR when he sees me. "I pray you to be well, Hector. Come in, come in. Do you bring news of Oedipus?" He moves out of the door, and we enter his living room. "Could I get you a glass of wine?"

My body is suddenly frozen from cold shivers going up and down my spine. I sit on the closest couch and gesture to the one across from it. "No wine, thanks. Sit. Please."

His shoulders tense, and he nods, taking a seat.

I jump right in, seeing no sense dragging this out. "I'm afraid I bring bad news."

Nicholas scrunches his eyebrows together. "Bad news? But yesterday you said you had a plan that would save Oedipus? Did you encounter a problem?"

I take a deep breath. This is going to be harder than I thought. "I'm afraid my plan failed. I tried to take the blame for Oedipus, but the prince did not back me up. He—"

Nicholas crosses his arms. "Your big plan was to take his place?" I nod, and he continues, "Oh, Hector, the prince was right not to support it. You cannot lie to save him. We will find another way, together."

"I'm afraid we can't," I whisper. "He was stoned yesterday, by order of Prince Paris."

Nicholas stares at me for a moment—his mouth agape. "Oedipus . . . is dead?"

"Yes. I'm so sorry, Nicholas." I move over and sit next to him. "I know what he meant to you."

He remains motionless, except for the trembling of his chin. Seeing my strong, confident friend so shaken causes tears to form in my eyes. I squeeze Nicholas's hand, holding it in mine, to remind him he's not alone.

"I went to see him yesterday," he says, his voice barely above a whisper. "He said he loved me, but I didn't say it back. I was scared to admit it. Our relationship . . . you know we both had to marry soon. Things had to end, but he died, not knowing how much I cared. That I loved him too."

"He knew," I say. "I saw how you were together."

He shrugs. "Maybe so, but I still should have told him. And now I can't. It's not fair."

I shake my head. "We don't always understand why things happen. But I have no doubt Oedipus will be waiting for you in Elysium, and you can be together again."

Nicholas pulls his hand from mine. "Hector, do not start preaching your religious nonsense to me. Not right now."

"You should find comfort—"

"There is no comfort in it if you don't believe in Elysium. There is no afterlife, and Oedipus is gone, Hector.

Just gone." He stands. "I need you to go. I want to mourn my friend alone."

He trudges up the stairs, leaving me in his living room. I contemplate following him, but it's probably better to let him have some processing time before attempting to comfort him again.

"I'm so sorry, Nicholas," I yell. "I'll check in on you later."

There's no response, but I'm not surprised.

I head outside, leaning against his wooden door and breathing in the fresh air. That was terrible. I knew about Nicholas and Oedipus's romantic relationship, but I didn't realize it was so serious. Nicholas never spoke of love before today. Of course, why would he, when they were both of marriageable age and their relationship had to end soon?

I remind myself my work still isn't complete. Taking a deep breath, I head to Oedipus's parents. They will appreciate an oracle's support, as true believers in the immortals.

I'M IN ARTEMIS'S TEMPLE WHEN I HEAR AN UNEXPECTED, OUT-of-place voice.

"Good afternoon, my boy," Jetta says, standing next to the goddess's statue.

"Jetta!" I say, embracing him.

He's dressed in a tunic, but his hair is still a disheveled mess. It warms my chest; it's good to see some things haven't changed.

But then it hits me; something must be very, very wrong. "Why . . . why are you here?"

"You know why, Villow," he says. "The Oldungur Council is furious Dameaon left for Sparta. They believe he abandoned his Guidance duties. You must bring him back."

I rub the back of my neck. "He's the one who left. Why aren't you telling this to him?"

"I saw your fight, Villow. You are the reason he left."

"You don't actually believe that? He left because he's selfish."

Jetta's eyes soften. "He left because you accused him of doing nothing as a Guide. You hurt him."

I take a step back and tilt my head. "I could never hurt him, Jetta. He doesn't care about me or what I think. Dameaon left because he wanted to keep having fun with Achilles."

"Is that why?"

"Yes. And furthermore, I had good reason to be upset with him. He killed Oedipus, but he didn't need to. We could have found another way to properly deal with the situation."

"Are you certain Dameaon killed him?" he asks, raising his eyebrows.

"Um, yes. He told me himself."

"Your twin is not as cruel as you think he is. He did not kill Oedipus. He exiled him, with a large sum of drachmas, giving him the chance to start a new life elsewhere."

I press my fist to my mouth and stagger backward. "W-What? Why . . . would he lie to me?"

"Probably because he knew you wouldn't rest until you found Oedipus and brought him back. And besides being bad for Troy, that would be a poor use of your limited time as a Guide."

I sway, dizzy from his revelation. I can't believe Dameaon showed Oedipus mercy—more mercy than I thought he was capable of. Perhaps I've been wrong about him. Perhaps he really did do what was best for Troy. Perhaps he has changed. If so, I need to fix this.

I push my shoulders back. "What do you need me to do?"

"Go get your twin. Convince him to return to Troy before the Oldungur Council demands I call you both back to Reos."

"I will do what you ask, Jetta, but first, I ask you to consider that his trip to Sparta could be good for Troy," I say. "We should allow him to continue, at least for a little while."

Jetta bites his bottom lip, contemplating what I said. "A Guide should remain with the civilization they are assigned to. The Oldungur Council won't like it."

"I went to Dardanus and Abydus."

"You were learning how to be an oracle. It benefitted your Guidance duty here."

"Well, now Dameaon is solidifying a relationship with an ally, and a strong military ally at that. There have never been two Guides before. Sell it as us dividing and conquering, to make Troy as successful as possible. Master Oldungur Cassandre will be open to it. You said it yourself. She is unconventional."

He ponders what I said for a moment and then shrugs. "While I would prefer him to come back, what you said has merit. I will do my best to convince Cassandre and the other Oldungurs this will work. Just remember, you need Dameaon for your report out, so he must be back at the end of your year here."

I nod. "If he's gone too long, I will go and bring him back myself. I promise."

He smiles warmly. "Thank you. I've missed you, Villow. You are changing the Trojans' culture, and I am so proud. Keep it up, and I have no doubt you will come home successful."

"I've missed you too. Do you have to get back right now?"

"I must return soon, but I can stay a few minutes. What do you want to know?"

"Have you seen my parents? Are they good?"

He nods. "Every now and then. And yes, they seem quite fine."

His words make me feel ten pounds lighter; my parents are still married, at least for now. "What about my classmates? Portia Sturling? Katarin De Legard? Dexter Khan?"

He chuckles. "I have my hands full with the two of you. I don't have time to keep track of other students."

"Of course," I say, pausing for a moment. "Can I ask a favor? Could you take a few notes back to Reos with you for my classmates? It would mean a lot to me."

He smiles. "As long as you make it quick. And don't include specifics about your Guidance duty."

I sit on the floor, removing some paper and a quill from my bag. I start with a note to Katarin. It flows easily, since I've thought about what I want to say to her at least a hundred times.

Kat,

I'm so sorry for how we ended things. You have always been, and will always be, my best friend, and I should have never reacted so poorly to your confession. I'll make it up to you. I promise. And don't worry, I'm still the same Villow I've always been.

—Vil

My second note is for Portia. It's tougher to put my thoughts into words, since she is a bit of an enigma. Finally, I go with honesty.

Portia,

I miss you, more than I can convey. While only three months have passed on Earth, it has been an eternity without you. I hope you are staying true to our promise and waiting for me. I am counting down the days until I see you.

Yours, Villow

Satisfied, I hand the two notes to Jetta. He hugs me, whispering in my ear. "I really am proud of you."

Tears form in my eyes; Jetta's belief in me is a much-needed courage boost.

"I'll see you back on Reos," I say.

Our Guru nods, touching his amulet and muttering, "Intoarcere, intoarcere." He fades—becoming more and more transparent—until he disappears completely. I wave my hand in the space where he just was. How I wish I could go with him, even for a day. I miss Reos so much my heart aches. But this is the life I chose. The life of a Guide.

"I pray you to be well, Oracle," a Trojan calls from the entrance. "Can I speak with you?"

The client is a reminder of how needed I am in Troy. This is my purpose. Where I belong. And Jetta said it himself—I'm doing well.

I gesture for him to join me. "Of course. Come in."

AND SO, LIFE MOVES FORWARD AT A FAST PACE, THE WEEKS turning into months. With Paris's absence, King Priam invites me to attend the daily strategy meetings. Through those sessions, I've grown to respect all the Elders for their thoughtfulness and commitment to Troy. And Priam is exactly what a ruler should be: open to others' input, strong but compassionate, and kind. In truth, he's become a surrogate father to me, which is much needed since I lost faith in Lord Drasko. Without Dameaon's company, Queen Hecuba invites me to join her on her nightly strolls. She is warm and caring—everything I ever wanted in a mother. Even so, I can't help feeling like a fill-in for my twin, only to be replaced when he returns.

Even Oedipus's "death" becomes easier, knowing he is really alive. Not that it matters to most of the Trojans. His parents do not want my sympathy, saying it was his foolish mistakes that caused his downfall. The field hockey players accept his death as fair punishment. The only misery surrounding the situation is Nicholas. His love for Oedipus remains strong, even now. But I can't risk telling him. Truthfully, it's better that Oedipus is gone. Nicholas was right; he will have to wed a woman soon, and their relationship would complicate his life.

Two months after Dameaon left, I'm confident that we've passed our trial. My visitors at the temple have dwindled, proof that the Trojans are solving their problems by themselves.

The only dark cloud is Priam's cough. It's worsening, causing concern for Hecuba, the Elders, and myself—even though the doctor insists it's only a lingering cold. While I hope it's true, I can't risk Priam dying and my brother becoming the king.

It's time for us to head home. I write my twin a coded letter, certain it will be read on its journey across the sea.

> *Paris,*
>
> *Things in Troy are running smoothly, although King Priam's health is a concern for both the royals and the citizens, especially with the disappearance of their prince. You'll be responsible for running a city soon, and I question your ability to do so. The gods came to me in a dream last night, reminding me that our journey together isn't over. It made me think about our time on Mount Ida. If we return to that icy peak and ask the gods to evaluate our efforts, I'm certain we will meet their approval.*
>
> *Sincerely,*
> *Oracle Hector*

After a month with no response, I'm convinced my twin is ignoring me. Then, one typical afternoon, Natham delivers Dameaon's letter:

> Neschume, *a sailing vessel, is leaving for Sparta tomorrow morning—be on it.*

Once again, Dameaon demands things happen on his terms. But Jetta's admission has given me a new appreciation for my twin, so I'm willing to relent.

I instruct Natham to make the arrangements and then spend the day at the temples. I have dinner with the king and queen, who are thrilled Paris has invited me to join him in Sparta—no doubt praying he will come back with me.

After a final night's sleep in Troy, I arrive at the docks the next morning, travel bag in hand.

"Good day, Oracle Hector. We're almost ready to go. Join us aboard when you're ready," the captain hollers from *Neschume*. Then he focuses on his crew, shouting commands that send the fifty Spartan sailors on deck running. I board, staying at the stern and out of their way.

A burly, sun-wrinkled fellow pulls a rope that drops the sail. The cool breeze fills it and propels us forward, starting the journey across the sea. The captain screams again, and most of the sailors go belowdecks, using oars to paddle on both sides of the ship.

I turn back to Troy, and that's when I see Nicholas, along with the rest of the field hockey players. They're on the dock, waving goodbye. I'm overcome with emotion and tears stream freely down my cheeks. If all goes well in Sparta, I'll only set foot on these shores to head to the Teleportation Machine.

If all goes well.

With Dameaon, well-laid plans have a way of falling apart. As if on cue, a solitary seagull releases a mournful keen, sending a shiver of foreboding down my spine.

Between its wind-filled sails and the crew's rowing, *Neschume* cuts through the waves effortlessly. Every morning, the sailors sing chanteys to Poseidon, asking for safe travel, and each day, their wish is granted. They praise me in hushed whispers, certain the sea is calm because I'm onboard.

For me, the surrounding blue vastness kindles an internal freedom I haven't felt since becoming a Seeker. With Troy's shores gone from view, it's easy to forget about my responsibilities and what is at stake if I fail. When our port of call appears a week later, I'm disappointed. I hoped our journey would take a few more days.

The crew clearly doesn't share my chagrin. They scurry about, steering *Neschume* into a harbor three times the size of Troy's, executing their duties at double the normal speed. Once the ship is secured, the sailors race down the ramp to their loved ones on the dock. Their joy is infectious, so I remain on the deck to watch.

The captain joins me. "Is everything all right, Oracle?"

"Ah, yes. I'm just enjoying the reunions. It's nice to see such happiness."

He scratches his ginger beard. "Our families worry whenever we cross the sea. Today, they can breathe again for the first time in a month." He clears his throat. "Speaking of, my wife and daughter are waiting for me. But I can't disembark until everyone else does, so . . ."

"Of course," I say. "Let's go."

I head down the ramp onto the dock. A little girl around four escapes from her mother's grasp and runs past me.

"Daddy!" she screams.

"I've missed you, Phoebe girl," the captain says, clutching her armpits and whirling her around in a circle. Her red hair fans out, and she releases a high-pitched squeal.

It rouses memories of my last day with Katarin, when I spun her around just like that. The loneliness inside me bubbles to the surface, cracking my facade of happiness. What I wouldn't give for a moment of real companionship with my best friend.

Jetta must have gotten my letter to her by now. Has she forgiven me? Does she regret not saying goodbye? Does she ever think about me? Maybe she's at the Summit right now, wishing I were there too. Or at Mage training, since her sixteenth birthday came and went. Perhaps she's—

My thoughts are interrupted by a broad forearm clenching me in a headlock.

"Guess who?"

"Hello, Achilles," I rasp.

He laughs and releases me. I place my hands on my knees and swallow three times to prevent a coughing spell.

When I straighten, I'm face-to-face with my twin. Even though he's scowling, it's a pleasant surprise. I assumed he would send a servant—if anyone—to meet me. "Paris, it's good to see you."

He rolls his eyes. "Let's get moving. It will take the rest of the morning to reach the palace, and I have better things to do."

Achilles gestures to three nearby horses. He hands me the reins of a brown mare. "This is Maeja. She's a good-natured beast with a smooth gait."

I pat her neck and mount her, following my brother out of the port. For all his bluster about being in a hurry, our pace suggests otherwise. We head northwest, ambling along a riverbank. The silver backs of hundreds of sprats shimmer just below the water's surface.

"You picked the perfect time to visit," Achilles says, riding next to me. "Besides the glorious weather—I mean, look, there's not a cloud in the sky—King Menelaus is returning today with his new bride. We're having a party in celebration. You'll get to taste our wine. Spartan vineyards yield the sweetest grapes in all the world.

"And wait until you meet Menelaus. Besides being a fantastic ruler, he's a dear friend. You'll love him. Everyone does. Paris told him so much about you—"

"Achilles, you're making my head hurt," my twin says. "Can you be quiet for two minutes?"

"Oh, Paris, calm yourself. You're just mad you had to get up early," Achilles counters.

But he stops talking, and we ride in silence. Soon, we leave the river's edge, heading into a flat plain. The grass is so high, it brushes against the bottom of my sandals as we ride. Eventually, the terrain to our left morphs into rolling hills, speckled with herds of sheep and goats.

Achilles points north to a distant complex on the other side of the river. "There's Sparta, the golden city."

Even from this far away, I understand the sobriquet; the sun's reflection on the buildings' roofs makes them sparkle with a honeyed sheen. I expect we'll cross the babbling water on the nearby wooden bridge, but Dameaon continues west.

"Paris, I think you missed our turn," I call. "Paris?"

He ignores me, so I turn to Achilles.

He grins. "Sparta is built on strength. We exhibit that to the world through the way we live."

"What does that have to do with us bypassing Sparta?"

His smile broadens. "Wait and see."

I don't want to wait and see, but I remain silent. We continue on, and twenty minutes later, an edifice appears on the horizon.

"That's where we're going, Hector," Achilles says. "It's Sparta's palace."

"But it's so far away from the city," I say.

"I told you, Sparta exhibits its strength through the way we live. There are no walls around our city or palace. Our superior army is all the protection we need." Achilles kicks his horse's sides and gallops toward our destination. "Last one there owes me a glass of wine."

Dameaon and I bring our horses to gallops, chasing after him. When we reach the palace, I dismount to grass so thick it's like carpet.

"Paris, you were last," Achilles says. "I'll expect my wine this evening at the party."

"The wine's free, so what does it matter?" Dameaon asks.

"It's not about the cost; it's about you hand-delivering it like my slave."

My brother scowls. "Your slave? I don't think so."

Luckily, we're interrupted by an ebony blur, running toward us and bleating the whole way.

"Hi, Aegidius," I say as he bounces at my feet. "You're just as spunky as ever."

I scratch his tuft of white fur, and he jumps into a nearby fountain, splashing me with cool water. Then he disappears into the herd of goats a few feet to my right.

"I trust you have a good excuse for missing my return," a stranger—standing in the palace door—crows.

Savage. It's the first word he evokes. It could be his menacingly tall structure. Or the golden crown—with six sharp points—on his head. Perhaps it's the intensity of how he's swinging his long arms as he charges forward. Or his deep scowl.

He stops in front of my twin, placing his hands on his hips. "Imagine my shock when I arrived home and found my two best friends were on a boondoggle. And this was after I sent word so you would be here to greet my new bride."

Dameaon juts out his chin. "I had things to do."

"Calm down, Menelaus. We're here now," Achilles says, punching the tall man's arm.

The savage man laughs loudly. "I missed you both. I trust this is the reason for your absence?" he says, pointing at me.

"This is Oracle Hector," Achilles says. "Hector, this is King Menelaus."

He turns his genial periwinkle eyes toward me. "This is the oracle you've been telling me about?"

My twin nods. "We were expecting him next week,

but *Neschume*'s captain sent word that they made great time and were arriving this morning. Needless to say, we couldn't leave him stranded at the docks."

"Of course not," Menelaus says. "Hector, I thank you for making the trip to Sparta. And your timing couldn't be better. I returned home to a slew of problems I could use the gods' guidance on."

Achilles throws his arm around the king's broad shoulders. "It's always about work with you, Menelaus. That can wait until tomorrow. Tonight, I promised Hector a real Spartan party."

"And where *is* the reason for the celebration?" Dameaon asks, fingering his gargoyle ring. "I need to meet the girl who snared a self-proclaimed lifelong bachelor's heart."

Menelaus's face lights up. "She's tired from our journey and is taking a nap." He puts his hand on his forehead. "How inconsiderate of me . . . Hector, you must be tired from your travels. I'm sure you'd like to rest for a while."

"Yes, that would be nice," I say. "But more importantly, I need a few minutes alone with Prince Paris. I have news from Troy that can't wait."

"Of course," he says. "Paris, why don't you get Hector settled in the room across from yours and then meet Achilles and me at the stables? It's the perfect day for a hunt."

Dameaon agrees, and we split up. My twin and I head down a corridor to my new quarters. It's double the size of my room in Troy and has three beautiful tapestries—all of Ares—on the walls. Besides a double bed, there's a nightstand, chair, and two large windows. I'll be quite comfortable for the short time I'm here.

He closes the door. "Okay, brother. I'm sure you have a lecture for me, as always, so let's get it over with."

"Why didn't you tell me the truth about Oedipus?" I say. "You didn't have him killed. You sent him away."

He scrunches his eyebrows together. "Who told you that?"

"Jetta." I expect him to be shocked, but he has no reaction whatsoever. "He came to see me when you left for Sparta, telling me the Oldungur Council wanted me to bring you back. But I convinced him you were here to help Troy."

"This is what you came to tell me?"

"No. I thought it was pretty clear in the letter I sent you. Priam's cough continues to worsen, and I've done everything possible to influence the Trojans to be self-sufficient," I say. "They will survive without a king. That means we passed our trial, and we can head back to Reos early."

He shakes his head. "Why would I head back before I need to? I'm having a great time."

My cheeks flush. "Dameaon, playing prince is bad enough. You've broken some of the Rules—probably more than I care to know about—but the Oldungur Council won't forgive you for becoming the leader. Is having fun really worth losing your Guidance duty forever?"

"I'm not worried about that," he says. "But let's say I'm willing to go along with your little plan. What are we supposed to do? Sneak off in the dead of night?"

"No, of course not. Everyone knows sea voyages are dangerous. We'll head back to Troy and, with any luck, hit stormy weather. We can fall overboard and swim to shore. It will be hard for the king and queen to lose their son, but it's the best solution."

He contemplates what I said. Then he opens the door. "All right, brother. Pretending to drown is a bit dramatic, but I'll play along. I'll alert the docks we're leaving tomorrow. Which means you'll only have one day in Sparta, so try to have some fun for once."

He shuts the door behind him, and I stare at the wood's grain. I can't believe it. He agreed to head back to Reos. And it was easy.

A little too easy.

With my twin, there is always a catch. But then I remember he demonstrated mercy with Oedipus, showing real growth. Maybe his time in Sparta matured him even more. This could be proof of a more logical, reasonable Dameaon. Or perhaps the threat of punishment frightened him. Either way, I can relax, knowing we'll start our journey home tomorrow.

Achilles elbows my ribs. "Are we boring you, Hector?"

I glance at my brother and him. They're both smirking, pleased they caught me spacing out. "Ah, no . . . I was just looking around."

"It's okay if you're bored, but don't lie about it," Dameaon says.

"I'm not bored," I say. "The party is just a little overwhelming."

And it is; between the extravagance and noise, it's a lot to take in—especially after Troy's more subdued gatherings. The palace's grand hall is made of gold, from the floor to the vaulted ceiling. The walls are adorned with tapestries of deep shades of red and purple. The square perimeter is lined with alternating statues of Ares—in different fighting stances with swords—and elaborate gold candelabras, bathing the room in a soft warm light.

Lively music provides a backdrop for their alluring dances. The wine—which is as good as Achilles claimed—is flowing freely. The fifty guests' singing gets louder with every glass. Everyone is swathed in exquisite silk chitons and robes—even Achilles, and it's odd to see him without his armor. Their hair is elaborately coiffed and garnished with gold jewelry, embellished with gemstones. There is no doubt that Sparta is a prosperous city.

"Greetings, my friends. Is everyone having a good time?" Menelaus asks, joining our small circle. The thin gold threads in his evergreen robe shimmer in the candlelight, accentuating his deep complexion.

"Hector isn't," Dameaon says. "He's bored."

"Enough, Paris," I say. "I already told you, I'm not bored."

Menelaus smiles. "Oh, Paris, stop giving him a hard time or he'll turn the immortals against you."

"I'm not worried," my brother replies. "You see, Hector *always* does the right thing, no matter what. And he's great at telling everyone else what's right for them, regardless if they want to hear it or not."

Menelaus scrunches his eyebrows. "As is his right as an oracle. It would do you some good to listen to him. Speaking of, Hector, I'd love to get your thoughts on some concerns I have for my people. Perhaps we could take a tour of my city tomorrow and I could get your advice?"

I glare at my brother, who looks up at the ceiling. Apparently, it's up to me to deliver the news. "Unfortunately, we're leaving for Troy tomorrow morning. King Priam isn't well, and Paris must return at once."

"Wow . . . so soon," Menelaus says. "That's greatly disappointing, but of course, I understand. Duty is more important than anything."

He raises his cup. "If tonight is our last night, join me in a toast. First, let's congratulate Achilles. I just received approval from the military council for your appointment to general of the army. It's quite an honor, especially at such a young age. You make Sparta proud, Achilles, and I'm glad you're on our side.

"Second, let's toast Paris. You have become a dear friend, and I have no doubt my time with you had a permanent effect on me."

"And you on me," my twin adds, clicking his glass against Menelaus's. "Now, let's move on to more important business. There are some new maidens here tonight. I assume your wife's ladies-in-waiting?"

Menelaus laughs, a deep-throated, infectious growl that reveals his sparkling white teeth. "They sure are. When my wife joins us, I'll have her introduce you."

"Where is she anyway?" Achilles asks. "I'm beginning to think you made her up."

"Oh, she's real and she's magnificent. Be nice, Achilles, or I'll tell her ladies-in-waiting to stay away from you. And trust me, those are maidens you want to know," Menelaus says, raising his eyebrows suggestively.

I'm certain he's hinting at their liaisons with women, and I have no interest in hearing the details. "I'm going to get some food."

Achilles nods. "I'll join you. I'm starving."

I make small talk on the way to the banquet table. "Congratulations on your promotion. What exactly do you do as general?"

"Same thing I did before: work hard and play harder," he says.

I chuckle and grab a bronze plate. It has Ares etched on its surface—just like everything else in Sparta. "Seriously. What are your responsibilities?"

Achilles starts down the opposite side of the buffet. "We have many enemies and never know when the next war is coming, so I train my troops extensively each day. Swordplay, archery, defensive tactics . . . you know, the usual." He jabs an imaginary sword across the table with his free hand, his arm muscles bulging.

I play along and duck to the side, causing my roll to fall off my plate onto the floor. "What about battle strategies? You train your troops on those too, right?"

He scrunches his forehead. "I lead the strongest army in all of Greece. We march in bravely and win, every time."

"I see," I reply, bending and picking up my bread.

When I straighten, he's staring at me. "Hector, if you have something to say, say it. Our society encourages healthy debate."

He asked for it. "I think your approach is one-dimensional. As a soldier, being strong is important. But it's equally important to think critically. If you understand your enemy's mind, you can figure out his weaknesses. That's the true key to winning any battle."

He builds a small hill of scallops on his plate. "It's an interesting point, but I'm not sure I agree. If you don't match your enemy's strength, you'll lose. Even if you know his weakness."

"Strength is important," I say. "But if you spend equal time teaching your troops to identify enemies' weaknesses, your army will be unstoppable."

Achilles thrusts out his chest. "And what happens if they don't have any weaknesses, like me?"

"Everyone has a weakness."

He doesn't respond. In fact, he's lost all interest in me, focused on something beyond my shoulder. I turn, searching for the cause.

Human sunlight—it's the best way to describe the woman who just entered. With each sashay, her wavy honey hair flutters back from her symmetrical tawny-colored face. And although her body is as thin as a willow tree, her white sheath's low neckline exposes a sizable, perky bosom.

To my right, Dameaon starts toward her like a wolf stalking its prey. But he's not the only one; he reaches her just as Menelaus does.

This isn't good.

I place my plate on the table and race toward them.

Menelaus is in the middle of introductions. "This is the man I was telling you about, the great and noble Prince Paris of Troy. Paris, this exquisite wonder is my wife, Queen Helen."

Helen kisses both of his cheeks. "It's a pleasure, Paris. My husband speaks of you like a brother," she purrs, her voice melodic and husky. "If there's anything I can do to make your stay more comfortable, let me know."

Dameaon flashes his most devious smile—no doubt ready to say something inappropriate—so I elbow him out of the way.

"Excuse the interruption," I say, "but I'd like to introduce myself. I'm Oracle Hector. It's a pleasure to meet you, Queen Helen."

Her eyes—the exact green as Menelaus's robes—lock on mine. She grasps my shoulders and kisses my cheeks lightly, wafting the sweet scent of honeysuckle around me. "It's an honor, Oracle. Truly."

She turns back to Menelaus, adjusting his lopsided gold crown in his scraggly mud-brown hair. He smiles at her warmly.

The band starts playing a slow song, and my twin flashes another devilish smirk, extending his palm. "Would you honor me with the first dance, Helen?"

Her rosy cheeks blush darker, and she places her dainty hand in his. I panic; this is a bad idea. A woman like this is easy to love—too easy. And according to Trojan gossip, my brother has made endless maidens fall for him.

Perhaps Menelaus realizes this too, because he lays his hand on top of theirs. "I'm afraid I can't allow that. I promised my wife I'd be her only dance partner for the rest of her life."

My twin's eyes darken, but he pulls his hand from the pile. "Of course. I'll find another dance partner. One who is more . . . available."

"Allow me to help you with that," Menelaus says, gesturing to a nearby teen. "Meet Acantha, Helen's most trusted lady-in-waiting."

Acantha curtsies in front of my brother, smiling shyly. With her black hair and alabaster skin, she would shine on any other night, but she's average next to Helen's beauty.

The king and queen head for the dance floor, and my twin and Acantha follow behind them. As Helen sways in her husband's arms, she steals glances at my brother through the crowd. Dameaon is far more obvious; he doesn't take his eyes off her.

Now—more than ever—I'm thankful we're leaving; there would be trouble if we stayed in Sparta.

FROM TWISTED ROOTS TO TWISTED ACTS

Curse my love for Spartan wine. Because of it, my head is pounding and most of last night is a blur.

I make a fist with my left hand and mutter, "Hura, hura, enray." My Crystal warms my body, healing my hangover. But even with my headache gone, my memories from last night are still vague. I remember joking around with Achilles, dancing with Acantha, and laughing with Menelaus. Only one thing stands out with shining clarity.

Helen. Even now, the thought of her fills me with warmth and desire. The instant I saw her, I felt as if we were connected by an invisible string. And when she looked at me, I know she felt it too.

But then Menelaus introduced her as his wife, and that brought on the heavy drinking.

My brother is right. We need to leave Sparta.

Forcing myself up, I splash cool water on my face. Then I throw on a scarlet robe and head to the dining hall.

Villow is already there, as are Helen and Menelaus—sitting at opposite ends of the table. I didn't believe it was possible, but Helen looks even more beautiful than last night. Her chocolate-colored robe accentuates her green eyes and tan skin, pulling me toward her.

One thing is certain—I can't go in there. With the bustle of the party, Menelaus didn't notice my attraction to his wife. In a group of four, I won't be so lucky.

I clear my throat, and they all turn to the doorway.

"I pray you to be well," I say, "but Hector and I must leave for the docks at once."

"Nonsense," Menelaus says. "Join us for a quick breakfast. If you're worried about time, we can take the chariot. Besides, you know the ship won't leave without you."

He's right of course; the captain has orders from the king to wait for us, and it won't set sail until we're on board.

Trapped, I enter the room and sit across from my twin. Villow hands me the bowl of grapes, raising his eyebrows in a hurry-up gesture. For once, we're of the same mind. I put two bunches on my plate, popping them into my mouth as fast as I can chew.

I risk stealing a glance at Helen; she smiles, and it takes all my strength not to caress her rosy cheek.

"I trust you slept well?" Menelaus asks.

"Hypnos himself blessed me last night," I say, thankful for the distraction. "Either that or it was the wine. What about you?"

He nods. "The sleep of the dead with my new bride beside me."

The thought of Helen lying against Menelaus appears

in my mind. To prevent myself from screaming, I clench my teeth—so fiercely my jaw erupts in pain.

"We should get moving," I say, putting my hands on the table and pushing to my feet. "I don't want to hold up the entire crew."

My twin stands. "That's thoughtful of you, Prince."

"It's too bad you cannot stay, even for a day," Helen says, placing her hand on top of mine. "I was so looking forward to getting to know you."

The skin she's touching is so warm, it's as if it's immersed in flames. I've never experienced a sensation like this, and I can't lose it. Not yet.

I turn to her husband. "Menelaus, what do you say to one more hunting trip, before we head for Troy?"

He smiles. "I would enjoy that very much, but I can't, in good faith, leave Helen alone on her first full day in Sparta."

"Nonsense. I'm so tired from my travels, I will probably sleep the whole day," she says, taking her hand off mine. "Spend time with your friends, and we can all have dinner together this evening."

Free from her touch, I can breathe again. I inhale sharply, and she smiles, as if she knows—and enjoys—her effect on me.

Menelaus moves around the table, standing next to Helen. "Not only are you fair, you are also understanding. I don't know what I did for the gods to bless me so." He kisses her—thankfully on the forehead.

"Paris, Hector, meet me at the stables as soon as you're done eating," he says, heading for the door. "Oh, and someone wake Achilles and see if he wants to come."

Villow rubs his neck. "Paris, your father needs you to return home. We cannot delay another moment."

"Might I remind you, I'm the prince of Troy, not you," I reply. "And as such, I say we can wait one more day."

He narrows his eyes. "You haven't been home in months, so how would you know?"

"This conversation is over, Hector," I say. "Make yourself useful and take a glass of orange juice to Achilles. He had too much to drink last night and could use something refreshing. He's in the guest room to the left of yours."

"It would be better if you did it," he says. "Achilles and I are practically strangers."

"Nonsense. You got to know him quite well in Troy." I point at the three remaining grapes on my plate. "Besides, I haven't finished my breakfast yet."

Villow looks at Helen and then at me; he wants to continue arguing, but anything he says will sound ridiculous. "Fine. I'll meet you outside in five minutes."

I hand him an empty glass. "Don't forget Achilles's orange juice."

His eyes darken, and he snatches it from me, filling it and then storming out.

Alone with Helen, I feel goose bumps rise on my skin. I won't waste a second, not when Villow will return any minute.

"So you and Menelaus, huh?" I say, offering her my warmest smile. "Seems a bit of an odd match to me."

She blinks rapidly—but then giggles, and it lights up the entire room. "You are quite bold to question my relationship with a man who calls you his brother. A man who is also a king, while you are just a prince."

"I will be a king soon enough," I say, pausing for a moment before continuing softly. "Perhaps too soon. According to Hector, my father is very sick."

She touches my hand again, and the burning sensation returns. "I'm sorry to hear that. Are you close?"

"I love him with all my heart."

"Love," she spits, pulling her hand back. "What is love, besides a lie we're taught to believe in from childhood?"

"Don't you love Menelaus? Or your parents, at least?"

"My parents saw me as a precious, beautiful jewel, whose only purpose was to make them look good," she says, lowering her head. "And I'm afraid my husband sees me the same way."

My heart aches for her; I know all too well how parents can shape our self-regard. "You're beautiful, Helen, but that's not what is most remarkable about you. In our short time together, it feels like I've found my home."

She offers me a sad smile. "You flatter me, Paris, with your lies."

"I would never lie to you," I say, leaning across the table and stroking her arm.

Her skin is soft and warm—just like I imagined. She locks eyes with mine, searching for something. Whatever it is, I hope she finds it.

"I wish you didn't need to leave tomorrow," she whispers. "I, too, feel at ease in your presence."

"Paris, I hate you," a voice says.

I remove my hand from Helen's arm and glance around. Achilles is in the doorway with his arms crossed.

Our conversation could sound bad, if it was taken the

wrong way. Okay, I'll be honest. Our conversation *was* bad, regardless of the context. How much did he overhear?

"Is that so?" I ask.

He nods, just slightly. "If you ever challenge me to a drinking contest again, remind me to say no. Is there any more orange juice?"

I laugh, but it comes out shaky. "Yes, of course. Come, join us." I pour him another glass.

He sits across from me, drinking the entire contents in two gulps. "Hector gave me strict orders to bring you to the stables. Are you ready?"

"You still look a bit green. Are you sure you want to go?"

"Nothing can keep me down. You know this."

He heads to the dining hall's entrance, and I follow him, turning back to Helen for a moment. "I know you plan on sleeping most of the day, but the palace's back gardens are best seen in the midmorning sun. Very secluded and private, if that's what you're looking for."

"Thank you, Prince Paris," she says. "I can think of no better way to spend my morning."

I smile at her and then join Achilles. We head to the stables, making small talk on the way. From his cheerful disposition, it's obvious he did not overhear Helen and me.

We join Menelaus and Villow, and the four of us ride our horses into the woods. Deep in the thicket, Menelaus dismounts and ties his horse to a nearby trunk, signaling for us to do the same. We walk a hundred feet, stopping near a clearing filled with wildflowers, grass, and a small stream.

"The deer often graze here," Menelaus whispers, removing his bow and quiver from his back.

We nock our arrows in our bows and crouch in the underbrush. As I hoped, a buck timidly enters the meadow a few minutes later. I aim and release, and a loud thunk implies a direct hit.

Sure enough, the bounding deer is now a motionless carcass. I head into the clearing to claim my kill, rolling my ankle and dropping to the mossy ground. Footsteps echo as my three comrades race toward me.

Villow reaches me first. "Are you okay?"

I wince, grasping my left ankle. "I hurt myself when I fell."

"Use your Crystal. Quickly."

"I can't. It's out of juice."

He raises his eyebrows. "What do you mean it's out of juice? How is that possible, unless you're abusing it?"

"Shh," I hiss. "They're coming."

"What happened?" Achilles asks, kneeling next to me.

"I tripped over a tree root," I say.

Menelaus squats and touches my ankle. "It's a bit swollen. Can you stand?"

"Let's see," I say, getting to my feet and cringing in pain.

The king grabs my waist, supporting me. "We need to get you to the doctor."

I lean against him. "While I appreciate your concern, I'd feel a lot better if you stayed and enjoyed the day. I'm sure my ankle will be fine, although I can't say the same for my pride."

"You are a brave soul," Menelaus says. "Come . . . at least let me get you to your horse."

He acts as a crutch, helping me to the thicket where my horse is tied.

Achilles boosts me onto its back. "Are you certain you don't want me to come?"

Villow is behind his right shoulder, glaring at me with suspicion in his eyes. I need to make sure he stays busy. "I rather you stay with Hector and show him a good time."

Achilles nods. "Okay, but see the doctor first thing. I can tell you from experience, ankle injuries are serious."

I agree, riding into the thicket until I'm out of sight. Then I embrace my Crystal, feeling its warmth surround me and heal my leg.

I have more exciting plans this morning than spending time with the palace doctor.

Reaching Sparta's palace within fifteen minutes, I leave my horse with the stable hand and head for the back gardens. As I approach, my palms begin sweating, and I feel a bit light-headed.

Did Helen understand what I was trying to tell her? And if so, will she be there?

I emerge through a grove of olive trees to a small courtyard in the middle of the garden. Helen is here—poised on a marble bench—and my heart flutters.

At that instant, the sun's rays burst through the clouds, encasing her in a warm glow. Her golden hair shines brighter, making her look like a goddess come to life.

"I pray you to be well, Helen," I say, stepping into view. "May I join you for a while?"

If she's surprised to see me, she doesn't show it. She gestures to the bench, and I sit next to her. "That was a very short hunt. Are the others back too?"

"No," I say. "An injury sent me back early."

She clutches her heart. "Are you hurt?"

I lock eyes with hers, and my entire body ignites with fire, but I can't look away. "No, I'm suddenly feeling much better."

Out of nowhere, a tiny black figure bounds between us, landing on the bench with a sharp *bah*.

"Hey, Butthead," I say, petting his tuft of white fur. "It's nice to see you too."

And I'm grateful you're here, I add in my head. Now that he's broken the connection I have with Helen, I can think clearly again. And I don't like what I'm doing—hitting on my good friend's wife.

I stand, walking a few paces away; there's safety in distance.

"Maybe someday you can visit Troy," I say. "The palace is smaller, but the gardens are just as beautiful. If not more so. Isn't that right, Aegidius?"

In response, he eats the flowers off a nearby alfalfa.

"That's goat for 'I agree,'" Helen says, and he bounces over to her. She pets his head. "Hello, little one. You are quite handsome, aren't you? You and I will become very good friends, I expect."

"That, unfortunately, is not in your future. Aegidius is my long-time companion and will leave with me tomorrow."

"Ah. Then I suppose I will miss you both."

Unsure if she's teasing me or not, I examine her face. Her eyes are shining, as if she's ready to cry.

"I'm certain you will forget us quickly," I say. "The palace is full of humans and animals alike who will want to spend time with you."

"I suppose," she says. "Although I'm looking forward to the time with the animals more than the humans."

I tilt my head. "Really?"

"I grew up on a farm with very few neighbors, so the animals were my friends. The horses and I went on adventures together. I shared my deepest secrets with the goats. And my father's dog went everywhere with me, protecting me from any harm. Because of that, I'm better at relating to animals, even if they don't speak our language."

Cinders and Kitsune flash before my eyes; I, too, found friendships with animals easier than ones with my peers.

"I wish I would have met you first," I blurt out, covering my mouth with my hands. I want to take it back, but it's too late.

She slowly rises to her feet. "What did you just say?"

I pace on the grass in front of her. "Forget it, please. It should have remained unsaid."

"But it *was* said. What did you mean by it?"

"I just . . . It's . . . Well, I wish I would have met you before Menelaus did. Before you were married."

"Oh, Paris, how I wish that too," she says. "But although it is a marriage of convenience, it is still a marriage and cannot be undone."

Her words cut me like sharp knives. "Do you love him?"

"What?" she whispers.

"Do you love him?" I ask, moving a few inches away from her.

"I-I barely know him," she says, staring at my chest.

"He is a gentle man and a wonderful friend," I say. "You could do much worse. I am half as good as he is."

"You are half as old too," she says, but then looks down. "That was unkind. I shouldn't have said it."

"The truth is often unkind," I say, shrugging. "He's at least ten years older than you. Makes for an unsuited match."

"Not according to my parents. A king was too favorable a match to deny. And you're right. He is a good man. He agreed to wait until I'm ready . . . to make our marriage bed."

A slow smile spreads across my face. Helen is my friend's wife, and I should want their marriage to be happy—in all ways—but that news fills me with relief.

As far as I'm concerned, until they consummate their marriage, my flirtation with Helen is not forbidden. Not completely. I haven't crossed a line. Not yet. And I won't.

But that doesn't mean I can't spend a little more time with her.

I offer her my arm. "Come, let's wander the gardens. We shouldn't waste our only afternoon together."

She pauses for a moment and then clutches my elbow. It fits perfectly, as if it's always belonged there.

HOMEWARD BOUND

THE LAST FOUR HOURS HAVE BEEN THE SLOWEST OF MY LIFE. After Dameaon claimed he tripped over a tree root, I surveyed the surrounding ground, confirming what I already knew; there wasn't a root in sight, and he was looking for an excuse to leave. And after seeing him with Helen this morning, I'm certain she is the reason why.

He has to be with her.

I contemplated faking my own injury, but it would have been too obvious. Plus, how much damage could my twin really do in one morning? Regardless, returning to the palace as quickly as possible still seemed like the best option.

When I suggested it, Menelaus and Achilles agreed, just as soon as they each captured a deer. Achilles felled one within an hour, but Menelaus proved a surprisingly bad shot for a royal. So here we are, hours later, still crouched in the thicket. Every time a deer appears, I launch a haphazard arrow, sometimes missing the meadow altogether.

It takes another hour before Menelaus successfully shoots his prey and takes pity on me, conceding to return to the palace. I ride at a full gallop and arrive at the stables long before Menelaus and Achilles.

After handing my horse's reins to the stable hand, I search for my brother. I start in the front courtyard, moving to his bedroom, and then the dining hall, followed by the gardens. With each empty spot, my anxiety rises. Especially since Helen is also missing. To keep from hyperventilating, I remind myself she planned on sleeping all day and is probably in her own quarters.

Once I've exhausted my search—visiting every location I can think of—I head to my room. My insides are quivering, and I need to lie down in the dark to organize my thoughts.

I throw open my door and step inside, closing it behind me. I shut my eyes, breathing in deeply to calm my nerves.

"About time you got back," Dameaon says. "I thought you got mauled by a lion."

He's sprawled out on my mattress, his left ankle elevated by a pillow. I rush to the bed, relieved to see him—alone. "What are you doing here?"

"Isn't it obvious? Resting."

I sigh. "Why are you in my room?"

He props up on his elbows. "Your bed is more comfortable than mine."

"I'm sure that's not true. And I'm also sure there weren't any tree roots where you fell."

"Maybe you didn't look hard enough."

"I did a thorough search. There was nothing to trip over."'

"If you say so," he says. "Oh, how I missed your condescending attitude. It must be exhausting, being an expert on everything."

"I'm going to pretend that was the pain talking, for both our sakes. How is your ankle, anyway?"

He stretches out his leg and rotates his foot clockwise. "Much better, thanks to a day of rest. It'll be fine by tomorrow morning."

The shutters are closed, so the light is limited to the oil lamp on my nightstand, but it does look better. "Were you serious when you said your Crystal is out of juice?"

He shrugs. "Why would I lie about that?"

"I don't understand how that's possible. You should have had enough Magic to last the entire year."

"They don't hold as much Magic as you think. Yours is probably almost out too. But it doesn't matter, since we'll be back on Reos soon."

"Reos?" I ask.

"Didn't you want to go back to Reos?"

I perch on the edge of the mattress. "Yes. I just thought it would be a fight after meeting Helen. It's . . . unexpected. I keep forgetting you've grown."

"What do you mean?"

"Guidance duty has changed you. You've become more . . . like a true Glanching. Thinking about the good of all instead of yourself. It's a welcome change."

He scrunches his forehead. "Is that supposed to be a compliment?"

"Y-Y-Yes."

"Well, it's not," he says, twisting away from me and facing the wall. "I'm still the same, brother. And, contrary to your opinion, that's not a bad thing."

I clench my jaw; we were making progress, and I messed it up. "You're right. I'm sorry. I really was trying to compliment you, but it came out wrong."

My twin continues staring at the wall, so I try another tactic. "I'm supposed to meet Achilles and Menelaus for a drink in the gardens. Why don't you come?" He remains motionless, pretending he can't hear me. I don't have time to play his childish games, not with our friends waiting. "Okay, fine, stay mad. I'll check on you later."

I head to the gardens, where Menelaus, Helen, and Achilles are already drinking.

Achilles smiles. "We thought we lost you, Hector. You took off quicker than a defeated army."

"Sorry, I was worried about Paris," I say.

Helen blushes at the sound of his name, and I'm suddenly glad he decided to sulk in my room.

"Is he all right?" Menelaus asks, handing me a glass of wine.

He's changed out of his hunting chiton and into a navy one, with a silver crown on his head. He looks extremely regal.

And old.

Menelaus is at least thirty, while Helen is eighteen at most.

"Yes. He's resting his ankle so we can leave tomorrow," I say.

Menelaus furrows his brow. "I was hoping you would stay a few more days."

I shake my head. "Unfortunately, we need to get back. As I said, Paris must see his father as soon as possible."

"Understood," he says. "It's time for Paris to ascend to his rightful place and serve his people."

Achilles raises his half-empty glass. "That's why I'm so blessed. I hang out with royals, but I'm not royalty myself. That means fun can be the most important thing in my life."

"I'll drink to that," Helen agrees, clanging her glass against his.

Menelaus drapes his arm around her waist. "That isn't the mindset the new queen of Sparta should have. You are responsible for an entire city now, and that should be your main focus. Speaking of, it would be a shame for Hector to head back to Troy without experiencing our fair city. Why don't we all take a tour right now?"

"I'd enjoy that," I say.

Helen places her hand on his chest. "Do you mind if I pass? I'm still tired from the journey here. Besides, I have the rest of my life to meet your people."

"Our people," Menelaus corrects. "You are their queen. And the sooner you meet them, the better."

She narrows her eyes, but then seems to catch herself, and smiles. "Let me have one more day's rest, and I'll spend the rest of my life living for them."

"I don't want to leave you by yourself again," he says, stroking her cheek. "You were alone all day."

Menelaus isn't the only one against that idea—not

after she blushed at the sound of Paris's name. I rack my brain for an excuse for why I can't go—especially since I just said yes.

Achilles frowns at his empty cup, and the solution comes to me. I hand him my barely touched drink. "I'm sure Achilles wouldn't mind staying here, to keep her company."

She clings to his arm. "What a wonderful idea. It'll give me a chance to get to know your general."

"Is that okay with you?" Menelaus asks Achilles, who nods. He continues, "It's a perfect solution, then. Let's head out before we lose the light, Hector."

I nod, and he kisses Helen's forehead. "I promise to be back by dinner."

We make a quick stop for horses and head west through the rolling meadows to the expansive fields surrounding Sparta. Their crops thrive from the fertile soil, and I can't imagine anyone going hungry with their bountiful harvests. Yet the farmers are ashen and gaunt, like they haven't eaten in days.

I pull on my mare's reins, halting her. "Your crops are quite prosperous. So why do your farmers look so haggard?"

He stops next to me. "Sparta doesn't have the sea and walls surrounding it like Troy. We're besieged by cities on all sides who would love nothing more than to capture our rich farmlands. I worry Troy may face a similar problem soon, after what you told me last night. If their crops become as fruitful as ours, your neighboring cities may try to seize them too."

I point at the half-starved men. "I appreciate what

you're saying, but you didn't answer my question. If your crops are so bountiful, why are they so frail?"

"We've fought many wars protecting our land," he says. "These men are the prisoners."

A hollow-eyed, skeletal man strains to lift his pick several feet and drops it, barely making a dent in the soil. He's so emaciated, I'm afraid he'll collapse any second.

"No man should have to live like this. They deserve to be free."

He shakes his head. "I didn't choose this for them, Hector. I've never initiated a single war, and I don't plan to. But when someone declares war on my city, what would you have me do? Not fight back? Surrender? Let the surviving men go free so they can band with our other enemies and attack again?"

"But you've taken everything from them. Including their pride. Surely there must be another way—"

"Yes, there is. I could kill them," he says. "But I'm not an immortal, and I don't have the right to kill unarmed men. As king, sometimes the best choice is still horrific. These men are a reminder of the cost of war with Sparta. They prevent future battles, saving lives."

I want to argue that kindness and compassion always win. That if he let the men return home, they'd be so grateful they wouldn't dream of attacking again. That they'd see his mercy as strength and respect Sparta for it.

But what if he's right and they do see it as weakness? What if they join with Sparta's other adversaries and attack again? Is the possibility of their rehabilitation worth the risk of his own people's lives? Would I take that chance if I were in his place?

"I'm glad it isn't my decision."

"I've had many sleepless nights because of it," he says. "It's difficult to be responsible for others and put their needs before your own. But it's a blessing from the gods to be king, and I never forget that. Now come. I still have much to show you."

We travel past the remaining fields and enter Sparta. There are rows of two-story houses made of stone and mud, and every Spartan is dressed in a silk chiton or robe and adorned with gold jewelry. "Where is the commoner part of the city?"

"There are no classes in Sparta. All capable men join the army, which makes everyone equal," he says. "Come. It's easier to illustrate it."

He leads me to a series of small barracks in the middle of the city. "Boys start their training at five years old, living here until they turn sixteen. Then they join the army, serving for at least ten years."

I dismount and wander around. To my left, young boys are engaged in an intense game of field hockey that makes the Trojan matches look tame. A group of teenagers straight ahead of me are sparring with dulled bronze swords. A nimble boy whaps his opponent's shield, shattering his brittle blade. On the far side of the camp, boys around ten are shooting arrows at targets, hitting bull's-eye after bull's-eye.

"They don't do anything half-heartedly, do they?" I ask.

Menelaus shakes his head. "Of course not. It's an honor to protect Sparta's freedom and their families."

Two teenage boys walk by us, holding hands. The taller one leans over and kisses his companion on the lips.

"Are they . . . together?"

He nods. "Yes. Sparta encourages its young men to explore all aspects of their lives while they can. Eventually, they will take wives and leave that lifestyle behind, but for now, they are free to date who they please."

My thoughts drift to Nicholas and Oedipus. Their lives would have been so much easier here—where they could have been open about their relationship. At least until they had to marry. Then they would have been ripped apart—just like in Troy. I never fully appreciated Reos's view of relationships, allowing any two adult Glanchings—regardless of gender—to marry. Of course, new Glanchings are created by the Oldungur Council, while Sparta and Troy depend on children to succeed and grow. It's no wonder they don't support same-sex marriages, regardless of how unfair it is. Still, perhaps I can influence Menelaus to be more progressive.

"Have you ever consi—"

A piercing wail explodes from a nearby barracks, interrupting me.

I dash toward the noise, Menelaus yelling to stop behind me.

Inside the building is the most horrific spectacle I have ever encountered. Boys no older than seven are strapped to poles while grown men flog their bare backs with leather whips, creating zigzags of bloody cuts and bruises.

I catch one of the boy's eyes; his fear and pain is so intense that I almost throw up. My fingers prickle, and it takes all my strength not to launch icicles at the men. Instead, I run outside, retching until my sides hurt. Sensing I'm not alone, I turn and face Menelaus.

"Did you know about that?" I scream. "You need to stop them. It's barbaric."

"No, it's humane," he says. "You've never been to war, have you? No . . . I know you haven't, because if you had, you wouldn't think this needs to stop. Our troops must learn how to block out pain to prepare for the harshness of battle. Sending them off to combat ill-prepared . . . that's barbaric."

"But they're only children! How can you allow them to harm precious children?"

He grasps my shoulder roughly. "Hector, stop. Just because something goes against your inclination of what is right doesn't mean it's wrong. I live in a different world than yours. I don't choose battle for my people, but I do prepare them for the lives they're forced into."

I jerk my shoulder back to remove his hand. "I will never understand the abuse of children, and you won't convince me otherwise. I want to go back to the palace. Now."

"As you wish. But answer this, Oracle. If our training methods are so wrong, why does Ares support us?"

I can't tell him Ares doesn't exist, so I use the gods to deliver a message. "You've brought the underworld to Earth, and you will pay for that someday. The gods will take notice. Mark my words."

I return to my horse and gallop back to the palace. The stable hand takes her just as Menelaus arrives. He calls to me, but I ignore him.

Even though it's early evening, I just want the day to be over. I head for my quarters and find Dameaon fast asleep in my bed. The last thing I need is another argument, so I retire to his room.

I can't wait until morning so I can leave the terrors of Sparta on their shore.

As our chariot barrels along, I stare out at the flat plains. They're just as boring as when we arrived, but it's still a distraction from the awkward silence inside our basket.

As we near the docks, Dameaon finally speaks. "Helen wasn't able to join us?"

Menelaus shakes his head. "She wanted to, Paris, but she isn't a morning person. And she said goodbyes are hard for her."

My twin slumps his shoulders but says nothing else, and we arrive at the harbor moments later. I stand apart from my companions and watch the passengers board our Trojan vessel, *Trireme*.

An old man in loose brown robes hobbles down the dock with the help of his cane. His hood is pulled over his head to block out the sea's icy breeze.

Fascinating. Besides the threat of storms, traveling on a ship is hard on even the hardiest of men, so the elderly rarely attempt it. But perhaps he's from Troy and desperate to see his family one more time before he dies.

Drawing strength from his imaginary bravery, I rejoin my companions. I don't want to leave without a proper goodbye, even if I am troubled by Menelaus's ruling methods.

"Don't slack off on sword practice, Achilles," Dameaon says, clasping hands with him. "We'll have a rematch next time you're in Troy."

Achilles hugs him warmly. "Looking forward to it. I'll miss you, Paris. And you too, Aegidius," he says, bending to scratch the small goat's chin.

My twin embraces Menelaus. "You've been so gracious. Thank you for everything, and I'm sorry."

Menelaus pulls away. "Sorry? What are you sorry for?"

"To cut my time short with you," he says, shrugging. "I promised to stay until spring."

"You're doing what's best for your family and Troy. Never apologize for that," he says, squeezing my brother's shoulder affectionately. "Become the king I know you can be."

Dameaon's eyes moisten, and he pauses—just for a moment. Then he charges toward *Trireme*, Aegidius jumping at his heels.

It's my turn to say goodbye, and it hits me. This is it. A *real* goodbye. When I left Reos, I said farewell to loved ones, but I knew I would see them again. And even though I said goodbye to some of the Trojans when I set sail for Sparta, I never truly thought Dameaon would agree to head to Reos, and I would return to the walled city. But this time is different. I am absolutely certain I will never see Achilles or Menelaus again.

Suddenly, this send-off weighs heavily on my limbs. It takes all my strength to move forward and embrace Achilles.

"We've come a long way from our first meeting when

you tried to get rid of me," I say. "Now, I would like to think we're friends. Remember what we talked about. Train your troops' bodies *and* minds."

"You're a good man, Hector. I look forward to the next time we meet," he says, punching my arm lightly. "Put in a good word for me with the gods."

"I will," I promise, turning to Menelaus. I spent two days with him, but in that time I grew to respect him very much. That is, until the horrors I witnessed in his barracks.

He offers me a weak smile. "Oracle, I've enjoyed our time together. Even if we don't agree on *certain* things."

"You are a good man, Menelaus," I say. "But you are a man, and that means you have flaws. Reevaluate your decisions and don't put your people in intolerable situations for no reason."

He shakes his head, as if he's disappointed in me. "I have never harmed my people unnecessarily. Everything I do is for them. A friendly warning for you: Life has a strange way of presenting situations to help us grow when we're too stubborn to do it otherwise. You don't know what you're capable of until you have to make a decision from only bad choices."

"If any experience ever makes me support your treatment of children, may the immortals strike me dead."

He flashes a melancholy grin. "Fair enough. Farewell, Oracle."

I start toward the ship, but I don't want to leave. Not like this. I turn around and hug Menelaus.

"Be the king that Sparta deserves," I whisper and release him.

He nods, and I head down the dock and board *Trireme*. My twin is on the deck, watching Sparta's dock with slouched shoulders. This is hard for me, but I can't imagine how he feels. Achilles is his best friend, and he is also close with Menelaus. Truthfully, I've never seen my twin bond with anyone—besides animals—and he must be consumed by loss.

I pat his shoulder. "Jetta warned us saying goodbye would be hard. But remember, it's part of being a Guide."

My twin walks away, Aegidius hopping behind him. Once again, my attempt to be a real brother is met with his dismissal. He makes me want to scream, but the crew would think I went mad if I did. Instead, I take several deep breaths, inhaling the cold, salty air.

We sail out to the open sea, and I watch the harbor shrink to a small dot. It recedes from view, and eventually, the entire coast disappears. The breeze forms small ripples on the infinite water, lulling me into a calm hypnotic state. Even though it's early afternoon, I am ready to retire to my room.

"Excuse me, can you show me which quarters are mine?" I ask a nearby sailor.

"Yes, Oracle, of course," he says, leading me to a small windowless cabin belowdecks. He leaves his dimly lit oil lamp on the nightstand. "Is there anything else I can do for you?"

I nod. "Which room is Prince Paris's?"

"The last door on the left," he says. "I'm returning to the deck if you need further assistance."

I thank him and retire to the bed. I learned from my travel to Sparta that the more you sleep, the better.

Content our Guidance duty is back on track, I shut my eyes.

INTENSE SEESAWING WAKES ME FROM MY SLUMBER. I TURN THE lamp's knob up, illuminating the room. It's rocking back and forth, confirming the swells are gigantic.

When Dameaon and I were seven, our family visited the Abyssal Sea. When we ventured out on a boat, my brother became seasick—and that was on completely calm water. This must be torturous for him.

Lamp in hand, I head for his quarters. The ship is still teeter-tottering, so I lean against the wall to keep my balance. When no one answers my soft knock, I crack the door, just in case he's sleeping through this.

His room is empty, but something on the edge of the rumpled bed catches my eye; it's the brown robe the old man was wearing. And his cane is resting against the chair. The sailor must have been wrong about which room was my brother's.

Bang!

I jump and turn around. Thankfully, it was just the door slamming behind me from an especially large pitch. Still, I better get out of here before I'm caught in a stranger's quarters.

Just as I reach the door, the knob turns. I duck behind the bed, peeking around the corner. But there's no need to hide; it's only my twin.

I breathe out deeply. "You scared me. I thought I was in the wrong room." I hold up the brown robe. "Where did you get this?"

He lunges forward, as if he was shoved from behind. "Hector, what are you doing here?"

I stand slowly. "What's going on?"

In response, he steps to the left.

I gasp. Behind him is someone I never thought I'd see again. Someone who shouldn't be here. Someone who belongs in Sparta, on the arm of Menelaus.

"Hello, Hector," Helen says.

I look at the robe still clutched in my hands, and it suddenly makes sense; the old man at the dock was her in disguise. "Leave us. I need to speak with Paris."

Her chin trembles, but she follows my instruction.

Alone, Dameaon waves his hand dismissively. "I don't want to hear it, brother. I know what you're thinking and—"

"You couldn't possibly know what I'm thinking," I say. "You've done some selfish things, but this is the worst. How did you pull this off? More importantly, why?"

"You wouldn't understand," he says, pacing in the small cabin. "You never understand. But how could you? You're too busy judging everyone else to live your own life."

"That's not true. I live my life . . . I just don't wreak havoc along the way."

He sits on the edge of the bed. "Do you think I wanted this to happen? I couldn't help it. My life changed the instant I saw Helen. I'm not lonely anymore. And she feels the same way about me."

"She's married to one of our friends."

"She deserves more than Menelaus. He treats her like his possession, not as his equal."

"If that's true, I pity her. But it's not our problem. What will she do when we fall overboard and pretend to drown? Where will she go?"

"This changes things. We will return to Troy."

My anger floods back. "Our work is done there. We need to return to Reos."

He crosses his arms. "If you're ready to go back, feel free. I'm staying."

"You know I can't go back without you. While you were off in Sparta having fun, I spent three months helping the Trojans. They've changed for the better. And now, with one foolish decision, you're destroying everything. What do you think Menelaus will do when he finds out where Helen went? Sparta will declare war on Troy. And Troy will lose. Do you know what they do to remaining men after war? They enslave them."

My twin twists the gargoyle ring on his finger. "Menelaus is weak. He'll let her go. But if he doesn't, I won't give her up . . . even if it means war."

"Okay, then consider this," I say. "Do you really believe the Oldungur Council will forgive you for having a relationship with a human? You know it's in direct violation of Guidance Rule number six."

"First, I've learned the Oldungur Council is a bit flexible with the Rules. If they weren't, we wouldn't still be on Earth. Second, Helen is a Spartan, and our trial is to help the Trojans. A relationship with her falls into the gray zone. And, as you know, that is my favorite place to dwell."

Suddenly, I feel very stupid. After he showed mercy to Oedipus, I actually believed there was hope for him.

"You made a fool of me. I believed you changed, but you haven't," I spit. "You're still the same selfish Glanching you've always been."

"Say whatever you want. It doesn't matter. Not anymore, now that I have Helen." He stands. "You can't stop me, brother. Not this time."

He leaves the cabin, and I take his seat on the edge of the bed, overwhelmed by this turn of events. How could Dameaon justify breaking up a marriage? He knows how important it is—it's in the Glanching Code of Conduct. But then, maybe he's more like my father than I ever saw. Neither one seems to believe that specific Rule applies to them.

I know one thing; my brother is wrong. Menelaus won't give Helen up without a fight. With one selfish act, he has changed the course of Troy's future. And mine. If Troy falls, we will not pass our trial, and I will be banished to Rehuido.

That means Troy *cannot* fall.

As of this moment, I'm done letting things happen *to* me, especially when my twin is the cause. The Trojans deserve more in their Guide. I deserve more as a Glanching. I'll find a way to convince Dameaon to give Helen back. I'll figure out how to have Menelaus show us mercy. I will save the city I love.

And if I fail, at least I will go down fighting.

LIES IN THE NAME OF LOVE

A SWIFT, LOUD KNOCK AWAKENS ME. I UNTANGLE MY LIMBS from Helen's and stumble across the ship's cabin, opening the door a crack. My twin's disapproving scowl stares back at me—never a pleasant image—made even worse first thing in the morning.

"What?" I say.

"We're docked in Troy," he says. "Hesiod is on the deck. I suggest you head up and inform him how you're single-handedly destroying Troy. Unless you want me to tell him."

The last thing I need is one of the Elders hearing my brother's skewed version of the events. "I'll be right up," I say, slamming the door in his face.

Helen sits up in bed, her curls falling around her shoulders. I lean over, kissing her on the lips. "Welcome home."

"Home," she says, hugging her knees against her chest. "This is my home now, isn't it? Unless . . . What if your parents don't like me? What if they send me back to Sparta?"

We've had this conversation at least a dozen times over the last week, but I can't blame her for being nervous. She left behind a secure future for an uncertain one with me—all in the name of love.

"I've already told you, my parents adore me and want me to be happy," I say, sitting on the bed. "Besides, I can be incredibly persuasive."

Helen shakes her head. "If I stay with you, Sparta and Troy will no longer be allies. How can they support us?"

"Let me worry about that," I say, embracing her. "I promised I would take care of you, and I will."

"I'm sorry. I'm just so nervous. This is all I've ever wanted," she whispers into my chest. "Someone to take care of me. To love me."

"And now you have it." I release her and stand. "I need to head up to the deck and explain things to Hesiod before Hector does. Why don't you meet me up there in a few minutes?"

She gets out of bed, smoothing her wrinkled cobalt chiton. "No matter what else happens today, at the very least we can change our clothes. I've never worn the same thing for a week straight."

"It looks amazing on you," I say, kissing her again before leaving.

Up on the dock, Villow is standing with Hesiod and Pavlos. Hesiod's arms are crossed, and he's tapping his foot—no doubt because my twin already filled him in.

I join them, and their conversation ends abruptly. "I

don't know what Hector told you, but you need to let me explain."

Hesiod shakes his head. "We will deal with this . . . abduction situation later. Right now—"

"It's not an abduction, Hesiod," I say. "Helen is here because she wants to be."

"And I'm here to bring you to the palace," Hesiod says. "Your father is very ill. Honestly, I believe he's only held on this long in hopes of saying goodbye to you."

My throat and lungs ache with unshed tears. Villow said Priam was sick, but I didn't know it was this bad.

"Okay, let me tell Helen and—"

Hesiod looks down at his sandals. "He could pass at any moment, Paris. We cannot delay an instant longer."

"All right, I'm coming," I say, looking at Villow. He will try something foolish while I'm with Priam, if I don't stop him. "Hector, you must come with us. My father will want you there."

I turn to Pavlos. "Helen is in my room below. Take her to my palace quarters and don't let anyone speak to her until I arrive."

"Of course, Prince," he says.

With Helen in Pavlos's capable hands, I race down the docks to the palace and into the royals' wing. As always, a guard is stationed at Priam's bedroom door.

"Prince, thank the gods you have returned," he says. "I will announce your arrival."

"There's no time for such formalities," I say, pushing past him and inside.

The putrid stench of rotting meat invades my nostrils,

and any doubts about Priam's health disappear; he's dying.

The once-strong king of Troy is now a small mound under the blankets in his bed. Hecuba is sitting on the mattress next to him, stroking his hair.

"Father," I say, rushing to the bed and kneeling beside him.

"P-Paris?" he asks hoarsely. "Paris, is it really you?"

Despite her tears, Hecuba manages to offer me a smile. "Priam, it is your son. I told you he would make it home."

He struggles to lift his head, and Hecuba places a pillow behind his neck. With Priam now propped up, his ashen complexion and sunken cheekbones are even more pronounced.

"You are home," Priam says.

"I am so sorry, Father," I choke out. "I never should have left. Maybe if I stayed, I could have done something."

"Nonsense . . . It is my time, son. Thank the gods . . . I can say goodbye and I will die . . . knowing Troy is safe."

He squirms, managing to free his arms from the three layers of blankets, taking his wife's hand in his left one. "Hecuba . . . I love you. You have . . . been the best wife and queen for our people. Thank you, my love."

She kisses his hand, her tears streaming down her cheeks. "I love you too, Priam. And if the gods have mercy, we will be together again in the paradise of Elysium."

Priam grasps my hand in his right one, and I cringe; he's ice-cold, as if he's already dead. "And Paris, I was . . . so disappointed when you left to be a shepherd. But it . . . was for the best. You came back from Mount Ida . . .

changed. The time we spent . . . after that was the best we had together. I love you . . . for who you are . . . and who you will become."

I swallow twice, forcing my sobs back down my throat. I cannot break down—not now when he needs me to be strong. "I don't know what I did to deserve you as a father, but I am so grateful for the time we had. You have changed me forever and made me a better man."

He squeezes my hand. "I hope . . . in time, you find someone to share your life."

His words bring Helen to mind. She must be in my quarters by now. "I already have, Father. I returned with someone I love very much."

He pats my hand. "That's . . . wonder . . . ful, Paris. Love . . . her with . . . all your heart. It is the . . . greatest gift we have."

"I cannot wait for you to meet her. And we'll marry right away, so you can be there." I stand. "Let me go get—"

"There . . . is no time for that," he says, his voice no louder than a whisper. "Treat her . . . well, son. Love her . . . with all you are. Promise me."

I kneel again, kissing his forehead. "I promise, Father."

He smiles and then sucks in an uneven gasp. His hand slackens in mine, and his dull gaze points at the ceiling.

"Father?"

Queen Hecuba shakes her head. "He is gone, Paris." She looks at Priam's face and touches his cheek. "He is . . . gone," she repeats, collapsing on his chest.

He's gone. I stand and take three steps backward. My entire body is chilled in an instant, as if I'm the one who died. Tears form in my eyes, and my chin trembles. Priam was more of a father to me than Lord Drasko ever was, and now he's gone.

A hand squeezes my left shoulder, offering comfort. It's Villow, who has joined me next to Priam's bedside.

"Are you all right?" he asks.

"No," I say. "He can't be gone. I need more time with him."

"I know," my twin says. "But your return brought him peace. He knows you'll do anything to keep Troy safe. Even if it requires personal sacrifice."

His message is clear—he expects me to give Helen up. And he's probably right. It certainly would be the smart decision. But I can't lose her, not after losing Priam.

Pulling out of his grasp, I address the guard near the door. "Assemble the Elders at once."

THE THRONE ROOM SEEMS SMALLER AFTER RETURNING FROM Sparta. Or maybe it's just because the walls are closing in on me, now that Troy is my responsibility.

The Elders are already around the table. I join them, sitting in the head chair. Priam's chair.

I never wanted to be king, but now, I have no choice; it's the only way to keep Helen. Which means I need to convince the Elders her abdication was justified.

"What is the urgency, Paris?" Pelagios says. "We must notify Troy of your father's passing and plan his burial."

I steeple my hands. "I will let you get to your duties soon, but this cannot wait. I have returned from Sparta ready to be Troy's king. And there is reason to celebrate. I've brought home the woman I will make my queen."

"A Spartan royal?" Lycus asks, his eyes shining. "That would be advantageous for Troy."

Thaddaeus leans forward in his chair. "Is it Menelaus's sister?"

"Far from it," Hesiod says. "He has stolen Menelaus's bride."

The gasps around the table are audible. Seleucus slams the table with his fists. "You cannot be that foolish. Stealing the king of Sparta's wife? That would send you straight to the underworld."

"I did not steal her; she came willingly," I say. "And Menelaus and Helen never consummated their marriage, so I would argue it's nulled."

"Prince, you know very well that doesn't null their marriage," Deiphobus says.

I cross my arms. "I will remind you that I am king now, Deiphobus, and should be addressed as such."

Thaddaeus shakes his head. "Paris, you must send Helen back. We cannot go to war with Sparta."

"Let me handle Sparta," I say. "Menelaus sees her as a possession. He will let her go for a large amount of gold and riches."

"Even if that is true, the gods will punish Troy for this," Hesiod says. "You cannot take another man's wife. Especially a king's."

The mention of the immortals gives me an idea. "Menelaus is not who you believe. He is an abusive husband and tyrant ruler, who uses his power to enslave men. They work in the fields fifteen hours a day and are whipped if they stop. He leads the Spartan army into neighboring cities, murdering their citizens. I don't believe the gods would look favorably on us for turning a blind eye to his behavior."

Deiphobus nods his head; he always wants to believe the worst about everyone. "When I visited Sparta last year, I felt there was something a bit off about him."

Hesiod presses his fingers against his closed eyes. "I want to do what's right, Paris, but how can we stand up to Sparta?"

I stand. "Deiphobus will travel to Sparta with gold and jewels in an attempt to negotiate an exchange with Menelaus. At the same time, we will assemble an army, in case Deiphobus's negotiation skills are as weak as I fear they are. Sparta's power grows each day. It is only a matter of time before they attack us, with or without Helen."

Deiphobus shrinks in his chair. "What will stop Menelaus from murdering me as soon as I set foot on his soil?"

"We are saving Helen from Menelaus's abuse," I say. "The gods will protect you."

"As you wish," he says, but his voice is unsteady.

"It is my wish, yes," I say. "Are we united on this strategy?"

The Elders mumble half-hearted words of agreement, but it's the best I can expect given the circumstances. "It is decided then. Deiphobus, you will leave for Sparta at once. Thaddaeus and Seleucus, you are in charge of Priam's funeral. Hesiod, lead the effort to assemble and train our army. And Lycus and Pelagios, you can work with Hecuba to plan my marriage to Helen. I'll leave you to get started."

They all remain sitting—probably confused about how they agreed to this plan.

I rush out of the room before they can recover and argue with me. Besides, Helen is waiting.

My arm is quivering. My twin towers above me, shaking me awake. Which is astonishing, since I banned him from the palace four weeks ago. I raise a finger to my lips and roll Helen off my chest. Slipping into my robe, I lead him onto the balcony.

"The world better be ending, brother," I say, closing the door behind us.

"In some ways it is," he says. "We lost today. Badly."

"How is that possible?" I ask. "Hesiod sent word we outnumbered their army three to one."

"Achilles tricked us. He kept most of his troops hidden until our scouts left."

Once again, the Elders' deficiencies hurt Troy. "Hesiod should have been smarter than to fall for that."

My twin rubs the back of his neck. "He's doing the best he can, but he isn't a seasoned war veteran like Achilles."

I rest my arms against the balcony's railing, looking out at the sea. The full moon illuminates the purple waves, making them appear as if they're battling on the choppy surface. "What's our next step?"

"I know you don't want to hear this, but you must return Helen."

I shake my head. "That is not an option."

"War is not an option either," he says. "We only have sixty men left. Do you hear what I'm telling you? Over two hundred men lost their lives today . . . all for the sake of your mistress."

I stiffen my spine. "Be careful, brother. She's not my mistress; she is my wife."

"Wife? Wife!" he exclaims. "She can't be your wife. She's already married to Menelaus. You must return her. Deiphobus told us that is the only way Sparta would relent."

I lower my head to my chest. "I can't. I need her."

He throws his hands up. "You're a Glanching, and she's a human. You have to go back to Reos when the Oldungur Council says so. What then?"

"After our report out, I'll come back here. To Helen."

"You're assuming we'll get to choose when and where we'll return. Or that we'll even pass our trial."

I scrunch my eyebrows. "We'll pass."

"How? Troy is going to fall. We won't survive that."

"I'll figure something out."

"No, you won't. You are dooming us to mine Magical Ore the rest of our lives. But the Oldungur Council may forgive you, if you return Helen and end the bloodshed."

My eyes blaze with anger. "I won't give her up. If you don't like how things are going, desert Troy. But remember, that means you leave your precious Trojans alone with me."

"You're impossible," he says, throwing open the balcony door and stalking into my room.

I follow him, worried about Helen. She is cowering in bed, the blanket pulled up to her nose.

"Today, your selfishness brought death to Sparta and

Troy," he says. "It will continue until you go back to Menelaus."

She bursts into tears, placing her hands over her face.

"Leave! Now!" I scream.

He charges out, and I sit on the bed and cradle her in my arms.

"Don't cry. It's okay."

"How?" she says between sobs. "He's right. I need to go back to Sparta."

I still. "You want to go back?"

"Of course not," she says, clutching to my chest. "I love you. But no one should have to die for us to be together."

"And I love you for saying that, but Menelaus won't give up. Not at this point. This war won't end until one of our cities is victorious."

"It's just—this is so hard. I didn't expect the war to create a wares shortage. I haven't gotten a single new robe or piece of jewelry in a week."

I still; we're at war, and Helen is worried about her wardrobe? But then I remember her upbringing and soften. To Helen, material things equal self-esteem.

"You know we must keep all the wares to buy the neighboring cities' loyalty and convince their men to serve in our army. And our love is more important than a new robe, is it not?"

"Of course," she says, kissing my cheek. "I'm just tired and talking nonsense. Forgive me."

"There is nothing to forgive," I say. "And don't worry. I'm going to make sure Troy wins this war. Soon. So go back to sleep."

"Okay," she whispers, and we lie down again.

Almost instantly, she falls into slumber beside me, her breaths steady and even. Sleep does not come as easily for me; I can't silence Villow's voice inside my head, insisting Menelaus would end the war if he only got her back.

Even if that's true, I can't live without her.

I won't.

THE LOST KING IS FOUND

LAST NIGHT, THE CITY STREETS WOULD HAVE BEEN BUSTLING with activity. Now they're deserted, with the Trojans at home, mourning the loss of their loved ones. The emptiness is a painful memento of the battle hours before. As is the putrid smell of death, still lingering on my skin.

I was certain I was ready for war, but I was wrong. No matter how hard I try, images from combat replay in my mind: the terror on men's faces as blades slashed open their throats; the sickening suction of my blade as it sunk into a Spartan soldier's eye socket; and the ear-piercing wails from the mouths of the injured and dying.

I desperately want to head to Nicholas's house—where I've been living since Dameaon kicked me out of the palace—but the Trojans may want to seek comfort in the immortals. So instead, I trudge through the streets to the northern hills.

Even from a hundred feet away, I can see someone inside Apollo's shrine. I hurry, racing up the hill. The Trojan is leaning his left shoulder against one of the temple's pillars, his hair falling in scraggly tangles down his back.

"I pray you to be well," I call.

He turns to me, and I stumble backward. It's Guru Jetta, and he looks terrible—with stooped shoulders and dark shadows under his eyes.

"I'm afraid I'm not well. Not well at all," he says.

"Hello, Jetta. Yes, I can't imagine you are well. And I can't say I'm surprised to see you."

If anything, I'm surprised he waited this long to come. For the last month, I've barely eaten or slept, certain my Crystal would glow at any moment, summoning me back to Reos for an early report out with the Oldungur Council.

He frowns. "Things have certainly gone rather . . . badly, haven't they?"

"That's a serious understatement," I say. "My brother's selfishness has brought war to these shores. I've tried to stop it, Guru, but Dameaon will not give Helen back. And I fought next to the Trojans, but we're no match for the Spartans. My twin is dooming Troy, and us as Guides in the process. All for the *love* of one human."

"I'm not here to question you, Villow," he says, his voice unusually monotone. "I know you've tried to fix things. As have I. I just came from your brother's quarters, but he wouldn't listen to reason." He sighs. "I fear there is little left to do."

My heart flutters against my chest. "Are you . . . telling me we've failed?"

"No, not yet. But I was summoned to Kapitala earlier today, where the Oldungur Council and I discussed your Guidance duty at length. I reminded them this was the humans' last chance at re-creation, so the Council reluctantly agreed to see this trial through to fruition.

"But Cassandre is furious, especially since Dameaon is deliberately disobeying the Guidance Rules by having a relationship with Helen. She believes he is being purposely impertinent."

I rub the back of my neck. "I don't think it's that simple. Dameaon has convinced himself that Master Oldungur Cassandre will overlook his relationship with Helen because she's a Spartan and our trial is to help the Trojans. Truthfully, he's gone a bit mad. Helen has possessed him in a way I never thought possible."

"He believes he loves her, and that is a powerful Magic indeed," Jetta says. "Regardless, your twin is no help to you now. You must find a way for Troy to survive this war. Win, lose, it doesn't matter, as long as they have a future when your tenure is complete."

"There's nothing else I can do, Jetta," I say, wringing my hands together. "I'm out of ideas. The Oldungur Council has lost faith in me, and I fear you have too. Hope is lost."

Jetta doesn't respond. Instead, he moves over to the statue of Apollo, staring up at his angelic face. "Apollo, the god of light and healing. We could use a little bit of both those things right now."

He returns to the front entrance, where I'm still standing, and pulls his amulet out from under his shirt. "What do you think would have happened if the cyperus tree hit with lightning gave up? We wouldn't have the malaa'ig tree, and Relken might not have resumed his experiments. Perhaps Magic would still be a mystery.

But the tree fought back because it wanted to live. And it regrew, better than it was before." Jetta puts his amulet back and pulls me close. "Hope isn't lost, Villow, not while you are alive. And I haven't lost my faith in you. Far from it."

Tears form in my eyes; Jetta's encouragement renews my faith in myself. He's right. Things have seemed bleak before, but I've always fixed them. I can still turn this around—for my sake and the humans'.

I pull from his embrace and nod curtly. "I'll do everything I can to end this war."

"I know you will. You must. You are too talented to end up in Rehuido," he says, squeezing my shoulder. "Oh, I almost forgot." He pulls a letter out of his sleeve and hands it to me. "News from home."

I'd been so preoccupied with my Guidance duty, I'd forgotten I sent letters to Katarin and Portia. But Jetta only has one for me.

"Were . . . both of my letters delivered?" I ask, fingering the edge of it.

"Yes, but only the redhead gave me one in return," he says. "She is a fiery little thing, isn't she?"

"She sure is," I say, biting the sides of my mouth to keep from chuckling; I can only imagine the conversation that sparked his colorful description.

Jetta nods. "Well, my business is done here, so I'll head back to Reos now. Good luck to you, Villow. Do everything you can to save your Guidance duty. But remember, do not break any more Rules. Cassandre has no patience left for disobedience."

"Thanks, Jetta. I won't let you down."

He clutches his amulet and returns to Reos, leaving me alone inside the temple. Its cavernous space never seemed so cold. I would give anything to go home too and be surrounded by my family and friends.

But if I left now, I'd fail my trial and be banished to Rehuido. I would never get to see my loved ones again, and that can't happen. I need to figure out a way to fix this—all of it.

Before I can do that, I need to know if Katarin forgave me. I carry my torch outside, climbing up to Apollo's annulus and sitting on the top step. Wiping my sweaty hands against my chiton, I open the letter and read:

Villow,

It was so nice to hear from you. I hope everything is going well with your trial. Of course I forgive you, but I also can't lie. Your words still sting, and it will take time to recover completely. But I'm glad to know the truth. If you don't love me, then we weren't meant to be. In time, I'm sure we can return to the place we've always been. You're still my best friend too. Always.

—Kat

The corners of my lips turn up into a smile. Katarin and I are still best friends. And it's okay Portia didn't respond. Perhaps she didn't think Jetta would be returning to Earth. Or maybe she just doesn't like to write letters. I won't assume the worst until I hear it directly from her.

Regardless, I need to pass my trial, so I can return to those I care about most.

Between Jetta's faith and Katarin's forgiveness, my hope is renewed. Although things are bleak—okay, they've never been bleaker—I can turn this around.

I can do this.

I have to do this.

THIRTY-THREE. THAT'S HOW MANY DAYS HAVE PASSED SINCE our first battle with Sparta, where we lost over two hundred Trojan lives. All capable men were immediately drafted to fill the vacancies, with only the Elders, palace guards, blacksmiths, and doctors spared from service to their king. But it didn't matter. The Spartan army was much stronger, and every fight brought more deaths, leaving Troy short of men and vulnerable to future attacks. The Elders sent urgent messages to the neighboring cities, begging for help. Two kings answered, providing troops in exchange for vendible wares.

This afternoon, we head into battle again with an army made up mostly of foreigners, whose only alliance to us is the promise of continued merchandise from Troy's trade ships. It's not exactly an army destined to win.

"You about ready, Hector?" Nicholas says, pulling me from my thoughts.

He's already dressed in his armor—minus the helmet—while I'm still in my silk chiton. "Sorry. I was just thinking."

"About what?" he asks, throwing his shield's strap over his shoulder so it lays against his back.

"We weren't able to defeat Sparta with an army of Trojans, who were fighting for their home and loved ones. What chance do we have with an army of strangers?"

Nicholas places his helmet on his head and shrugs. "They come from cities with real armies and have trained their entire lives. That counts for something. Besides, I'm feeling lucky today. Now, get dressed and meet me at the amphitheater. We're leaving in a few minutes."

"I'll be right there, General," I say.

He heads out, and I dress in my armor, racing out the front door and through the streets to the amphitheater. On the way, I pass the field where we used to play field hockey.

My heart aches for those simpler times, when my biggest worry was a black eye. Now, I spend my days training for battles where I watch my friends die.

In the amphitheater, Nicholas is already on his horse, Celer. When he sees me, he lifts the goat horn off his shoulder and blows three short notes. The cluster of men move into rank, forming thirty straight lines, ten rows deep. We begin our march, heading out of Troy's northern gate to the field outside the walls.

We don't have far to go. A week ago, Achilles moved his army five miles south of Troy, no doubt as a public display of Sparta's strength. Not that we need it; the absence of so many Trojans is a constant reminder.

The flat fields offer no cover, so the Spartans have ample warning we're coming. Achilles blows three short notes into his trumpet, and his army falls into organized ranks, standing ready for us.

Nicholas blows one long and two short notes into

his horn. We raise our shields, forming a protective wall above our heads, and charge forward. Shrill pings ring out as the arrows bounce off them. Every few minutes, a wail conveys that an arrow penetrated our makeshift barrier.

I hold rank, extending my ash-wood spear through the gap between my shield and my neighboring soldier's. It plunges into soft flesh, followed immediately by a loud howl. The dripping red tip confirms it lanced a Spartan.

My first kill of the day but certainly not my last.

I swallow forcefully and thrust my spear forward again and again. As with the prior battles, our converged armies become so jumbled that the wall of shields is rendered useless. I toss my spear aside, throw my shield onto my back, and draw my short sword.

A Spartan engages me, swinging his blade at my neck. I dodge easily, plunging my sword into the slit in his helmet. Blood spurts out of his eye socket, as proof of his death, but another soldier is on me immediately. I fall into a steady rhythm, expunging Spartan after Spartan.

Seven. Eight. Nine.

My kill count rises as the stench of bloodied sweat promulgates the massive losses on both sides.

But then searing pain pierces my neck, surging through my entire body and bringing me to my knees. I have been injured many times during battle but not like this. I collapse, fading in and out of consciousness. In my delirium, I'm certain my chest is consumed by fire. The clang of metal upon metal besieges me, as do the haunting screams of the dying. Yet I am unable to move, paralyzed from agony.

After what feels like an eternity, the pain subsides

enough that I can sit up. I brush my fingers against my neck, but there's little more than a scratch. My Crystal is still warm against my chest—confirmation of its healing power.

Those around me haven't fared as well. Hundreds of dead bodies lie between the clusters of fighting soldiers. To my left, Nicholas—still on Celer—is surrounded by three Spartans. He thumps the tallest one's helmet with the hilt of his sword, and the man stumbles away. The other two seize Nicholas's waist and pull him to the ground.

"Nicholas!" I scream.

He upsurges, plunging his blade into one of their necks. I strike the other on his breastplate, swinging again to open his jugular. Then Nicholas and I stand back-to-back, bringing down a continuous stream of adversaries.

"We need to win today," he says, "but most of our men are dead."

"There's nothing we can do, Nicholas," I say. "We're outnumbered. Call the retreat, and I'll cover you."

"Damn this war. Find me on the other side," he shouts and strikes a Spartan's legs.

I swing wildly, diverting the nearby soldiers' attention. Nicholas leaps onto Celer and blows four long notes into his horn.

Our army races across the field toward Troy, but the horde of Spartans wallop them from behind. There will be no one left at this rate, and I'm certain the war will be lost.

Right here. Right now.

I shut my eyes, unable to watch the slaughter of the remaining troops.

But then three long blasts ring out, and the Spartans retreat to their camp. Across the field, Achilles nods at me—still with his trumpet in hand. I bow my head, acknowledging that even now he's showing us mercy.

"Hector! Come on," Nicholas hollers, pointing to where the rest of our army is waiting.

I start north, but a loud wail stops me.

To my left, Nicholas's face is contorted in pain.

"Noooooo!" I cry, rushing forward to catch his limp body in midair as he falls off Celer. Laying him on his back, I discover why he screamed—there's an arrow protruding from his neck.

He gasps for air. "Hector . . . I . . ."

I place my shaking fingers against his wound, attempting to slow the bleeding.

"It's all right. You're going to be fine. But I need to get you out of here," I say, lifting his shoulders. He screams, so I lower him back onto the ground.

"It's too late . . . for me, Hector," he pants, red liquid trickling out the right side of his mouth. "My time . . . on Earth is over." He pulls his ring with three intertwining olive trees on the face off his left ring finger. "Give this to my parents. Tell them . . . I'm sorry . . . and I love them." I secure his ring on my right pointer finger, and he continues, "Promise me . . . you won't let my death be in vain. You must lead . . . our troops to victory."

I grasp his hand firmly. "Yes, I'll avenge you. I promise."

"You know . . . I've struggled with my faith. But perhaps . . . I was wrong. Pray . . . there's another world . . . and the Furies judge me favorably. I hope . . . Oedipus is waiting for me in Elysium."

My chest tightens, and I avert my gaze. It's crushing, knowing Oedipus is alive, while Nicholas believes he's dead, wishing for their reunion. But no good would come of telling him. Not now.

I take a deep breath and squeeze his hand. "I'm sure he will be."

"I . . . did the best I could with my life," he says. "I hope . . . it was enough. Oh, by the gods, I'm not ready to die."

And then he's gone—just like that.

I lower his eyelids with my fingers and collapse on his chest. My body convulses, overwhelmed with the anguish of losing him. It's too much to bear. He was my best friend on Earth and also my hope for Troy. Nicholas was a born leader, and I anticipated he would rebuild the city after the war.

Without him, my efforts are worthless. Even if we survive the war, there are no men strong enough to carry the burden of rebuilding. The city will be lost, and so will my Guidance duty.

But it doesn't matter. I promised Nicholas I would avenge him, and I owe him that at least. Taking several deep breaths, I force myself up and place his corpse across Celer's back.

I hoist myself up behind him, and we gallop over to the remaining army.

Forty, maybe fifty troops are all that's left, and at least half are injured. The healthy soldiers are bandaging the wounded and trying to stifle the bleeding from their missing appendages.

I summon what little strength I have to address them.

"Soldiers, you fought bravely today, but we lost many, including our general." I point at Nicholas's still body in front of me. "I was with him at the end, and his dying wish was to avenge those we lost. Remember, Troy has the favor of Apollo, and he'll be with us when we strike back. But for now, we must retreat."

We trudge back slowly—the injured setting our pace—reaching Troy just before dusk. At this point, very few Trojans gather outside the gates—because most of the army is made up of strangers—but Nicholas's parents are always there, anxiously awaiting the return of their son. Sure enough, Thaddaeus and Rosa are up ahead, smiling and waving wildly.

It dawns on me—with my helmet concealing my face and riding Celer, they think I'm Nicholas. Cursing myself for giving them false hope, I tug off my helmet.

Thaddaeus's smile fades instantly, and he braces his wife's shoulders.

I dismount in front of them, holding out Nicholas's ring. "I'm so sorry."

Thaddaeus takes it from me and clutches it in his right hand, while Rosa crumples into a ball at my feet. "No, no, no, no," she whispers over and over.

"It's all right. It'll be okay," Thaddaeus coos. "It will all be okay."

He's lying; for the two of them, nothing will ever be okay. They'll never hear their only child laugh again, never see him get married, never have grandchildren. The war cheated them of their future—and it's just not fair.

Rosa looks at me with glazed eyes. "Let me see my son."

"As you wish," I say, sliding Nicholas off Celer and onto the ground next to her.

She lifts her head and releases a scream—a hair-raising, wretched shriek—worse than anything I heard in battle. Rosa falls on top of her son and sobs loudly, replicating my earlier breakdown. Thaddaeus remains standing, staring at both of them, while silent tears stream down his cheeks.

I look up at the stars—just visible in the fading light—trying to block out what's happening, but I'm certain the image of Nicholas's grieving parents will revisit me in my nightmares, just like so many other horrors from this war.

"What's wrong with his hair? It won't move," Rosa asks, attempting to brush a strand off his forehead.

It's stiff from the blood that flowed from his neck wound. "Um," I say, looking at Thaddaeus.

He seems to understand, because he kneels and embraces her. They rock back and forth, remaining entwined until their crying lessens. Then they unyoke and rise.

Thaddaeus wipes the tears from his cheeks. "He fought bravely, no?"

I squeeze his arm. "Your son was the bravest of all. As always. And Nicholas found his faith, right before death. I was with him at the end, praying for his safe passage to Elysium."

Rosa's breathing slows. "Thank the gods. That gives me such comfort." She clutches her husband's hand. "We'll bury our son tomorrow. Tonight, I want my Nicholas home with me."

"One more night with him," Thaddaeus says. "Yes . . . that feels right."

I lift Nicholas onto Celer and hand Thaddaeus the

reins. He places his arm around Rosa's waist, steering her down the street. They limp along, as if each step causes them pain. But this war has taught me well. There is no greater loss than that of a child.

Nicholas's death remains with me, and it hits me; I can't go home, not without him there to greet me. The emptiness would be the final blow to my already fragile fortitude. Unsure what else to do, I stroll aimlessly through the streets.

Troy is going to fall—of that I'm certain. There are no more men to add to our army, and our neighboring cities have already dispatched the troops they are willing to spare. Sending more would leave them exposed to Sparta, and they won't risk their own safety for ours.

Reaching the front gate, I follow the wall along the southern part of the city. The rounded bulwark shimmers in the full moon's light.

Of course.

The walls. They're strong enough to hold off the Spartan troops—at least for a while. And we can use our fleet of ships to continue bringing in supplies while I persuade Dameaon there is no choice now—he must return Helen.

I trace a crack in the walls' surface. Knowing my brother, I can only hope they're as sturdy as they appear.

THE VAST SEA, WHICH ONCE FILLED ME WITH SUCH HOPE, provides no solace now. Still, I stare at the water like I've done every day since returning to Troy, waiting for buoyant tidings that never come. The claret sun casts its light onto the choppy waves, turning the water into blood.

It's an apt allegory. Two days ago, Achilles sent one of his scouts to Troy's gate, delivering a message: *I'm coming to end this. Surrender, or no one will be spared.*

Within hours, the Spartan army relocated to a field outside the city, docking their battle ships in our harbor. Now, the walls that kept us safe trap us. Our weakened army and trade ships are no match for their strength, and even if the Spartans don't penetrate the bulwarks, our food won't last more than a week.

There isn't much left I can do for the Trojans, except for my oracle duties. The dire circumstances have heightened the need for the immortals, so I spend practically every moment at the temples, channeling the gods and relaying sanguine messages: promises that the war will end soon, that no innocents will die, that Troy will come back from this.

I glance at the sea once more before heading to Apollo's temple. His angelic concrete face makes me long for my own peace. How I wish he were real; Troy could use a miracle right now.

"I was hoping I'd find you here, Oracle."

Helen is standing between two of the temple's pillars, appearing uncertain if she should enter or not. I shake my head at Apollo. "I asked for a miracle, and this is what you sent me?"

"What?" she asks.

"Nothing," I say. "What are you doing here?"

She moves inside the temple, joining me by Apollo's statue. The strains of war haven't dulled her beauty, but she holds no appeal to me anymore. Her selfishness makes her repugnant.

"I bring sad news," she says. "Aegidius was in the courtyard when an arrow breached the wall and pierced his heart." Her voice catches. "I'm told he didn't suffer, but he was my only friend in all of Troy."

I clench my hands into tight fists. "Over a thousand Trojans have died, but it took the loss of a goat for you to get upset? How many more need to die before you surrender yourself to Sparta? Before you do the right thing?"

She lowers her head, speaking in a whisper. "That's why I'm here. I'm ready to go back, but I need your help."

I blink slowly, trying to clear the black spots in my vision. Even in my wildest imaginings, I never thought Helen would agree to go back. Or enlist my help to do so.

"What's changed that you want to return to Menelaus?" I ask. "Has your relationship with Paris soured?"

She shakes her head. "It's because of Paris I need to go back. Troy is going to lose this war, and when it does, he will be killed for treason against Sparta. If I surrender myself, the terms will require sparing Paris's life."

"If what you're saying is true, why do you need my help? One of the Elders can negotiate with Achilles."

Helen stiffens her spine. "The Elders might tell Paris, and he needs to remain uninformed until the negotiations are complete. If he knew, I'm afraid he would stop them, and that can't happen. And you are the only other person I trust in Troy. Will you help me, Oracle? Please?"

"What makes you think Paris will let you go, even after negotiations reach consensus?"

"Because I will tell him whatever it takes to be set free. Even if it makes him hate me."

Dameaon won't like this. In fact, he'll hate it. But I

can't worry about his feelings right now; there is too much at stake, and this is the perfect solution, provided I can get Achilles to agree to my terms. But I need to know Helen has thought this through before I pin my hopes on her.

"What do you think will happen, if you return to Sparta?" I ask.

She shrugs. "I honestly don't know. Menelaus claimed to love me once, but my betrayal will not have done me any favors. It matters not. I will deal with whatever consequences await me."

"Even death?"

"Death would be a welcome escape from living without Paris."

I draw my head back. "You really do love him, don't you?"

Tears well up in her eyes. "With all my heart. He's everything I ever wanted. In Paris, I found my home. That's why I can't be the reason he dies."

Helen is saying all the right words, and she seems sincere. More importantly, she's offering me a way to save Troy from this endless war.

I shut my eyes and clutch my ankh amulet. "I will help you, but only because it's what's best for Troy."

"Thank you, Oracle, truly," she says, handing me a lion-crested ring. "Take this. It will identify you as an agent of the palace who can negotiate on King Paris's behalf."

I nod. "I'm sorry you must lose the man you love, but you're doing the right thing. The good of one cannot outweigh the good of the whole."

She offers me a wobbly smile. "That may be true, but

I'm doing this for Paris. Good day, Oracle," she says, leaving me alone.

The ring in my hand is the miracle I've been searching for; it's the tool to stop the war, but that's only the first step in passing my trial. I still need to find a way for the Trojans to come back from this. While I can help them, I only have a few months left before my trial is up. It's not enough time to secure their future—not without a strong leader to continue when I'm gone.

Nicholas was my solution, and his death complicates matters. Any other young men who could have taken charge perished during battle. And between Priam's death and the war, Hecuba has become a shell of a human being—barely able to get up in the mornings.

Worse, once the Spartan army leaves Troy's shores, there will be nothing stopping the neighboring cities from invading and capturing the harbors. I could ask Achilles to leave some of his men behind, but there's danger in that too. Without his leadership, they may turn to wickedness. And there's no way I will be able to get Achilles to agree to stay in Troy a moment longer than he has to.

Unable to find a good solution, I decide to head home for lunch and brainstorm again with a full stomach. I stop by the market to light my torch in the Eternal Flame. The once-vibrant shopping center is quiet now. With the shortage of supplies, only half of the shops are open, and there are very few customers. The Eternal Flame is the only thing that remains unchanged, burning as brightly as ever. I dip my torch into the pyre, and it ignites.

"I pray you to be well, Oracle," a merchant to the south bellows. "How's your day?"

"As good as it can be, I suppose," I say, making my way to her shop of handcrafted wooden figurines. "I'm surprised you're still open."

"Carving has always calmed me," she says. "And during these troubling times, I need a lot of calming. Even if I don't sell anything, it fills the time."

"Baaah," her four-year-old son says, playing with a wooden shepherd and a flock of sheep on the street next to her.

She smiles at him, but then her face darkens. "Elpidius used to have a promising future. Now, my son has no future at all."

I crouch next to him and tousle his white-blond hair. Towheaded and pink-cheeked, he's still the definition of innocence—even with a war raging around him. Elpidius takes a figurine off the table and gives it to me. Then he returns to his play, moving the shepherd around his wooden lambs.

I look at the tiny figurine in my hand, and my heart surges with hope; it has given me the answer to rebuilding Troy. I place the wooden toy in my bag and toss a couple drachmas on the counter.

"There's still hope for Troy's future," I say, handing her my lit torch and sprinting away. "I must go. But thank you."

After a brief stop at Nicholas's parents' house, I head out of Troy on Celer. When I near the Spartan camp, I raise my white flag high above my head. It billows in the cool afternoon breeze, announcing my peaceful approach.

Even so, the two soldiers who ride out to meet me draw their swords.

"What are you doing here, Trojan?" a soldier with a bushy gray beard asks.

"I come in peace, to negotiate the end of this war," I say. "I must speak with Achilles at once."

The homely, wide-nosed man scoffs. "And what makes you think we would let you anywhere near our general?"

"Because of this," I say, showing them the lion-crested ring on my finger.

The Spartans exchange glances, communicating silently.

"We need to check you for weapons," the homely one says.

I hand him my sword. "This is my only weapon, but search me if you must."

I dismount, and Homely frisks me, roughly. Satisfied I'm unarmed, they escort me into their camp—Gray Beard in front of me and Homely behind. The Spartan soldiers emerge from their tents, emitting hateful glances.

Gray Beard sticks his head inside a tent in the middle of camp. "General, I have a Trojan who claims he's here to negotiate peace. He has a ring with the royal crest."

"Negotiate? Oh, this ought to be good," Achilles calls from inside.

He throws open the tent flap and emerges. While we've fought in five battles, I haven't seen Achilles up close since I was on Sparta's shores; his curly hair falls in a tangled mess below his shoulders, and he's lost at least thirty pounds. Once he was striking, but now, like everything else, he is ravaged by the war.

"You? What makes you think I have anything to say to you?" he says.

I hold up my hands, palms facing him. "We must speak privately."

The usual light in his blue eyes is replaced with clouded hatred. "Why would I give you a second of my time?"

"Because you once called me your friend. That has to count for something. Please, Achilles, I want to end this."

Achilles whips back the tent flap, motioning for me to go inside. There isn't much; a small hay-filled mattress on the floor, a square table with two chairs, and a basin of water—certainly not the kind of accommodations he's used to.

He enters behind me, arms crossed in front of his chest. I gesture to the chairs, and he shakes his head, not moving from the entrance. "You have five minutes. This better be good, Hector."

"If you think a truce is good, then yes, it's good," I say. "This war has gone on too long, and it's time it ended."

Achilles releases a wicked cackle. "I've lost six hundred and seventy-two soldiers. Six hundred and seventy-two! It should have never begun."

"Menelaus declared war on Troy, not the other way around."

"Because Paris stole his wife! You were there. Why didn't you stop him? And even if he wanted to, you know Menelaus couldn't just let her go. He would've appeared spineless."

"I knew nothing of Paris and Helen's plan. And there's

been bloodshed and loss on both sides. Paris is ready to negotiate a truce to end the war."

"A truce? You think I can sell a truce to Menelaus? Get real. I can't leave until Troy is defeated and Helen is reclaimed."

I shrug. "Helen will return and be the loving wife Menelaus always wanted, provided Sparta leaves Troy and inflicts no harm on Paris."

He places his hand on his forehead. "Oh, well then, I guess everything is fixed. Hey, while we're at it, why don't we pick some daisies and skip off to play hopscotch? Give me a break. That won't work. Not at this point."

I figured it was a long shot, but I had to try. "Fair enough. What if Paris declared you the victors?"

He collapses onto the chair behind him. "The great Paris admit defeat? No . . . I know him better than that. What's the catch?"

I sit in the other chair. "There is no catch. His people suffered because of his selfishness. He's trying to make things right . . . something he should have done long ago."

He stares into my eyes. Perhaps he discerns my honesty, because his expression softens. "If you're sincere, let's ride to the palace together, right now, and declare Sparta the victors. My army will stay in Troy a month or so for appearance's sake, and then, with Helen and a substantial amount of gold, we'll set sail for Sparta. I'll convince Menelaus that's sufficient penance upon my return."

I think about the slaves in the Spartan fields. "How can I be certain you won't take our men prisoners?"

"You'll have to trust me, the same way I'm trusting you.

Troy is across the sea, so we can take pity on you. Besides, you have very few men left."

What he's saying makes sense. And as far as I know, Achilles has always kept his word. More importantly, I have no choice but to believe him. "Okay, Achilles, I'll put my faith in you. But I need a week to gain consensus from the palace for surrender. Then I will return, to execute your plan."

He jumps out of his seat. "You must think I'm an idiot. I know a trap when I hear it. I'm not giving you a week to find new allies."

"You have my word, as an agent for the king, that's not what I'm doing," I promise. "And even if I wanted to, there aren't any cities left to appeal to."

"Then why do you need a week?"

I came prepared for that question. "You know Paris's stubbornness. And there are six Elders. It will take time to gain full alignment."

He shrugs. "That is not my problem. You have three days."

"That's not enough time—"

"Three days, no more. If you don't return with my terms agreed to, I will march on Troy and burn it to the ground," he promises, flinging open the tent.

I sigh. It's not enough time, but what choice do I have? "Fine. Three days," I say, ducking under the flap and going outside.

Gray Beard and Homely are waiting nearby.

"Escort him to the edge of camp, then come right back. Troy will surrender to us in three days' time, so we must start preparation for our departure," Achilles says, turning to me. "Hector, I'm trusting you. Don't betray me."

He darts inside his tent, and the two soldiers lead me out of camp.

"Thanks for accompanying me, but I can take it from here," I say. "Tell Achilles I'll be back before time runs out."

Gray Beard nods and turns back toward camp. Before I can move, his homely comrade presses his sword against my throat.

"What are you doing, Ward?" Gray Beard asks.

"What Achilles wasn't brave enough to do," Ward says. "He called him Hector. As in Oracle Hector. If we kill him, the Trojans lose their liaison with the gods. It could end the war. We could go home."

Gray Beard places his blade against Ward's neck. "You are a fool. Our general just said Troy is willing to surrender. That means the war is already ending. But what do you think Troy will do if we kill an agent of the palace? You must let him go."

Ward does nothing for a moment and then lowers his weapon. "I promise you, Layland, he's up to no good. You're making a big mistake."

"It's my mistake to make," Layland says. He glares at me. "Go . . . before I change my mind."

He doesn't need to tell me twice. I kick Celer's sides, and we head toward Troy.

After a few minutes, I turn back, confirming Ward and Layland returned to camp. I steer Celer south, and we gallop as fast as we can, racing toward Mount Ida.

Once we reach the hills at the edge of the mountains, I begin my search, scanning the terrain for a flock of sheep.

Time passes quickly, and the more crests we climb, the more panicked I become. My skin tingles from the sweat that pours out of me, but I keep going. There's no time to waste. Still, when darkness comes, I'm forced to stop and make camp.

Lying near the fire, I reminisce about my first night on Earth. My future was uncertain then, and my biggest worry was creating a believable backstory. Now, disaster is crashing all around me. I won't find the real Paris in time, and even if I return to Achilles, Troy will still fall. Worse, the Oldungur Council will deem our mission unsuccessful, and that will be the end of humans as an Original Species. And my future will be ruined, as will the Verchant name.

Searching for solace, I dump out the contents of my shoulder bag. The small rock I brought from the Summit's stream bounces on the dirt. I palm it and rub my thumb against its smooth surface. It transports me back to my afternoons in the Summit with Katarin. I grab my friendship bracelet from the ground and put it on my wrist. If she were here, she'd remind me I'm a Glanching, meant to do good, and all is not lost. Not yet.

But there aren't many possibilities left. If only I could start over, I'd do things differently and make better decisions. Of course, Dameaon caused all of this, so unless he altered his behaviors, it wouldn't matter. Besides, Glanchings know better than to mess with time travel Magic.

Magic.

I grab my potion box from the ground and open the lid, removing the purple potion. Its liquid sloshes against the sides of the bottle. Jetta told me not to break any Rules, but there aren't any humans in sight; that makes it a bit of a gray area. Besides, this is the only chance I have of finding Paris.

I pour it out and hold my breath. A small puddle forms in the dirt and trickles out in thin, crooked lines. And then—nothing.

I chuckle; what did I think would happen? It shows how desperate I am, putting my faith in Dexter's potions.

But then the liquid rises from the ground, glowing brighter each second. It shoots west, creating a semitransparent magenta path across the mountains.

I jump on Celer's back and follow the beam of light, beseeching it to lead to the lost shepherd of Troy.

THE MORNING SUN'S RAYS DISINTEGRATE THE POTION'S BEACON, but it doesn't matter; after riding all night, distant bleats are my compass now. Sure enough, after ascending the next peak, fluffy white sheep speckle the grassy terrain below. I kick Celer's sides, and we sail down the steep hill.

Their shepherd is nearby, sitting casually on a boulder. His hair falls halfway down his back, but it's definitely the lost king.

"Paris!" I scream, dismounting and running toward him.

He jumps to his feet. "Villow? Is that you? B-B-By the gods. What are you doing here?"

He's afraid—and he should be; I'm going to destroy his peaceful existence. "I'm here to bring you home. It's time to embrace your destiny."

"The mountains are my home now, and I no longer go

by that name," he says. "I'm Erebus the shepherd, and your brother is the prince."

"With all due respect, you made a mistake," I say. "Dameaon is a fake king . . . unfit to lead anyone."

He raises his eyebrows. "King?"

I lower my head; I wanted to break the news gently, but in my haste, I let it slip. "Yes . . . king. Your father passed away a few months ago. I'm so sorry."

He closes his eyes and takes a deep breath. "No. That can't be. The last words I said to my father were 'I hate you.' But I didn't. I just . . . needed him to understand I didn't want his life," he says, his voice quavering. "I didn't get to say goodbye. Or tell him I loved him."

"Paris—"

"I'm Erebus, not Paris. And it doesn't matter. This is where I belong. Your brother is the king now. I—"

"My brother stole Menelaus's wife and started a war with Sparta. Troy lost over a thousand men."

All the color drains from his face. "What? But . . . the gods favor him. Why else would they give him the power of transformation? Besides, he said he would be a better leader for Troy."

The revelation that my twin knew Paris was the prince when he agreed to take his place makes my blood boil, but I have bigger issues to focus on right now. "He was wrong. He isn't fit to be king and he's ready to make things right. But you must return with me. Now."

He shakes his head. "I'm not strong enough to lead. I never have been. I'm sorry, Villow, but Troy is better off without me."

"Better off? As we speak, the Spartans are camped

outside Troy's gates and their ships are in the harbor. Even if they don't attack us, everyone will die from starvation soon. Does that sound better off to you?" I take the wooden figurine out of my bag and place it on the boulder. "A merchant's son gave this to me yesterday. An innocent child, who somehow remains pure, even with all the destruction around him. Can you honestly stand by and doom his future?"

"Troy was doomed the moment Sparta declared war on it. I know Achilles . . . He won't stop until his army is victorious," he says. "Even if I did come back, there's nothing left for me to save."

"That's where you're wrong," I say. "I arranged a deal with Achilles, but it won't work without you. Left without a leader, Troy could very easily fall victim to an invading army. And their fields are decimated. After Sparta returns home, you must negotiate with the peaceful rulers of the neighboring cities for food while we replant our crops.

"I know you're scared, Paris, but you can do this. The gods have a plan for you. Be the ruler you're meant to be. Come with me. Now. Save your people."

He picks up the little figurine, closing his fingers around it in a tight fist. "Okay . . . what do I need to do?"

"I knew you'd make the right decision," I say, renewed with hope. "We'll ride Celer. We can reach Achilles by mid—"

"We can't leave my flock," he says.

I press my palms against my forehead. "I'm sorry, Paris, we can't be slowed down. Troy has no future if we don't reach Achilles by nightfall in two days."

He gestures to the sheep and goats. "I understand.

But my flock is my family, my friends. They'll be eaten by the lions, and without them, there is no future for me."

I estimate our current location; it's not ideal, but if we focus, we could lead his flock halfway out of the mountains by nightfall. That *should* leave enough time to escort them to the base of the mountains *and* for Paris to reach Achilles. Plus, it gives Celer a much-needed break from galloping.

"All right. If you insist, we need to get moving at once."

"Understood. Let's go," he says. He uses his staff to drive the sheep and goats into a manageable circle, and we start up the hill, leading them as far as we can before darkness comes.

In the glow of the fire, I fill Paris in on everything that's happened in Troy—both the good and bad. Somewhere in the middle of it all, an inner determination steels his body; his shoulders square, his head rises, and his eyes glint with an intensity they never had before.

When we reach the base at midafternoon the next day, I use a sharp rock to cut off his hair and give him the lion-crested ring.

I tickle Celer's muzzle. "You've been so strong. I need one more favor. Take Paris to Achilles as fast as you can, and then you can rest."

He snorts in response, and I pat his neck. Paris mounts him, and I hand him the reins. He looks like the king he's always been—deep inside.

"Achilles's camp is just outside Troy's gates," I say. "Don't forget what we discussed. Tell Achilles you came yourself because it was the kingly thing to do. Once you enter Troy, find Helen. She will help you convince

Dameaon to hide until my return so you can take your rightful place as king."

"Thank you for helping me save Troy," he says. "You are a true friend. I won't forget what you've done for me. And my people."

"The gods are with you," I say. "Don't forget that."

He points at his flock. "Take good care of them. I'll see you soon."

He kicks Celer's sides and gallops away. I watch until he's out of sight and then, shepherd staff in hand, lead his flock across the field.

WRONG AGAIN

THE PALACE GARDENS THAT ONCE BROUGHT ME HAPPINESS ARE now haunted by Aegidius's spirit. Every corner holds memories of my little goat—from the fountains he splashed in to the alfalfa he munched. Even the ground below my sandals is a reminder of the delight he used to get from rolling in the grass.

I hate being here. But I can't leave. Not until I talk to Helen. She's perched on a marble bench surrounded by flowers, her serene face turned toward the sky.

If my instincts are correct, her peace will be short-lived.

I clear my throat, and she smiles. "Oh, Paris. What a pleasant surprise. I thought you were meeting with the Elders. Come, join me." I remain standing by the olive tree, and she scrunches her nose. "Paris, what's wrong?"

"We promised we would never lie to each other," I say, "so I'm going to give you one more chance to be honest. You've been acting strange since you returned from your walk two days ago. What happened that you aren't telling me?"

She sashays toward me, wrapping her arms around my neck. I keep my hands at my side, refusing to reciprocate. She pulls away, searching my face for answers. "I've already told you. Nothing happened."

"Really?" I pull a letter from the folds of my chiton. "Then maybe you can explain what this is about?"

Helen takes the paper from me. When she's read half of it, her shoulders tense and the corner of her left eye twitches. Subtle tells—but I know her well enough to recognize she's scared.

"Why would I know anything about this?" she says, trying to hand the letter back to me.

I refuse to take it. "I don't know, Helen, but the Elders were just as surprised as me when it arrived."

"I . . . I don't know what you want me to say."

"How about the truth? The ring that I keep on my night table—you know, the one with the royal crest—is missing. Only you and Pavlos have access to it. His loyalty is unquestionable. You . . . I'm not so sure about."

She crosses her arms, clutching her shoulders with her hands. "I . . . I took it. I gave it to Hector. I asked him to negotiate with Achilles on my behalf. To find a way to end this war."

"What were your terms?" I ask, my voice barely above a whisper.

"It's all here, in the letter," she says, holding it up. "I would surrender to the Spartan army. In return, we would set sail for Sparta, and Achilles would spare your life."

I snatch the letter from her, rereading the contents.

"How could you make this decision without me? We can handle anything, as long as we do it together."

She places her left hand on my chest, smiling wistfully. "There was no decision to make. Sparta has surrounded us, and our food is almost gone. The people of Troy are starving. We've lost the war, Paris." She nods at the letter, clutched in my right hand. "Clearly, Achilles has accepted my terms. This is the best resolution we could possibly hope for."

I put my hand on top of hers, still on my chest. "Best for who? There is no living without you. There must be another way. We can run away together. Regroup in a neighboring city. We'll return and rebuild Troy once Sparta leaves."

"The Spartans will not leave without me, Paris."

"You don't know that. We have to try."

Helen pulls her hand from my grasp. "I was hoping I could spare you the truth, but it's clear you need to hear it. I *want* to go back to Sparta. This is all . . . too hard. I thought you were all I needed, but I was wrong. I'd rather have security. Comfort. Menelaus can provide that."

I scrunch my eyebrows. "Do you really think he will forgive you? You ran away with me, Helen."

She shrugs. "I can be very persuasive. It's a chance I'm willing to take."

"You once told me nothing else mattered as long as we had each other. That our love could conquer anything."

"Well, I was wrong. Honestly, I'm not sure I ever loved you."

I bend over, placing my hands on my knees. My throat burns with the bitterness of Helen's weakness. I risked everything for her, and this is how she repays me? By going behind my back—with my brother no less—to save herself? She's weak—much weaker than I ever thought possible—and there is very little I hate more than that.

I take three deep breaths and straighten my spine, glaring at her with cold eyes. "I knew you were a bit shallow, but I didn't think you were a coward. If you don't love me, I don't love you. Go. Get out of my sight."

Helen stumbles backward, and her chin begins to tremble. But I have no sympathy for her. Not now.

"Go! Now!" I shout.

"I'm so sorry, Paris," she cries, running toward the palace.

I stand in the gardens—alone. Well, except for the portentous letter still clutched in my hand. I reread it for the hundredth time:

> *King Paris,*
>
> *As I discussed with Oracle Hector, as an official agent of the palace, Troy will declare Sparta the victors of this war. In addition to the surrender of Queen Helen, Sparta demands full access to your treasury and will take what is necessary to fulfill payment for losses procured during battle.*
>
> *I am speaking as an agent for King Menelaus, so if these conditions are met, the war will henceforth be resolved and Sparta will return home.*

As was conveyed to Hector, if I have not received word of your agreement by sunset tomorrow, Sparta will treat that as a refusal and descend upon Troy with all of our might and fury.

—General Achilles

The reality that Helen made this happen hits me, and my chest tightens to the point I can barely breathe. I collapse on the bench where she was sitting moments ago—when I still had hope she wouldn't confirm my worst fears.

The flowers encircling my seat are just starting to bloom in the warmth of springtime. Their white petals and vibrant yellow stigmas identify them as narcissus. How appropriate. The flowers' beauty masks the poison found in their bulbs—just like Helen. Her external beauty masked her toxicity.

She single-handedly took away everything else good in my life. Because of her, my relationship with Achilles shifted from best friend to worst enemy. Aegidius, an innocent goat, was killed by the indiscriminate hand of battle. Hecuba, the only real mother I've ever had, is practically mad from the worry the war created. And the Trojans lost—some their lives, and those remaining, their security and future. My Guidance duty is no doubt in jeopardy, all for a woman who never loved me.

I look at the letter again; as furious as I am, my twin's betrayal was a blessing. It showed me Helen's true nature. If she wants to return to Menelaus, there is no sense waiting until tomorrow. I will end this now.

PAVLOS READIES OUR HORSES, AND TOGETHER WE RIDE OUT TO the Spartan camp. As if he was expecting me, Achilles stands at the edge, just beyond the tents.

The war has changed him; he was once compared to Adonis, but now he's barely more than an ashen, haggard skeleton. His vibrant eyes have darkened from all he's been forced to live through. I avert my gaze, unable to bear the guilt. My selfishness did this to him, to the man who once called me brother.

When we reach him and dismount, two Spartan soldiers rush forward. Achilles holds up his left hand, demanding they halt their charge.

He approaches me, releasing an ugly laugh. "The great King Paris has finally decided to leave the safety of Troy's walls and grace us lowly Spartans with his presence. How nice of you to come instead of sending the oracle again."

I shrug. "I figured I had the time, so why not? It's good to see you, Achilles."

He shakes his head. "Let's drop the pleasantries. I have no interest in any conversation with you, unless it's to hear you accept my conditions."

"I have your word . . . No Trojans will be harmed if I surrender?"

Achilles looks down at the scraggly grass between us. "I once thought of Troy as my second home. I have no interest in killing another one of its citizens. I never wanted this war, Paris. You started it."

"As much as I hate to admit it, you're right," I say. "This is my fault. You don't need to spare Troy, and for that, I am more grateful than you know." I hold out my hand. "I accept your terms. Let's return to Troy, and you can claim your well-gotten spoils."

He extends his hand but stops inches from taking mine. "By the gods," he says, gaping at something behind me.

I follow his gaze. A man is dismounting from a horse a few feet away, so I don't see his face. Not at first. But when I do, my blood runs cold.

Suddenly, Villow's plan becomes crystal clear. After negotiating a peaceful surrender, he found Paris—the real one—so he could ascend the throne and restore Troy to its former greatness. It's a good plan—probably the best one under the circumstances—except for the fact I'm here and the Spartans are staring at two Parises.

The real king starts toward us, pausing for a second when he sees me, shutting his eyes. Then he continues forward; what else can he do, really?

Achilles gawks at the two of us—duplicate bookends—standing side by side. "I . . . I . . . don't understand. What sorcery is this? How are there two of you?"

One of his soldiers—an ugly brute—steps forward. "This is clearly a trick. Permission to kill them both, General, before they turn their magic on us?"

"Stand down, Ward," Achilles says. "I need a minute. Something is not right, but one of them must be the real king of Troy." He thinks for a moment, then he points at me. "What was the name of the lake at the military camp we attended when we were twelve?"

I have no idea what the answer is, and even if I did, I wouldn't say. This is my chance to put Villow's plan back on track. I snort. "That was a long time ago. How could I possibly remember?"

He points at the real Paris. "You, what is your answer?"

"Lake Trichonida," he says. "It's where you got bitten by that snake, thanks to me convincing you to sneak out."

Achilles nods—pleased with his answer—and draws his blade, holding the tip against my chest. "I don't know who, or what, you are, but it is clear he is the real Paris. To the underworld with you."

I'm in for intense pain, but I don't care. Paris will survive and take his rightful place. Helen will be surrendered and head back to Sparta. Troy will be safe and start to rebuild.

Achilles swings his sword behind his back and then forward, toward my neck. I finger my Crystal; it's about to exert some serious healing Magic. But then Achilles falls to his knees, dropping his weapon mid swing.

Pavlos is standing behind him, holding the hilt of the dagger embedded in Achilles's neck.

"Pavlos, no!" I scream, but it's too late.

Blood gushes out of the wound, covering the front of Achilles's breastplate. I fall onto my knees, cradling his head in my lap. Pavlos's body drops beside me, his throat sliced wide open.

I glance up, just as Ward's blade slashes into my forehead. Blood gushes into my eyes, blurring my vision, and everything goes dark.

When I come to, the moon is shining in the aubergine sky. I place my fingers above my left eye, but the only indication of my wound is a small raised line. Achilles and Pavlos aren't so fortunate; they both lie dead next to me. My stomach twists into knots, and my eyelids are hot with unshed tears.

They were both virtuous and loyal and deserved so much more than me.

I gently shut Pavlos's eyelids with my fingers. He killed Achilles but only because of his fidelity. "I'm so sorry, my friend. You believed it was your duty to protect me, and it cost you your life. I won't forget you. I promise."

I move to Achilles, taking his cold hand in mine. "You always said my reckless nature would get me killed someday, but you were wrong. Instead, it's killed everyone I loved. I caused this with my selfishness. All of this. You deserved more in a best friend. But I'll do better from now on. I promise."

Turning my face to the stars, I let my tears flow freely, mourning their premature depature from this world. Who knows what they could have accomplished if they hadn't died so senselessly? Just like so many other young men in both armies.

The army! A quick glance around confirms the Spartans are missing—as is Paris. They must be inside Troy's walls.

I stand. I have to leave, but I don't want to. Achilles and Pavlos deserve a proper burial, beneath the ground, where the wolves won't be able to feast on them. But I don't have time for that—not now. Not when Troy needs me.

"Goodbye, my friends," I whisper. "I'll come back for you as soon as I can. I promise."

THE BLOWS KEEP COMING

AFTER A TWO-DAY TREK, TROY APPEARS ON THE HORIZON. THE Spartan camp is gone—as if it never existed—which means Paris reached Achilles in time. I laugh and cry simultaneously, my tension melting away. Leaving the flock grazing in sparse grass south of the city, I set out to find the rightful king and share a celebratory glass of wine.

The moment I enter the gate I feel it; something's amiss. A familiar yet unplaceable odor permeates around me, and the air is infused with negative energy that makes every hair on my body stand on end. As I jog through the streets, the ever-present noises—horse hooves against the stone roads, animals caterwauling, and human chattering—are absent, and I don't encounter a single Trojan.

The narrative darkens when I emerge into the market; the vendors' stores are toppled, and broken pottery is scattered everywhere. The Eternal Flame—the constant burning light of Troy—has been smothered. I drop to my knees next to it.

A few paltry ashes smolder at the bottom of the pit, evidence it was extinguished not that long ago. The stone walkway beneath me is a shade or two darker than normal. I trace my fingers against it, covering them in a rusty film. Suddenly, I'm able to place the metallic smell.

Blood.

After months of war, I know it well. My worry transforms into panic.

I hop up and reach Iris and Theos's house in a flash, hoping they are safe inside. They have to be; the alternative is too dire, considering they are my only Trojan friends who are still alive. I race through their house, frantically searching the rooms. Iris is in her bedroom, staring out the window.

"Iris?" I say timidly. "Are you okay?"

She turns. Her greasy hair hangs loosely around her puffy face, and her chiton is soiled with dirt and dried blood. Her eyes slowly focus on me. "You! How dare you come here? After everything that's happened, I never want to see you again."

Iris lunges, punching my chest over and over. I restrain her arms as gently as I can, and eventually, she stops fighting and collapses in my arms.

"You promised me Troy was favored," she whispers, "so why did the gods let this happen?"

Her hair's muskiness is overpowering, so I turn my head away. "Let what happen?"

She steps out of my reach. "Let the Spartans kill Theos."

"Theos is dead?"

"All of Troy's men are. They killed them. All of them."

My stomach churns, and I swallow to prevent myself

from throwing up. "B-B-But I negotiated a truce with Achilles on behalf of the king. I don't understand what could have happened."

"The almighty Oracle Hector always thinks he knows best. Obviously, Achilles didn't like your terms because the Spartans marched to our city's gate and demanded entrance. And the guards had no choice but to let them in, since Paris was their prisoner."

I tremble at her account of the events, uncertain how to make sense of them. Achilles would never have betrayed me like that. Not when he gave his word. He's too honorable. And Paris knew his role; he wouldn't have deviated from the script, not when there was so much at stake.

Something is amiss, but I don't have time to figure it out. Not right now.

"Is Paris dead too?" I ask.

She shakes her head. "I don't know, but if I had to guess, he's being held at the palace, along with Helen. I would give anything to exact revenge on the man who killed Theos. I'm sure Menelaus feels the same way and wants to deal with them personally."

If Paris is alive, there's still hope.

Speaking of Paris, where is Dameaon? With no Magic left in his Crystal, he must still be disguised as the prince of Troy. That means hanging around the palace would be dangerous. But I'm not worried; my twin always finds a way to save himself.

I nod. "Thank you, Iris. I know everything is terrible right now, and I'm so sorry for that. But you must remember, pain is a part of life. You loved and were loved, which is more than most people get in a lifetime. Perhaps you will love aga—"

"Oh, quiet, Hector. I'll never love again, I promise you that. Since all of our men were murdered, some Spartan soldiers are staying in Troy and claiming the women as war trophies. So don't you dare preach about love."

"By the gods," I whisper.

This is even worse than I thought. Iris is right; her life is over. The thought of her going from a loving relationship with Theos to a forced one with a Spartan soldier is too much to bear.

But maybe there is something I can do to help—or rather, something a god can do. Although Achilles deluded me, he's still a reasonable man. If a god were to demand it, he would let Paris go and take his whole army back to Sparta. I'm certain of it.

"I'm so sorry for everything, Iris," I say. "I can't bring Theos back, but I will get the Spartans out of Troy."

She turns to face the wall. "I'll believe it when I see it, but frankly, Hector, all you seem to do is make things worse."

There's no point in arguing or trying to defend myself. She's lost everything, including her faith in me—and who can blame her?

With a clear purpose and fierce resolve, I set out for the palace.

I SPRINT THROUGH THE STREETS, THANKFUL THAT THE ROADS are still empty. Outside the palace gates, I clutch my Crystal and transform into Ares, the Spartans' favorite immortal. Although becoming a god is definitely against the Rules, I'm past caring. There's very little chance I will pass my trial anyway. All that matters is saving Paris and the Trojan women.

I knock on the door and cry out to open it, but the only response is the roar of the crashing waves on the shore. I clench my palm into a fist and open it, hurling a jagged hailstone at the entrance.

Taking heed of the splintered wood, I crouch and sidle through the blasted hole. The courtyard is surprisingly tranquil, which seems appropriate for a makeshift graveyard.

Iris said the Spartans killed all the Trojan men.

Common sense should have prepared me for this. That many bodies would have to be piled somewhere. But the copious number of Trojan corpses—stacked in haphazard pyramids—is horrific. My heart pounds in my chest, and bile burns the back of my throat. I hold my chiton to my nose in a pathetic attempt to block out the fetor of decaying flesh as I venture farther inside. Sheer terror is plastered on the men's faces; their deaths were slow and painful.

The fountain I froze with Magic so long ago still flows, only now the water runs red from spilled blood. It's encircled by seven pikes, with a decapitated head displayed on each one like a grotesque wildflower. One, two, three, four, five, six—each of the Elders are accounted for.

The seventh skewer is mounted with Paris's head, and my hope for Troy dies.

"Oh, Paris," I whisper. "Forgive me."

His tongue is lopped out the side of his mouth like an

overheated dog. I try to remove his head from the pike, but his blistering flesh peels off in my hands. A cockroach wriggles out of his left eye socket, and I stumble backward, heaving until my sides hurt.

And then I remember Dexter's potions. I hastily dump out the contents of my bag and open the potion kit, removing the red one. I manage to wrench Paris's head off the skewer and lay it next to his neck before pouring the potion over him. Nothing happens, but then, it took a moment for the first potion to work too.

After a minute passes, I resign myself to the truth—even Reos's Magic has limits and cannot bring a human back from the dead.

I shut my eyes, trying to calm my racing heart. Two days ago, Paris was smiling. He was happy, until I sent him to his death. If only I had left him on Mount Ida, tending to his sheep. He would still be alive now.

Straightening, I notice the small mound in the far-left corner.

It's the male children of Troy, flung in a careless heap. Elpidius, the carver's son, is in the stack, his little hand resting against his cheek—now green with mold, instead of vibrant pink. I raise my face to the sky and scream as loudly as I can.

Thwack!

An arrow whisks by my left ear, shot by a Spartan behind me. Several more soldiers emerge from the middle palace door, swords drawn for battle.

The intense rage inside me bursts out, filling the sky with gunmetal clouds that shroud the world in shadow. I aim my right pointer and middle fingers at the advancing soldiers, hurling icicles into their eyes. After three of his comrades fall, the archer drops his bow.

He raises his hands above his head. "Please . . . Ares, I didn't recognize you. Show mercy."

"You don't deserve mercy," I spit, executing him.

He topples to the ground, but more soldiers emerge. I continue my assault until there are no Spartans left alive.

I stand for a moment, surveying the courtyard—now a wasteland of broken statues, icy fountains, frosted barbs, and bloodied Spartans. Satisfied, I enter the middle palace door. The royal wing is untouched—filled with artwork of the immortals—and there are no Spartans in sight. It's surreal, as if everything that happened was a nightmare. If only that were true.

In some sort of poetic justice, Ward and Layland are standing guard at the king's suite. My thirst for vengeance has subsided enough that I don't have the desire to hurt them. Plus, I need them alive.

"Ares," Ward says, bowing his head. "By the gods, is it really you?"

Layland falls to his knees in reverence.

"Take me to your general," I say. "I must speak with Achilles at once."

They don't move, immobile from their awe. I freeze Ward's legs—in part to deliver a message and also in payback for holding his blade to my throat. "Let me speak with him, or I'll freeze you both to death."

Layland closes his eyes. "Ares, Achilles is dead."

I take a step backward. "No. How?"

"Paris's guard killed him," Ward spits. "Or should I say the imposter's guard."

"Imposter?"

Ward snarls his lip. "Yesterday, Paris and his guard showed up at our camp and told Achilles that Troy agreed to the terms of surrender. But then, in the middle of their meeting, another Paris showed up—obviously the work of some evil sorcery.

"Achilles identified which Paris was the fraud and tried to kill him, but the Trojan guard stabbed our general first. At least I was able to avenge him by killing the guard and the imposter."

And just like that, the missing piece falls into place. Somehow, my twin discovered my plan. For reasons unknown to me, he went to see Achilles, oblivious to the fact the real Paris was on his way to the camp. And when he showed up—well, I can't imagine how duped Achilles felt. No wonder it ended in bloodshed.

What's worse, Ward said he killed the fake Paris, which means Dameaon could be really injured—with no Magic left in his Crystal to heal himself. I need to finish this, so I can go and find him.

"If Achilles is dead, who are you guarding?" I ask.

"Queen Helen," Ward says. "We are taking her back to Sparta so Menelaus can deal with her treachery."

After everything that's happened, Helen has managed to stay alive. "I demand to speak with her."

Layland opens the door and moves out of my way. "Of course, Ares."

Inside, Helen is lying on the bed, facing the far wall. I shut the door behind me, and she turns, propping herself up on her elbows. "Ares? What are you doing here?"

"Oracle Hector sent me," I say.

"Hector?" she asks, sitting up and perching on the edge of the mattress. "Do you bring word of Paris? Was he able to escape? Is he safe?"

I still; I have no desire to deliver more bad news, but it's better if she believes he's dead. "I'm sorry, Helen, but he has passed on to Elysium."

She clutches her heart and shakes her head. "He can't be dead. He can't. I tried to end this war for him. I said things that made him hate me, but I didn't care, because it kept him safe. But now, if he's dead . . . I did it all for nothing. Not if he died hating me. If he died not knowing how much I really loved him."

Helen's selfishness caused this war, but my heart still aches for her. She tried to do the right thing in the end, and it wasn't enough. Unless . . . maybe she can help both cities. "It is so. But I promise you, he is in a better place, and you will be reunited with him someday. Provided you dedicate the rest of your life to doing good."

"Doing good?"

I sit on the mattress next to her and clutch my ankh amulet. "Yes. You have an opportunity to help Troy. The Spartans killed the Trojan males, even the children. And some of the soldiers are staying here and taking the women as their war prizes. When you return, you must convince Menelaus to forget about Troy's indiscretions. They have lost enough."

"I want to help you, Ares, truly. But I am going back as a prisoner," she says. "I doubt that Menelaus will listen to anything I have to say."

I hate to admit it, but Helen has a point. Menelaus is a kind man, but he's also proud. And ruthless. He won't forgive Helen for her betrayal, even if he still loves her. But he's also a devout believer in the immortals, and I can use that. "I'll tell the soldiers Aphrodite put a love spell on you, and I just broke it. As long as you never tell him the truth, he will show mercy."

She scrunches her eyebrows together. "Are you certain he will believe that?"

"He will want to believe it, Helen," I insist. "He loved you once, and he can love you again. Consider this your penance for betraying your marriage to him. Persuade Menelaus to have mercy on the Trojans. Help the Spartans learn compassion. Be the queen both cities need to move on."

She nods. "If this is what the immortals ask, I will comply."

I was hoping for a more enthusiastic response, but at least she agreed. "It is, Helen," I say, standing. "I will be watching from Mount Olympus, so don't disappoint me."

I head for the door, but she calls to me. I turn around. "Yes?"

Her eyes are wet with unshed tears. "For what it's worth, I am sorry. For all of it. I didn't mean for this to happen. I just . . . I just wanted to be happy."

"If you mean that, truly mean it, take this opportunity to change."

She clenches her hands into small fists on the sides of her body. "I promise to do the best I can."

I open the door. "That's all any of us can do. Good luck, Helen."

Outside, Layland is attempting to defrost Ward's legs by rubbing them.

"Queen Helen's love for Paris was not her fault," I say. "Aphrodite cast a spell on her, which I have just removed. She is ready to return to her real husband and resume her marriage. No harm should come to her because of the goddess's actions."

"Aphrodite did this?" Ward asks.

I nod. "By the word of an immortal, it is true. I demand you gather all your troops and leave for Sparta with Helen. If you don't depart tomorrow, the wrath of the gods will fall on your city. And if you don't believe me, take a look at the courtyard. It was your well-deserved punishment for killing the men and boys of Troy."

Their terrified expressions make me confident they'll follow my orders. Having done everything I could for the remaining Trojans, I head out to find my brother.

I don't have to go far; Dameaon is in the courtyard, fury in his eyes.

THERE'S ENOUGH BLAME TO GO AROUND

I REEL AROUND IN A CIRCLE, SCRUTINIZING THE FROSTED wasteland that was once the palace courtyard. Only one thing could cause this much damage. Magic.

The nearby door creaks, forewarning me someone is coming. I duck behind a now-headless Artemis statue and peer around the goddess's left arm.

It's Ares—or rather, my brother disguised as the god of war. Besides the fact the immortals aren't real, I'd recognize his self-righteous visage anywhere.

I charge at him. "You're insane. You have to be, to kill these men with Magic."

He points to the courtyard's left corner, where small bodies are piled into a pyramid. "The Spartans deserved it. They murdered all the Trojan men, including the male children."

I throw my arms up. "That doesn't give you the right to play god, even if you look like one."

"You're one to talk," he says. "And don't think I didn't notice you turned back into your Glanching form. So much for your Crystal being out of Magic. Just another lie in the millions you've told me. And your interference in my plan got Achilles killed and ruined any chance Troy had at survival. What were you thinking?"

"I could ask you the same thing about Helen. You went behind my back to conspire with her. What were *you* thinking?"

"You can't be serious," he says. "Helen came to me for help."

I shrug. "If that's your story."

He points at the corpses again. "Why didn't you use Magic to save them? You've broken every other Rule. Why stop there?"

"Gee, I'm sorry, I was a little busy hemorrhaging blood from my forehead, you know, after being stabbed. Besides, while most Rules are nonsense, I do follow my own moral code. And that includes fair fights. I know you think the worst of me, but I'm not a savage." I gesture at the courtyard. "Unlike you. I can't believe you did this."

He shifts his eyes. "It's your fault I was in this situation in the first place. If you hadn't stolen Helen, none of this would have happened. Look what you caused. And for what? For *love* with a human?"

There's truth in what he's saying, of course. But I won't give him the satisfaction of agreement. "The Helen thing got a little out of hand, and that's unfortunate."

"Unfortunate?" he says, tugging at his hair. "That's a bit of an understatement, don't you think?"

"I suppose. But we'll do better with the next civilization."

He straightens his spine, and his shoulders stiffen. "You are delusional if you think we're going to get another chance. This is it for us. We failed."

I jut out my chin. "Maybe. I would argue our trial goal was to make the Trojans more self-reliant. We did that."

"The Trojans aren't self-reliant anymore, Dameaon. They have no food. No men. No leader. We're going home to be banished. Or worse. Maybe we'll be annihilated. And it's all your fault."

"You chose to be a Guide, brother, just like me. If we fail, it's both our faults. And if I'm annihilated, at least I won't have to listen to you a min—"

A warm sensation on my left pointer finger stops me in my tracks. I hold up my hand, displaying my Crystal, glowing with a soft purple light. "Guess we'll find out soon enough."

My twin licks his lips. "We aren't due to go back yet. We can't. We have to help Troy first."

"Help them how? There isn't anything left we can do. Besides, the Rules dictate we must return to Reos the moment our Crystals glow," I say, mimicking him. "And I'm guessing the Oldungur Council is mad enough already. We don't want to keep them waiting."

"This is the moment you decide to start following the Rules? Come on, Dameaon, help me. Please. We owe the Trojans that."

"You're so certain we aren't going to pass this trial. If you're right, humankind will be destroyed, so anything we do to help the Trojans will be pointless anyway."

He shakes his head. "It's still the right thing to do."

"You've lost sight of the big picture. Our best chance

to help the humans is to go back and plead our case. Now. Troy is lost, but maybe we can persuade Cassandre into giving humankind another chance. Giving them a future."

My twin looks at the ground. "If we do nothing for Troy, *I* have no future. I can't abandon them."

"And I can't stay here," I say, backing away from him. "I'll be back on Reos, when you come to your senses. Until then, best of luck, brother."

FRATERNAL DEFIANCE

In the ominous silence of the palace courtyard, my brother disappears through the jagged hole in the door, abandoning Troy, his duty, and me. An uncontrollable shudder courses through my body. His apathy is despicable, but I have bigger problems right now.

Even though I eliminated the threat from the Spartan army, Troy is still in jeopardy. The fields are decimated, and while the harbor will be usable once the Spartans leave, all the fishermen lie dead around me. In addition, when the neighboring cities learn all of Troy's men are dead, there will be nothing left to stop them from invading. Especially since some of the kings believe Troy is beholden to them for sending troops.

Troy's best chance is reestablishing its seaway trade passages, to import merchandise from far-off lands. They could exchange those goods for food and livestock and slowly rebuild their wealth. Unfortunately, the merchantmen are also dead, and the stockpile of olive oil—Troy's main commodity—was drained long ago.

What the Trojans need is an ally—one with the resources and men required to restart their trade ships—who won't pillage the city while they are at their weakest.

Dardanus.

Just north of here, it's one of the cities I visited while learning how to be an oracle. It's small—at most, half the size of Troy—and their king, Erichthonius, has little desire for prestige or power, but a fondness for wealth and possessions—making him a perfect choice. But he's also a man who avoids risks—at all cost. He will need a good reason to help Troy, and Oracle Hector won't be able to persuade him. It will take someone with a bit more . . . intimidation capability. Fortunately, I have a whole arsenal of immortals to choose from to pull this off.

Confident I've come up with a solid plan, I race down the streets of Troy to Iris's house. Every second counts right now, but I have one more task to complete before heading to Dardanus. With any luck, Jetta has stopped watching the Viewing Sphere, assuming we are on our way back to the Teleportation Machine.

When I reach Iris's front door, I pause. She isn't going to listen to me. Not as Hector. Not when she's so deep in her grief. I clutch my Crystal and transform into Aphrodite, heading up to her room.

She's still where I left her, staring vacantly at the wall.

"Iris?"

She turns and falls to her knees. "Aphrodite? What are you doing here?"

I take her hands, pulling her to her feet. "After all you

have been through, child, you bow to no one. I am here for you. You think the immortals abandoned Troy, but we haven't."

"Forgive me, goddess, but if the immortals were still on Troy's side, you would have intervened sooner. Before our great city fell into the hands of the Spartans."

"The immortals have infinite power, but we use it in mysterious ways. Did I not make Theos fall in love with you? Did you not have a blessed marriage with him?"

"Yes," she says, shutting her eyes, "but it wasn't enough time."

I touch her cheek. "It never is. Humans' lives are short. You must cherish the good times and remember, when the bad times come, they don't last forever. Once you have grieved Theos, I hope you will open your heart to the possibility of loving another."

She crosses her arms in front of her chest. "I'm sorry, Aphrodite, but I will never love again."

"Never is a long time, especially when you're still so young. One as generous as you should not live their life alone."

"I doubt there is much time left for me, goddess. And the time I do have will be under Spartan rule."

I rub my neck. "I told you, the immortals have not abandoned Troy. The Spartans will be leaving for home at once. And Dardanus will send help to your gates in two days' time."

"I don't understand?" she says. "Why would the Spartans leave? Or Dardanus help us?"

"Because the immortals demand it," I say. "And you play a pivotal role in our plan. You must help the other women overcome their grief and encourage them to embrace the Dardanian citizens. Rebuild Troy and make it a stronger city than it ever was. Can I count on you, Iris?"

"Yes, goddess," she says. "I will try my best."

The coldness in her eyes remains—and I imagine it will take a long time for it to wane.

If ever.

I offer her a half smile. "I have one more request. Find a way to forgive those whose actions took so much from you. Hatred will poison you if you can't find a way to let it go."

She nods but refuses to look at me. I'm certain she can't imagine a time when she won't be angry.

"My work here is done for now," I say, "but I will watch over you from Mount Olympus. Farewell, Iris."

"Farewell, Aphrodite," she says, but I'm already halfway down the stairs.

Out in the street, I take a moment to collect myself, slowly breathing in the crisp air. Seeing vibrant, upbeat Iris so broken was devastating. I can only hope my words will make a difference—someday.

Once my knees stop quivering, I use my Crystal to transform back into my Glanching form. Then I remove my amulet, placing it in my shoulder bag.

I cannot risk Jetta bringing me home, not until I speak to King Erichthonius.

From the couple weeks' time I spent in Dardanus, I'm familiar enough with its layout to expeditiously navigate to the palace. Thankfully, there are no walls to infiltrate, and the outskirts are practically barren during the early evening hours.

I race through their cobbled streets, past their singular temple—dedicated to Apollo—to the palace at the northeast corner of the city. Finding cover in a grove of olive trees, I take my amulet from my bag and place it around my neck. I clutch my ankh in my right hand and transform into their most revered immortal. Then I charge toward their palace.

The guard stationed by the main door bows his head. "Apollo, w-w-what are you doing here?"

I don't have time to be polite, not when the Oldungur Council is waiting. "Bring me your king. Now."

He bows again and charges through the door. I tap my foot, wishing he would hurry, especially since my Crystal is back around my neck.

One. Two. Three. Four.

Five minutes pass; I'm ready to head inside and find the king myself when the guard returns—with Erichthonius.

The king bows before me, displaying his completely bald head, adorned with a simple gold crown. "Apollo, blessed of all gods, we are humbly here to serve you."

"I am glad to hear that, King Erichthonius, because I bring troubling news," I say. "As you know, Troy has been battling Sparta for many months. Unfortunately, they lost the war."

He pales, licking his thin lips. "By the gods, will they come for us next?"

"No. The immortals have intervened, and hope is not lost. The Spartans are, as we speak, leaving for home. Your city is safe, and Troy can rebuild."

"A blessing from the gods indeed," he says.

"Which brings me to why I am here. The Spartans murdered all of the Trojan men, and the women will not survive without your help. You must unite the two cities. Supply half of your current olive oil so that the trade ships can resume their routes. Provide them with all the goats and cattle you can spare. Send half of your men to Troy to help the women restore their city. Some of your citizens used to live in Troy and made their living as fishermen and sailors. Make sure a few of them go back and teach the others. In return, half of what used to fill Troy's coffers from trade will now fill Dardanus's."

His eyes light up at the prospect, but then they darken. "Forgive me, Apollo, but what if no one wants to go?"

"Many of your people will enjoy the opportunity to start over. They know of Troy's harbors and trade. Some will come. I have no doubt."

He nods. "As you wish, Apollo. I will execute your orders."

I straighten my back, narrowing my eyes. "These resources, including the men, must arrive at Troy's gates in two days' time. I will be watching from Mount Olympus. Do not fail me."

"I-I won't," he says, extending his shaking hand.

I grasp it firmly, closing our deal. He is terrified of me. Good—that means he will comply.

My work here is done; Troy will survive, at least for now.

"Then I will take my leave," I say, turning and walking away.

I only make it a few paces. Then my vision blurs, and everything around me disappears.

I MATERIALIZE IN THE BACK OF OUR GUIDE CLASSROOM. JETTA is a few feet away, pacing next to the Viewing Sphere. The combination of his deep scowl, down-turned lips, and dark eyes leaves little doubt—he's furious. And who can blame him? Dameaon and I have been disappointing Guides—in every way.

Speaking of my twin, he's leaning against the wall behind Jetta. He frowns and faintly shakes his head.

Our Guru throws his hands into the air. "What were you thinking, Villow? How could you stay on Earth after I called you back?"

I clutch my Crystal and change into my Glanching form. "I had to. If I didn't, the Trojans would have been doomed. And my plan worked. They—"

"You made things so much worse for yourself," he says. "You made me use a Transmission Potion to get you back here when you should have used the Teleportation Machine. The Oldungur Council demanded we head to Kapitala for your report out immediately upon your return. Now I will have to explain why we're late."

"Immediately?"

He nods. "Yes, immediately. That does not bode well for either of you." He grabs a potion off the table and pours it into the top of the Teleportation Machine. "Nor does the fact we are going by potion."

Sweat forms on my forehead, and my knees become too weak to hold me up. This is more dire than I thought. Normally, Guides complete their report outs within three days of returning from their planet. And using Transmission Potions for travel between places on Reos is considered wasteful, since the train can travel anywhere in six hours or less. This means the Oldungur Council wants our report out completed as soon as possible.

We failed.

There is no other reason to rush it. The only outstanding question is, will we mine Magical Ore for eternity or be annihilated?

I steal a glance at Dameaon, but his hair has fallen into his eyes and I can't read his mood.

Our Guru steps into the Teleportation Machine. "This goes without saying, but don't talk unless spoken to. I will do everything in my power to gain the Oldungur Council's mercy, but you must be obedient and remorseful." He looks pointedly at my twin, who crosses his arms in response.

"I'm serious, Dameaon," Jetta says. "Your very existence hangs in the balance. Listen to me for once. Obedient and remorseful. Even if you aren't. It's your only chance. Understood?"

"Yes, Guru," I say, stepping inside the Teleportation Machine.

My brother mumbles incoherently, but at least he joins us.

"Okay, my boys, here we go," Jetta says, pushing the button.

As the world fades, I can't help thinking this will very likely be our first—and final—judgment.

WE REAPPEAR JUST OUTSIDE THE OLDUNGUR COUNCIL'S EDIfice. It's always been my favorite building at Kapitala; besides being the location where the Council completes all its official work, its impressive size and onyx surface convey the Oldungurs' power and influence over the Glanching population.

"Come," Jetta says, stepping out of the Teleportation Machine and toward its entrance.

My fear transforms the building's triangle visage into a pointed dagger, piercing into Zon's amber surface in the violet sky. An empty pit forms in my stomach, and I have the irrational desire to flee. But where would I go? The Council's reach is omnipresent, and they would find me in no time. Besides, running away from problems is not a Glanching thing to do; it's time to face what I've done.

I force my shaking legs forward, following Jetta through the main doors—etched with our ancient language—into the octagonal lobby. Jetta heads inside the back door to alert the Council of our arrival, leaving Dameaon and me alone.

The lobby is filled with display cases that tell the Glanching's rich history and house wonders from every corner of Reos. On a normal day, I could spend hours here, moving from case to case, gleaning new information I somehow missed the first fifty times.

But right now, I don't feel like reveling in Reos's

history—not when I no longer have one of my own. I collapse on a nearby bench, grateful to be off my feet—even for a moment. Dameaon leans against the wall across from me, looking completely relaxed.

Heat flashes through my body. He's the reason we are going to fail, and somehow he's completely calm.

"Why aren't you upset?" I ask. "We're about to get banished. Or annihilated. And we destroyed our Original Species forever."

He shrugs. "You don't know that for sure. Besides, worrying never did anyone any good."

"Maybe if you had done a little more worrying while we were on Earth, I wouldn't be so panicked now. Your careless attitude is the reason we're here."

"Of course," he says. "Everything is my fault. As always."

I jump to my feet, placing my hand on my forehead. "It is your fault! If you didn't steal Helen, the war wouldn't have happened. And we would pass today, no question."

"Oh, right. And I'm sure the complete ruin you caused in the courtyard with Magic will score us high marks. That was well played, brother."

I tug my hair. "Stop acting like this is some kind of game."

"Are you sure this *isn't* a game? You're the one who constantly refers to the Rules."

"The Rules are there to help us. If you—"

The door lets out an audible rasp, and Jetta returns with Oldungur Mekhi.

I haven't seen the latter since our Path Ceremony—almost a year ago—but his surly expression is uncharacteristic. As the Guide Oldungur, he's responsible for all his Seekers and is likely certain we will make him look bad in front of the rest of the Council. And he did just interrupt a fight between Dameaon and me—who are due to report out any minute.

Mekhi remains by the door, but our Guru crosses the lobby to where we're standing.

"The Council is ready to hear your report out," Jetta says. Then he continues, his voice at a whisper, "Mekhi believes our best bet is to focus on the Trojans' level of goodness and try to avoid the topic of the war as much as possible. And he says we're in luck. Cassandre is in good spirits today."

My stomach flutters with the slightest ounce of hope. Maybe, just maybe, we can survive this.

"Let's head inside," he says. "And remember, do not speak unless you are spoken to."

I follow Jetta across the lobby, and Mekhi leads us inside the door, entering Hotarare Hall. Since the chamber is only used for Seekers' report outs, I have never be granted access before.

It's even more intimidating than I thought it would be. The circular walls are made of solid onyx, and it's cavernous, with a ceiling three times as high as the room is round. There are four curved benches near the entrance and a small jade podium in the middle of the room. The far end has a six-person granite desk on a ten-foot-high platform, where the Oldungur Council—minus Mekhi—are already sitting. Their significant height advantage makes them even more imposing than normal.

Our footsteps echo inside the hollow space—amplifying

the soft clicks of our heels into loud booms—as Mekhi ushers us to the front bench. Dameaon and I sit next to each other while Jetta continues forward to the podium. Mekhi moves behind the platform, sitting in the open seat on the far right of the desk.

Oldungur Mekhi turns to his right and addresses his peers. "Good afternoon, fellow Council members. Today, on the twenty-fifth day of Janner, Guide Seekers Dameaon and Villow Verchant come before us for their first report out. Jetta Kuo, their Guru, is here to present their case. As a reminder, the twins' goal was to influence the Trojans to become more self-reliant, while still keeping their goodness, so when their leader passed, they could survive. Please remember this goal as their Guru takes us through their performance. I'll now turn it over to Jetta, who can take us through—"

Cassandre holds up her left hand, silencing him. "We are well aware of what the twins' trial goal was, Mekhi. We don't need to waste our time with a play-by-play. We know how many Rules they have broken, and we know Troy is practically in ruins—from a war Dameaon caused, no less. Jetta, what, if anything, can you offer as a reason they passed this trial?"

Jetta clears his throat. "Thank you, Master Oldungur Cassandre," he says, and I place my hand over my chest. Only his back is visible to me, but I can tell his shoulders are rigid from tension. Yet his tone offers no indication of his nerves. "I can give you two reasons. First, the Trojans remained a civilization of goodness, even when faced with the horrors of war. In their darkest hours, they showed great bravery and loyalty to their king and city. That is not an Original Species who is evil, but rather one that has hope for future goodness. It's proof that the humans have a real shot at re-creation. And you know the situation with their Essence Orb. This is their last chance, so I believe allowances must be made.

"Second, there have never been co-Guides before, and there were clearly some . . . bugs that had to be worked out. I am certain you remember your promise of mercy, Master Oldungur Cassandre, when Villow and Dameaon agreed to this arrangement."

Cassandre rests her chin against her steepled hands. "My promise of mercy did not give the twins free rein to do whatever they wanted. Surely you're not bold enough to ask for that much mercy, Jetta?"

"I am, Master Oldungur. The twins made mistakes, yes, but they showed moments of promise too. Dameaon expanded Troy's trade enterprise to include far-off cities, increasing both their wealth and their commodities. Villow helped make their land fertile so the Trojans could plant crops and bolster their food source. And in the end, he convinced Dardanus, a neighboring city, to help rebuild Troy even after the war devastated their city. So, yes, I do believe they deserve mercy."

"Convinced Dardanus?" Cassandre says. "Villow pretended to be Apollo. They could hardly say no to a god, could they? Really, Jetta, that's not compelling."

I sag back on the bench, suddenly feeling very hollow. I was so proud of my resolution, but she dismissed it like it was trivial. Unimportant even.

"If this is Cassandre in a good mood, I would hate to see her in a bad one," Dameaon whispers in my ear.

I hold my pointer finger to my lips, reminding him to be quiet. The Council doesn't need one more reason to be upset with us.

Jetta bows his head. "With all due respect, Cassandre, it *is* compelling. His devotion to the humans, even when all hope was lost, is admirable. Dameaon and Villow have it in them to be strong Guides and deserve another chance as Seekers." He pauses, continuing in a softer voice. "If you need additional justification, I ask you to consider Project Hara-kiri."

Project Hara-kiri?

While I'm certain I've never heard of it, the Council clearly knows what it is. All the Oldungurs—minus Cassandre—shift their eyes.

She frowns and lifts her right palm. "Enough, Jetta. We have let you speak, but it is our turn now. I call for a yay or nay vote to determine Dameaon and Villow Verchant's fate. Remember, you must judge them based on their actions. Ask yourself if they met the requirements of their trial and if they measured up to the Guide Seeker standards of rectitude.

"Oldungur Simyager, you have seniority so you will begin. Yay or nay?"

Simyager peers over his glasses at us, curling his lips. "Villow had the audacity to use potions on Earth. It's a definite nay for me."

Dameaon elbows my ribs, no doubt because Simyager cited me as the cause of his vote. But even if I hadn't used potions, he still wouldn't have said yes. He's been the Alchemist Oldungur for hundreds of years and is a bit of a dogmatist. Dexter has never said anything positive about him.

Dexter.

I hope Simyager doesn't figure out where I got the potions; I would hate to take my friend down with me.

Cassandre turns her head to the left. "Mekhi, as the Seekers' Oldungur representative, you are next."

Mekhi offers us a weak smile. "While I agree the twins made many mistakes, Jetta raised solid points, and I believe they have promise. It's a yay for me."

One to one.

Our odds could be worse.

"Oldungur Hana, you have next seniority," Cassandre says.

Hana, the Mage representative, offers us a sympathetic half smile. "I'm sorry, but it's a nay for me."

"Oldungur Gregg, you are next," Cassandre says.

He shoots daggers at my twin; apparently, he's still furious about his Soldier Class defection. "It's a definite no for me. Someone obviously didn't select the right Path."

"Siva, 'tis your turn," Cassandre says.

The Performance Class lead strokes her pointy chin and gazes at us, pondering her answer.

One to three.

If we get one more nay, we are finished. But Siva is allegedly the most easygoing member of the Council. There's still hope.

Finally, Siva turns to Cassandre. "While I believe Villow and Dameaon have potential, I cannot move past their reckless abandonment of the Rules. It is a no for me."

Four nays.

My face burns with embarrassment, and my eyes are hot with unshed tears. It's as if I'm suddenly on display. We are failures—and the whole room knows it.

"The Oldungur Council has spoken," Cassandre says. "Since my vote will not make a difference, I will show you the mercy of refraining. Let it go on record that Dameaon and Villow Verchant have failed their trial and are declared unfit as Seekers. The humans' Essence Orb will be destroyed, removing them from existence forever. All that remains is the Council's decision if banishment or annihilation is most appropriate for the Seekers' performance. Jetta, take the Seekers to the lobby while we deliberate. You are dismissed."

I lean forward, draping my limp hands over my knees. I can't believe it—all hope is lost. While I knew there was a good chance we would fail, deep down I was convinced my final acts would save us. And the Trojans.

But now, they—along with all the other humans—will be annihilated. The Verchant name will be tarnished forever. I'll never see my family or friends again. I won't get to tell my father that, despite everything, I still respect him. Or Katarin that she was the best friend a Glanching could have. Or Portia that I love her. Or Dexter how talented he is.

Tears form behind my eyes, but I won't fall apart. Not in front of the Council. I push up onto my feet and offer them a flinty gaze before heading toward the door.

Halfway there, I realize my twin is still seated.

"Dameaon," I say, my voice just above a whisper. "We have to leave. Now."

My twin turns to me, and I step backward, shocked at the heat radiating from his amber eyes. He shakes his head—once—standing.

Jetta reaches him and grabs his shoulders, trying to pull him backward, but Dameaon shakes him off and advances to the podium.

If we weren't destined for annihilation before, this should clinch it for us.

"I know you don't want to hear from me, but that's too bad." He turns to look at me for a moment before continuing, "For as long as I can remember, I've never measured up to my twin. At home, in school, in every aspect of life. And I never realized how lonesome it was. Not really.

"Then I went to Earth and was surrounded by humans. For once, I fit in. They brought out the best in me, and I really did do everything I could to help them. But when I met Helen, the loneliness inside me was replaced by true acceptance. It made me weak and selfish. The Trojans suffered for my happiness, and I realize how unfair it was. I would do it differently if I could.

"You can punish me however you see fit, and I'll deserve it. But please, don't blame the humans for my actions. Do not destroy their Essence Orb. Assign a new Guide, a better Guide, to lead them to goodness. I know they can do it."

Cassandre offers him a weak smile. "I appreciate your bravery, Dameaon, in speaking on behalf of the humans. Frankly, it is one of the traits I most admire. But it changes nothing. We don't reassign an Original Species to a new Guide when theirs fail. It is not the way things are done."

My brother shrugs. "Then change it. It seems like the Rules can be bent whenever it suits you."

She stiffens, raising her eyebrows. "While I respect bravery, I don't have the same affection for insolence. We were gracious enough to let you speak. Now wait outside while we deliberate, before I lose my patience."

Jetta darts forward and grabs Dameaon's arm, tugging him backward. This time, he comes willingly.

I trail behind, as memories of our trial on Earth invade my mind. Dameaon's insistence of using the Trojan ships to increase trade always felt a bit selfish—as it made him rich—but what if it really *was* to increase their independence? And his attempts to form an army always felt illogical, but what if he was only trying to keep Troy safe? I return to Sailing After Dark, when Dameaon put Oedipus under arrest for Dareios's death. I was furious at the time, but his quick reaction stopped the fighting and kept Troy safe from Spartan retaliation. Stealing Helen was careless—okay, it was downright dangerous—but he did a lot of good too.

Further, what he said about his life was true. Our parents always favored me, and that couldn't have been easy. And if I'm being completely honest, I haven't always been the best brother.

But I have a chance to make it up to him now.

I set my jaw and turn around, facing the Council. "Punish me and spare Dameaon."

Cassandre's eyes widen. "What did you say?"

"I-I'm sorry for speaking out of turn," I say, moving to the podium. "But I can't remain silent. Not after Dameaon's admission. My twin has never taken the blame for anything in his life. But he just did. Surely you can understand how changed he is. The humans did that. I believe, with all that I am, if you give him another chance as their Seeker, he will succeed.

"But I know too much has gone wrong for there to be no consequences. I joined the Trojans in battle after battle. Because I didn't trust my brother, the real Paris was killed and the Spartans were able to invade Troy. And I broke the Rules too. I used Magic to kill the Spartans. I pretended to be the immortals to save Troy. Let me bear both of our punishments, so Dameaon can continue to be the humans' Seeker."

Cassandre rises to her feet and points one long finger at the door. "Out. Now."

I wince. Her tone is clear; she was mad before, but now she's furious.

Bowing my head, I rush from the room.

JUDGMENT DAY

IF ANYONE TOLD ME MY TWIN WOULD STAND UP FOR ME SOMEday, I would have called them insane. But Villow is defending me right now—to the Oldungur Council no less. It's foolish but incredibly brave. And dare I say, even loving. It almost makes all the anguish—Aegidius's slaughter, Helen's betrayal, Achilles's death, and failing as a Guide—sufferable. Everything, that is, except getting the humans destroyed.

Inside Hotarare Hall, I can hear Cassandre dismiss my twin. He dashes out to the lobby, and the door slams shut behind him. Villow places his hands over his face and shakes his head.

He's not used to being insubordinate. Lucky for him, I'm an expert.

"Not too bad for a Rule-following know-it-all Glanching," I say. "How did it feel, standing up to the Oldungur Council?

He removes his hands and lets out a small cackle. "Honestly? It felt . . . good."

I pat his back. "I knew if you spent enough time with me, I would rub off on you."

"Boys, please," Jetta says. "This is serious. I fear you made a bad situation even worse."

I shrug. "We're about to get annihilated, Jetta. It doesn't get much worse than that. You need to learn when to let things go."

He crosses his arms. "This is not a joking matter, Dameaon."

I offer him a half smile. "It has to be. Otherwise it's just . . . sad."

"Not only is this sad, it's also unfair," Jetta says, turning his back to us. "In all my years as a Guru, I've never seen such courage. Such true selfless leadership. I am so proud of you. Both of you." He faces us again, wiping at his eyes.

Villow puts his arm around his shoulders, hugging him—his own tears flowing freely. "Thank you, Jetta. We couldn't have asked for a better Guru. Or friend."

An uncomfortable lump forms in my throat, making it almost impossible to contain my sobs. But I refuse to receive my sentence as an emotional wreck.

I swallow a few times, and the lump subsides. "Stop with all the waterworks, you two. We haven't been sentenced to annihilation. Not yet."

Villow smiles—as if he knows I'm trying to lighten the mood—and releases Jetta.

"Of course, Dameaon," our Guru says, drying his cheeks with the sleeve of his linen shirt. "You're right."

My twin rubs the back of his neck. "Jetta, you mentioned Project Hara-kiri during our report out. What is that?"

"Over the last year, fifty Seekers have disappeared, along with their Olemasolu Statues," he says. "It's not uncommon for one trainee to will themselves out of existence every now and then, but not fifty. The Oldungur Council is obviously concerned, and it's made them laxer with their judgments. I was hoping mentioning it would buy you a bit of mercy."

Fifty Seekers willed themselves out of existence, just like Sariel. If Katarin is aware, perhaps knowing her sister wasn't alone in her decision has brought her a little comfort. I hope so, for her sake.

The door to Hotarare Hall opens, and a stone-faced Mekhi steps into the lobby. "The Council is ready for you," he says, going back inside the room.

For all my bravado and sarcasm, my pulse is suddenly racing. I clench my jaw, backing away from the door in quick, jerky steps. If by some miracle we aren't sentenced to annihilation, we will still be banished. Nothing will ever be the same—and either way, I'll never see anyone I love again.

My twin squeezes my shoulder, pulling me from my thoughts. "It's okay, Dameaon. No matter what happens, we're in this together."

I place my hand on top of his and squeeze it warmly. "There is no one else I'd rather be with, brother." Then I turn to Jetta. "I need one favor. Can you tell Cinders I'm sorry I didn't make it home? Let him know that I tried to keep my promise and that he was the best friend I've ever had."

He scrunches his nose. "Cinders. I'm not sure I know him. Does he go to Moudrost?"

I can't help but smile. "No, he's my family's wyvermalkin."

"Ah, of course," he says, piling his hand on top of Villow's and mine. "I will make sure he knows."

I nod, and Jetta heads for the door. Villow falls in line behind him, and I take up the rear. The Oldungur Council is still seated at their desk, and although I search their faces for clues, they are impossible to read. We reach the front bench, and I perch precariously on the edge.

"I do not believe in dramatics for dramatics' sake, so I will get right to the point," Cassandre says. "Your selflessness moved us. Dameaon, your intense belief in the humans gave us hope for their future. Villow, your willingness to sacrifice yourself to save your twin showed your compassion and love. It evoked our mercy, leading to a revote."

My heart flutters so hard against my chest it echoes in my ears. A revote. The tiniest seed of hope takes root inside me, and I hold my breath.

"This time, the vote resulted in three yays and three nays. As Master Oldungur, any stalemates are decided by me." Cassandre rests her hand on her chin and continues, "Against my better judgment, I approved you for a second trial as Seekers. There will be some modifications to your training, determined by Oldungur Mekhi and your Guru. But be aware, there will be no mercy next time. For now, you are dismissed."

Next time. My life isn't over. Nor is my brother's.

A huge grin forms on my face. We passed!

Jetta stands, nodding at the Council. "Thank you for your mercy. The boys will not disappoint you again."

He points to the exit, and we follow him down the aisle. Halfway to the door, I steal a glance at Cassandre. She shakes her head, but the corners of her lips turn up. I return her smile and then practically run from the room.

We don't stop walking until were outside the Oldungurs' building.

"Did that really just happen?" Villow asks, shaking his head.

Jetta releases a shaky laugh. "It did, my boys. I am so relieved. The thought of losing you . . . Well, no matter. We have been given a reprieve, and we won't waste it."

I offer him a weak smile, but something still feels off inside me; my tension hasn't dissipated like it should have.

"Are you okay, Dameaon?" my twin asks.

I tilt my head. "I guess I'm still in shock."

"I think we all are," Jetta says, rubbing his forehead with his palm. "I'm afraid I have a bit of bad news to share, now that you've passed your trial. Your parents . . . well, they got a divorce, and your father lives in Kapitala now."

My entire body suddenly chills, and I sway on my feet. "Wait, what? When?"

"Six months or so ago," he says. "In any case, I have your father's new address if you want to see him before heading back to Belkin."

"No, I think it's best we head home at once," my twin says. "I'm sure Mother will be eager to see us."

I glance over at him; he seems surprisingly calm for someone who just learned his parents split up. Too calm.

Jetta nods. "I have some business to attend to with Mekhi, so I will see you back in Belkin. We'll reconvene after I figure out the new terms of your trial." He hugs us both and then continues, "I am so proud of you, boys. Enjoy your time off. You earned it."

We bid him farewell, and I'm left alone with my twin.

I study his face for a moment, but he's still not showing signs of shock—or panic.

"Why don't you seem surprised Mom and Dad got divorced?" I ask.

He looks down at the ground. "I . . . I knew Father was considering it. But I didn't think he would actually go through with it."

"You knew? For how long?"

"About a month before we left for Earth. But he didn't tell me. I overheard a conversation and confronted him. Eventually—"

"You knew this whole time and didn't tell me?"

"I didn't tell *anyone*. I was hoping he would change his mind. Besides, it wasn't exactly like we trusted each other. Not back then. But things are different now. We—"

"You always think you know what's best," I say, backing away from him. "And your speech in front of the Oldungur Council tricked me into believing you might actually want to be a real brother for once. But this . . . deception reminds me of who you really are."

"That's not fair," he says, touching my arm. "Things *are* different now."

I pull out of his grasp. "I'm going to the train station. Don't get on the same car as me."

"Dameaon, wait—" he calls, but I don't stop.

There's nothing left to say. Just when I started believing Villow and I could be a real team, reality slaps me in the face. As bad as our relationship has been at times, I never would have kept something like this from him. It's just one more example of the betrayal he is capable of.

But I won't be fooled—not again. My time on Earth taught me well. I put my faith in the wrong people there too, and it almost got me annihilated. Still, many of the humans were loyal and honest, even to the end. I'll be smarter next time and choose the right ones to trust.

For now, it's back to Belkin. It's not a visit I'm looking forward to. While I never understood my parents' marriage, I can't imagine my mom is coping well without my dad. And even though we never got along, Spektrolith will be empty without him.

Still, there's a little wyvermalkin eagerly awaiting my return, and that counts for something.

In fact, it's everything.

A PERMANENT REMINDER

I WATCH MY BROTHER STALK DOWN THE STREET, UNCERTAIN IF I should follow him or not. He's wrong about our relationship; it *is* different now, after our report out. I need to make him understand before—

A hand covers my eyes, blanketing my world in darkness.

"Guess who?" the Glanching standing behind me whispers in my ear.

The voice is female—but I can't place it from a whisper. I press my fingertips against her hand. The skin is soft and smooth, but it's still not enough of a clue. Then I breathe in.

Lupinus flowers.

"Portia?" I ask.

"You passed the test," she says, removing her hand from my eyes.

I turn around, and my heart freezes; she hasn't

changed a bit since I left for Earth. "It's nice to see you, but I don't understand. What are you doing here?"

She laughs, revealing her dimples. "I knew you'd be here, darling."

"How?"

She leans in closer, speaking in a whisper. "Colton is here training, and I came to visit. He overheard his Guru talking about you and Dameaon. He said Oldungur Mekhi called you home early and you were in trouble. So I've been hanging out here because I wanted to make sure you were okay. But you don't seem happy to see me."

"No, of course I am," I say. "I'm sorry. I've just been through a lot."

"Me too. Look," she says, pulling back her hair to reveal the remaining Elemental symbols tattooed on her nape. "I've learned all the Level One Elemental spells and am now officially a year-two Seeker."

I lower my head and break eye contact. It's not fair, but her comparison is disheartening; I watched friend after friend die—and was almost annihilated—while she learned a few spells.

"Hey, what's going on?" she asks.

I attempt to block out my dark memories and kiss her lips—once—quickly. "I'm sorry, was that okay?"

She pulls me back and kisses me again. "It was more than okay. I am your girlfriend after all."

I squeeze her hand. "When you didn't respond to my letter, I got worried."

"You know I'm not one to write. I told you I would be faithful and I have been."

I smile. "I need to see my mother, but first, there is something I must do. Will you join me?"

She nods, and we head down the street together.

Thirty minutes later and fifty kala gulas poorer, Portia and I exit Den of Inktiquities.

She holds up my right hand, pointing at my wrist. "I'm glad you got a tattoo, but I still don't understand what it is."

"It's a Trojan horse," I say, taking the wooden figurine from my bag. "A young boy gave it to me when all hope was lost. It inspired me to make a decision that almost cost me everything. It's a reminder of my mistakes, so I don't repeat them."

She shrugs. "I suppose that's okay, but I still think you should have gone with the Guide crest."

I offer her a forced laugh and take her hand, heading for the train station.

The carriage is practically empty, so we have our choice of seats. We select two in the back, and Portia leans her head against my shoulder, falling into a blissful slumber.

I try to remember the last time I slept that well. It might have been the night before my Path Ceremony and my premonition of doom. But my omen was right; that night did mark the end—of the naive, childlike Villow. Since then, a lot of bad things happened; Katarin and I had our first big fight, my parents got divorced, I watched hundreds of humans die, and I almost failed as a Guide. But some good things happened too; I discovered an internal strength I never knew I had, found love with Portia, and even saw goodness in Dameaon.

Almost a year has passed since that night, but that time has changed me—more than the rest of my life put together. Zon's bright rays shine down through the train's window, warming my bare arm. It's a reminder I'm home—for a little while—and should enjoy it as best I can.

Home.

There is no better place in the universe.

THE END

ACKNOWLEDGMENTS

LIKE ALL OF THE GREATEST THINGS IN LIFE, WRITING IS BEST done in the company of others. I would like to thank those who cast their magic into my life and made this novel possible.

To my husband, Ben, who participated in endless brainstorming sessions and read multiple iterations of this manuscript. Your feedback was invaluable and shaped key moments in the story. Your tireless patience and kind heart are no doubt the closest reflection of a Glanching on Earth.

My deepest gratitude to my mother, the antithesis of Lady Actavia in every way. You've always put your family's needs first, and I'm so fortunate you are my mom and best friend. Thank you for always believing I could finish this novel, especially when I lost hope.

I am eternally grateful to my father for instilling your love of the written word in me. Even while working two jobs and attending graduate school, you still read to me. Luckily, you're not like Lord Drasko, except, of course, in your love of books and cigars.

Thanks to my brother, Joe, who was my constant companion growing up. Our endless hours of make-believe and fond childhood memories will forever be cherished by me. Because of you, I never knew Dameaon's loneliness.

To my mother-in-law, Nancy. Your constant enthusiasm and support drove me forward, even on the hardest days. Most of all, thank you for raising your son to be an exceptional person who makes every single day brighter.

Thanks to the entire team at Writer Therapy. Chersti Nieveen, without your guidance, I would still be stuck, certain the story was missing something but unable to identify what it was. Emily Pearce, your invaluable feedback on the plot and characterization shaped the novel to what it is today. And sincere gratitude to the rest of the team—Jennie Stevens, Kristy S. Gilbert, and Jill Sorensen—for pushing my debut novel over the finish line.

Special thanks to Casey Gerber at Casey Gerber Creative. Your vision designed a cover that captured the essence of the book in a way I didn't know was possible. Thank you for lending your talent to this project.

And finally, to my three cats, who are a constant source of laughter and love. Thanks for keeping me company in the wee writing hours of morning, as only crepuscular creatures can. Without you, there would be no Cinders.

Made in the USA
Middletown, DE
04 May 2021